RX FOR CHAOS

Baen Books
By Christopher Anvil

☙ ☙ ☙

Pandora's Legions
Interstellar Patrol
Interstellar Patrol II
The Trouble with Aliens
The Trouble with Humans
War Games
Rx for Chaos

RX FOR CHAOS

BY
CHRISTOPHER ANVIL

EDITED BY
ERIC FLINT

BAEN

Rx FOR CHAOS

This is a work of fiction. All the characters and events portrayed in this book are fictional, and any resemblance to real people or incidents is purely coincidental.

A Baen Book Original

Baen Publishing Enterprises
P.O. Box 1403
Riverdale, NY 10471
www.baen.com

ISBN 10: 1-4165-9143-5
ISBN 13: 978-1-4165-9143-6

Cover art by Clyde Caldwell

First Baen printing, February 2009

Distributed by Simon & Schuster
1230 Avenue of the Americas
New York, NY 10020

Library of Congress Cataloging-in-Publication Data: t/k

Printed in the United States of America

10 9 8 7 6 5 4 3 2 1

TABLE OF CONTENTS

Acknowledgments

"Cinderella, Inc" was first published in *Imagination*, December 1952.

"Roll Out the Rolov" was first published in *Imagination*, November 1953.

"The New Boccaccio" was first published in *Analog*, January 1965.

"A Handheld Primer" was first published in *Amazing*, January 1978.

"Rx For Chaos" was first published in *Analog*, February 1964.

"Is Everybody Happy?" was first published in *Analog*, April 1968.

"The Great Intellect Boom" was first published in *Analog*, July 1969.

"Interesting Times" was first published in *Analog*, December 1987.

"Superbiometalemon" was first published in *The Magazine of Fantasy & Science Fiction*, July 1982.

"Speed-Up!" was first published in *Amazing*, January 1964.

"Rags From Riches" was first published in *Amazing*, November 1987.

"Bugs" was first published in *Analog*, June 1986.

"Positive Feedback" was first published in *Analog*, August 1965.

"Two-Way Communication" was first published in *Analog*, May 1966.

"High G" was first published in *IF*, June 1965.

"Doc's Legacy" was first published in *Analog*, February 1988.

"Negative Feedback" was first published in *Analog*, March 1994.

"The New Way" was first published in *Beyond Infinity*, November/December 1967.

"Identification" was first published in *Analog*, May 1961.

"The Golden Years" was first published in *Analog*, March 1977.

"No Small Enemy" was first published in *Analog*, November 1961.

"Not in the Literature" was first published in *Analog*, March 1963.

Mating Games

Cinderella, Inc.

The girl was sallow and scrawny, her face as unattractive as two pills in a smear of mustard. She squinted up and down the street before she hustled across to a wide doorway under a glowing sign:

CINDERELLA, INC.

She hurried through the door and up to a handsome male attendant standing near a hotel-like desk. "At your service, madame," he crooned.

She fumbled in her pocketbook and brought out a piece of torn telescript. She crammed it into his hand. "Can they make *me* look like that?" she demanded.

He unfolded the paper and glanced at the lush advertisement. He smiled and returned it. "Yes," he said, "but it will be expensive."

"Oh, I've got the money."

He raised his hand in an imperious gesture, and a round purple and gold couch whirled down from above. "Seat yourself, madame, and be borne on your voyage to beauty," he said grandiosely. In a sort of mesmeric trance she flopped down on the couch and it whisked away with her.

The couch vaulted through a wide oval opening into a rose colored room ringed with mirrors. From a hidden opening in the ceiling a grayish-green light rayed down on her. "Behold yourself as you are," said a taunting female voice.

3

The girl glanced with irritation at the mirror. "You don't have to sell me," she snapped, "I know what I look like."

The couch started forward with a jerk and slid toward a mirror, the image enlarging as it approached. The mirror swung up and the couch slid through to halt before a desk in a softly-lit room done in gray. A window looked out over the city. A man in a white coat rose from his desk and offered her a chair facing him. His eyes went over her impersonally.

She got up from the couch and sat down beside the desk.

"What is it you want?" the man asked.

"This," said the girl, and spread the advertisement before him.

He studied the picture for a minute then looked the girl over again. "Stand up, please." She stood up. "Now turn around. Mm-hm . . . Well, sit down." He bridged his hands and looked at her. "I think we can do the body, but I'm not sure of the face. This will cost money. Ah, we insist on a cash payment . . ."

"How much money?" She watched him tensely, opening her pocketbook.

"One hundred thousand."

She took out ten crisp bills and spread them on his desk. He nodded, scribbled a receipt, and took her back to the couch. It whirled her out the door and down warm, gaily-lighted perfumed halls to another hotel-like desk where two pretty young girls sat on the counter with their short-skirted legs swinging back and forth. They jumped to their feet and went to the couch. Automatically she showed them the receipt.

"Oh," said one of the attendants, "you've already paid?"

"Yes."

"Well, then we can forget the sales talk." They glanced at the receipt, and their eyes widened. "You get the *full* treatment!" They looked envious.

"Don't you think I need it?" she said coldly. "Why don't we get started?"

"Don't you be nervous," said one of the girls sympathetically. "You'll come out all right. Joanie and me looked almost as bad as you do when we got the treatment." She straightened and turned around slowly, then laughed in vibrant happiness. "And we didn't get the *full* treatment!" They climbed onto the couch and waved to an attendant who set it whirling down the hall . . .

It was twenty days before she returned to consciousness, and it was thirty days after that before the doctors and attendants could be sure of the results.

At last she stood in front of the mirror, naked, and saw what she had hoped. She was, in physical existence, what men with overactive glands and vivid imaginations dream of. She moved sensuously and the male attendants hastily left the room. Her throaty laughter followed them out the door.

Later she was called for her final interview. "Please sit down," said the woman doctor, frowning at a sheaf of papers on the desk. The doctor picked up a clinical photograph and showed it to her. "Do you recognize this woman?"

"Of course," said her sensuous voice. "That was I." She laughed huskily.

"Quite a transformation. Sometimes I think I'll take the treatment myself." The doctor ran a hand across her face, with the fingers spread out, massaging. "Now you'll admit, there's been quite a change."

"Of course."

"It would be unpleasant to change back."

There was a momentary silence. "Change *back*?"

"Yes, yes, I know," said the doctor, "this sounds like a scene from a horror teleshow. But the fact is that the, er, change was brought about, among other things, with the use of glandular secretions. A few chemicals were even used that don't ordinarily exist in the adult human body. Now our doctors have stabilized your physique as effectively as they can." She shuffled through the papers. "But you'll need to use a jectokit. We have yours here."

She handed across a small cream-colored plastic box. "The directions are indented into the box, so you can't make any mistake if you read them. Your body can store some of these substances for a time, but don't go longer than ten days without them. Don't get cocky. You're a beautiful woman now, but remember, your beauty rests on that little box. After six months, we'll give you a refill, or one of our branch stores will. You're safe, so long as you do as I say." The doctor looked up to see how her listener was taking it. She received a breath-taking smile in return.

"I'm off," said the new beauty, "to find a man."

"That won't be hard," murmured the doctor a little ruefully.

The wedding, three months later, was a striking one. The women stared enviously at the tall handsome breadth of the bridegroom, and the men watched the bride with bulging eyes. When the ceremony was over, and the couple occupied the bridal suite for the night, there was a momentary interlude.

"Darling," murmured the bride, "forgive me for a moment. I want to pretty up."

"You're pretty enough to eat," said the groom huskily.

She laughed and slipped past him to the bathroom door with her travel case. "Compose yourself," she smiled. "I'll be out in five minutes."

The groom smiled back. "Five minutes, then."

Once inside, she locked the door and brought out the little yellow plastic box. She clicked open the cover and looked at the photograph snapped inside. "Cinderella, Inc." said the legend, "*reminds you.*"

"I remember," she said, and began her ritual.

In the bedroom, the groom was in his shirtsleeves whistling and unpacking his suitcase. Suddenly he stopped and stared at a little brown plastic box rolled up in his bathrobe. "By George," he gasped, "I almost forgot."

Hastily, he rolled up his sleeve....

Roll Out The Rolov!

Maryn was bored. She emerged from her bath dripping and unattractive, and waited resignedly as the Warm-Dry blew her lank young hair back from her forehead. The autotape whipped out and took the measurements of her immature figure.

From the bedroom nearby, the memory box spoke with her mother's recorded voice: "Hurry up, Maryn."

"Yes, Mother," said Maryn obediently, knowing the memory-box would record her answer.

"It's almost eight," said her mother's voice, timed to go off when it was almost eight.

"Yes, Mother," said Maryn obediently.

"Well, you'd better hurry. Jackson won't want to be kept waiting."

"Yes, Mother," said Maryn. She pressed her hand along the flat length of her body and found she was dry. She waved her hand through the light beam and the Warm-Dry clicked off with a dying sigh. Maryn stepped on the travel-rug and pressed with her toes. The travel-rug slid with her into a luxurious bedroom.

"Jackson won't want to be kept waiting, Maryn," said her mother's voice from the memory box.

"No, Mother," said Maryn. The "Jackson" her mother referred to was young Jackson Mellibant VII, just down from Herriman College. To her mother's delight, he had asked Maryn for a date.

"Remember," said her mother, "the Mellibants are very influential. You may not have another chance like this."

7

"No, Mother," groaned Maryn. She pressed down with her heels and the rug stopped before a pastel pink egg about five feet high. Maryn pressed down with the toes of her left foot and the heel of her right. The rug pivoted her around. Maryn passed her hand through a beam of blue light and the egg snicked open. Maryn stepped in and it closed around her, leaving only her head outside.

"Maryn," said her mother's voice, "I do think you should hurry. Are you getting your foundation yet?"

"Yes, Mother," said Maryn, who was now being buffeted about slightly, within the egg. Inside the pastel pink, egg-shaped machine, her body was being, as the advertisement put it, reborn.

"Remember," said her mother, "you must look your best, Maryn."

"Yes, Mother."

"Now, Maryn," said her mother's voice from the box, "remember if he gets—forward—you aren't to be naive."

"No, Mother," groaned Maryn.

"Lead him on, Maryn. Remember, the Mellibants are very influential."

"Yes, Mother."

"And Maryn, if he should—if he should—well, come up after your date, you're to use the rolov, do you understand?" Her mother's voice rose warningly. "Not yourself, do you understand?"

"Yes, Mother," Maryn mumbled.

"I don't want you to feel hurt, Maryn, but you simply would-n't do. What's the use of having these great technical advances, if we don't use them? I've set the rolov so it will have your exact foundation, and he'll never know the difference. That way you'll both have a better time. Well, I'm glad that's settled. Have a good time, dear."

"Yes, Mother," murmured Maryn. The egg snicked open and Maryn stepped out. She raised her hands and felt the soft voluptuous curves of the dead plastic fastened upon her. She was now, according to the advertisement, "—Reborn—With mystery, with glamour, with the body beautiful to make men lie at your feet and cry aloud for your favor." She had, according to the advertisement, left behind the drabness of her "everyday self." Well, most of it anyway. Maryn stuck her head into another pink pastel egg to get rid of the rest of it.

"Hurry, Maryn," said her mother, as Maryn stood with her head in the egg.

"Glub," said Maryn. The egg ejected her head.

"Hurry," said her mother's voice.

"Yes, Mother," said Maryn. She stepped on the rug, dug in her toes and slid to the dressing machine. This sat like a great metal spider behind a flowered screen in the corner of the room. All the craft of a hundred designers had yet to make a dressing machine attractive, and Maryn approached it with the remains of childhood dread. Once she had started it, the long shiny metal arms flashed over her and Maryn lost her fear in boredom. She was always at first a little afraid the machine would spin a cocoon around her and hang her up for a trophy, but as usual it dutifully spun a dress about her. This time Maryn was surprised to find the dress a trifle tighter than usual.

"Maryn," said her mother's voice.

"Yes, Mother?"

"You're in the dressing machine, aren't you?"

"Yes, Mother." Maryn raised her legs alternately for the shoes and stockings.

"Hurry," said her mother. "And don't reset the machine. I have it set properly now."

Maryn stood stock still till the dressing machine went *click* and a series of chimes played a tune, signifying that milady might now profitably move on to the finisher. Maryn pressed down heel and toe and slid around the screen to a pastel rose-and-gilt box about the size and shape of an upended coffin. Double doors popped open and a light lit up the wine colored interior. Maryn stepped in.

"Hurry, Maryn," came her mother's muffled voice.

"Yes, Mother," said Maryn. She shut her eyes and stood still as a hundred tiny nozzles opened and squirted perfume. A hot breeze fluffed her hair.

Somewhere outside, a chime announced the arrival of Jackson Mellibant VII.

"*Hurry*, Maryn," said her mother's voice, in a special peremptory tone. As a child, Maryn had been greatly impressed by the memory box. Now she understood that her mother had merely sat down for a minute and rattled off her comments, touching the spacer button to put three minutes between this one and the next, and setting a special comment to be made when the dressing machine went on and another to be said when the front door chimed.

The finisher opened up and Maryn stepped out onto the travel rug. On her way out, she had a brief glance at herself in a full length mirror. To an outsider, the effect was designed to be one of lush beauty, combined with serene sophistication and impeccable breeding. Maryn herself had the impression she was watching a popular solido heroine setting out on her stereotyped adventure for the Caswell Brewing Co.

"Remember, Maryn," hissed her mother's voice, "use the rolov, not yourself."

"Yes, Mother," groaned Maryn, as she slid out the bedroom door and down the hall to the living room. She sighed miserably and ran her tongue over her teeth. Their surface felt unnaturally slick and slippery, and Maryn realized that somewhere along the line they had received a coating of Shinywhite. She wondered where. Momentarily distracted by this question, she did not at first see the tall, handsome, sophisticated, and impeccably-bred figure of Jackson Mellibant VII. She caught only the tail end of his flashing smile as he pivoted on his rug and raised his arm. Together, the two of them slid out the door and down the spiral ramp to the waiting car.

The evening passed in stifled perfection. Jackson Mellibant VII said precisely the right thing at exactly the right time. Maryn, well-drilled at the Lacemont Finishing School, found it impossible to give anything but the perfectly right reply. She and Jackson whirled around the dance floor with marvelous grace and precision, their feet locked to smooth metal disks, their motion controlled by the electronic calculator in the nightclub basement.

At the table, Maryn and Jackson drank a good deal of champagne, which was automatically removed from their stomachs by the teleporter. The drive home in Jackson's car had, therefore, no element of hazard, since Jackson had no difficulty punching the proper destination on the keyboard.

On the drive home, carried out at precisely the city speed limit, Maryn sat in futile boredom as Jackson took up her hand and made a lyrical speech concerning it. Maryn's mouth opened and gave a neatly-turned reply. This led coyly on from stage to stage according

to the established routine of Caswell Breweries' heroines, till at last
they reached home. The car stopped itself by the walk. "My, the house
seems lonely," said Maryn, with the correct degree of impropriety. She
studied her gloves. "My parents," she added, "never get home till
round three."

"Perhaps," said Jackson, "I might come up for a few minutes. Just
to see that everything's all right."

"That," said Maryn, who felt like screaming and hammering on
walls, "is very thoughtful of you." They slid up the ramp together.
Maryn turned to Jackson and flashed her Shinywhite smile at him. In
turn he bent and kissed her plastic shoulder.

Together, they slid in through the living room. Maryn glanced
sidewise at Jackson as they slid past the sofa. She was afraid he might
choose to continue operations there. A moment later, they entered
the hallway. This evidently required more intimacy, as he now put
his arm around her waist.

At the bedroom door, they came to a halt. "You'll wait here for a
moment?" she asked, putting her hand on his arm.

"Don't be long," he whispered.

In the living room, there was a faint rumble.

Maryn stiffened. "Did you hear that?"

"What?" asked Jackson, standing with one hand in his side
pocket.

"That noise," said Maryn, becoming alarmed. "In the living
room," she whispered. "Would you—"

"I most certainly shall," said Jackson, gallantly. He slid off down
the hallway and Maryn waited in rising alarm till he called, "Perfectly
all right. Nothing here."

"Thank Heaven," said Maryn, feeling her first genuine emotion
of the evening. If Jackson had been on hand, she might have thrown
her arms around him and kissed him, but he was still in the living
room. Relapsing into boredom, Maryn slid into the bedroom and
pulled back the covers. There on the sheets as a reminder was the
small flat black box that controlled the rolov. Maryn stabbed one of
the buttons, and the discreetly hidden door by the bed opened up.
Out rumbled the life-like rolov, and Maryn sat it on the bed, swung
its feet off the travel platform, and slid the platform back into the
closet. She closed the closet door, and worked the controls so that the

rolov clumsily got into bed and lay down on its side. This part of the rolov's repertoire was not automatic, and took a certain amount of facility with the control box. Maryn, seeing how awkwardly the rolov got into bed, was grateful she did not have to make it walk anywhere. She stood looking at this model of her present appearance and had to admit that, except for the eyes, it looked lifelike. She laid her hand on its shoulder. It was cold as an oyster.

A gentle tap sounded on the bedroom door.

"Just a minute," breathed Maryn, hastily stabbing the warm-up and breathing buttons. She flicked off the lights.

The door opened, and a dark form slid quickly in.

"Over here," whispered Maryn, crouching by the bed.

"Darling," murmured the passionate voice of Jackson Mellibant VII.

Maryn pressed the automatic button.

"Darling," breathed the rolov, in a voice like pure fire.

Maryn, unable to stand it, slipped out of the room. She did not doubt she could leave this end of the evening to the built-in skill of the rolov, but she did not think she could bear to watch it. With the hot murmurings still faintly audible behind her, she tiptoed wearily down the hallway and walked into the living room.

On the sofa, reading the night's paper, sprawled Jackson Mellibant VII, his face a study in boredom.

Maryn stood transfixed.

Jackson, flipping the paper, glanced up, snapped the paper around and looked at it. An instant later he glanced up again at Maryn. "Eh!" he gasped, his eyes wide.

"Well!" said Maryn.

For a moment they stared at each other. "You're not in there!" Jackson commented stupidly.

"What about you?" snapped Maryn.

For a moment, they stared at each other vacantly, then Jackson's face took on a look of shrewd calculation. "Come on," he said. She followed him down the hallway, holding tightly to his hand. They bent to listen at the bedroom door. Giggling murmurs came from within.

Jackson started to shake silently. He pulled her back to the living room and burst out laughing.

"I don't see anything funny about it," snapped Maryn. "Who's in there?"

Jackson sank down on the couch and laughed all the harder.

"Some *friend* of yours?" Maryn demanded icily.

Jackson choked and gasped for breath. "Whew!" he said. "Friend?" He tried to stop laughing and failed. He put his hand on Maryn's arm, as if for patience, and she struck it away angrily. She stamped her foot.

"Maryn," said Jackson between bursts of laughter, "did you put a rolov in there?"

"What if I did?" she demanded angrily. "That's better than you— you—"

"No," said Jackson, "you don't understand." He took a small flat black box out of his side pocket and held it up. "*I* put one in there, too," he said.

As Maryn stared, he started to laugh again. "Two love-making machines," he gasped, "locked in steely embrace. Ye gods, there's progress for you."

"I don't think that's very funny," said Maryn. "Why did you have to send a machine in?"

"Oh," said Jackson. "The Murches are very influential people. Miss Maryn Murch must have nothing but the best."

"But—" Maryn stared at him. Jackson Mellibant VII was the precise image of exact physical and social perfection. Very clearly, he *was* the best. Maryn said so.

"Oh no," said Jackson. "Don't judge others by yourself. I'm all sham and pretense. You don't get strong leading the lives we lead today. I couldn't compare with that machine."

"You mean," said the startled Maryn, "that you're *made-up?*"

"That's it," said Jackson, rising sadly to his feet. "I'm a fraud, a fake. Well, I'll get my machine and be going."

"Wait a minute," said Maryn, taking him by the arm.

"What?"

"I want to talk to you."

"Still?" he looked at her in surprise.

"Yes."

"What about the machines?"

"Oh, they can blow a fuse for all I care," said Maryn. "Won't you sit down?"

"M,m. All right," said Jackson.

She smiled at him and rested her head on his shoulder.

It was well into the morning when Maryn's mother returned, went directly to the memory box in the bedroom and ran it through. "Well," she said to Maryn, "everything seems to have gone off very nicely. Did he ask for another date?"

Maryn nodded.

"That's good," said her mother. "Remember, Maryn, the Mellibants are very influential people. You must *still* do your best."

"Yes, Mother," said Maryn, obediently. "I will."

The New Boccaccio

Howard Nelson shook hands with the white-haired man who stood behind the desk. "Nelson," said Howard, introducing himself, "of Nelson and Rand, Publishers."

"I'm Forrick," said the white-haired man, smiling. "Well, we of United Computers seldom meet a publisher. We're usually called in to straighten out production difficulties."

"That's my trouble exactly," said Howard.

"Really? You said you were a *publisher*?"

"That is correct. Publishers publish books, and books have to be produced. Let me assure you, we have production difficulties. But my specific problem at the moment is our monthly, *Varlet*."

Forrick smoothed his white hair with one hand. "Oh yes," he said, smiling. "*Varlet*. I bought a copy the other night on my way to the train and rode three stops past my station. Very fine magazine." He cleared his throat, and blushed slightly.

"I'm glad you've read it," said Howard. "You can understand it's hard to obtain material that's just right for *Varlet*. What we like is a humorous, sophisticated, but high-powered approach to sex."

"Fine art work, too," said Forrick approvingly. "But I don't see where we can help you."

"Didn't I read somewhere recently that you folks claimed you could make a machine that would play chess?"

"Why, yes, and we could. But there's been no demand for that sort of computer." Forrick frowned in puzzlement. "What does that have to do with your magazine?"

"Let me tell you some of the difficulties we have in producing *Varlet*," said Howard, "and you'll see what I'm driving at."

"Go right ahead," said Forrick. "I'm interested."

"To start with," said Howard, "our need is for a very specialized type of material, and writers only occasionally hit on exactly the right blend for us. This made it hard enough when we first came out, but we managed by using the best original material we could obtain, and by reprinting other stories and articles that happened to meet our requirements. But now—" he spread his hands—"there's not only *Varlet* on the stands, but also *Rascal*, *Sly*, *Villain*, and I understand there's one coming out next month called *Devilish*. How are we supposed to compete with that field when there isn't enough to be bought in the first place? It's impossible."

"I see your point," said Forrick, frowning. "You'd have to lower your standards. But *that* would hurt sales."

Howard nodded and sat back.

"It *is* a production problem," said Forrick thoughtfully. "Hm-m-m." He reached for a telephone. Soon he had a phone in each hand. "Meigs," he roared at one point, "that's our motto! If the job is impossible, we'll do it anyhow!"

Howard sat tight. Eventually Forrick put down the phones and mopped his brow with a large handkerchief.

"We've got the boys working on it," he said. "I'm glad you brought this to us, Nelson. It looks like a real challenge."

They shook hands.

Howard was cursing dismally over a piece of miserable art work some months later when they brought it in. He watched in amazement as the workmen set the glittering machine by his door, then he got up excitedly. The thing looked like a combination electron microscope and spin-drier, but plainly on the front of it in shining chromium was the word: Writivac-112. He walked over to look at it.

"Say, not bad," he said.

The technicians plugged it in and carried out tests with little meters and lengths of cord. Howard watched interestedly.

There was a discreet cough at his elbow. He glanced around. "If you'll just sign here, sir."

"How much?"

"Total cost, installed, is $5,750. Is that satisfactory?"

"Is it satisfactory?" Howard stared at him for a moment. To be able to just set dials and get exactly what he wanted? "Is it satisfactory?" He grabbed his pen, read rapidly, and signed his name.

As soon as they cleared out, he approached the Writivac-112. A little instruction book dangled beside it. "Fred! Don!" he yelled. "Get in here!" He got his two top men into the room, and then they locked all the doors and went to work.

The machine had several dials and settings. According to the little instruction book, the three knobs lettered A through C on the front determined the proportion of sex, adventure, and mystery in the story. The fourth knob, lettered D, handled special types, all the data for which had to be put in a feed-in slot at the top of the machine, and the feed-in switch thrown to the right. If a large amount of such special material had to be fed in, both memory and feed-in switches were turned to the right. Then the length and spacing switches were to be set, the On button pushed, and the user must be sure the ink reservoir was full and the paper dispenser loaded.

"Oh, boy," said Fred, who was art editor. "Check the paper reservoir, chief." Surreptitiously he turned dial A (sex), all the way to the right.

"I notice there's no humor dial," said Don coldly, looking over Fred's shoulder. As fiction editor and part-time writer, he did not look on the machine with enthusiasm. "It'll be a hell of note if this thing doesn't turn out humor," he said. "I hope we haven't got a white elephant here."

"One way to find out," said Howard. He opened the cabinet in back. "Plenty of paper and ink there."

"Let's go," said Fred. "Can I push the button?"

"I'll push it," said Howard. He glanced at the settings. "A little one-sided, but let's see what happens." He pushed the On button.

There was a soft, continuous, muffled clacking sound, and a faint sliding noise of sheets of paper slipping over one another. At one point the Writivac hesitated and then went on, just like an author hunting for the right word.

"Sounds O.K." said Fred eagerly.

"Maybe it'll hatch an egg," grumbled Don.

"I don't like your attitude," said Howard, thinking of the $5,750 he had tied up in this.

"Sorry," said Don.

The machine whirred on.

At length there was silence. Then there was a loud plop, and a massive stack of papers dropped into view through the Out slot. A bell rang once, like the timer on a stove.

Fred and Don and Howard looked at each other.

Howard recovered first and reached in the slot.

Fred coughed. "Should we say some historic words?"

"I can't think of any," said Howard.

"Wait till later," said Don ironically, "and we can have the machine run some up for us."

Howard glanced at him suspiciously, then pulled out the paper. The first sheet was a title page. In the exact center of the white sheet, capital letters spelled:

LUST

They huddled around the stack of paper at a large table, and Howard cautiously removed the title sheet to glance at the first page. Immediately his face reddened. Fred's eyes bulged out like onions. Don pursed his lips and made as if to blow live steam out of his mouth.

After a lengthy silence interrupted only by the turning of pages, Don reached out a shaky hand to the carafe and poured himself a glass of water. Howard grabbed it. Fred quietly appropriated the rest of the manuscript.

"*Whew!*" said Howard. "I feel scorched."

Across the room, the machine rang its bell.

"What did you set the length for?" asked Don.

"I forgot to set the length," said Howard. He leaned forward and squinted.

"You've got a novel coming up," said Don, staring at the machine. "But we still don't know if the thing will write stuff for *Varlet.*"

"Boy!" said Fred, looking up. "Where's the rest of it?"

"There's another ten thousand words or so in the Out slot," said Howard.

Fred shot across the room, and wandered back, reading as he walked.

Howard glared. "Don't hog it!" he roared. "Over here with it!" The three of them hunched over the new set of sheets as the machine clacked busily across the room.

The sun was a faint glimmer in the west as they finished the last page. Howard cleared his dry throat, and squeezed a last drop of water from the carafe. He glanced at Don. "What do you think?"

"My eyes feel like sandpaper just from reading it."

"How about it," said Fred. He made motions with his hands in the air. "A half-dressed babe on the cover, her negligee down over one shoulder. LUST in big red letters behind her. Nothing else. No background. No nothing. Just a plain cover with the babe and LUST. How about it?"

"It'll be banned in Boston," said Don dubiously.

"So what?" said Fred. "That's good advertising."

"We'll have to sell it under the counter," said Don. "We'll have to ship it out in lead-lined trucks and have it hustled over the state line by men in asbestos suits."

"Oh, it's not that bad," said Howard. "We'll say it's frank and outspoken, a down-to-earth novel. Could we call it a 'psychological study'?"

"I doubt it," said Don.

Fred shook his head reluctantly.

"All right," said Howard, "then it's a down-to-earth, plain-spoken novel about the stuff life's made of. We'll say it's a first novel, a masterpiece by … ah … by the new Boccaccio!" He looked up in triumph. "That's exactly the note to strike. Boccaccio's respectable. We'll say this is the work of a modern Boccaccio, that's all."

Don eyed the machine sourly and said nothing.

"Well," said Howard, "we'll rush it through the presses and publish it in the fall. Can you have that cover ready, Fred?"

"You bet," said Fred, grinning and raising his thumb and forefinger.

"I thought we got this thing to write stories for *Varlet*," said Don.

"Precisely," said Howard, "but we have to have enough breadth of vision to fit it into the big picture, too."

"A stroke of genius, chief," said Fred on cue.

"Thank you, Fred." Howard looked at Don hopefully.

"There's bound to be a catch in a thing like this," said Don.

Howard looked hurt. "Did any of your writers ever produce a book like that ... or any kind of a book, for that matter ... right on order in an afternoon?"

"No," said Don.

"All right. Now don't worry about *Varlet*. We'll set it up for *Varlet* next."

Fred sneaked a glance at this watch. "That book gave me an appetite," he said. "Why not let Don go out for some food?"

"I'm not leaving this room," said Don. "If anyone isn't needed here, it's the art editor."

Howard said mildly, "You can both go. It'll take two of you to bring it back." He pulled over a pad and scribbled his order. "Here, and don't lose the paper."

After they had left, Howard made careful adjustments on the Writivac. He fed in several exceptionally good issues of *Varlet*, three of *Playboy*, two copies of *The New Yorker*, and an old issue of *Esquire*. He replenished the paper supply, checked the level of the ink, and set the length for two thousand words. Then there was a commotion at the door, and he looked up to see Don and Fred come in with covered trays.

"Well, we eat in style," he said. "You were fast enough."

"We naturally wanted to get back in time to see our next issue," said Don.

"You set it up yet?" asked Fred.

"Just finished." Howard pressed the button.

They had hardly uncovered the tray when the Writivac-112 rang its bell. Fred started eagerly across the room.

"Wait a minute, will you?" said Don. "Once we start reading that stuff we'll never get to eat."

Howard started buttering a roll. "Come on back, Fred. It can wait a minute."

Fred came back reluctantly. The minute they finished the food and piled the trays to one side, Fred was across the room again. The three of them crowded over the printed sheets. On the title page appeared the words:

THE PARK IN SPRINGTIME

"Could be anything," said Don.

"It sounds promising to me," said Howard.

They leafed through the sheets with intense interest, three pairs of eyes moving as one.

When they were through, Howard looked up exultantly. "We're in!"

Fred looked dazed. "Boy," he said at last. "Boy!"

Don nodded reluctantly. "It's good," he said.

They clapped each other on the back, Fred and Howard happily, and Don resignedly. Mentally, Don was filling out a correspondence school coupon for a course in welding. Finally they all went home and fell into an exhausted sleep.

The next six months, for Howard, were a triumphal march. *Varlet* was coming out twice a month, and arrangements were being completed to bring it out as a weekly. The magazine had so much advertising that it was as thick as a phone book, and desperate TV executives were petitioning Congress to pass a law against it. Just in case, Howard was planning a home-type magazine. He and Fred were making final arrangements on the format of *The Saturday Reader's Companion*.

"We won't get many ads at first, of course," Howard was saying, "but after the first couple of issues—" He was interrupted by someone rapping the outside of the door with his foot. "There's Don with the food." He started to get up.

"I'll get it," said Fred, springing to his feet.

Don came in carrying a stacked tray balanced on a pile of magazines. He was grinning like an imbecile.

"You out of your head, boy?" said Fred. "Watch that tray!"

Howard scowled. "What are all those magazines? What are you bringing them in here for?"

Don shrugged. "I told you a thing like that had to have a catch in it." He plopped down the stack of magazines.

"*Varlet*," he said. He tossed a copy onto the desk. "*Devilish*." He tossed a copy of *Devilish* onto the desk. "*Sly*." He tossed a copy of it on the desk. "*Villain*." Another copy. "*Slicker*." Another. "*Hellion, Rascal, Knave, Cheat*." He tossed them on the desk in rapid succession.

"Open any one," said Don. "Look at the stories. Good stuff."

Howard blinked.

Fred closed the door furtively and locked it. "What are you getting at?" he asked. "We've still got the *Reader's Companion* coming out."

"I think *I* get it," said Howard slowly. "What's that last thing you've got in your hands there?"

Don held it out for him to see. "The *Publishers Gazette*." He opened it to an ad on an inside page.

Howard took it and read:

"Writivac-120, the new all-purpose electronic writer, composes stories typed, double or single-spaced, adjustable margins. Neat copy. Choose one of several styles. Mystery Master, at $3650, is a sound low-priced machine. Can be converted to any other standard type by inserting pop-in coils (available at extra cost). Genre King, at $5750, supplies the best in versatile production-ability with complete control over content. Flexible. Swift. Reliable. Get yours today.

"Available with pica or elite type. Prices slightly higher west of the Mississippi."

"Well—" said Howard.

"I knew there was something fishy," said Don. "What they did was give us a pilot model and watch to see if we complained of quirks while they got their production lines tooled up. Now they're in mass-production. If they get the price down far enough, or the payments spaced out long enough, there'll be one in every living room in the country. We've had it."

Fred stared at the floor.

Howard cleared his throat. "How's that welding course coming?" he asked hopefully. "Is there room for two more in the class?"

A Handheld Primer

How many of us, the last one or two Christmases, have shared that sinking sensation on being grabbed by a junior member of the family who looks up with a piercing gaze:

"Can I have a handle for Christmas? *Can* I? *Glenn Thomas has got one.*"

A "handle," of course, is a "handheld," known also as a "magic box," "thinkbox," "pocket brain," or "PERM" (Pocketable Electronic Reference Module). This is one of those things that was impossible five years ago, scientifically unthinkable ten years ago, and twenty years ago it was science fiction. The possibility of it has been so well debunked by now that it is a little unnerving to run into it in fourteen different models at one end of the camera counter.

It was the thought that others must have found themselves equally unprepared that led to this article, which should give, at least, a better picture of the handheld.

First, the essentials.

The *price* ranges from the collapsed levels of remaindered products of the industry's latest bankrupts into the realms of fantasy. In short, you can buy them from $4.95 *up*. The highest price for a standard job—an all-purpose multiprogrammable financial, real-estate, and stock-and-bond-market model with built-in expandable reference library of data and programs—is $45,000.00. But then there are custom-built models, with no price limit in sight.

The best bet seems to be to stay under twenty bucks for the first one, particularly if it is a present for someone not yet nearly old enough to vote, and most particularly if the someone happens to be a small boy. There is something about an expensive handheld that can translate the merely obnoxious to levels truly intolerable.

Next—*where* to buy it?

If you want a reliable one, stay away from discounters, particularly those with a truck parked near the front door, decorated with an overgrown bedsheet reading:

HANDHELDS!!
TRUCKLOAD
SALE!!!!!!

The truckload lot will almost certainly be from some outfit in bankruptcy, and while the merchandise may be all right when you get it home, what do you do if it isn't?

If you want a good model, try a camera shop, a book store, or, better yet, a camera shop or book store *on a large college campus*. There you can expect to find a merchant with a discriminating— even spoiled—clientele, that will not hesitate to speak up or even boycott him if he doesn't back the product.

This brings us to the heart of the subject.

Which one to buy?

It is here that the worst mistakes can be made—mistakes even worse than paying fifty bucks for an OG-53 Experimental that will give wrong answers if you so much as bump it, and if you send it back to be fixed, they will return it unfixed by barge line. To avoid such things, look over what's available *before* buying.

Most handhelds fall into some special-purpose category, such as:

1) The descendents of the *calculators* of the mid-seventies. These are too well known to need description.

2) Historical Daters—Relatively simple and inexpensive—and said to have served as a training ground for making the more complex types. You punch the buttons and the screen lights up with the outstanding events of that date. Hit 1-4-9-2, and across the screen from right to left goes: "Christopher Columbus discovered America." A cheap dater may do nothing further. The better models have a wide button lettered "MORE." Tap it repeatedly, and you get:

"Columbus sailed the Atlantic seeking a westward route to Asia . . . He had, in his first expedition, three ships: *Santa Maria* (100 tons), *Pinta* (50 tons), *Niña* (40 tons) . . . He was backed by Queen Isabella and King Ferdinand of Spain . . ." The more expensive models go into incredible detail.

—If you buy one of these, watch out for the "bear-trapped" jobs, whose manufacturers smilingly put sixty percent of the machine's capacity into a few standard dates—knowing that those few dates are the ones most of us will try before buying.

There are scientific daters, military daters, religious daters, and so on. The latest is the "PHD" or "Personal History Dater." With this, you feed in the interesting events of the day before you go to sleep. Then later on, you can review your life by date—and so, of course, can anyone else who gets hold of this electronic diary. It's worth the extra money to get the kind that takes a look at your retinal patterns before it will talk.

3) "Pocket Prof" of "2SR" (Special Subject Reference). In a way, these are the most amazing of the handhelds. Take, for instance, the "GenChem I" put out by the most reliable and expensive U. S. maker. This is said to contain the equivalent of all the facts and data in the usual college course in general chemistry. Its main advantage over a textbook consists in its *indexing*. Though you can look up references by getting its index on the screen, there is another way. Tap the "CC" (Chemical Compound) button, then hit, say, H-2-O, and facts about water will be flashed on the screen as long as you care to persist, until every reference, direct and indirect, has been sought out and shown. Tap the "El" (Element) button, then tap C-A, and the same thing will be done for calcium. To find references to reactions or other relationships between calcium and water, tap these two sets of buttons, and also tap "Cnc" (for "connection"). References that concern both water *and* calcium will be flashed on the screen. Few books have an index even remotely as complete, and with the handheld you have only to glance at the screen to see if the reference shown is the one desired. This is an improvement over hunting up, one at a time, a long list of page numbers.

The GenChem I model, incidentally, uses the broad screen with adjustable flash-time, and a hold button, instead of the reel-type screen, across which letters flow from right to left.

These handhelds have made a considerable dent in textbook sales, though as hard-core book-lovers like to point out, very few textbooks have ever been known to fade away at two a. m. the night before the exam, just when someone has unauthorizedly borrowed your recharger.

But, as the handheld enthusiasts ask, how many books can be programmed to give a vocabulary and grammar review in a foreign language, with practically unlimited numbers of questions in randomly varied order, and in whatever form you care to try? There's even one that will speak the words aloud—while research continues on another to independently check the user's pronunciation.

4) Novelty handhelds—These are the recreation and entertainment models, such as chess and checker players, go, bridge, pinochle, and "pocket casino" models. There are "scenic view" and "guided tour" models. And the "Favorite TV" and "Favorite Movie" series. And, of course, the notorious "Pocket Burlesque Theater."

The latest versions of all these use the N-V viewer, unlike the bulky early models with large built-in screens. In the N-V system (the letters stand for "Natural-View"), a separate image is flashed into each eye, each view being separately adjusted to fit the user's vision.

The Scenic View II uses highly sensitive color apparatus, and an enormous repertoire of scenes—making, in effect, a modern compact replacement for the stereoscope.

The Guided Tour models put related scenes together, along with an earphone for the voice that gives the description. An interesting feature is the "branching" of the tours. Suppose a tour of Paris incidentally shows a famous restaurant. Press the appropriate button, and a new guide appears to express appreciation for your interest, and show you through the restaurant in detail. When now and then he asks, "Do you see?" it isn't a rhetorical question, but the sign of another "branch-point", where if you want you can get still more details.

Similar to this in principle, is the new "careers" model, meant to show what a person in any given line of work actually *does*. The first versions, to judge by the groans of the people really doing the kinds of work shown, fall considerably short of realism.

5) The so-called "trade" handheld—such as the Plumber's Helper, the Auto Mechanic, the Carpenter, the Contractor, and so on. These vary widely.

There is, for instance, a shiny model we can call the

WidgetMasTer. Suppose you want to learn from this model how to bend a widget, and so tap out B-E-N-D. If you hit two of the jam-packed keys at once, a red light flashes and an alarm goes off. This is, as the instructions explain, "for your protection."

After you tap out B-E-N-D, across the screen glides: "REFER TO ITEM REQUIRED."

Anyone used to book indexes will suppose this means to name the *noun* first—that is, "Widget, bend." But, if you tap out W-I-D-G-E-T, the screen replies, "STATE REFERENCE DESIRED."

Apparently, this must be the place to hit B-E-N-D. But then WidgetMasTer unreels: "REFER TO ITEM REQUIRED."

If you move fast enough, you *can* hit W-I-D-G-E-T-B- but then the red light flashes and the alarm hammers. There is no such thing as a "widgetb," and WidgetMasTer knows it.

The only way out of this impasse is to throw WidgetMasTer in the trash can (the preferred solution), or else fight your way through the instruction pamphlet. Eventually you will locate reference to a "GN" key (for "Generic Name") and an "Op" key (for Operation") and an "Sp" key (for "Species") and a "Q" key (for "Query"). It develops that all you have to do is to just press the Q key, and release it, then press the GN key and tap out W-I-D-G-E-T, then press the Sp key and tap our A-L-L, then press the Op key and tap out B-E-N-D, and then press the Q key again, and then, after a brief little two-minute pause while the red light blinks on and off to show how busy WidgetMasTer is, then there slides across the screen: "MAINTAINING PROPER CORRECT ALIGNING GRIP USING SPECIAL TOOL 2WB STEADILY AND FIRMLY APPLY ALTER-NATING PRESSURE USING SPECIAL TOOL A1WB. USE RED HEAT TO AVOID DOWLING CORKING AND CHIEFFERING. DO NOT FORCE THE BEND. CAUTION! NEVER HEAT TREATED WIDGETS!!"

Since the first part of this answer is gone from the screen well before the last part appears, you may think at first that that sense of confusion results because you missed something the first time around. All you have to do to check the answer is to go through the procedure again, wait till the red light gets through blinking, then watch closely as the answer glides past.

What, it *still* isn't clear?

The trouble seems to be that WidgetMasTer is, as they say in the handheld trade, "question-progenitive"—for every uncertainty you bring to it, it presents you with at least one new uncertainty. The only known way to get a clear answer out of this oracle is to have no uncertainties to begin with. If you already know the subject backwards and forwards, you can nearly always unravel its answers.

Very different from WidgetMasTer is the "Mechanic's Special." For instance, if you tap out, H-O-W R-E-M-O-V-E S-T-U-C-K N-U-T? the wide screen answers:

EXPERIENCE SHOWS IF YOU HAVE SIX NUTS, FIVE MAY BE EASY; ONE WILL STICK. IF THE BOLT HAS TWISTED OFF, REFER TO BROKEN BOLTS. IF NOT, AND YOU HAVE AN EXTRA NUT, REFER TO NUTSPLITTER. IF NOT, REFER TO HEAT. ALSO REFER TO DIRT, EYES, KNUCKLES, FIRST AID, VICEGRIPS, CHAIN WRENCH, LEVERAGE, IMPACT, BRASS NUTS, INACCESSIBLE, BLOCKED, RUSTED, SEIZED, ROUNDED, SLOW TUNES AND CAN PRAYER HELP?

One Mechanic's Special is worth many WidgetMasTers. But, so far, the trade market has a wider selection of WidgetMasTers.

Of course, whatever you're looking for, the device not only needs to be good in itself. It also has to fit the situation. If, for instance, what you are looking for is a gift for a younger member of the family, considerable thought may be needed.

A checker or chess-playing model, for instance, can often keep a boy happy and out of trouble for upwards of half-an-hour at a time—but be sure to get the kind that can be "backstepped" to show previous moves. Otherwise, there will be howls that the handheld *cheats*. Incidentally, the "Disrupt" button, that knocks a temporary hole in the chess handheld's calculating ability, is not to be sneered at. It gets tedious pushing the "Reset" button to start a new game.

Any game-playing model, of course, may seem "non-educational"; but then, nearly everyone agrees that a dater *is* educational; and do you really want:

"Say, do you know what happened in 1066? . . . No, no. *Everybody* knows *that*. I mean, do you know what *else* happened? You *don't*? You *don't know*? You mean to say *you don't know*? Well—"

Then there is the very educational "Historical Facts" model:

"You've heard of Robert E. Lee and Ulysses S. Grant, haven't you? . . . Okay, quick—What do the 'E' and the 'S' stand for?"

Avoid like poison the "Political Science" jobs. Those so far available obviously were put together either with the kindly help of the Central Committee of the Communist Party, or by charter members of the Death-To-Taxes League.

All these specialized models are, at least comparatively speaking, standard traditional devices. So are the:

6) Pocket computers. Most of us have had some chance recently to find out what can happen when we first design our own programs. The newer handhelds of this type may have a still larger storage capacity, faster speeds, easier programs, newer microtapes with more ingenious prerecorded programs, crystal-needle master programs, new sensing and acting attachments, independent detachables—and with all this extra latitude, it is, of course, possible to get into a worse mess; but, at least, it is still a mess of a familiar kind.

It is the recently marketed "companion computer" or "pocket buddy" model that adds the tricky new dimension to handhelds. With *these* you can lose more than your money and your disposition.

Take, for instance, the "CCI," which is "Mark I" of the new "Constant Companion" series. This device fits in your shirt pocket, has a "receptor"—a kind of little eye on a flexible stalk—that sticks over the pocket's edge—and a grille that "hears" and on occasion "talks."

CCI was introduced at a price of ten thousand, now sells for six thousand five hundred, and, to the non-enthusiast, it is well worth this price *not* to have one. It is rumored that the price will come down further in the near future. The value of not having one seems likely to stay up.

How does CCI work?

There is the first catch.

No explanation of its construction is given, and curious competitors have found that it self-destructs when opened. This means you do not really know its strengths or limitations. It is *rumored* by the salesmen that the device is in contact with a ring of satellites which in turn are in touch with four gigantic interconnected computers.

And what does CCI do? A quote from the brochure will give the idea:

". . . your Constant Companion is at all times on the alert. Beyond the reach of human failings, he (*sic*) never forgets, never falters, and never fails . . . If you have an appointment or a birthday to remember, your personal friend and pocket private secretary will prompt you at the proper time . . . If you wish to review a scene or an event, CCI has it. If you want to reexamine a spoken agreement, test again the nuances of personal expression, your Constant Companion will unfailingly help you . . ."

CCI is a personal portable combination reminder service, bug, and memory. But, how does it work? How, for instance, does the device communicate with the ring of satellites? What if you drive through an underground tunnel, or board a submarine for a submerged cruise? Does CCI somehow stay in contact with the ring of satellites? If not, why don't the instructions warn you? If so, the Defense Department will be interested.

Incidentally, CCI is already reported to be the subject of study by a government "task force" to determine the legal and technological means to, in effect, *subpoena* your "Pocket Pal," in case you ever land in court.

Meanwhile, if you have an argument with someone who insists you said what you know you didn't say, you can "back-key" to the appropriate stage of the argument, set the device for "Databanks—Repeat Conversation" and have the indescribable thrill of hearing your own voice blow your own argument to bits.

As if they had not done enough already, the manufacturers of CCI are out with a handheld boasting "extended capabilities." This is CCCI—"Constant Companion *and Counselor*, Mark I." This device incorporates an earphone on a cord that goes down the back of the neck under the shirt collar, to just behind the shirt pocket, where a pin-type connector passes into CCCI itself. The cord and earphone permit CCCI to talk directly into your ear.

CCCI has its own sensing apparatus, plus tiny skin and pulse attachments, and a set of special glasses ("two hundred flattering styles available"). Its sensing apparatus follows what's happening, its skin and pulse monitors watch your emotional reactions, and the special glasses enable the device to tell where you are looking; the device's circuits then correlate what is going on outside with your inner responses.

That it can do this is, of course, impressive. But do you want it doing it to *you?*

CCCI was, naturally enough, made to sell, and to do that somebody has to buy it. It is priced at twenty-five thousand. There is a little problem there. *Who* will pay for it?

Two answers seem to have been arrived at.

First, it can be *rented*. Under a "special introductory offer," you can now use it for a week for "only three hundred and fifty dollars." That's the first answer.

In groping for a second answer, the planners seem to have asked: What *might* lead anyone to pay the price?

To see the answer arrived at, consider the slant of this sample from the advertising brochure, which incidentally is headed, "You Don't Have Everything If You Have No Constant Companion To Guide You In the Most Intimate Affairs of Your Life." The brochure reads:

". . . In this ultramodern era, the powerful logic and memory capabilities of the high-speed electronic computer have long since revolutionized manufacture, transportation, and communication— but they have left mankind still wandering in jungles of personal emotional ignorance.

"NOW, with the scientific miracle of CCCI, for the first time the mighty djinn of the Computer Age stands at your side to guide you adroitly through the mazes of ignorance to mysterious pleasure palaces of the senses. The jeweled secrets of ecstasy, hidden to others, are opened to you, who know their value to be beyond price.

"Where others blunder and hesitate, your guardian djinn guides you on a magic carpet to the heart of whatever tempestuous interest rouses your imperious fancy.

"Wise in the ways of human nature, encoded deep in its capacious memory banks for instant reference and lightning retrieval, CCCI represents a fusion of new knowledge and ancient wisdom, of—"

In case anyone hasn't caught on, the following paragraphs get the idea further pinned down for the wide-eyed reader, using words like:

"Houri . . . enchantment . . . delights . . . forbidden knowledge . . . wisdom . . . harem . . . silken . . . seductive . . . sensuous . . ."

Without ever exactly getting to the specifics, the general idea planted in the mind of the prospective buyer is clear enough. And— Who knows—this approach may make sales.

But what is the device worth?

Consider the experience of an acquaintance we will disguise as "S. L.," for "Secret Lover."

S. L. was secretly fascinated by a certain brunette, but was also sunk in tortured despair because of his own inadequacies. The exact nature of S. L.'s inadequacies can be left to the imagination, the *important* thing being that, to deal with them, he rented CCCI for a week, and at once confided his troubles to his new "constant companion and counselor."

"I'm scared," he concluded, after unloading his store of tortured doubts into CCCI's capacious memory banks. "What if she rejects me? What can I *do?*"

Into his ear there spoke a wise elder-statesman voice:

"Success is impossible at a distance. Closeness creates opportunity."

This sounded reasonable. So, after some further vacillation, S. L. got himself invited to a party whose only redeeming feature was the likely presence of the brunette. As S. L. circulated amongst the guests, the wise elder statesman voice in his ear was reassuring:

"Confidence is the key. You are assured and confident. There is every prospect for success. You *will* succeed . . . That is she? . . . Yes, pulse, respiration, visual focus, and all other indicators agree. The subject is now being fixed for reference in memory banks, and all channels are—*One moment—*"

The elder-statesman voice suddenly sharpened, freezing S. L. to the spot as he stared at the girl, who also froze, staring wide-eyed at him, while in S. L.'s ear, CCCI poured out urgent warnings:

". . . Attention! Subject is equipped with an Allectronics Elder Brother Mark III Protector! This is a dual-function device to guard against emotional entanglement in the user while repelling external advances, using high-voltage fine-wire shock prods!"

S. L. stared, paralyzed by this intelligence.

The girl stared back, blushed, winced, and suddenly whirled and walked fast toward a door leading to an inner hall of the apartment. CCCI was pouring instructions into S. L.'s ear:

". . . pursuit is inadvisable! The Allectronics Mark III will deliver a warning shock to subject if she has any interest, and will deliver a severe shock to you on contact. This will condition subject against you, and you against subject. The correct tactic is to withdraw at once, and attempt to determine—"

S. L. abruptly jerked the plug out of his ear, and went through the door after the girl. Totally forgetting CCCI, he called out in a low angry voice, "What are you running away for? *I* haven't done anything!"

"Because," came the angry reply, "every time you looked at me, I get an electric shock!"

"Well—that isn't *my* fault!"

"Well, it certainly isn't mine! All I'm trying to do is protect myself! You've got *Wolf Wiring!*"

S. L. had never heard CCCI spoken of as "Wolf Wiring" before. But the unexpected exhilaration of the conversation carried him past the confusion:

"If you don't like Wolf Wiring, I'll get rid of it. At least, *I'm* not a human lightning rod!"

"Ouch! *Damn* this thing!"

"Why not send Elder Brother home, too?"

"All right! I can't stand *this!*"

Anyone who considers this incident can decide for himself just what CCCI and Elder Brother Mark III Protector are *actually* worth.

The thing to do seems clear enough. Stick to handhelds of types that have been around for a while, and try one at twenty bucks or less first. That makes it easier to get an idea how they work, what the one you have lacks, and what you want, before you spend more.

As for any existing model that will benevolently run your life for you—Well, as they say: "This approach shows great potential promise for the future; at present, however, considerable further development work appears to be needed."

The last word on this subject seems to be that there isn't any last word *yet*; but keep your eyes open and your guard up—They no doubt are already struggling with that "further development work" that appears to be needed.

The Drug
Factory

Rx For Chaos

Morton Hommel, Ph.D., Director of the Banner Value Drug and Vitamin Laboratories, Inc., pressed himself flat on the floor as the bullets stitched a line of holes through the laboratory wall at about waist height overhead.

A foot away, against the wall, sat a sample of the cause of the trouble, and as Hommel lay pinned from either side by his breathless assistants, he could not help seeing the label on the little bottle: DE-TOX The Antacid Detoxifier. Take one to three tablets per day as required, to counteract harmful mental effects of mild overindulgence in alcoholic beverages, sleeping pills, stimulants, stay-awake pills, nicotine, tranquilizers, etc., etc. De-Tox is a new formulation, designed to fortify the critical faculties of the human brain. Used in moderation as directed, it will overcome that groggy, fuzzy feeling that follows mild over-indulgence. . ..

Hommel had thrown himself under the table with the haste of a man who has only a fraction of a second to pick his spot and dive for it. Now that he was under there, he remembered the half-full carboy of sulfuric acid that was in the lab somewhere. Was it on a neighboring bench, or was it directly overhead?

He lay paralyzed, hardly able to breathe, with his heart hammering to the whine of the bullets, the clatter of breaking glass, and the smash and rattle of falling plaster. A heavy thud made the floor jump beneath him. Viola Manning clung moaning and trembling to his left arm, and Peabody, his fanatical young research chemist, kept trying to mumble the results of his latest experiments in Hommel's right ear. And all the while, scarcely a foot away, that bottle of little pale-green pills stared him in the face. The flag at the bottom of the label, and the motto underneath, seemed to jump out at him:

"A Banner Value Product of the Banner Value Drug and Vitamin Laboratories, Inc. At all better druggists, everywhere."

That, he thought, was the trouble. The stuff was all over the world, like aspirin. No, even that didn't do it justice. It was more widespread than aspirin. Any place where they ate, drank, or breathed anything that befogged their wits, there was a ready-made market for De-Tox.

Hommel experienced the fervent wish that he'd thrown the original report in the wastebasket. Or touched a match to it. Or just slid it in a drawer of his desk, ignored its possibilities, and put the men onto something else. In the beginning he could have suppressed it in any number of ways. Instead, never imagining how it would turn out, he had gone straight out to the golf course, where old Sam Banner himself instantaneously saw the commercial possibilities, and said, "O.K. Push it."

Hommel had come back with a faint professional contempt for Banner's apparently snap decision, but quickly lost that as the old man breathed fire down his neck. Meanwhile, the work unfolded like a freshman laboratory exercise, no untoward side-effects showed up, and the next thing Hommel knew, they were in production.

After that, it was a succession of new sales records, bonuses, and salary raises, plus fantastic coverage in national magazines, with Banner himself turning down honorary degrees, and trying to explain that he was a business man, not a Benefactor of Humanity. Banner solved the problem by shoving the credit off on Hommel, while Hommel, who would willingly have kept the credit, had it violently wrenched away from him by the chemist who had sent in the original report.

The uproar finally died down, the new drug became a standard household item, and there was nothing to do but work the cash register, and send out friendly reminders that De-Tox was a registered trademark, and not to be referred to as "de-tox" or "detox."

It was not many months after this that Hommel, a little before noon one morning, got word to come to Sam Banner's office without delay.

Banner was seated at his desk, swirling a glass about half-full of water, and staring out the window. He glanced at Hommel.

"Something funny about these De-Tox pills."

"What do you mean?"

Banner swung his chair away from the window. "This psycho thing. They can't put the subject under after he takes the pills."

Hommel frowned. "You mean, the drug interferes with induction of the hypnotic trance?"

"Can't put them under," corrected Banner, who had a distaste for long words. "They go through all the usual stuff, and the subject won't go under. Even when they've got him trained to go under at the snap of a finger. Funny."

"Hm-m-m," said Hommel. "That is curious."

Banner nodded, and set down his glass. "TV sales are down."

Hommel blinked, but said nothing. If there was a connection, it would appear shortly.

Banner said, "New car sales are down. Used car sales up. Liquor sales way down. Movies are in trouble. Buying on time is down all across the board."

Hommel started. "Are you saying there's a connection between the fact that hypnotic suscept . . . er . . . that it's hard to put the subjects under, and that there's been a change in sales patterns?"

Banner nodded. "You've been tied up, Mort, so I don't know if you noticed it. But not long ago, the biggest car maker in this country came out with a campaign to put over a new style car design. For a month, anybody who used TV, radio, newspapers, magazines, or looked at a billboard was blind, deaf, and dumb from having the thing thrown at him. You know how many of this new style they've been able to unload so far? Eighteen thousand."

"That's fantastic."

"You bet it is. You study enough sales charts, and you'll see things that will stand your hair on end. People just don't react the way they used to. Not since we came out with these pills."

"But are we sure there's a connection?"

Banner tossed over a professional journal opened to an article titled, "Complex Interrelations of Social Phenomena and Waking Suggestibility."

Hommel frowned at it. It was out of his field, and the style made it abundantly plain that the article wasn't intended for the general public.

"Hm-m-m," said Hommel a few minutes later. "Well, I'm afraid I'm not familiar enough with the terminology—"

"Take a look at the footnote on page 1040, Mort."

Hommel dutifully turned pages, and read:

"Curiously enough, the proprietary preparation known as 'De-Tox' was found to affect negatively all the above-mentioned correlations. The values given are, therefore, those obtained when both experimental and control groups had refrained from the use of 'De-Tox' for a period of fourteen weeks."

Hommel hunted through the body of the article, written in a far less congenial manner than the footnote, and after a brief hard struggle, gave it up.

Banner smiled. "You have to crush all that wordage through a hydraulic press to get the meaning out of it."

"But what *does* it mean?"

"In his words, 'progressive and ordered civilization depends for its smooth functioning upon the existence, in a sizable proportion of the populace, of an extensive degree of waking suggestibility, and in some cases a mild state of hypnosis.'"

Hommel thought it over. "And he says, just incidentally, that our De-Tox cuts down this suggestibility?"

"That's it."

Hommel groaned.

"Nice, isn't it?" said Banner. "The pills are all over the world."

"Do you suppose he's right?"

Banner scowled. "That's a good question. Do you get out much, Mort?"

"Well . . . lately, since we've been working on this new hay-fever drug . . ."

"I know," said Banner. "I've been tied up lately myself. You've just been going back and forth between your office and apartment, right?"

"That's pretty close to it."

"Read the papers?"

"Just the headlines."

Banner tossed over a folded newspaper. "Take a look at the car ad on the back page."

Hommel turned the page over, and read:

QUALITY, COMFORT, DURABILITY

Abelson's presents the first choice of long-lasting motor vehicles. The price is low but the value is high. Every interior is cleaned, all fittings tightened, and all moving parts lubricated. Why pay $4,000.00 and up for "newness"? Who cares if the fenders sweep up, out, or down? What's a little rust? A car is transportation. Who cares if the style is boxy, stretched-out, flattened, or flaring? Let's be frank; Do you want to buy a new car and look like a fool to the neighbors? Drop in at Abelson's Used Car Lot and see our selection of best buys from the best years.

You'll be glad you did.

Hommel looked at the picture above the advertising message. The picture showed an exaggeratedly modern-looking car, with a grille like two rows of teeth, and the ends of four bills, each labeled $1,000, sticking out between the teeth.

He read the ad over and over again, and one line stood out:

"Let's be frank: Do you want to buy a new car and look like a fool to the neighbors?"

Hommel scratched his head. "I certainly seem to have missed *something.*"

Banner glanced at his watch. "Let's go into town for lunch. We can circulate around a little, and look things over."

Banner Laboratories was located well out of town, so it was after noon when they got there, and the best eating places were crowded.

Banner said, "If you can hold out for an hour or so, Mort, it might be a good idea to just look around."

"Suits me."

Banner parked the car, and they got out, across the street from a large new-car showroom. The big window was plastered with bright stickers, and the face of the building was hung with pennants and streamers.

Hommel felt the usual quickening of his pulse as he and Banner approached the door. They stepped in, to be assaulted by a glitter of polished metal, a fresh new-rubber smell, and the impressive sight of a brand-new car slowly revolving on a turntable.

Across the room, four or five salesmen sat hunched around a table, their ties loosened, coats hanging over the backs of their chairs, and smoldering cigarettes drooping out of the corners of their mouths as they played a listless game of pinochle.

The door clicked and banged shut.

The salesmen looked around, blinking. There was one swift complex movement, a momentary waving of arms, sawing of elbows, scraping of chairs, and a salesman, exhaling a cloud of smoke but with no cigarette in sight, came neatly, briskly, across the floor toward them. His step was confident, and his manner friendly, but his eyes suggested a boxer who had been thrown three times by a judo expert, and is coming out for the fourth time.

"Good afternoon, gentlemen. You want to look at a *new car*?"

Banner nodded.

"Well, sir, we've cut the price on this model to $2,895.00. For your money, you get something no used-car dealer can offer—newness. The style, of course, is a little different from past years. But what is style but *proof of newness*?"

He maneuvered them around to a sleek, dark-blue model, and opened the door to show a lush, expensive interior.

"Granted," he said, "it's a little extreme, but . . . ah . . . look how new the upholstery is! Look at the floor mats, and the brake pedal—"

Banner, obviously patterning his reaction after the advertisement they'd read earlier, shrugged. "Who cares about the upholstery?"

"Ah, sir, but remember, it's more *proof of newness*! Of course, what counts in a car is the running gear. But one of the most important factors in the condition of the running gear is its freeness from wear and misuse. It's *newness*, in other words. And you'll find no newer car anywhere than—"

Banner peered inside.

"Fantastic dash. Everyone will laugh like—"

"A car, sir," said the salesman quickly, "is a long-term investment. Would you permit uninformed neighbors to decide your choice of stocks and bonds? Of course not! Why, then—"

Like two fencers, Banner and the salesman thrust and parried in a rapid exchange of arguments that lasted five minutes, with the other salesmen listening breathlessly, and the owner wide-eyed in a glassed-in cubicle to one side. At the end, Banner conceded that he hadn't heard such good reasons for a new car in years, but he still wanted to look around. The salesman handed over his card, and managed to shake hands with both of them on the way out, while telling them how welcome they'd be when they came back.

As the door swung shut, a voice could be heard in the background, saying, "We've got to tone that dash down, *somehow*."

Banner and Hommel glanced at each other after they'd gone a few steps.

"If," said Banner, "*that* salesman can't sell new cars, who could?"

Hommel said uneasily, "How do we know where a thing like this is going to stop?"

"That's the trouble. We don't."

They walked on in silence. Then Banner cleared his throat.

"Look there. Down on the next block."

Hommel glanced at a huge sign:

BEST YEARS—BEST BUYS

Twenty or thirty customers were unhurriedly making their way through a large used-car lot. Here and there, attendants were polishing and waxing cars. Salesmen were raising hoods, and helpfully taking off brake drums so customers could see the condition of the brake lining.

As Hommel and Banner walked past the car lot, Hommel became conscious of some odd quality about the appearance pf the customers. "They look—" he hesitated.

"Neat," said Banner, frowning, "but shabby?"

"I think that's it."

Hommel studied a middle-aged man by a nearby car. He was wearing a clean, frayed, black sweater with three yellow stripes on the sleeve and a big yellow "W" on the back. He was saying expansively to a salesman, "So the wife says, 'Charles, you can't wear that old thing. What will people think?' And I said, 'This sweater's as warm as a new one. They'll think I've got sense, what *would* they think?'" He shook a little greenish object out of the bottle, shot it into his mouth, crunched it up, and offered the bottle to the salesman.

"Don't mind if I do," said the salesman. He shook the bottle over his open hand, tossed a little pale-green pill into his mouth, chewed contentedly, and handed back the bottle. The word "De-Tox" was momentarily visible on the label. The customer slipped the bottle in a side pocket. The two men chewed placidly.

Hommel and Banner stared.

"Ah," said the customer, "that old stuff really knocks the horrors in the head, doesn't it?"

"Good stuff," agreed the salesman.

"So they drop the bomb—" said the customer.

"Sure. So what? You're no deader than if a truck hit you."

"How much you want for this clunker?"

"Nine hundred. Good tires, good battery. The engine's smooth. Standard transmission, so you got no worry there. Heater. Radio. If you listen to that junk anyway."

"I used to listen to the news. But why bother?"

"Sure. What happens, happens."

"So the Arabs *are* mad at each other. What can I do about that? How's she start?"

"Fast. We take care of that."

"Jack her up. Let's jerk a wheel off to begin with."

"Yes, *sir*."

As the customer bent over to examine a tire, the neck of the pill bottle thrust out of his pocket.

Banner tore his gaze away with an effort.

Hommel let his breath out with a hiss.

They walked on, feeling stupefied, and caught sight of a "Bar and Grille" sign down the street.

"Let's go in there and eat," said Banner. "I want to sit down and think this over."

"It will certainly bear thought," said Hommel. "Did you see how casually they shook out those pills?"

"'Really knocks the horrors in the head,'" quoted Banner. "What was it he called them?"

"'That old stuff,'" said Hommel.

"It sounds like some kind of liquor. Of course, it could be that that was just an exception."

Hommel was feeling more and more sure of it as they put the

car lot farther behind them. "After all," he said, "some people chew garlic—"

Banner put his hand on Hommel's arm.

Hommel looked around.

Coming out of the doorway of the bar was a man with ruddy complexion and bloodshot eyes. He pressed his hand to his mouth, tilted his head back, and chewed with a solid crunching noise. With his other hand, he held onto the doorpost. "Ah," he murmured, swallowing repeatedly, "that licks it." He reeled out onto the sidewalk, tilted expertly, banged into the building, and walked along with his feet tilted out and hands moving along the brick face of the building as if it were on wheels and he was shoving it to the rear. As he came closer, he saw Hommel and Banner, and muttered, "'M all right. Don't worry. M'body's drunk, but my head's cold sober."

An aproned figure appeared in the doorway. "You take those pills, Fred?"

"Sure, sure. You think I want to get run over or something?"

He reeled out past a storefront with a plate-glass window, staggered over to a door leading to a flight of stairs, expertly grabbed the handle on the third try, tilted forward, and vanished inside.

The bartender mopped his brow with a big handkerchief, and went back into the bar.

Two men in their early twenties came out, absently tossing pale green pills in their mouths, and strolled off down the street.

Hommel looked in the doorway, and saw, beside the cash register, a glass dish of pale-green pills with a cardboard sign, rudely lettered:

"Dettox. Take some."

Banner glanced in over his shoulder. "Let's eat some place else."

Hommel looked down the street. On the corner at the far end of the block, a sign read, "Soda-Pharmacy-Lunch."

Hommel pointed. "How about that?"

"Fine. A sandwich is all I want."

They walked in silence for a moment, then Banner said, "This thing is a lot more widespread than I imagined."

"We might *still* be getting an exaggerated picture of it."

"Maybe. But it's one of those things you can discount by fifty per cent, and *still* have too much."

They pushed open the door of the drugstore, sat down at the lunch counter, and ordered ham sandwiches and milk shakes. Hommel gradually relaxed, and was moodily contemplating his sallow and unsatisfactory image in the drugstore mirror across from the counter, when he felt Banner grip his arm. He turned, and Banner murmured, "Look at that boy and girl."

Seated at a table between the soda fountain and a display of alarm clocks were a boy and girl with glasses of some kind of dark-brown carbonated drink. The boy raised his eyebrows at the girl, who giggled as he solemnly dropped two pale-green pills, one in his drink, one in hers. To the accompaniment of a violent effervescence, they crushed the pills with their spoons.

Hommel was momentarily paralyzed. Then he glanced around, horrified that no one was doing anything to stop them.

At the soda fountain, a boy in a light-brown jacket was turned away, just taking two milk shakes from the mixers. At the prescription counter at the far end of the room, a man in a white jacket was handing a woman a package, and smiling at her owlishly through thick lenses. He raised one finger of each hand.

"*One* for *one*. You'll be tranquil, but not dopey." He laughed. "No, madam, they won't fight each other." He turned to the next customer. "Yes, ma'am?"

Hommel let his breath whistle out through his teeth. The boy and girl had set down their empty glasses, and were now watching each other expectantly.

For an instant, they both straightened with a look of mutual disapproval. Then a kind of greenish light came into the boy's eyes. The skin at the corners of his eyes tightened up as his ears pulled back. He opened his mouth and made a "*whooo*" sound, as if blowing out live flames.

Arm in arm, the boy and girl went out the door.

Hommel stared after them. "Great, leaping—"

Banner growled, "That boob at the prescription counter is packaging De-Tox with the tranquilizers."

Hommel started to get up.

Banner gripped his arm. "Hold on. You stop a fan by pulling out the plug, not grabbing the blade."

Another customer was approaching the drug counter. Another

large bottle of De-Tox was wrapped up and handed over. The cash register jingled merrily. Another customer stepped up.

"I see what you mean," said Hommel slowly.

Just then, the boy behind the lunch counter set down their milk shakes and sandwiches. They ate somberly, then started back to the plant. On the way, they stopped for gas, and were treated to the sight of a yawning truck driver swallowing a pill to keep awake, and following it with two pale-green De-Tox pills.

Banner and Hommel pulled through the gates of the Banner Value Drug and Vitamin Laboratories, Inc., in silence and a state of profound gloom.

The next six weeks passed with Hommel running a big program to search out the effects of chronic overdosing with the pills, and, if possible, to find some antidote. While Hommel suffered from the gradual discovery that half his research staff was doped to the ears, Banner piled up frustrations trying to get official recognition of the possible dangers of the drug.

"*Phew!*" said Banner. "How do you convince them when they're already on the pills themselves, with their critical sense working overtime? It was all I could do to get the drug barred from the armed forces. One of the boobs even told me I should 'take medication to quiet an excessively active imagination.'"

"What I've run into is just as bad," said Hommel. He opened a portfolio, pushed some bulky reports out of the way, and pulled out a folder of large glossy photographs. "We've found out what chronic overdosing with the drug does. Here, for instance, we have a dog massively doped with the pills."

Banner leaned forward, and the two men looked at a photograph of a large lean dog inside a square, fenced-in pen, with the fence completely removed from the side behind the dog. The dog was looking hungrily through the woven wire at a bowl of what appeared to be big chunks of meat covered with gravy.

"Hm-m-m," said Banner. "All he has to do is to go back through the open side of the pen, go around the other side, and he's got the meat."

"His approach was different," said Hommel, and handed over another picture.

This photograph showed large and small stones, gravel, and dirt thrown back from the fence, a shallow hole dug under the fence, clumps of fur sticking to the bottom wires of the fence, and the dog, scratched up and exhausted, bolting down the food.

Banner stared. "Is this what it does to people?"

"Well, here are some first-rate chess players, who originally got started on the pills because they wanted to be clear-headed during a tournament."

The photograph showed half-a-dozen intellectual-looking individuals peering over each other's shoulders at a chessboard where a White Pawn sat on Queen's Knight 2, with the White King right beside it on QB2. Arrayed against White was the Black King on QB4, Rook on K4, Queen on K8, and Knight on QKt6.

"Whose move?" said Banner.

"Black's. Now, all that these doped-up chess players had to do was to find a good move. Three of them favored K-QB5. That's a stalemate. One liked Q-Q7ch. That loses the Knight. Another favored R-K7ch; that's another way to lose the Knight. The last one got excited and figured he had checkmate. He moved Q-B6ch. White has four different ways to get out of check, including a choice of two ways to take the Queen."

Banner passed his hand over his face.

Hommel pulled out a photograph of three mechanics squinting under a raised hood. The engine showed up clearly. Hommel said, "Look at that distributor."

"Hm-m-m. The high-tension wire from the coil is interchanged with one of the spark-plug wires. They've plugged into the wrong connections on the distributor cap."

"Right. These expert mechanics figured it out, too—in an hour and forty-seven minutes."

Banner shook his head. "What's that next one?"

"A highly-competent chemist who used the pills to improve his objectivity, and was so pleased with the effect that he gradually increased the dosage."

The photograph showed a man in a laboratory jacket holding a dripping Bunsen burner by the base. Before him was a distilling flask fitted with upright reflux condenser. A length of rubber tubing supplied water to the top of the condenser's water jacket. This water ran down through the water jacket, and was carried off by another length of rubber tubing, which coiled around and connected to the side-arm delivery tube on the distilling flask. Everything was thus neatly connected up, including the pointless side arm. The water from the jacket obediently flowed in through the side arm, filled up the distilling flask, rose up through the inside of the condenser, overflowed at the top, like a fountain, and poured down the outside.

"Ye gods," said Banner, "surely he could figure *that* out!"

"I think he secretly thought he was witnessing the spontaneous generation of matter."

"But how does this come about? The drug starts off by *stimulating* the critical faculty."

"Yes, and following repeated overstimulation comes fatigue, exhaustion, and malfunction. Eventually, people get into such bad shape from overdose of the pills that if they stay off them for a while and start to recover, the first flickers of returning intelligence strike them as 'weird ideas,' instability, and so on. They're afraid that they're getting 'strange.' So, they take more pills."

Banner shook his head. "What's that next picture?"

Hommel handed him a photograph of three keen-eyed men, one gnawing the end of a lead pencil, and all studying a circuit mounted on a board.

Banner said, "What's the difficulty?"

"It doesn't work."

Hommel watched Banner's face change expression as his gaze shifted from one part of the picture to another.

"Where's the power supply?" said Banner.

Hommel laughed dryly. "They overlooked that."

Banner shook his head and turned away, to gaze out the window. "This thing has got to be stopped. If we were the only people making the drug, we could shut down our plant to stop it." He banged his fist into his hand. "What we need is some kind of dramatic incident, to jolt people to their senses! But what—"

A pill-colored, pale green sound truck went by off beyond the fence, on the road that paralleled Banner Drugs' main building. Pale-green pennants whipped from poles mounted on the fenders and at the corners of the truck's roof. Banner and Hommel followed it with their eyes as it passed, reading the big sign on the side:

8:00 p.m.   Tonight
THE
SOLID
PHALANX
Be at the Stadium to hear Big Jim!

They stared after the truck as it disappeared down the road.

"What," said Banner, "is the Solid Phalanx?"

Hommel scowled. "I've heard our men talk about it. It's apparently a pseudo-Nazi organization of dead-end pill-addicts looking for someone to blame. 'Big Jim,' I think, serves as imitation Fuhrer, and blames all the troubles in the world on 'eggheads.' The last I heard, his supporters were supposed to get guns and ammunition, and be ready for The Day."

"What happens then?"

Hommel shrugged. "I don't know."

"Hm-m-m," said Banner. "8:00 p.m., in the stadium. Pill addicts." He glanced thoughtfully at Hommel. "Mort, could you make up a few bottles of imitation pills? The same color, size, shape, and flavor—but without the drug?"

"Ye-s," said Hommel, "but—"

"It might pay us to find out more about Big Jim."

Eight o'clock that night found Banner and Hommel getting out of their car in a big parking lot, bottles of fake pills clinking in their pockets. They made their way with a stolid mass of dour-faced people, past black-uniformed guards wearing black leather belts, black boots, and black-and-white armbands, and who relieved them of fifty cents apiece, into a stadium full of silent people, whose only visible movements consisted of breathing, tossing pills into their mouths, chewing, and swallowing. The only perceptible sounds in the stadium were the moaning of the wind, and a continuous low crunching noise, like twenty or thirty cars rolling slowly downhill on a gravel road with their engines off.

The dour faces and endless working of jaws began to get Hommel after a while. He could feel himself starting to get a little choked. His hand wasn't quite steady as he tossed fake pills in his mouth. His stomach muscles twitched in incipient spasms. The effort to keep his face straight was becoming a struggle.

All around him, the *munch-munch* sound went on endlessly.

Hommel could feel the irresistible burst of laughter build up. Desperately, he told himself what the consequence of that would be.

Munch-munch-munch-munch-

Just as his self-control neared the snapping point, there was a movement down below. Instantaneously, everyone around Hommel, including Banner, only a fraction of a second late, sprang to their feet.

What happened was a little hard for Hommel to follow, because he was still struggling not to laugh. Between sudden shouted roars of approval, that ended just as abruptly, he could hear a voice shout:

"Who made the first gun?"

The crowd roared. "Eggheads!"

The voice shouted, "Who made the first plane?"

"Eggheads!" roared the crowd.

"Who made the first bomb?"

"*Eggheads!*"

The *munch-munch-munch* was clearly audible in the pause between shouts, and Hommel, gagging and straining, was only vaguely conscious of the progression through poison gas, germ bombs, intercontinental missiles, and radioactive fallout, which led to the comparison of murderers and eggheads, which in turn brought up the question of punishment, and "execution of The Plan."

By this time, Hommel had himself in hand again, heard the rousing unified scream of "Death to the Murderers!" and something in the atmosphere of the place got across to him so that he had no further temptation to laugh.

"Big Jim" now finished up with the command to buy more guns and ammunition, and announced that armbands would be distributed on the way out.

Hommel and Banner found themselves sitting in the car a little later, holding black armbands marked with a large "X," which symbolized what The Solid Phalanx was supposed to do to all eggheads at no very distant date.

Hommel had expected Banner to be worn out by all this grimness and activity, but as the old man contemplated the armband, he gave a smile that Hommel would have hated to have inspired, and was cheerful all the way back to the plant. Hommel couldn't get a word of explanation out of him.

Next day, ground was broken for an addition that reached at right angles all the way from the main building to the front fence bordering the road. This addition, seen from above, formed an upright to the long crossbar of the main building, to make a sort of massive T, the lower end of the upright of the T toward the road, and the crossbar parallel with the road and well back from it.

The new addition was wide and deep, massively built, with a broad ramp that led up on either side to a huge loading deck, so that trucks could drive in one electrically-controlled gate in the extra-heavy fence, roll along the curved drive, up the ramp onto the loading deck that ran through the building in a wide tunnel from one side to the other, load or unload, roll down the other ramp, along the other curved drive, and out the second gate to the street.

There was no doubt in Hommel's mind that this addition could serve five times Banner Drug's present needs, to say nothing of some enigmatic fittings in the ceiling of the loading tunnel, that could serve no useful function Hommel could think of.

Hommel, however, had no time to ponder this. It was at this point, with the Phalanx growing daily more formidable, and with a monster rally scheduled for early the next afternoon, that Banner chose to appear on a TV program and remark that Banner Drugs appeared very close to having an antidote to the De-Tox pills.

This was news to Hommel, whose effective research staff was reduced to himself, Viola Manning, and young Peabody. Worse yet, it dawned on Hommel that the people behind the Phalanx would not take kindly to this mythical antidote that would cut their following out from under them. But Banner didn't stop there. When asked about the Phalanx, he referred to them offhand as "a mass of addled brains. I hope we can cure them soon." "Big Jim" got passing mention as "that vulture." Banner finished the interview with the remark that, "I hope we can collapse the Phalanx bubble sooner than anyone expects."

The next day, the big parking lot at Banner Drug was all but empty, as frightened employees stayed away.

Shortly after time for the Phalanx's monster rally, a long line of cars stopped along the road outside the gates, and a crowd of men with black-and-white armbands climbed out carrying guns, and headed for the fence. To Hommel's horror, someone threw the switch that opened the electrically-controlled gates. The mob poured through, spread out, and swarmed toward the main building, directly in front of them.

Hommel, lying under the table, with Viola Manning clinging to his left arm, and Peabody muttering something about pills in his right ear, was just living from moment to moment. It was obvious to him that Banner's foolhardy actions had doomed them all. He felt a momentary pity for the old man, at this moment cowering, no doubt, in his office.

An electrically-amplified voice, unmistakably that of Banner, boomed out over the din. With a kind of pitying contempt, it demanded:

"What's wrong, you poor boobs, can't you find us? Afraid of eggheads? *Come on*! Let's see if you're yellow."

The volume of fire that answered this left Hommel all but deaf. But after the first few moments, not a shot came into the room. Hommel's curiosity got the better of his judgment, he pulled loose from Viola and Peabody, stood up in a half-crouch, and peered out the window.

Gun-carrying figures wearing armbands ran past outside.

Banner's amplified voice rose over the din:

"You want to fight, do you? O.K. *Here we come!*"

A host of armbanded figures sprinted toward the sound of the voice.

The building trembled continuously.

Peabody's lips were moving, and Viola had both hands pressed to her ears, her face contorted.

It made no difference. All Hommel could hear was one continuous crash and roar, that left him dazed and unconscious of the passing of time.

Finally it came to Hommel that the noise was dying down.

Someone tapped Hommel on the arm. He looked around.

Banner, an old but efficient-looking Springfield .30-06 in one hand, and a bandolier of ammunition slung across his shoulder, jerked his head toward the door. Dazedly, Hommel followed him outside.

When they were a few yards from the door, Hommel came to his senses. "Listen . . . *that mob might—*"

"Not for a while."

Hommel followed Banner's gaze toward the massive new addition. Its walls were pitted and pockmarked all over. There was scarcely a sliver of glass left in a window from one end of it to the other. The ramp was littered with knots of men, their eyes streaming, blindly hammering at each other with gun butts, breaking apart to reel over the edge of the ramp, and fall flat in the dirt. A multitude of struggling figures could be vaguely seen through the grayish haze that drifted out the entrance of the loading dock.

Hommel stared. "*Who are they fighting?*"

"Who do you think? They're drugged. That addition splits the ground here into two parts, with a gate on either side. They came in through both gates, ended up on both sides of the addition, went into a rage when I spoke through the loud-speakers that are under the roof on both sides of the addition, and fired at the building from opposite sides. Some of the shots sprayed through that cloud of tear gas in the loading tunnel, they charged in, couldn't see who they were fighting—"

"They're fighting *each other?*"

Banner nodded with satisfaction. "At their own cost, they're making a nice big mess that can't be ignored." He glanced around. "Look there."

Way out by the far end of the fence, wary reporters and cameramen could be seen coming forward very cautiously.

Banner took one last satisfied look at the struggling, retching, helpless tangle, and opened the door. "Once word of this mess reaches the majority of people who use only a mild overdose of the drug, they'll drop it like a—"

Peabody, on the way out, all but knocked them down in his haste.

Somewhere, there was the blast of whistle. Hommel glanced around, to see heavily-armed troops well spread out, coming across the open ground to the south.

With a sensation of relief, Hommel knew the mess *was* coming to a close. He remembered Banner's remark that he had barely gotten the drug barred from the armed forces. By that narrow margin, they should be able to get through the final convulsions. Then the thing would be over. Hommel promised himself that if ever again some wonderful new drug should appear—

Vaguely, he became conscious that Peabody was earnestly talking to Banner. Peabody had been trying to tell Hommel something earlier. Hommel, thoroughly skeptical of the unpromising sidetrack Peabody had insisted on following, now listened curiously.

". . . And *then* tried the methyl ether, instead," said Peabody, happily holding up a little, pale-pink pill. "I was hoping to get the antidote, but Dr. Hommel was right. It isn't that. But there is a mental effect. This acts to *stimulate visual memory.*"

Viola Manning shut her eyes.

Hommel gripped the doorframe.

"Hm-m-m," said Banner, eyeing the pill.

Peabody said, "I tried it first on rats learning a maze. The effect was unmistakable. I tried it on myself, and I could see almost any page of my college organic text, just as if I were holding it in front of me. The effect lasted almost four hours. Sir, it could be tremendously useful. Students, engineers, doctors—"

Earnestly, Hommel stepped forward to protest—and then paused.

He always *had* wanted a good visual memory.

Banner was saying thoughtfully, "Not quite as big a market as . . . er . . . some we've had, but still—"

The three men huddled around the little pale-pink pill, looking at it as Eve may have looked at the apple.

There was a slight commotion, and they glanced around.

Viola had passed out cold.

Peabody went for water.

"Women," said Hommel, "are illogical."

"True," said Banner, "but why so, particularly?"

"Well, she came through all that trouble. She didn't faint *then.*"

Banner nodded. "I see your point."

They glanced back at the new pill.

"She only faints *now*, when there's nothing to be afraid of."

Is Everybody Happy?

Morton Hommel, Ph.D., Director of the Banner Value Drug and Vitamin Laboratories, Inc., beamed proudly as old Sam Banner, the company's founder and president, sat back and squinted at the little bottle of dark-purple pills.

"They *what?*" said Banner.

"Eliminate the allergic response."

"You mean, they *cure* hay fever?"

"They do. And not only hay fever, but the entire spectrum of—"

"Hold on a minute. They *do* cure hay fever?"

Hommel got control of his enthusiasm.

"They alleviate the *distress.* They . . . ah—"

"Stop the sneezing?"

"Yes—and the other symptoms."

"How about the side effects?"

"Well . . . there we have a—" Hommel hesitated. "There seems to be only one side effect."

"What's that?"

"Well, it's . . . nothing uncomfortable. No sensation of tightness in the head, or sleepiness, or anything that can be classified as *distressing* in any way. Quite the contrary."

Banner set the pills on his desk.

Hommel struggled on. "It's . . . ah—Well, it's unusual, and yet, it s highly bene—That is, it's a *good* side effect."

"What is it?"

"There's an extremely pleasant sensation of . . . well . . . friendliness and fellow-feeling. Possibly, to some extent, this is a reaction from the distress experienced by the allergic individual—"

"If you've got hay fever and you take these pills, the pills *make you feel friendly*?"

Hommel hesitated. "Yes."

"Friendly toward *what*?"

"Well—There's a pleasant slightly euphoric—"

"Never mind the gold paper and fancy ribbon, Mort. You feel friendly. Is that right?"

"Yes. It's a . . . very pleasant sensation of fellow-feeling."

"Do you see things?"

Hommel blinked. "What—"

"Does the lamp post grow big violet eyes? Do you get swept off on a wonderful voyage of discovery, and learn the inner secrets of the universe, which evaporate after you get back?"

"No. It's definitely not hallucinogenic."

"You just feel *friendly*?"

"Yes."

"Friendly towards *what*?"

"Well . . . it's hard to define. It's a sense of fellow-feeling. By no stretch of the imagination could it be considered a *harmful* side effect."

"You think it's a *good* side effect?"

"Frankly, yes."

"Then let's nail down what it does."

"I don't know how better to describe it than to say it's a sensation of *warm fellow-feeling and friendliness*."

"You've taken the pills, yourself?"

"Yes. And they relieved my hay fever completely. I'm sure if you'd care to try the—"

Banner said dryly, "I don't have hay fever. Now, since you've tried it yourself—"

"And we've thoroughly tested it. My report—"

"Your report read like a banquet with all the delicacies—cooked in the cans. Kind of hard to digest."

Hommel opened his mouth and shut it. "I don't know how else to express it. You feel *friendly*. We *need* more friendliness in the world."

"Suppose you drive somewhere, and take this pill so you won't have hay fever?"

"Your reactions to driving situations are perfectly normal. There's no falling off in reaction time, no sleepiness, no feeling of unreality. You do feel more friendly toward other drivers. You're more likely to be accommodating, and less likely, for instance, to try to beat them at the light. We find the drug makes the user, indirectly, a more careful driver. This isn't its purpose, of course; but I don't see how it could be considered a *harmful* side effect."

"This feeling of friendliness—Do you feel friendly toward your car, for instance? Or just toward other people?"

"Possibly it's correct to say that a man is incidentally more *careful* of his car. I suppose that might be interpreted as friendliness. But the inner sensation is a sense of *fellow-feeling*, for other human beings."

Banner sat back and scowled at the bottle of small dark-purple pills.

"If it were entirely up to me, Mort, these pills would go straight down the nearest drain. Unfortunately—"

Hommel was astonished. "Why should we try to suppress this?"

"The question is academic, because we can't. But bear in mind, we get paid for killing germs and easing pain. Uplifting human nature is not our line of work."

"But—"

"If we're going to stay in business, we can't ignore a money maker like this. But we're going to have to find out if we can get hay fever relief *without* incidentally making the customer feel friendly."

"But why eliminate a *good* side effect?"

"The customer isn't asking for it. The ideal drug does exactly what the customer buys it to do, *and nothing else*. He buys drugs to relieve an ache or kill a germ, not to have his head feel tight, to get sleepy, or to have green fur grow on his tongue."

"This is different."

"And, since we probably can't get rid of this side effect, we'll start work on an antidote."

Hommel felt staggered. "*Antidote?*"

"Right, Mort. An antidote. Just in case."

Despite Hommel's objections, Banner insisted. Being the boss,

Banner got his way. The problem itself proved as interesting as the original problem, so that Hommel soon forgot his objections.

Meanwhile, the new drug appeared on the market, and Hommel exasperatedly read the label:

Nullergin-20

For relief of Allergy Symptoms. Take one to three tablets per day as required, to relieve symptoms of hay fever, or allergic response to dust, cat hair, egg white, or other causative agent. Nulllergin-200 is a new formulation, designed to overcome symptoms of allergic response to a wide range of substances. Like all drugs, it should be used in moderation. *CAUTION*: In some persons, Nullergin-200 has been found to apparently induce a sense of friendliness; discontinue use where this side effect is undesirable.

Where, Hommel asked himself, *would a sense of friendliness be "undesirable"?* Then he shrugged. The *main* thing was, this blessing for allergy sufferers was on the market.

The sales of Nullergin-200, with a minimum of advertising, picked up steadily. By hay-fever season, the cash registers were ringing all over the country. It was then that Banner called Hommel into his office.

"How's that antidote coming?"

"It's quite a complex problem. But we're making measurable progress."

"Measurable progress? Well, put all the man power on it you need, because we're getting into a measurable mess."

Hommel looked blank. "What do you mean?"

Banner had several newspapers on his desk, and tossed one over. "Look at the headlines."

Hommel read:

ULTERIOR STRIKE SETTLED
Management Yields After Long Struggle

Banner said, "Take a look at that picture."

Hommel frowned at a photograph of two men, the first grinning in triumph, the second smiling benevolently, with his arm around the other's shoulder. Behind them stood several rows of men, some smiling, some scowling, a few with handkerchiefs at their faces.

Hommel said blankly. "I see it. But—"

"Look at the part of the story that's circled."

Hommel spotted several paragraphs marked in heavy pencil:

> Mr. Scharg explained that he wished the union well, and hoped the company would be able to offer a similar raise every year.
>
> Asked for his comment, Mr. Kraggenpaugh, the union representative, expressed contentment with the contract "for the time being. If the management had accepted this offer earlier, it would have saved everyone trouble. This proves they could have done it all along."
>
> Not available for comment was Maurice De Pugh, executive vice president, who earlier argued that accepting the union's demand would put the company out of business.
> Mr. Scharg's sudden reversal took everyone by surprise. The question now raised is how Ulterior, in light of the latest drop in sales, can afford a pay raise it rejected last year, when it was making a profit.
>
> Mr. Scharg's report to the upcoming stockholders' meeting is eagerly awaited.

Hommel frowned, and looked back at the photograph. The man smiling in friendship was identified as Mr. Scharg. The man grinning in triumph was Mr. Kraggenpaugh.

He studied the photograph more closely, and noticed that, of the men who had handkerchiefs raised, two apparently were blowing their noses, and one had his eyes shut, as if sneezing violently.

Banner said, "Kind of an unusual thing, Mort."

"It certainly is." Studying the photograph, Hommel could see a bulge in the pocket of Scharg's suit coat. It could be a pair of gloves. But who would carry gloves in hot weather? It could be a handkerchief. But Scharg did not look as if pollen were bothering *him*.

Or it *could* be a pill bottle.

Banner said, "Mort, this stuff doesn't put a man into a stupor, does it?"

"No."

"What happens if he takes an overdose?"

"Well, the more he takes, the greater the . . . the effect."

"The more pills he takes, the friendlier he gets?"

Unwillingly, Hommel said, "Yes."

Banner handed across another paper.

Hommel was confronted by large headlines:

KIDNAP VICTIM SAFE!
Police Recover Youth
In High-Speed Chase
Father Hugs Kidnapper

A photograph showed a well-dressed man pumping the hand of a tough-looking individual handcuffed to an astonished policeman. Hommel glanced at the text:

> ". . . But this is the man who kidnapped your son!"
>
> "I don't care," the boy's father told the police officer. "I just feel friendly toward *everyone*."

Hommel looked up. "We don't *know* he was using our product."

"Can you think of some *other* explanation?"

"No." Hommel looked puzzled.

"Neither can I. And here's something else I never heard of before." He handed Hommel a page torn out of a magazine.

Reluctantly, Hommel took it, to see an advertisement showing a cheerful overalled figure holding an electric drill, a section of an article about a high-speed passenger train, a small ad for a suction-plunger to clean out drains, and finally a paragraph circled in heavy pencil:

LONELY? NEED FRIENDS?
Our method brings Guaranteed Results. No need to exchange photos. This is not a pen-pal club. This method is New and Proven. You pick *who you want* for a friend *in advance*. Then take our Mystery Substance and *use* it. That's all. Now you have a friend! Can be used on anyone.

Sex, age, social class, do not matter. Sound great? It *is* great! Full instructions included. Send $2.25 to Friendly Universe, Box 250, Dept. W3 . . .

Hommel looked up dizzily.

Banner pulled open a desk drawer, took out a small stamped package, opened it up, removed a stoppered vial from a cardboard tube, and unfolded a large sheet of paper labeled: "Now—A *Friendship* Essence—Here are your Instructions!"

Hommel swallowed hard, and read "Now, an ancient mystery from the mysterious East, but guaranteed by Modern Science, makes it possible for anyone—*even you!*—to have friends! And it is so easy! . . . Contained in this vial is the Mysterious Miracle Essence compounded from an ancient formula . . . some say the mysterious vital essences of Earth, Air, Fire, and Water are condensed into it by magically enchanted *strictly scientific equipment* . . . but we say only, it *works*, and it's *wonderful* . . . All that you need to do is buy a simple atomizer at any drugstore, and spray this Mystery Essence around the room before your chosen friend gets there. Or, you go where they are, and squirt it around when they aren't looking . . . The *Mystery Essence* will do the rest. It never fails! . . . There is no law against this. It is perfectly legal, and *you are doing them a favor* . . . The power of the Mystery Essence *will secretly protect* your chosen friend against *hay fever, cold and poison ivy!* Refills available at $2.25 each from Friendly Universe, Box 250 . . ."

Hommel looked up in stupefaction. "Great, holy, leaping—"

Banner said, "You see, Mort, it *isn't* such a harmless side effect, is it?"

"I never imagined—" He stared at Banner. "Could *you* foresee all this?"

"Not the details. But if you should come in here with a little pill that cured headaches, and had no side effects, and nothing wrong with it, except that if you hit it with a hammer it would blow out ten city blocks . . . well, no one might be able to foresee the *details*, but they could tell *something* would happen when it went on the market."

"Yes, but this was *friendliness.*"

"Are you saying, Mort, that friendship isn't a power in the world?"

"No. But—"

"Then, you see, these pills *exert power*. Just as surely as if they were TNT."

Hommel sat back in bafflement. "I see it. But it doesn't seem right."

Banner nodded. "*If* these pills were used right, there'd be no great problem. *Some* people will use them just as they should. But I would bet you, Mort, that right this minute there are others mashing these pills into a fine powder, touching a match to the powder, and then sniffing the smoke to see what happens. If one of these people dives out a tenth-story window because he has turned into a bird, and another starts eating ground glass because he can't be hurt, who do you suppose will get blamed?"

Hommel only nodded his head.

"Right. Keep working on that antidote."

Hommel did as he was told. Fueled by a large proportion of Banner's profits, the "antidote" project forged ahead at a strenuous pace. But Nullergin-200 went faster.

As the hay-fever season ended, the common-cold season took over. It developed that Nullergin-200 eliminated most of the symptoms of an ordinary cold. Sales increased.

Hommel, more and more immersed in his work, paid little attention to the outside world. But it was impossible to ignore it completely.

On his way to work one morning, he nearly smashed into the car in front, which had stopped considerably in a long line of traffic to let a second car back out of an alley. The driver of the second car, in his friendly appreciation, walked back to thank his benefactor. As Hommel stared in disbelief, this first driver got out to shake hands, and the two beamed upon one another until some unregenerate ten cars back let go a long blast on his horn.

Farther on, two small children were playing in the middle of the street, and all the traffic laboriously detoured around their cardboard tent. A large oil truck, in front of Hommel, had to back and fill to get around, and finally came to a stop. The driver, a large, tough-looking man in a worn leather jacket, walked over to the two children, bent down, and rumpled their hair. He smiled at Hommel in pure friendship.

"You live for your kids. Right, Jack?"

Hommel stared at the truck driver's massive shoulders, and snarled, "*Right.*"

When Hommel got to the plant, he was an hour late. He wasn't in a very friendly mood himself.

Banner at once called him to his office.

"How's that antidote coming?"

"Our program would go a good deal faster if we had less socializing and more work."

"Our own people are taking the drug, eh?"

Hommel nodded. "They say it cuts down the symptoms of the common cold. That may be true, but—"

There was a brief tap at the door, and Hommel glanced around. The door opened, and Banner's secretary looked in, to gush, "Oh, Mr. Banner, I just *had* to come in for a minute, to say how much I *do* enjoy working for you."

Banner looked at her coolly. "I appreciate that, Miss Hemple, but—"

"I just *love* every minute here. And I think you're just the *kindest* employer. There, I *had* to say it. Thank you *so* much, Mr. Banner, for everything."

The door shut, and Banner stared at it.

"Is that what you mean, Mort?"

"That's how it starts. It gets worse when everyone tells everyone else how he enjoys having him for a co-worker. You take half-a-dozen people, and the permuta—"

"The *what*?"

Hommel paused. "There are thirty different ways they can congratulate one another on being good co-workers. At *least* thirty different ways."

Banner said soberly, "I've heard of the world ending by disasters. It never occurred to me it might end in a handshake."

Hommel started to reply, but was interrupted again, this time by a woman's scream echoing down the hall outside.

Banner and Hommel were on their feet at once. Banner seized a heavy cane he used for occasional bouts of rheumatism, and they went through the outer office, and reached the hall door just as there was a louder scream.

Hommel threw the door open, to see Viola Manning, one of his assistants, rush past.

Right behind her came Peabody, Hommel's promising young research chemist. Peabody's eyes were lit up in a kind of greenish murky light. Both his hands were stretched out after Viola Manning.

Hommel shouted, "What *is* this? *Stop!*"

Peabody didn't stop.

Banner shot out his heavy cane, entangling Peabody's legs.

Peabody's arms flailed, he hurtled forward off balance, and hit the floor with a crash.

Banner recovered his cane, and watched Peabody alertly.

Peabody groaned, sat up, and felt cautiously of his nose and face. He staggered to his feet.

Hommel eyed him coldly. "And just what the devil were *you* doing?"

"I . . . ah—"

From somewhere came a sound of sobbing, and a reassuring feminine voice giving words of comfort.

Peabody glanced around nervously. "Did I—"

Hommel said angrily, *What were you doing?*"

"I . . . I was dissolving some powdered Nullergin-200 in ethyl alcohol, and I . . . it occurred to me to wonder what the physiological effect—"

"You *drank* it?"

Peabody stared at his toes. "Yes."

Banner said, "How much?"

"Just a little . . . a few milliliters . . . hardly any—"

Hommel said, "You were dissolving it in pure ethyl alcohol?"

"Yes, but I diluted it. I poured in some water, shook in a little . . . er . . . sucrose . . . and—"

Banner said, "How many pills did you grind up in this punch?"

"The . . . the dissolved Nullergin-200 couldn't have been the equivalent of a tenth of a pill."

Hommel said grimly, "Then what happened?"

"I . . . ah . . . Viola—She had just come in, and—All of a sudden I saw her in a different light—" His face reddened. He said helplessly, "It was like friendship—only a lot more so."

Hommel said disgustedly, "Next time, stick a little closer to the planned experiment."

"Yes, Dr. Hommel. I will."

"Does Viola realize what happened?"

"I—No."

Banner said, "Did you drink up all of that stuff, or is there some left?"

"There's some left."

"Save it."

Hommel nodded. "And write it down, as accurately as possible, the quantities you used. Then you'd better take a few minutes to decide what you'll say to Viola Manning."

Peabody nodded grimly.

Hommel said, "I'll try to explain to her that it was a . . . er . . . toxic effect. Possibly you can find some better explanation."

When Peabody had gone off, pale and shaken, Banner went back into his office, and Hommel had the job of explaining to Viola Manning.

That evening, when Hommel got back to his apartment, the daily paper told of a town in the mid-west that had found the way to peace and friendship—through putting Nullergin-200 in the water supply.

When he got up the next morning, the news broadcast told of two daring bandits who, late the previous afternoon, had walked into a bank in a friendly town in the mid-west, and cleaned it out. The bank guard explained, "I just felt too friendly to stop them."

What riveted Hommel's attention was the bank president's comment: "The trouble with those boys was just that they haven't been drinking our water. I wonder if there's any way to spray the friendship medicine in the *air*?"

"'Friendship medicine,'" muttered Hommel. Then he headed out into the morning traffic jam. This business of waiting out delays at intersections, while drivers politely waved each other ahead, was getting on his nerves.

Late in the week, Banner called Hommel to his office.

"How's the antidote coming, Mort?"

"Assuming there *is* an antidote, we might find it faster with . . . ah . . . fewer complications in interpersonal relationships."

"How's Viola Manning taking it?"

"She looks around with a start when the door opens."

"How about Peabody?"

"He's drowning himself in work," said Hommel.

"Good." Banner picked up a newspaper. "If you'd just glance over the items circled on the front page, Mort."

Hommel glanced over the front page, to notice to his horror that practically every news item was circled:

NO STRIKE, SAYS UNION
Accept Voluntary Pay Cut
RACE WAR ENDS
"We Love Each Other" Say Rival Gang Chiefs
PEACE FORCE ENDS STRIFE
"Friendship Bombs" End Long-Drawn War
Guerrillas Emerge From Jungle Hideout
COMMON COLD LICKED BY RESEARCHERS
Nullergin-200 Gives Double Dose of Blessings
No Sniffles No Snarls
URGE NULLERGIZATED CITY WATER SUPPLY
Ends Colds, Strife With Same Method
PETTIBO STORES HEIRESS FOUND
Eloped With Garbage Collector
Class No Obstacle To True Friendship
IS PEACE PACT REAL?
Soviets Claim Treaty Sprayed With Superdrug

Hommel looked up dazedly.

Banner said, "Things are picking up, Mort."

"But is it better, or worse?"

"Take a look at the folded page."

Hommel turned back to a page with the corner folded, to read:

INDUSTRIAL OUTPUT DROPPING AGAIN
Productivity Per Man-Hour Hits New Low Again This
Month

Hommel read the article, certain comments standing out boldly:

". . . Blamed on on-the-job socializing and increased hesitancy of supervisory personnel to force the pace . . . 'After all, we're all one happy family,' says the superintendent of the Boswah Corporation's East Steelport plant . . . claimed it is possible to keep production lines moving but only by slowing them further . . . 'There is a much nicer atmosphere around here,' comments one worker, sipping her coffee as the line idles by, 'It used to be hurry-hurry-hurry' . . . Executives agree, 'Our competitors have the same problem. Why would we want to hurt *their* business by stepping up productivity. They're basically very nice people.' . . . Dissenter is the crusty, hard-lining president of Kiersager Corporation, who insists, 'We will fire every one of these pooped-out friendship addicts that turns up for work. This mess of flabby hand-shakers is so much clotted blood in the arteries of commerce.'"

Hommel looked up. "Is it like this all over the country?"

"Can you think of anyone who doesn't want to avoid colds?"

"No. Everyone wants to avoid them," Hommel said.

"And how many people are there now who are against taking drugs on principle?"

"Not many."

Banner nodded. "This was bound to come along sooner or later. If people would only use the stuff in moderation, there'd be no problem. But they figure if two pills are good, four pills are twice as good."

Hommel said glumly, "At least it isn't habit-forming."

"No, but if you take two pills before breakfast long enough, you've got the habit whether the pills themselves are habit-forming or not. And if without the pills you snarl at people, and with the pills you feel friendly, which way will most people want to feel?"

"Friendly."

"Right. And if things get so exasperating they stop feeling friendly, they take *more* pills. And it's a little hard to regulate it, when the friendly authorities are using it themselves. Worse yet, supposing every factory on earth stopped making the pills tomorrow? First, the stuff is somewhat cumulative, and second, consider the uproar when it suddenly wore off. What we need is something so we can come out of this *slowly*."

Hommel stared at the paper. "But it's doing *some* good."

"So does a dose of castor oil. But one dose is enough. Keep hunting for that antidote."

Time passed, and more and more money and effort went into finding an antidote. Peabody, driven by a compounded sense of humiliation, seemed to think he could only justify his existence by finding the antidote, and was working day and night with every sign of being close on the trail of *something*.

Meanwhile, in case their attempt to find an antidote should prove useless, Hommel in desperation was following up an improbable project designed to produce some *natural* antidote. The drug overcame hay fever, the argument went, so maybe a stronger causative agent for hay fever might overcome the drug. Since anything seemed worth a try, some two hundred isolated acres of unsettled land were given over to ragweed culture. Some fields were studded with the housing of potent radiation sources, while others were sprayed with special chemicals. While a desperate watch was kept for promising mutations and hybrids, the mere sight of these fields, with dark-green monster ragweeds looming twenty feet tall, and others creeping mosslike along the ground, was enough to give chills to anyone who remembered when hay fever had been a real complaint.

At present, of course, only the stubbornly individualistic suffered from hay fever. These sneezed their way through life, observing with acid contempt the deterioration in quantity and quality of goods and services. Where others offered an eager handshake, this minority shoved its way past with a snarl.

Banner and Hommel, one summer afternoon, drove toward town to send a telegram. They cautiously detoured cars stopped by motorists who just wanted a little talk for friendship's sake, and stopped warily for traffic lights that didn't work, and were flagged down by friendly truck drivers who wanted to share their cargoes.

Laden down with watermelons, hundred-pound boxes of nails, a five-gallon can of asphalt roof-coating, two crates of chickens, and a tin of frozen blueberries, they finally made it to the telegraph office, and stepped inside, to find a woman clerk chatting on the phone.

A tall thin man wearing a green eyeshade got up as they came in.

Banner said, "We've got a carload lot of chemicals we want to trace. We haven't been able to reach anyone by phone. What's the chance of a wire getting through?"

"Depends on who's on the other end." The man removed his eyeshade and glanced pointedly at the woman clerk. Her conversation was clearly audible:

". . . They're the nicest people. We just told them we couldn't pay it, and they said to forget it. The bank has lots of money anyway, and they didn't need it. . . . Then Howard got his bill from the *hospital*, and that was two thousand seven hundred, and we were just *frightened*, what with the plant closing and all—but that nice Mrs. What's-her-name in the office there said she'd just drop our record right out of the file. What does anyone need money *for*, anyway? Aren't we all friends? So then . . ."

The three men glanced at each other. Banner cleared his throat.

"Well, it won't hurt to try."

The telegrapher slid over a pad of forms and a pencil. "Speaking of lost cars, they're getting fairly common. As I understand it, the solution is to accept a carload lot of whatever happens to be lost in your neighborhood. Somebody somewhere else takes your carload lot which is lost in his territory." He added dryly, "It's the *friendly* way out. Saves the railroad a lot of trouble."

Banner tore a form off the pad. "A slight complication in the manufacturing process."

"Yes, I think that *is* starting to show up. Possibly you gentlemen can identify this for me." He reached under a counter, and produced a bottle labeled, "Count Sleek—The man's hair tonic that's friendly to your scalp. Invigorates. Refreshes. With RB 37."

Hommel took the bottle curiously. The liquid inside appeared clear, save for a few black specks drifting around in it. He unscrewed the plastic cap, noted a little whitish crust on the rim, and what appeared to be small transparent grains of some kind on the thread. Frowning, he sniffed cautiously, but noticed no odor. He screwed the cap back on, and stood weighing the bottle in his hand. For its size, it felt heavy.

The man behind the counter said, "I've used that brand of hair tonic before. This stuff doesn't look right or smell right, and the bottle doesn't even *feel* right."

Frowning, Hommel took a piece of tissue paper from his pocket—put there in preparation for the approaching hay-fever season—folded the tissue, unscrewed the cap from the bottle, and poured a few drops of the liquid on the folded paper. The liquid, which had seemed watery in the bottle, looked oily on the paper. The wet paper promptly turned brownish.

Scowling, Hommel wiped the bottle with an edge of the folded tissue. The paper dissolved away, leaving, one beside the other, four curved blacked edges with a charred look. The large oily drop in the center of the paper sat there as the paper beneath turned black, then suddenly, the paper shrank away in a thin film to expose the next layer.

From the tissue arose a sharp pungent odor.

Behind the counter, the telegrapher watched alertly.

"I've seen hair tonic I liked better."

Hommel cleared his throat. "My guess is, it's concentrated sulfuric acid."

Banner said, "They sold it in *that* bottle?"

"They did. I suppose a shipment of the wrong stuff reached the place where they make that—or maybe some chemical factory got a load of the wrong bottles. If enough people will just be obliging, practically anything can happen."

Banner and Hommel went soberly back outside.

"Are we," said Banner, "near even a partway-workable solution?"

"We're *near* half-a-dozen different solutions," said Hommel hauntedly. "But they're completely worthless until we arrive at something actually usable."

The rest of the month passed with slow breakdowns that roused little notice, because—who would be so unfriendly as to complain?

Hommel, sneezing violently during hay-fever season, but avoiding Nullergin-200 as he would avoid poison, was among those who did not feel friendly when he bought gasoline and got kerosene, and when he went to a store to purchase some staples, and found a can swollen out at both ends as if packed under high pressure.

"What's wrong," he asked. "Did they overload these cans?"

"It isn't that they put too much in the cans," said a clerk, in a friendly way, "it's just that everything inside is spoiled, and that makes gas."

That night, nothing else having worked yet, Hommel prayed long and earnestly for a solution.

The next day dawned with an impressive pollen count, and the rest of the week went by with Hommel progressively more miserable. He had scarcely walked into his air-conditioned office one day when Peabody, dark circles under his eyes, came in.

"Unless I'm completely insane, which is possible, I've got it."

Hommel stared at him, afraid to speak.

Peabody said, "I mean, the Nullergin-200 antidote."

Hommel said dizzily, "That's wonderful. Did—"

The phone rang. Hommel picked it up, and motioned Peabody to sit down.

An excited voice demanded, "Hello? Morton?"

"Speaking."

"This is Arthur Schmidt, out at the test plot. Look, Morton, we have a plant here that makes everyone sneeze . . . *Do you hear me?*"

Hommel stared at the phone. "What is the effect on . . . ah . . . disposition?"

"Terrible. With that first sneeze, believe me, all that friendly accommodating feeling evaporates."

"That's wonderful. Listen, you've isolated the particular plant that—"

"Yes, we know which one does it. It's quite a remarkable thing. A very ordinary, unprepossessing little plant, but it releases veritable clouds of extremely fine pollen. An unusual thing about this—it reproduces also, and I must say prolifically, not only by wind-borne pollen, but also by a kind of tumbleweed layering effect."

"By a—*what?*"

"And some of the other plants have evidently hybridized."

"Wait a minute. This thing reproduces *how?*"

"To put it plainly, parts of the stalk grow constricted when the plant reaches a height of approximately eight inches, and a blow or moderate wind causes it to break off. The plant has quite a light-weight structure, you see, Morton, and as a result of the construction of the stem, apparently it becomes partially desiccated—that is, dried out."

"I know what desiccated means," snapped Hommel. "Then what happens?"

"Then the . . . er . . . dried-out portion of stem and leaves is carried off a considerable distance, tumbling, rolling, being lifted up by the wind—"

"*Then* what?" The air-conditioner in the room was providing pure, pollen-free air, but Hommel could feel his nose tingle. "What happens when this thing goes tumbling—"

"Why, bits of the leaves break off, somewhat in the manner of— Possibly you're familiar with a plant commonly known as . . . ah . . . the 'lawyer plant,' I believe, or possibly it's called the . . . let's see . . . 'maternity plant,' which—Are you acquainted—"

"No. What does this have to do—"

"Why, essentially the same mechanism, Morton. When the leaf finds a little moisture, a suitable bit of ground—it takes root, and grows. A new plant, you see."

Hommel had a mental image of the world covered with a rolling carpet of ragweed.

"Listen, if you break a piece of leaf off of this super-ragweed, *the piece of leaf grows into another super-ragweed*?"

The reply was cold. "Rather an imprecise way to express it, Dr. Hommel, but—Yes, *essentially*, that is correct."

Hommel got control of himself. "Excuse me, Dr. Schmidt. My excitement at this, ah, this extraordinary achievement—So timely, too—You understood."

"Certainly, Morton, certainly. Forgive me if I seemed a trifle sharp. I misunderstood."

"Will you excuse me now? I want to inform Mr. Banner of the achievement."

"Banner? What does *he* know about it? Oh, he has money . . . but in a scientific sense, he is an ignoramus."

"Yes, of course. But when a piece of research particularly impresses him, he often provides more . . . ah . . . funds, to extend—"

"Yes, yes, Morton. I understand. Yes, I think he *should* know."

Hommel hung up. "My God! Little ragweeds all over the place!" Despite the air-conditioning, Hommel sneezed.

"Dr. Hommel?" said Peabody blankly.

Hommel stared at him, then said abruptly. "You say you have the 'antidote.' You were looking for some chemical that would stimulate the function the Nullergin-200 depressed?"

"That didn't work. I went back to another idea—something that would go right into the body and break up the Nullergin-200. Well, I've got it."

"What are the side effects?"

"That's one of the things that's taken me so long. So far as I can see, there are no noticeable side effects. You see, this is similar to an enzyme. A comparatively small amount will break down any quantity of Nullergin-200, given time. But, in the body, the enzyme is itself slowly broken down. Since only a comparatively small quantity needs to be used, the side effects are negligible, so far as I've been able to find out."

"And the decomposition products?"

"They're excreted."

"Is this enzyme hard to produce?"

"The process is partly biological. Temperature, pH—quite a number of factors need to be carefully controlled to get a good yield. But there's nothing particularly *hard* about it."

Hommel sat back. "Have you thought how we might use this?"

"Well, if for now we put it in the coating of the pills, the pills will still work—but the effect will wear off faster. And the more pills taken the more quickly the following pills will wear off, because the Neutranull, as I call it, will accumulate. By varying the proportion of Neutranull to Nullergin, we determine, subject to individual variation, *the length of time a given daily dosage will be effective.*"

"And," said Hommel excitedly, "since hay-fever season lasts only so long, *this is what we need.*"

A little work with pencil and paper, with Peabody providing the constants involved, suggested that varied proportions of Neutranull would eliminate the Nullergin-200, as slowly or rapidly as desired, and that the only way to get protection after a given time was to increase the dosage. If this was carried far enough, the effect of the Nullergin could be strung out for a long time—but as a result the Neutranull would build up to such a point that it would still make trouble during the next attack of hay fever.

"Well," said Hommel, "if anyone takes a reasonable dosage, he'll be all right. Good enough. Now, can we market this in time?"

Together, they went over the details. Then they went down to Banner's office.

Before the day was out, Banner Drugs was hard at work on the new process. But, as Banner pointed out, their problems were not solved.

"Even if we get this distributed without any trouble, Mort, there's still Schmidt's improved ragweed. If that pollen is blowing around, how do we stop it?"

"Possibly, it was developed indoors, in a greenhouse," said Hommel grimly. "At any rate, there isn't much of anything I wouldn't be prepared to try to stop it."

"Luckily," said Banner, "we are now well enough known to get our suggestions listened to. Maybe we can get this genie back in the bottle. Get Schmidt on the phone—if you can get him on the phone—and have him come down here. If he drives at night, he may be able to make it without getting glued fast in friendship along the way."

Late the following afternoon, Banner and Hommel met with a tough-looking individual who arrived wearing his hat like a uniform cap, a suave personage who smiled easily and radiated power, and a bulky glum-looking man with a Russian name. There were also three technicians and a quantity of electronic equipment.

As Banner explained courteously to Schmidt. "This is in your honor, Dr. Schmidt. These people are here to learn about your . . . ah . . . epochal discovery. This is General Harmer, Mr. Hall, and Ambassador Kurenko. Your description of your discovery will be simultaneously broadcast and recorded as you give it. Thanks to your reputation, there, of course, is no doubt as to the reality of your achievement. Nevertheless, there are experts of various nationalities listening in, and they may want to ask some questions, which they can do over this hookup. Your words will be translated, incidentally, as you speak them"

Schmidt looked impressed. "May I ask, Mr. Banner, what is the advantage of having a military man here?"

"General Harmer is the President's personal representative. The President couldn't come himself."

"Ah—" said Schmidt. "I see. Excuse me. Well, gentlemen—Shall I begin?"

Banner glanced at the technicians, who nodded.

"Start whenever you want," said Banner, "and just tell us in whatever way you want."

"Well, then—I will begin with *method*. Knowing time was short, I decided upon a brute-force approach. Not so crude, perhaps, as adopted by the well-known innovator, Edison, but using the same general principle, developed more scientifically. I decided to try *every conceivable method and combination of methods*, possible in the space and time, and with the equipment available, sacrificing precise determination of the interrelations of the causative factors involved, in favor of—results."

Schmidt then proceeded to describe, in short clear language, a set of procedures designed to produce the maximum possible genetic variation in the shortest possible time. At the end, he concluded, "With such methods, success or failure depends on chance and the unknown. Our tools are still too crude, and our knowledge too imprecise to enable us to proceed on a basis of exact knowledge. However, the method that worked for Edison has also worked in this instance, as I shall demonstrate. We now have, gentlemen, a variant of the common ragweed that no drug on earth can resist. For the record, I here produce a sample of biologically-inactivated pollen." He removed a small, thick glass tube, about the size of a two-inch cut off a lead pencil. "Is anyone here subject to hay fever?"

Banner, Hall, Harmer, Kurenko, and the three technicians all shook their heads. Hommel reached into his side pocket, said, "I am," and shook three small old-style pills of Nullergin-200 into his hand. As Schmidt nodded, and began to pull the stopper out of the vial, Hommel, who know Schmidt as a demon experimenter, at once took the pills. A warm feeling of friendship spread through him, reassuring him that the Nullergin-200 had taken effect.

"Ah," said Schmidt, "here we are. You see, the biologically inactive pollen, still—" He got the stopper out of the bottle, and instantly shoved it back in again.

A sensation like a double-prong fork made of red-hot pepper moved up Hommel's nose. His vision blurred as a layer of burning dust seemed to coat his eyes. His ears itched. The inside of his mouth felt as if he had just eaten two large plates of overseasoned chili. The room rang with violent sneezes from Banner, Harmer, and everyone save Schmidt. Through a sea of tears, Hommel could see Schmidt stretched out on the floor, his face covered with red blotches.

Every breath Hommel drew was like a breath of finely-ground pepper. He sneezed until he ached so that he didn't dare to sneeze, while at the same time he *had* to sneeze. His throat constricted so that to draw a breath was like sucking a half-frozen drink through a flattened straw.

Something flashed across his wavering field of vision, and there was the crash of breaking glass.

For a brief instant, Hommel could see Banner, his heavy cane upraised, knocking out one window after another, in a room full of choking, gasping, strangling men.

Then Hommel drew in the wire-thin end of a breath of air so cool and uncontaminated that it seemed as sweet as fresh spring water to a man dying of thirst. Then everything whirled around him.

Hommel came to fitfully several times, and finally awoke in a pastel-green room, where several other pajama-clad occupants crowded around a big TV.

Banner, wearing a blue bathrobe, prodded Harmer and Kurenko to move apart, leaving a slot through which Hommel could see a stretch of barren lifeless landscape, across which there slowly came into view a small figure in some kind of dully-glinting suit, carrying a kind of wand in one hand. As this figure passed out of Hommel's range of vision, there appeared a large-wheeled slow-moving armored machine.

The whole scene looked so alien to Earth that Hommel said, "What is that—the surface of the Moon?"

"No," said Banner, "that's what's left of the ragweed test site. They're checking for radioactivity right now."

Hommel leaned back. They could take the whole site and throw it into orbit beyond Pluto as far as he was concerned.

Banner said thoughtfully, "It's an odd thing. Progress is generally supposed to mean, *moving forward*. Once a scientific development appears, for instance, you generally can't suppress it. You have to adapt to it, and go on."

"Let's hope," said Hommel fervently "that we can suppress one or two of these latest developments."

Banner nodded gravely. Then he said in a low voice:

"Sometimes, if you can even move backward, *that's* progress."

The Great Intellect Boom

Morton Hommel, PH.D., director of the Banner Value Drug and Vitamin Laboratories, Inc., proudly put the bottle of yellow capsules on the desk of old Sam Banner, president of the company.

Banner glanced at them dubiously.

"What are they good for, Mort?"

Hommel said, with quiet pride, "They increase intelligence."

Banner looked up.

"What's that again?"

"The drug stimulates intellectual activity. It channels energy from gross physical pursuits into imaginative creativity."

Banner looked at him alertly.

"Have you been taking it?"

"No. But we've carried out exhaustive—"

"It *works*?"

"It's extremely effective."

Banner sat back, and studied the capsules.

"Well, a thing like this would sell to students. Lawyers would want it. Doctors, engineers—Just about everybody could use more brains these days. Quite a market." Then he shook his head. "But it might be that what we've got here is a catastrophe in a bottle. How did we get into this, anyway? I don't remember any work on brain pills."

Hommel winced. "We prefer to think of it as a *drug mediating the enhancement of intellectual activity*."

"That's what I say. Brain pills. How did we get into this in the first place?"

"Well, you remember that problem of parapl—"

"Put it into words an ordinary human can follow, Mort."

Hommel's face took on the expression of a truck driver faced with a detour off a six-lane highway onto a mountain road. With a visible effort, he said, "I mean, that problem of broken nerve tracts that wouldn't grow together."

"I remember *that*. So what?"

"We thought we had a promising lead. It had seemed satisfactory with experimental animals. What we wanted, of course, was something to stimulate the broken ends of the nerve, to cause them to grow and rejoin. We thought at first this would have to be administered locally; but we found, purely by accident, that it could be given by mouth. When we had every reason to believe that the drug would prove successful, we tried it on a human volunteer. This volunteer . . . ah . . . had evidently lacked proper motivational opportunities for educational develop—"

Banner stared. "He *what*, Mort?"

"He'd lacked the proper motivational opportunities for educa—"

"Was the fellow stupid?"

"Well, I'd hesitate to say he—"

"Mort," said Banner, "a junkyard is a junkyard—whether you decide to call it a junkyard or a 'storage module for preprocessed metals.' Was the fellow stupid, or wasn't he?"

Hommel blew out his breath.

"He wasn't the brightest person I ever met."

"All right. What happened?"

"He'd been badly injured. Yet it certainly seemed, from our previous work, that the drug ought to produce a cure. But it didn't."

"The broken ends of the nerves didn't grow together?"

"No."

Banner nodded sympathetically.

"What then?"

"Well, we were very much disappointed. But we were also surprised, because the patient suddenly seemed to gain insight into his accident. Prior to this time, he'd simply blamed the other driver."

"How did he get hurt?"

"He was driving in heavy traffic, got on the wrong turnoff, and tried to get back by making a quick U-turn in a cloverleaf intersection."

Banner looked blank.

Hommel said, "Not only that, but he was convinced that the other drivers owed him a lifetime pension. After he'd been treated with our drug, he saw there was another side to the question."

Banner glanced thoughtfully at the capsules. "Maybe we have something here, after all. What happened next?"

"Well, at first we didn't realize what had happened. But we continued treatment, still hoping for a cure. The patient enrolled in a correspondence course and completed his high-school education. Meanwhile, we'd started treatment on another patient, who read comic books at the beginning of the treatment, and was studying medieval history at the end. It began to dawn on us that there might be some connection. After that, we carried out thorough investigations, and found that there is invariably a marked increase in the patient's intellectual activity. It's no longer possible to think of this as a coincidence. The increase in intellectual activity is caused by our drug."

"Any side effects?"

"In some few patients there's a rash. Occasionally, there's a complaint of a temporary numbness—a sense of being removed from reality. The rash subsides in a day or two after discontinuance of treatment. The numbness fades away in a few hours. Neither reaction seems serious, and neither is especially common."

"How about this increased intelligence? Does it fade away when the patient stops taking the pills?"

"There's a drop, but there's also a residual increase that remains. One of the men on the hospital staff compared intelligence with the amount of traffic a road network will bear. The 'mental traffic' will depend on the mental 'road system'—the number and condition of the brain's nerve cells and connections. The drug speeds up mental 'road building.' When the drug is discontinued, this 'road building' drops back to a much lower level. Those 'roads' only partly finished quickly become unusable. But those already finished remain in use, allowing an increase in 'traffic'—intelligence—over what there was to begin with, although lower than at the peak."

"How much of an increase can there be? What's the limit?"

"We don't know. But it can be substantial, from what we've seen. And happily this all fits right in with current recognition of the importance of education. Quite a few of our patients have gone back to school or college, where they're all doing well. The drug fits in perfectly with the needs of the day."

Banner shook his head.

"It *sounds* good, Mort. And *maybe* it is. But we want to take a few precautions, just in case. Keep working to see if there are any side effects we don't know about, especially any that build up slowly. And start work on an antidote."

Hommel looked dumbfounded.

"But—an *antidote* to this would be a *stupidity drug*."

"It might be and it might not. Who knows how it would work? But we'd better find one." Banner smiled suddenly. "By the way, Mort, have you thought what to name this? How about 'Super Mentalline'?"

"Surely we ought to take a more conservative approach."

"With this," said Banner, "that may prove harder than it looks. But we'll see what we can do."

The drug, when it appeared, was modestly advertised. And Hommel thought the label on the bottle *too* restrained:

CEREBROCREATINE
A Mental Stimulant
Take one to two capsules daily as required, for mild stimulation of intellectual activity. Especially recommended for students, teachers, and others engaged in pursuits requiring increased mental activity.
Caution: Some individuals may be allergic to these capsules. Appearance of a rash, or a temporary feeling of numbness, should cause reduction of dosage or discontinuance of use.

Sales got off to a sluggish start, and remained dull until a sensational Sunday supplement article appeared, titled: "Breakthrough in Brains—New Drug Dramatically Boosts I.Q.!"

That got the ball rolling. Soon, brief "special reports" on radio added to the attention. Television news announcers began introducing humorous items on "I.Q. Capsules," for light relief from a steady diet of disasters.

Sales started to pick up.

Students with half a semester's work to do the night before the exam instantly recognized the possibilities. The results were so delightful that the news spread fast.

Sales of Cerebrocreatine began doubling from week to week.

Banner found himself reading with close attention a letter that gave an idea what was going on:

> Dear Sir:
>
> I am writing to thank you for your help in passing German I. The night before the midyear exam, I could scarcely tell the difference between "f" and "s" in that weird type they use in our reader. But I ate up about half a bottle of your I.Q. pills, holed up with the text and the reader, and by the time Old Sol crawled up over the tree-tops next morning, I was a new man, *Ja wohl*!
>
> I'm pretty well covered with red spots right now, and for a while there I kind of felt like I was packed in ice, but I got past the midyear's exam, and it was worth it.
>
> This German, by the way, is interesting, once you get into it.
>
> Yours in *Gemutlichkeit*,

Banner read this letter over and over again, then called Hommel in to find out how work was coming on the antidote.

Hommel was cheerful.

"We've had some brilliant suggestions, and some really stimulating discussions on the subject, and that sort of beginning can lay the groundwork for some genuine high order achievement later on. I'm sure we'll have real progress to report before long, considering the caliber of the thought that's been shown recently."

Banner frowned.

"That's nice, Mort. But what's been *done* so far?"

"Well, as you realize, this is an extremely difficult problem to deal with. There are a great many ramifications, of really extraordinary subtlety. To put it in layman's language, it pays to clear away the undergrowth before plunging into the thicket."

Banner looked at Hommel attentively, then held out the letter.

"Take a look at this, Mort."

Hommel read the letter quickly, with a faint air of negligent disinterest.

"I'm sorry we didn't have this when I was going to school."

Banner said dryly, "Personally, I'm glad it waited until now." He studied Hommel's expression alertly. "You haven't tried this stuff yourself, Mort?"

"I've made rather extensive use of it. The results have been most gratifying. It's highly stimulating mentally."

"I see. But no actual *work* has been done on the antidote?"

Hommel frowned. "No, I admit, but—"

"Quite a few weeks have gone by."

"I realize that, and we've found some really interesting approaches, that I think should enable us to solve the problem much more rapidly than if we had simply gone at it blindly, more or less by trial and error."

"Maybe. Well, keep at it. And Mort—"

"Yes?"

"If I were you, I'd go a little easy on those pills."

"We've found no harmful side effects, other than those that are strictly temporary."

Banner nodded. "I could be wrong, Mort. But bear in mind that the dosage we suggest on the bottle is 'one to two capsules daily,' and here we have a letter that says, 'I ate up about half a bottle of your I.Q. pills.' We could get something unexpected out of this. If so, we want people here who aren't worried about getting a dose of the same thing themselves. How about your star chemist, Peabody? Is he using the stuff, too?"

"I'm sorry to say Peabody has acquired an irrational distrust of drugs."

"He won't use it himself?"

"No. And I have to admit, he shows up rather poorly by contrast with those who do."

"He does, eh? Well, Mort, do as you think best. But I'd advise you to think this over."

After Hommel had left, Banner called in Peabody.

"I'm told," said Banner, "that you don't think much of our new brain-booster pills."

Peabody looked harassed.

"It isn't that, sir, but I . . . ah . . . I think I'm probably allergic to them."

"Have you tried them?"

"No, sir."

"Don't you feel that, out of loyalty to the company, you ought to eat up at least a bottle a week?"

"I wouldn't want to eat even one capsule a week."

"Why not?"

Peabody shook his head.

"You never know what the side effects may be."

Banner leaned forward.

"What do you think of the work that's been done in finding an antidote?"

"What work? No work *has* been done."

"Even by you?"

"I've groped around some. I've gotten some ideas. But I can't say I've actually accomplished much yet."

"What do you think of the suggestions that have been made?"

"Oh, some of the *suggestions* have been brilliant. They might take a hundred years, all the laboratory facilities and chemists in the country, and a trillion dollars, but some of the suggestions have really sounded good."

"A little impractical, eh?"

Peabody nodded. "Brilliant, though."

"Just between the two of us, Peabody, how many pills do you think the average person who uses this stuff takes?"

"Two with every meal, and two when he goes to bed. That night, he dreams of waking up with an I.Q. of 1,500, and when he gets up he chews up two or three extra for good luck."

"*Does* it make him smarter?"

Peabody scratched his head, and looked exasperated.

"Yes, it does, but—I don't know."

"At least, the pill is useful for learning, isn't it?"

"I suppose so. Everyone says it is. It must be. But is learning supposed to be an end in itself? Once they get started on this stuff, they don't stop."

Banner nodded slowly. "We have to have an antidote."

"There may not *be* an antidote. The effect may be irreversible."

"But we have to look, because that's the only way to find out— and there's another thing that might help, if it's taken care of in time."

"What's that?"

"Where does Hommel keep his personal stock of brain pills?"

Peabody's eyes widened.

"In a drawer of his desk—You mean the Cerebrocreatine?"

"Yes. Now, of course, Peabody, I don't want to suggest that you—or anyone, for that matter—might make up a batch of these pills at considerably reduced strength, and put them in place of the pills Hommel has right now. Naturally, I wouldn't suggest such a thing. Nevertheless, if somebody *did* do that, it might just possibly do some good. Of course, if anyone did do it, he would want to think it over carefully first. Peabody, I admire people who get things *done*. By the way, it seems to me that it's about time you got an increase in salary, isn't it? Yes, I think so. Well, it's been nice weather lately, hasn't it? If we come up with one more drug like this, I think I may just go into the business of manufacturing fishing rods. Of course, there may be something wrong with that, too. If people would chew their food more before they swallow it, they wouldn't *need* so many pills in the first place. And a little exercise wouldn't hurt, either. What the devil are they doing with these things, anyway, Peabody? Are they trying to see who can get to be smartest by eating the most pills?"

Peabody, listening wide-eyed, swallowed hard, opened his mouth, shut it, recovered his breath, and said, "Yes, sir. They seem to use longer words every day."

Banner nodded. "I've always thought there must be a hole in this somewhere. Well, you think over what we've been talking about, and decide what you want to do. The more people we have actually *working* on this antidote, the better."

Peabody squinted in concentration, then nodded determinedly.

As time passed sales climbed to a stunning figure.

Hommel told Banner that he'd evidently reached "some kind of a saturation point" with the drug, which no longer seemed to have any effect on him.

Peabody received a raise.

Hommel reported that a number of his more outstanding men seemed to have "reached the saturation point."

Peabody received a bonus.

Hommel stated exasperatedly that there was "no word of anyone *else* having reached the saturation point"—only he and some of his best men. And wondered why should that be.

Banner wondered aloud if possibly there could be anything about working in a plant where the drug was manufactured that could have anything to do with it.

Hommel seized on the idea as a possible explanation, and determined to look into it once work on the antidote could be got moving. Save for Peabody, this was still on dead center, no one being able to figure out how to put his grandiose research plans into effect.

"The trouble," said Hommel, "is that there are so many very interesting and exciting alternative approaches to the problem—we scarcely know where to start."

"In that case," said Banner, "start anywhere. But for heaven's sake, *start*."

"Many of the more promising methods might prove prohibitively expensive."

"Then forget about them. That simplifies the problem."

Hommel looked puzzled. "True," he said, as if he could not quite grasp the concept, but recognized somehow that it was valid.

After Hommel had gone out, Banner stared at the closed door, then shook his head.

"Well, if that's brilliance, let's hope it wears off pretty soon."

More time went by.

Work on the antidote got sluggishly under way, by fits and starts, and with baffling setbacks, as if the work were dogged by gremlins.

Banner, meanwhile, tried to rouse, amongst those in high places, some awareness of possible future difficulties. Those in high places were not aroused, except by enthusiasm for Cerebrocreatine.

Meanwhile, in colleges and universities throughout the world, bell-shaped curves were being knocked into weird corrugated forms. Ranks of straight-A students moved triumphantly toward graduation. Newspaper and magazine articles predicting the arrival of the millennium multiplied like rabbits.

Banner, meanwhile, had trouble with his car. Having had it inexpertly repaired while he was away on a trip, now that he was back he called up to get it taken care of, and invited Hommel to come along with him.

"All that needs to be done," said Banner, as they walked onto the company parking lot, "is to adjust the carburetor. That shouldn't take too long. We can have lunch a little early, and if they don't have the work done, we'll come back in their courtesy car. I'd adjust it myself, except that they've made so many improvements in the thing that it scares me every time I look under the hood."

Banner got in, and reached over to open the door for Hommel, who by now was seeming more like his usual self. As Hommel slid in and slammed the door, Banner turned the key in the ignition. The engine choked and gagged into life, to run with a galloping rhythm as clouds of black smoke poured out the tail pipe. Like a malfunctioning oil burner on the move, they pulled out onto the highway.

The drive to town turned into a thrilling trip. The car lacked acceleration, and had a tendency to cough and quit. A police officer soon motioned them to the side, parked in front, red light blinking, walked back to their car.

"You're creating a serious hazard in the area of air pollution."

Banner adopted the humble attitude suitable to the occasion. "I'm very sorry, Officer. I made an appointment to get it fixed, and I'm on my way there right now."

"You realize that it's as essential to maintain a vehicle as to purchase it in the first place?"

"Yes, Officer," said Banner humbly.

Just then, a car streaked past at about seventy.

The officer straightened up, hesitated, then said, "As I look at all this traffic, it's impossible not to imagine what it would be like to strip away wheels, trim, and car bodies, leaving only the engines and tail pipes of all these vehicles, pouring out clouds of gaseous contamination. Such a situation would never be tolerated. Yet, the fact that the contamination is incidental, that one contaminating vehicle moves on, to be replaced by a new one, that the source of contamination is covered by trim, and incidental to the purpose of individualized transportation—all this caused the damage inflicted to be overlooked for decades. One wonders what other sources of trouble are similarly concealed by externals."

Banner opened his mouth, and shut it again.

The officer said, "Not long ago, it was necessary for us to learn some new police procedures, and to assist in acquiring the proper degree of mental readiness, I made considerable use of what are known as 'I.Q. capsules.' Quite a number of surprising thoughts occurred to me, based on things I'd heard or read, and hadn't connected together. Were you aware, for instance, that the civilization of ancient Rome may have collapsed because of contamination of the drinking water with lead, which was extensively used for water pipes? And have you considered that an ingredient used extensively to prevent 'knocking' in modern motor fuels contains lead? Could our air supply be contaminated as was the Romans' water supply?"

The officer shook his head and glanced around. "Rectify that condition as soon as possible. If I should see it again and it hasn't been alleviated, I'll be compelled to give you a summons."

"Yes, Officer," said Banner. "I'm going right down there."

The policeman nodded, got back in his car, and Banner waited for a break in the traffic.

"Those pills of ours, Mort, seem to get around."

"They certainly do. I wonder if there's anything to what he said?"

"I'll be frank to say, *I* don't know. But I did notice a speeder go past, and he missed it."

They drove into town, and found the car dealer's drive blocked with parked cars. Banner pulled off the road in an adjacent lot where the dealer sold his used cars. Frowning, they got out and walked back.

"It looks to me," said Banner, "as if he has enough work piled up to last for the next three months."

They were walking along a row of used cars, and passed one where a puzzled customer looked into a car's engine compartment, listening to the salesman:

". . . And another thing you might not know, and I wouldn't either, but I've been studying up on it lately, and that's this power brake. Now, you tend to think a power brake *applies power* to the brake, but that's not how it works. What happens here is that the power brakes create a vacuum on *one* side of the piston, while atmospheric pressure—"

The customer looked desperate.

"Look, all I *want*—"

Banner shoved open the door of the showroom, nodded to a group of salesmen leaning against the trunk of a new car, and walked past toward a short hall leading to the garage. From behind came the voices of the salesmen:

"... And when he did that, she had him dead to rights."

"Sure. It was the same in Schlumberger vs. Mallroyd."

"Oh, I don't know. The decision there was adverse."

"*Was* it? What do you say, Phil?"

"Well, I'd hesitate to go into that. I'm not far enough in the course to say about that. I *thought* so. But I realize there's a lot involved in that. It depends on whether a higher court—"

Banner shoved open another door, walked down a short hall past the open door of an office where a stack of mail lay unopened on a chair, pushed open another door, and he and Hommel walked past a counter where parts were sold, into the garage itself.

Here they were momentarily struck speechless by a roomful of cars with the hoods up, the mechanics seated at a bench where all the tools had been shoved off onto the floor. The men, comfortably seated at the bench, had books open, writing furiously.

Banner eased through the jam of cars, and peered over their shoulders. They were all working on different pages of separate copies of the same book, a text on calculus. As they filled up the sheets of paper with finished problems, they put them on top of a large stack of such papers, and tore off fresh sheets. Several unopened packs of paper, containing five hundred sheets to the pack, sat on the back of the bench.

From the service manager's cubicle across the room came the ring of a phone, then an obliging voice:

"Sure, bring it right in. We'll get at it first chance we get."

Banner stared across the room, to see the service manager put down the phone, and turn to contemplate a skeleton on a stand. His voice came faintly across the room:

"Clavicle, scapula, sternum, rib: frontal, parietal, occipital, squamous temporal, mastoid temporal, nasal, zygomatic, maxilla, mandible . . ."

Banner eased through the jammed cars, motioned the stupefied Hommel to follow, shoved open the door to the short hall, walked through, shoved open the door to the salesroom, and was greeted by the words, "Was it ethyl ether, or was it a preparation consisting of ethyl ether? In the one case, what they'd run into . . ."

Banner stiff-armed the outer door, to find the same salesman and customer standing by the car. The customer, red-faced, was saying heatedly, ". . . All I'm *in* here for is a car I can use to get to work!"

The salesman nodded.

"But of course you can select a car more intelligently after you learn how they operate. And it's a fascinating study. You'll be surprised, as I was, once you get into it. For instance, were you aware that the present infinitely-variable transmission is a descendant, in a sense, of a development of the 1920s . . ."

Banner walked past to his car, got in, opened Hommel's door, then nursed the engine to life.

"Let's hope, Mort, that this place isn't typical."

"It couldn't be."

"You're right. If it was, the country would have collapsed by now."

They finally found a garage that could do the job, but the mechanic was overloaded with work, and it took a long time.

Somehow, the day's experience didn't seem to augur well for the future.

As time passed, the men working on the antidote began to see the importance of it, and developed a fervor that only Peabody had had before. But it took a long time for this fervor to produce any results.

"I hate to say it," said Hommel, "but it seems to me that this Cerebrocreatine of ours helps study, but somehow prevents *work*."

Banner handed over a newspaper. "Take a look at this, Mort."

Hommel glanced at the paper, to find an article marked in pencil:

SAUGASH AREA BOASTS FOUR COLLEGES!

Saugash, April 22. Work began today on a new neighborhood college, to supplement the Saugash Community College completed here last fall. This brings to four the total of higher educational facilities in the Saugash area, counting Saugash University and Saugash Teachers College.

Dr. Rutherford Dollard Ganst, VI, President of Saugash University, presided at the ground-breaking ceremonies, which were attended by the mayor and many other notables, and a crowd of interested persons estimated at over four thousand.

President Ganst, in a short and memorable address, stated: "Nothing is more important in this day of rapid scientific advance and complex societal change than an informed citizenry. Education alone can create an informed citizenry. Thus the need for education becomes no less vital and urgent than the need for air or water, for food or any other necessity of life. Education has become the basic prerequisite for life today. Nothing is more important. Today, educational qualifications are vital to everyone, from the manual laborer at the bottom, to the head of the great educational system at the top. Employers will not accept the unqualified, because they are seriously lacking in qualifications. Without qualifications there can be no success. Mere ability is no longer enough. Indeed, with sufficient qualifications, one may dispense with ability. It is the *qualifications* that are vital, and only educational institutions may grant qualifications. Thus Education is no longer the necessity of youth alone. Education is now the essential and inescapable concomitant of progress and indeed of existence for every man and every woman of each and every age and condition of life, without exception, from the cradle to the grave. The gigantic dominating growth of our education system, swelling like a tide to overwhelming proportions never before conceived by the mind of man in all recorded history, cannot be resisted! Nothing can stop it. Nothing can stay it. *Education will be served*! Science requires it. Technology demands it. The towering giants in the field of the hierarchy of education itself mandate it! *Education will conquer all!*"

❧ ❧ ❧

Hommel looked up dizzily.

Banner said, "When you first told me about this pill, Mort, you said, 'It stimulated intellectual activity. It channels energy from gross physical pursuits into imaginative creativity.' The trouble seems to be that it channels a little too *much* energy."

"But what can we do?"

Banner shook his head.

"Keep working on that antidote."

As the days passed, the situation didn't stand still. On a drive to town one afternoon, Banner and Hommel were nearly run off the road by a truck whose driver was studying at sixty miles an hour. A few minutes later, on the flat farmland below the highway, Hommel saw a farmer driving a tractor, reading a book strapped to the steering wheel in front of him. The tractor ran into an electric pole, the book and the farmer were knocked off. The farmer picked up the book and went on reading.

Banner parked on the shoulder of the road behind a car with a flat tire, and looked where Hommel pointed.

He shook his head, then glanced up, and murmured, "Now, what's *this*?"

The car in front had the left rear tire flat, and three men were standing around the open trunk of the car. They seemed to be arguing in a languid way.

"Oh, no," one of them was saying, "I'm sure the essential thing is to *first* jack up the car."

"You mean, *elevate the car on a jack*."

"Well, my terminology may have been a little imprecise, but—"

The third man broke in. "It's incorrect, in any case. The essential prerequisite is removal of the bolts while application of vehicular weight precludes rotation of the wheel."

"Rotation of the wheel? Yes, yes, we're overlooking something. Due to the fact that the wheels are fastened on opposite sides of the car, they rotate in opposite senses, and to prevent inertial loosening of the fastening nuts or cap screws—cap screws in this case, I presume—the 'handedness' of the screw threads is reversed on opposite sides of the vehicles. Now, to loosen a cap screw successfully, it must be rotated in the proper direction. Yet, the thread is screwed in out of sight in the brake drum. *It is not subject to visual observation.*"

"That *is* important. How can we determine the handedness of the threads?"

A perspiring woman stuck her head out the car window.

"Oh, hurry. *Please* hurry."

One of the men sluggishly got out the jack and stood holding it.

"Does anyone have a text, or repair manual, that might clarify this point?"

The woman put her head out the window again.

"*Please* hurry! The pains are coming closer together!"

One of the men looked around severely.

"Now, don't interrupt. We have a difficult problem here."

The man with the jack leaned it against the bumper, then all three men knelt to scratch diagrams in the dirt on the shoulder of the road.

Banner and Hommel hadn't changed a tire in years, but they could stand it no longer, and got out.

Banner grabbed the jack, and fitted it under the rear bumper. Hommel pulled out a combination tire iron and lug wrench, popped off the wheel cover, and loosened the wheel. Banner jacked the car up. Hommel took the wheel off. Banner got out the spare, and Hommel put it on while Banner put the flat into the trunk, then let down the jack. Hommel banged the wheel cover into place. Banner put the jack in the trunk. Hommel tossed the tire iron inside, and they turned away.

The other three men stood staring. One of them shook a yellow capsule out of a bottle, tossed it into his mouth and swallowed.

"Would you be prepared to do that again? I'm not sure that we've learned all the essential manipulations."

The woman put her head out the window. There was a note of desperate urgency in her voice.

"*The pains are getting closer together!*"

As the car disappeared down the highway, Banner and Hommel stood staring after it.

"How near, Mort, are we to that antidote?"

Hommel had a haunted look.

"No one could say. Peabody seems to be closest. But he could run into trouble any time. Besides, his solution seems to be the least desirable."

"Don't worry about that," said Banner with feeling. "Just as long as we get it while there's time to use it."

Several more weeks crawled by, so slowly that they seemed like months or years. Meanwhile, the gradual overall disintegration turned into specific failures in production and distribution. Little notice of this appeared in newspapers, general magazines, or on radio or television, which were preoccupied with more intellectual matters, particularly "adjusted voting." Under "adjusted voting" each person would cast a number of votes in accordance with his "intellectual level." The more degrees, the more votes. Television networks were carrying the "Debate of the Century" on this plan, the object of the most acrimonious dispute being how many votes should be allowed for publication in professional journals. No one dared to disagree with the principle of the plan, lest he label himself as "undereducated." To be "undereducated" was a serious business. The social stigma attached to it was about equivalent to having served two terms in prison for robbing gas stations and grocery stores.

In the midst of all this, with consumption of Cerebrocreatine mounting from week to week, with gigantic new campuses looming over the landscape, with the airwaves thick with learned discussions as the means of existence crumbled, Hommel and Peabody walked into Banner's office.

"Well, we've got it. It's practically a stupidity drug, but it *works*."

Banner got the new drug on the market in record time. Advertised as "Super*Ak*tion, for active people—instant-acting stimulant to healthful practical activity," it was wholesaled at a very modest profit in "superinhalator bottles," supposed to be used by spraying into the nose and throat.

"For the love of Heaven," said Hommel, "why don't we sell it in *capsules*?"

"It isn't going to sell like wildfire, Mort. Not in the present state of affairs. What one-hundred-percent intellectual is *interested* in healthful practical activity? And what is Cerebrocreatine turning the average person into?"

"I know. We should sell it in some different form. If only—"

Banner shook his head. "Since it will have only a very limited sale, we've got to make the most of it." He picked up a sample inhalator. It was shaped like a small gun, made of violet plastic, with the label on the side of the grip. Banner aimed it across the room, and squeezed the trigger. There was a *squish* sound, and a fine jet of liquid shot out, to leave an oval of tiny droplets on the wall.

Hommel frowned, and looked at the "superinhalator" again.

"When in doubt," said Banner, "rely on human nature. *Real* human nature, with its high points and its low points. Bear in mind, there are likely to be a few unregenerate bullheaded individualists around, regardless of anything formal education can do, even backed up by a thing like Cerebrocreatine."

"I still don't—"

From the window came a rude roar of exhaust, and a screech of brakes.

Banner looked out, to see a truck marked "Central Plumbing" slam to a stop in the drive below. Three men in coveralls jumped out, went around to the rear, yanked out a blow torch, a suction plunger, a coil of wire, and a tool case, and headed for the front door.

Hommel looked out.

"About time. That drain has been plugged for three months." He shook his head dispiritedly. "But I still don't see any way that we can hope—"

From a window down below boomed a rough profane voice:

"Where's the drain? We haven't got the whole ___ __ _ ___ day! Great _____ ! Look at all these stupid _____ !"

There was a faint but distinct *squish squish squish* sound.

Hommel stared at Banner, then at the "superinhalator" on his desk.

Banner said, "Practical men use practical means, Mort."

There was a thunder of feet on the staircase down the hall.

Banner and Hommel went into the hallway, to find a research chemist named Smyth looking around dazedly as he tossed yellow capsules into his mouth and contemplated some complex theoretical problem.

Up the stairs burst a couple of brisk men in gray lab coats, followed by three more in coveralls.

Smyth looked at this crew as at a colony of tame ants that has gotten out of its jar.

One of the men in overalls shifted his blowtorch to the other hand, and aimed a small violet gun at Smyth.

"*Squish!*"

Smyth staggered back against the wall. He sucked in a deep breath, and suddenly his expression changed from dreamy contemplation to astonishment. He banged his fist into his open hand.

"Why am I just standing here *thinking* about it? Why not *do* it?"

He strode off down the corridor in one direction as the plumbers vanished around the corner in the other direction.

From around the corner came a sucking pumping sound, followed by a gurgling noise, more sucking and pumping sounds, a good deal of profanity, then a shout of triumph.

"She's unplugged! O.K., boys, let's go!"

Banner nodded.

"That's more *like* it!"

Hommel looked down the hall where Smyth had disappeared.

"Wait a minute. What's he working on—"

There was a thundering noise on the stairs, then the roar of exhaust.

Smyth came hurrying back up the hall, carrying what looked like a silver-coated round-bottomed flask in one hand, and in the other a small bottle of yellowish oily liquid. From the mouth of the silvered flask came a wisp of whitish vapor.

Hommel stared. "Great, holy, leaping—"

"You see, Mort," said Banner, a little expansively, "we've provided the few remaining practical men with the means to convert *intellectuals* into practical men. They, in turn, will be irritated by the intellectuals around *them*. There's the answer to our problem."

Hommel was watching Smyth.

Smyth vanished into his laboratory.

Banner went on, "The trouble with Cerebrocreatine was that it undermined necessities of life at the same time that it gave us fringe benefits we could get along without. That's not progress. Progress is the product of a new advantage *compounding advantages we already have.*"

He paused as Smyth came out holding in one gloved hand a shiny rod bearing at its end a clamp. The clamp gripped a small unstoppered bottle of yellowish oily liquid.

Smyth insinuated the rod around the door frame, peered into the room, drew the door almost shut, turned his face away, and tilted the rod.

BAM!

The building jumped. Fire shot out around the edges of the door. Black smoke rolled out behind the flames.

Smyth threw off the smoking glove, sniffed the air, then sucked his fingers.

"Well, *that* didn't work."

He turned away, drew in a deep breath, then went back into his laboratory. There was immediately the whir of a powerful draft sucking up fumes.

"Hm-m-m," said Banner looking thoughtfully at the partly opened door.

Smyth reappeared, unrolling what looked like a small coil of bell wire. He tacked a loop to the door frame, then, still unrolling wire, went back into the laboratory. Wisps of smoke were still trailing out around the top of the door, but this didn't seem to slow him down. He came out, cut the loop, stripped the insulation off the two ends, pounded in another tack, and hammered it flat to hold the two wires. Then he bent the ends of the wires, so they wouldn't touch—yet.

Hommel cleared his throat.

"Ah . . . Dr. Smyth . . . I wonder if perhaps . . . a little more theoretical consideration of the thermodynamics of the reaction—?"

"Theoretical considerations be damned," said Smyth. "The only way we're going to find out is to try it and see what products we get."

He raised his left arm over his head, shielding one ear with his shoulder, and the other with his fingers, then he touched the bare ends of the two wires together.

BOOM!

The building jumped.

Cracks shot up the wall.

There was a heavy shattering crash from overhead.

As the roar died away, the smash and tinkle of breaking glass could be heard throughout the building.

Smyth shoved the door slightly open, and a grayish cloud poured out. He wafted some of the fumes in his direction, and sniffed cautiously.

His face lit in a triumphant smile.

"*That* saves some time!"

He pulled the door shut, and headed toward the stockroom.

Hommel turned to Banner, "How is *this* an improvement? We were better off with theorists!"

"We've overshot the mark again. This stuff is too strong."

"There's a threshold effect. If you don't use enough, you get no result you can detect."

A small crowd was gathering in the hall to see what was going on. Banner separated Peabody from the pack.

"Peabody, my boy," said Banner, "we've got this last problem pretty well licked, thanks to your antidote. But there's still one little loose end that we've got to take care of."

Peabody looked apprehensive.

"What's that, sir?"

Banner shook his head.

"*Now* we need an antidote for the antidote."

Science at Work

Interesting Times

Alex Bohlen, bioprogrammer for Xpert Systems Implants, sat a few yards from the boxing ring and watched Reinhardt Magnusgarten climb through the ropes. In the seat to Bohlen's right, even as the crowd around them let out its roar of approval, Ed Norton, implant surgeon, gave a grunt of disgust.

"That SOB can't stop clowning."

Bohlen noted Magnusgarten's nose-thumbing gesture across the ring toward Bisbee, the champion.

Bohlen shook his head. "The implant doesn't affect his natural ebullience."

"Ebullience? The guy thinks he's unbeatable. When they weighed in, he laughed in Bisbee's face."

Around them, the shouts of the crowd were rising to a new pitch, and Bohlen listened wonderingly:

"Okay, Maggie! Kill the bastard!"

"Magic Garden! You're in the Garden, boy! You've made it! Hey, hey! Magic Garden!"

"Come on, Maggie! Show him! We're all champs now!"

"One round, Maggie!"

Bohlen leaned toward Norton. "Are all these people crazy?"

"I don't think they are. But I think Magnus may be."

In the ring, Magnusgarten had shrugged off his robe to reveal a large pale physique, and, as the crowd gave a roar of laughter, he patted his none too muscular midsection. He then danced somewhat tipsily around in his corner, and Norton suddenly sprang to his feet, to shout to the trainer, who shook his head and leaned over the ropes to answer:

"Just the usual! You know Maggie!"

Norton sat down, and Bohlen said, "What was that?"

"I thought Magnus might be drunk. Tab says he's just horsing around, as usual."

"That's a relief, at least."

"There's a lot riding on this. Magnus could show a little seriousness."

"That would be nice. But he's done all right so far."

"Sure. Against second-rates. Strictly thanks to the implant."

"True."

In the ring, an official, arms raised, was trying to quiet the crowd. The crowd chanted back, "Fight! Fight! Kill him, Maggie! Fight! Fight! Kill him, Maggie! Fight! Fight! Kill him, Maggie!"

Someone tugged at Bohlen's left sleeve. He turned, to smile at a pretty blonde girl in the seat beside him.

"Bo," she said, "I'm scared."

"I told you you might not like it. But don't worry. It's always like this. A lot of noise and emotion. It's just the way it always is."

She shook her head. "I don't mean that. I'm afraid for Magnus. He can't possibly stand up to that man."

Bohlen followed her gaze, to see the two fighters in the center of the ring, right hands outstretched. The contrast jarred him. There in the blaze of the lights was the champion, Bisbee, a light sheen of sweat over powerful muscles, plainly trained to the peak of condition, his face blank, his gaze alert. He had a look of power and lightning reflexes.

And there was Magnusgarten, large, but more lightly built, his muscles less developed, pale, slightly pudgy, a silly faintly nasty grin on his face as he said something to the champion.

By some freak of acoustics, Bohlen caught the words.

Norton swore. "What did the overconfident ass do now?"

Bohlen shook his head. "He said, 'Sweet dreams,' to Bisbee."

"Great. He thinks the implant's magic. He doesn't know the difference between the second-rates he fought to get here and the champion of the world. How could I be so stupid?"

"You? What did you do?"

Norton shook his head. "I bet on him."

Bohlen grinned. "On Magnus?"

Norton nodded. "And it wasn't pennies."

The crowd was shouting and laughing. The girl said in a low voice, "Oh, Magnus." Bohlen turned to reassure her. There was a bell. A huge shout went up. Bohlen looked around.

Bisbee was in the center of the ring, his muscular arms raised to shield his head as Magnus with incredible speed landed blows to the champion's arms, shoulders, and when Bisbee tried to strike back, to his briefly uncovered head. When Bisbee turned, as if to get away, Magnus was already there, blocking him, smashing at Bisbee's well covered head and body.

The crowd screamed, "Maggie! Maggie! You've got him!"

The girl was on her feet with everyone else, clutching Bohlen's arm.

Norton was shouting with the rest of them. "Put him down, Maggie! Put him down!"

Magnusgarten hit Bisbee again and again. Bisbee kept backing and turning, keeping his head well covered. Magnusgarten hit him on the biceps, the shoulders, landed a blow to the midsection. Suddenly, Bisbee lashed out, and his punch missed, pulling him a little off-balance. Magnusgarten hit him to the eyes, and again to the eyes. Bisbee covered his face with his gloves, the sweat running down his well muscled body.

Magnusgarten laughed, stepped close, said something to Bisbee, then stepped easily around the big muscular fighter, and smashed him in the side.

As Bisbee retreated across the ring, Magnusgarten followed, hit the upraised arms, then the midsection. Bisbee covered himself with gloves, forearms, and elbows. Magnusgarten hit him. Bisbee gave with the punches.

Norton said, "Damn it! Why won't he go down?"

The big crowd fell silent. For several moments there was nothing but the sound of the blows. Then, from somewhere to the rear came an elderly, somewhat cracked male voice:

"Keep it up, Champ! He's wearing out!"

The bell rang.

Magnusgarten, breathing hard, sank onto his stool. Bisbee, the champion, sat down and leaned back. His eyes were puffed, and blood trickled from a cut in his lip.

Norton said uneasily, "This is the first fight to go a full round."

Bohlen said, "Well—Bisbee is the champ."

"I don't like the looks of it. Magnus acts tired already."

Bohlen leaned close to Norton's ear. "Remember the program."

Norton nodded, but said moodily, "If there had been more strength in Magnus's blows, Bisbee would be down by now."

"He's no weakling. He's hurt Bisbee. You can see that."

"I know he's no weakling. But he doesn't do his part. Tab has to train him playing games and he has to do it between parties. Magnus throws the whole burden on other people."

"The reporters love it. So does the crowd."

"That won't help him if Bisbee connects."

There was the sound of the bell.

Magnusgarten came unsteadily to his feet. He sucked in a deep breath and blew it out, looking across the ring at Bisbee.

The champion, hands partly raised, stalked warily across the ring.

The cracked voice called from the back, "Watch him, Champ! He's not that bushed!"

The champion's guard jerked up higher.

At the same instant, Magnusgarten pivoted. Bisbee reeled back, hands in front of his face. Magnusgarten laughed, stepped aside, struck Bisbee's gloves as if to knock his guard down, hit him in the side, in the elbows, hit the raised gloves, smashed Bisbee in the ear, struck again to the head, where the upraised arms soaked up the force of the blows, smashed him on the biceps, again on the biceps, as if to lacerate the muscles, to destroy Bisbee's power of defense—

Bisbee backed, moved with the blows, covered himself, retreated around the ring as Magnus advanced.

The crowd screamed for action. Time and again, Magnusgarten lashed out, breathing hard, and the champion slipped away.

Among the shouts of "Yellow!" "Coward!" "Come on and fight!" came a cracked voice, "That's it, Champ! Wear him down!"

The bell finally rang.

A shout went up.

Norton sat back. "My God!"

From the rear of the arena, as the shouting died down, came the cracked voice, "He's slowing, Champ. Next round, push him a little."

Norton twisted in his seat. "Who is that? Damn it, I wish he'd shut up!"

The girl said, "Is it true?"

Bohlen looked at her anxious face. "Is what true?"

"Is Magnus tired?"

"He's bound to be a little tired."

"But doesn't the—the chip—the implant—It makes him an expert, doesn't it?"

As Bohlen hesitated, Norton leaned across him to snarl, "The bastard won't train, that's the trouble. The implant steps up his coordination. It gives him skill he wouldn't have. But he thinks it's magic and he doesn't train."

"But couldn't the implant make him train?"

Norton glanced at Bohlen. "How about it?"

Bohlen hesitated. "Maybe some day. So far, we can't do anything for motivation. I never even thought of the problem." He frowned at Norton. "Did you?"

"I thought if we got someone big and strong, who knew the rudiments, who'd take the risk of the surgery, and if we could get the chip implanted—I thought that would do it."

"That's what I thought."

The bell rang.

Bisbee, his guard well up, cautiously crossed the ring.

Magnusgarten, breathing hard, his hands down, stood, legs slightly trembling, in his corner.

The thin cracked voice called, "Test him a little, Champ!"

Bisbee's left hand lashed out.

Magnusgarten moved his head and body just a little, slipped the blow, and brought up both hands. The champion's right smashed solidly into Magnusgarten's midsection. Magnusgarten went back on the ropes, bounced off, and as Bisbee swung a right that missed, the cracked voice yelled, "Cover, Champ!" Magnusgarten's fists flashed out to Bisbee's briefly unprotected head. The blows were solid, coordinated, and one followed another so fast Bohlen wasn't sure whether there had been three, four, or half-a-dozen.

Bisbee went down. The sound brought the crowd to its feet and silence to the arena.

Bohlen reached in his hip pocket, and brought out a handkerchief. He mopped his face and brow. "Close."

The girl said wonderingly, admiringly, "I never thought Magnus could do it!"

The worshipful tone irritated Bohlen, but he clamped his jaws shut. Norton, sweat running down his face, looking as if he had been in the ring himself, leaned across Bohlen to speak in a low voice.

"Magnus hasn't done a damned thing! Every move he's made has been programmed. I did the surgery, Bo here programmed the chip. The rest of the team sweated right along with us. And now the lazy bastard is supposed to get all the credit? When you see him, tell him to train! He could have lost this fight!"

There was an indrawn breath from the crowd. Bohlen turned back to look in the ring.

Magnusgarten, blood running from his nose and lip, leaning painfully on the ropes, stared as Bisbee stood up and the referee stepped back.

It suddenly dawned on Bohlen that the champion had stayed down for the count of nine voluntarily. Bisbee's face looked puffed around the eyes, and his lip was cut and swollen, but his movements showed no weakness.

The wondering murmur of the crowd sounded like the sea washing up on a long flat beach, and Bohlen thought of the turn of the tide.

Then the bell signaled the end of the round.

Norton leaned over to Bohlen. "Now what?"

Bohlen drew a deep breath. He kept his voice low. "The chip can judge the visual images, and give the commands to Magnus's muscles. If Bisbee knocks out Magnus's vision, or if Magnus's strength gives out, there isn't much the chip can do."

"Then it's up to Magnus?"

"What do you mean?"

"The champ's been soaking up punishment since the fight started. Magnus is worn to a thread dishing it out. This can't go on. Bisbee's going to connect. What good will the chip do then?"

"If the chip gets no input, it has him cover. That's all it can do."

"Then when it comes to the final settlement, it's up to Magnus?"

Bohlen frowned. "I'm not sure I follow. Magnus can override the implant any time. But I don't know what good that will do. We picked Magnus because he was a promising fighter. But the skills in that chip are distilled from every first-rate boxer we could get to cooperate. The only people who could hope to equal it would be first-rate champions themselves: Sullivan. Dempsey. Louis."

"And Bisbee?"

"Maybe. Especially since Magnus is out of shape."

The bell rang, and Bohlen looked up to see Bisbee come out of his corner, and Magnus, with a look of doom, motionless, hands down, still in his corner. Bohlen glanced at the girl. Tears were running down her cheeks.

Bohlen bent over, ignoring the ring.

"Are you in love with Magnus?"

She nodded hopelessly.

From the back of the arena came the cracked voice.

"Paste him around, Champ. Wear him down."

Norton turned around.

"Who in hell is that?"

Bohlen forced himself to watch.

Bisbee had moved close. Bohlen now saw an unexpected display of skill as Magnusgarten tied up Bisbee, robbed his punches of most of their force, took the heavy blows on his arms instead of his head, blocked, turned, weaved, slipped the blows, gasped for breath, wincing with the force of the punches that did get through, spending the round soaking up punishment and dealing out in return nothing that was any real threat to the champion. Finally, the bell rang.

Norton sank down in his seat. "I thought Magnus was done. But he's still alive. What now?"

Bohlen shook his head.

Norton said, "He's more worn out than when the round started. Bisbee looks fresher."

"I'm afraid Magnus is just a sparring partner to him now. But he's on his feet. He could still win."

"Bisbee batters him on the arms. What happens when he gets Magnus so numb and arm-weary he can't cover himself?"

"I'm afraid that's it."

"Nothing programmed for this problem?"

"The problem isn't cut and dried. There are stratagems, evaluations, sequences of moves. It depends on what Bisbee does. And boxing isn't all skill. It depends on condition, guts, will. We picked Magnus because he was a promising fighter. We didn't know he was going to take his training easy. I'm surprised he's lasted this long."

"I've got a lot on this bout."

"We all have. The press acts as if this decides it for skill implants."

Norton shook his head. "The technology will go on. Maybe some illusions will go."

"I can think of one—let technology do all the work. If Magnus loses, it will be that that did it."

The bell rang.

Magnus moved quickly out of his corner. After an exchange of blows in the center of the ring, the champion moved in impatiently. Magnus's brief show of strength gave out, but he succeeded in tying up the champion and slowing him down, though he himself landed few blows that had much force. The round passed in a silence from the crowd, and just as the next round started, a familiar cracked voice spoke up:

"Okay, Champ. Take him."

Norton gave a low curse, and crouched lower in his seat.

Bisbee crossed the ring before Magnus seemed to realize what was happening, then Magnus, nearby in the ring, pivoted to land a blow to Bisbee's head. Bisbee, seeming unaffected, smashed Magnus to the midsection, to double him over, then abruptly delivered a sequence of head and body blows that brought the crowd to its feet, and suddenly Magnus was down, near the edge of the ring closest to Bohlen and Norton.

Now, for the first time, there was a shout of "Bisbee! Bisbee!"

The girl, crying, stood up, clutching Bohlen's arm.

Bohlen realized the count had already reached three. He shook his head.

As the count reached seven, Magnus opened his eyes. He turned his head, to see the crying girl. At the count of nine, he struggled to his feet.

Bohlen, frowning, noted blood running from a cut above Bisbee's right eye. That must have happened in the exchange of blows just before Magnus went down. Bisbee, seeming unaware of it, forced the fight, and Magnus again showed his skill in defense. Just before the bell rang, Magnus landed a blow that hit the champion above the right eye. Then he dragged himself to his corner and dropped onto the stool.

Bohlen sank back in his seat.

Norton said grudgingly, "The skill is the chip's. But he's got guts, all right. I think I'd have stayed on the deck."

Bohlen nodded. "I don't know any way to program courage. Bisbee's eye doesn't look good, either."

"No. But this dents our slogan that 'Anyone's an expert with an XPert Implant.' There's more than skill involved. You can't turn everything over to the implant."

"No, I don't think anyone would care to try it. It isn't the chip that feels the blows."

The girl was sitting, trembling, with her eyes shut and head bowed. Bohlen looked at her thoughtfully, then heard the bell.

This time, both fighters were cautious, as Magnus circled to get a blow at Bisbee's eye, and Bisbee sought to prevent it. Bohlen, watching the seemingly academic series of combinations as both fighters boxed, was surprised to note how often Magnus, though plainly the weaker, still managed to score. By the end of the round, the cut over Bisbee's eye was visibly worse, and the eye nearly shut. But Magnus seemed scarcely able to stay on his feet.

Norton said, "Damn it, even if he half-blinds him, how will he put him down?"

"Be glad he's still conscious."

"If he lives through it, I hope next time he trains. Damn it, if he hadn't had an implant, he'd have trained!"

"Every time we get a technological advance, we lose something. People expect the technology to do it all."

"Ah, it's the usual thing. Tough barbarians from the northland erupt into the tropics, and conquer the weaklings lying around in the sun. A couple of generations later, they get whipped themselves by a fresh batch of barbarians. Now we make an oil burner and put the tropics into the home. The chip is the worst. It's supposed to do the thinking and planning. The problem has been around since the Vandals, and we're losing ground."

"I wonder if actually it might be possible to somehow program the training routine into the chip?"

The bell rang.

From the back of the hall, a cracked voice called, "Champ— You've got to force him."

Norton shook his head. "That guy ought to be in Bisbee's corner. If he'd just shut up, we might live through this yet."

Bisbee, seeming to pay no attention, tried to box Magnus at long range, while Magnus tried to circle, to take advantage of the poor vision of that swollen right eye. The fight turned into a sparring match, and Bohlen, groggy himself, watched with less and less attention. Toward the end of the round, he became aware that Magnus had just landed a blow to the head. Bisbee's broad back was to Bohlen, who didn't realize anything more had happened until he saw Magnus's head snap back, and Magnus went back on the ropes. Bohlen came awake to see Magnus, doubled over, take a murderous right uppercut that straightened him up, then he dropped unconscious to the floor.

Bisbee turned and walked across the ring.

The count, monotonously intoned, reached eight, and Magnus had yet to move or open an eye.

The bell rang.

Bisbee gave his head a slight shake, and walked to his corner.

Bohlen, groggy, glanced at the girl, who sat staring dazedly at her hands, as if afraid to look in the ring. Bohlen, who felt the same way, made the effort to look up.

In the ring, officials were conferring. Someone, apparently a doctor, was examining Magnus.

The bell rang.

Norton said, "What round is this?"

"Don't ask me."

"Wasn't that an unusually short break between rounds?"

"If you can still judge time, you're better off than I am."

Magnus, his guard up, was facing the champion, who bored in as Magnus gave an exhibition of skill that reduced Bisbee to a look almost of clumsiness. By the end of the round, Bisbee's right eye was nearly shut.

At the close of the round, as Bisbee and Magnus sank onto their stools, someone cheered, and the crowd joined in.

Norton leaned over beside Bohlen. "Not to take any credit away from Magnus, but I'm wondering. Speaking as a surgeon, a mere mechanic for bodies, it seems to me an opponent could beat Magnus to a pulp, and that chip would keep calculating moves for him. The chip isn't going to get dazed at all, is it? No matter how dazed Magnus gets?"

"I've taken it for granted that if he's groggy, he can't function. It looks as if I was wrong."

"The impression I have is that his skill improves after Bisbee knocks him half-unconscious. We never saw this before. No one ever got this far before."

"It's certainly a point. He acts dead on his feet, but his skill, if anything, improves."

"Well—let's hope he stays a little dazed. If Bisbee gets him again, I'm not sure the bell can save him."

"As it is, I think he's winning on points."

The bell rang. Again the two boxers approached each other. This time, Bisbee seemed determined to take advantage of his strength. Despite another display of skill from Magnus, the blows Bisbee dealt seemed on the edge of putting Magnus down. But when the bell rang, Magnus was still on his feet, and Bisbee's eye was almost shut.

Again the officials conferred, and now a doctor examined Bisbee.

The crowd, apparently worn out themselves, watched in silence.

The bell rang.

As the fight resumed, again Magnus was able to hit almost at will, as Bisbee covered himself, retreated, backed away, and suddenly, as if out of nowhere, smashed Magnus with his left hand, sprang forward, and moving too fast to be clearly seen, landed a sequence of murderous blows.

Again, Magnus was on the floor.

Bisbee stood over him, breathing hard, as the referee tried in vain to get him to move away. Finally, with a heavy sigh, Bisbee turned and walked away.

The count started, and reached eight.

Magnus tried to get to his feet, and failed.

The referee counted, "Nine."

The bell rang.

Bohlen sat unmoving, dazed. Around him, there was a near-total silence. Again the officials conferred. A doctor examined Magnus.

Norton nudged Bohlen. "Let me by. I think she's fainted."

Bohlen looked dully at the girl, slumped in her seat.

Somewhere, a bell rang.

Bohlen sat in a daze, then looked up without curiosity at the ring.

The two fighters were circling each other, both wary, exchanging blows meaningless to Bohlen. It dawned on him that he had missed something. Now the fight seemed almost even. It had obviously been Bisbee's at the end of the last round.

Bohlen looked away, and wondered idly if there was some food around somewhere. Then he asked himself why he felt as he did. Next he wondered how he did feel. It took a while to find a comparison. He felt as if he were a reporter in the Second World War, and the slaughter was still going on now after decades of fighting, and he still didn't know who was going to win.

The bell rang.

"Good God," said Norton.

Bohlen felt a twinge of curiosity, and glanced at the seat to his left.

The girl was gone. "What did—"

Norton said, "I sent her out. It was killing her."

Bohlen nodded absently, "Not a very doctorly way to put it. Your professional manner is underdeveloped."

"I don't feel very doctorly. I feel like a wet rag. How would you put it?"

The bell rang, to signal the beginning of another round.

Bohlen's thoughts moved like glaciers. After a while, he said, "I'd look profound, and say she was being emotionally traumatized by this experience."

Norton, watching the ring, nodded judiciously. "There's still time for you to go to medical school."

There was a crash from just above them, in the ring, and a murmur of voices, then someone said, "One."

Bohlen looked up.

Bisbee lay outstretched on the canvas.

Bohlen stared, trying to see Magnus lying there, because it was Magnus he expected to see. But the fighter stretched out there was Bisbee.

At the count of seven, the champion tried to get up. As he turned his head, Bohlen could see that now his left eye was swollen almost shut. Bisbee fell back onto the canvas.

At the count of nine, he scrambled to his feet.

Magnus crossed the ring, hit Bisbee, and hit him again. The blows weren't heavy, but Bisbee couldn't defend.

Bisbee then covered his head. He was fighting now as he had fought in the first round, but now both eyes were swollen, and blood was trickling down as Magnus methodically opened up a cut over his left eye.

Bisbee lashed out at his tormentor, who moved easily aside, and struck back to catch Bisbee in the mouth. Again Bisbee covered himself.

Magnus hit Bisbee, hit him again. Magnus, though obviously tired, was moving with smooth coordination. Suddenly he laughed.

"Sweet dreams," he said, and landed a sudden heavy blow to the side of Bisbee's head.

Bisbee staggered.

The bell rang.

Norton said, "They've got to stop this."

A few moments later, they declared Magnus the winner, and he stood with upraised fists, smiling, as the cheers echoed around him. But Bohlen could see no one close to the ring who was cheering. He glanced at Norton, who shook his head.

Bohlen said, "What happened?"

"What do you mean?"

"Bisbee had him. Then I looked away. I was tired of watching it."

"You should have bet on it. You wouldn't have looked away."

"The last I saw, Magnus was on the mat. What happened?"

"It was the same thing again. Magnus was out on his feet, but he moved like a dream. Bisbee couldn't connect. His eyes were swollen shut, and he couldn't follow what Magnus was doing."

"I suppose I should be glad," said Bohlen.

Norton grunted. "At the end, I was hoping Bisbee would win. It would have cost me money, but it would have been worth it. Look at Magnus."

Bohlen didn't look at the ring. "He won on luck. And guts, give him that. But the bell saved him at least twice."

"That's not what he thinks."

Bohlen looked at Magnus. "He thinks he's unbeatable. Damn it! It's the implant!"

Norton said, "And you programmed it."

"Not alone," said Bohlen defensively. "It wasn't my idea."

"I'm not blaming you. What I'm saying is, he's standing up there, taking the cheers. It was luck and the implant that saved him, and you programmed the implant, and I put it in. I tell you, one slip, and he wouldn't be here. He wouldn't have lived through the operation. But is he giving anyone else credit?"

"No."

"There's a problem here, Bo."

Bohlen said, "I won't argue with that."

"It never hit me we were making a Frankenstein's monster."

"Well—I wouldn't go that far."

"I would. This isn't the only expert chip there's going to be. This is just the first. This guy is a Boxer. Pretty soon we're going to be making Soldiers. Somewhere, right now, they're doubtless asking how to make Assassins. Sooner or later there'll be a Ninja implant chip. What's it going to be like to live in the same world with this stuff? For the first time, anyone with the money, or who has a backer with the money, will be able to acquire real skill without making the effort to earn it."

Bohlen stared at Magnus, saw Magnus smile easily, condescendingly, to the reporters as they crowded around, asking him to make a muscle, snapping pictures of him with fists raised. Magnus's lip was swollen, and one of his eyes was partly shut, but that didn't dent the easy air of superiority.

Norton said, "How does he look so casual when Bisbee had him on the mat twice?"

"Three times."

Norton blinked. "That's right."

Bohlen shook his head. "Maybe it's just his personality. This may not happen with everyone who gets an implant. He's the first. There will be others. It could even become commonplace."

"Not for a while. There aren't enough surgeons who want to do the operations."

"Yeah, but—"

Norton looked at him.

"But what?"

"That's the next expert implant—the surgical chip."

"You're serious?"

"I wouldn't make this up. It's perfectly logical. The bottleneck, all along, was the interface. A big part of that is the process of implantation. We need capable surgeons. Therefore, develop an implant to increase the number of capable surgeons. That will end the bottleneck. Q. E. D."

Norton swore.

Bohlen said, "Will you refuse the implant?"

"I don't end to end up like Magnus."

"Then you'll be passed by colleagues less capable now than you are."

"I can think of the very cretins who'd jump at the chance." He looked at Bohlen, and suddenly his eyes glinted. "And when does the programmer's chip implant come up?"

Bohlen shook his head. "Third on the list. Another bottleneck."

Norton smiled. "Programming should be a natural for this technique."

"I'm not certain it can be done. But I wouldn't bet against it."

"There are a lot of angles to this thing. Magnus has the idea he is different and superior. I wonder how competition would hit him. I think Bisbee deserves the chance to even things up."

"Would he do it?"

"We could find out."

Bohlen laughed. "It may end up like college. Almost everybody has to have a degree, now. I can see it a few years from now: 'What field is your implant in?'"

"Not so fast. Even with lots of willing surgeons, there's still the operation. Who wants it?"

"It could end up like tonsils and adenoids. Then, after a little more improvement in technique, like going to the dentist."

"People will send their children to the chip-implanter?"

"Why not?"

Norton gazed off into the distance, and shook his head.

"There's one thing we can be reasonably sure of."

Bohlen nodded. "In one sense or another, this technology will be very educational."

Superbiometalemon

Riveracre Farms, R. D. #1
Hewitt's Corners, MN
August 18, 1998

Interdisciplinary Genetronics
Transportation Division
100 Bionutronics Drive
Detroit, MI

Attn: Gene-Splicing Dept.

Dear Sirs:

I am once again writing to you, with considerable reluctance, and more in sorrow than in anger, but I believe you will see, if you will kindly *read* what I am saying, that I have good reasons.

In simple justice, not to mention your own self-interest, I think you *should* for once read this letter. I am not only a customer, but happen to have been one of your earliest supporters. I was all in favor of giving you a chance when you were just an idea pleading for a hearing. I had, at that time, no premonition that you would turn into a gigantic world-devouring monopoly, and I wrote more than my share of letters on behalf of the New Life Bill that finally enabled you to go ahead and show what you could do. Now all *I* am asking of you is a hearing, such as I helped obtain for you.

This is my fifth letter of complaint to you, and I think you had better read this one, at least, carefully. You would not be the first idea to turn into a monopoly and then get shrunk back down to size in a hurry.

To help you get the idea, I want to mention that I AM SENDING COPIES OF THIS LETTER TO THE PRESIDENT, TO APPROPRI-ATE COMMITTEES OF BOTH HOUSES OF CONGRESS, AND TO THE ATTORNEY GENERAL'S OFFICE.

If I now finally have your attention, I will mention, parenthetically, that copies are, of course, also going to all appropriate state officials, and there are quite a few of *them*.

Since my four previous letters were answered by routine computer printouts from either your promotion or your legal department, I suppose I had better summarize everything I said in those letters, which have probably long since been shredded and fed to your secretary's cute little lemon-yellow sports coupe.

In chronological order, here is a summary of my four previous letters:

1) "I am a dairy farmer, and recently purchased one of your new model Superbiometal Traction Servalls. As an admirer of your early Biotank models, I want to complain about your phasing out of these models. Their advantage over the usual all-mechanical tractor in times of fuel scarcity was enormous, since at night you could put a stack of hay, corn stalks, straw, wood chips, or what-have-you on the tank-feed mechanism, and in the morning the biotank would have converted the stack into fuel, and the tractor would be ready to go. With one or two supplemental biotanks, most of a farmer's fuel problem was solved. That was good enough, and this new improved series with so-called 'self-repairable modules' represents a complication I don't need and don't want."

2) "I want to again urgently request that you bring back your Biotank model. I could take an ordinary wrench to that model and fix the usual problems. At worst, I could nearly always take it apart and fix it. If, finally, *I* couldn't do the job, I could get hold of some-one who could. But if this present Superbiometal thing, with its 'self-repairable modules,' happens to be set wrong at the factory, and I reset it, *it* then reresets itself to the wrong setting, and neither I, nor my brother with forty years experience on engines, nor your

biobefuddled Superbiometal factory-trained regional representative, can figure out what to do. At present, it insists on running too rich; nothing we do fixes it; it leaves a rolling cloud of fine soot behind it, and drinks fuel like an eight-armed alcoholic; it runs feebly at best and jolts to a stop with a cough and a hiccup if there's any serious work to be done. I am not the only one with this problem. You had better straighten this out, or you will be hearing from our lawyers. P.S. Do you realize that if a sharp rock gets flung up, this Superbiometal tractor *bleeds!*"

3) "Kindly do not send me any more self-congratulatory press releases, slick brochures on New Superbiometal Products, or threatening legal form letters with enclosures that I am supposed to humbly fill out and send back to you by return mail. Everything non-legal goes straight onto the tank-feed stack. The legal junk goes to my lawyer, who is beginning to wonder whether an actionable case for mail fraud can be built up out of it. Instead of wasting time with all this mulch, kindly clear up the problem I have been trying to call to your attention: *Your Superbiometal Traction Servall is a disaster.* I am now farming with my old Biotank model, which is in very worn condition, but which works far better than this fuel-eating soot-machine that can barely crawl around the field. There may be someone who admires your Biotechnological Sophistication, but it isn't me. Don't send me any more slick testimonials from your paid admirers. I know what the truth is: The present model is worthless, and all its 'sophistication' won't grow a hill of beans. Bring back the Biotank model! It *worked.*"

4) "As you will have found out by now, I have traded in your fuel-guzzling Superbiometal Traction Servall for a new improved even-more-sophisticated Superbiometal Powercat. This is no sign of faith on my part so far as the Powercat is concerned. It is just that the Servall was totally worthless, and it seemed that the Powercat might at least be an improvement. It certainly appears 'more aggressive, lean, and powerful,' as your literature claims, but I frankly don't like the looks of the thing. I also don't care for this proliferation of bio-metal sports coupes, roadsters, and so on. Though I was one of your earliest supporters, I never expected you to rush all this stuff into production. It is perfectly obvious to anyone who uses your products that you are getting results beyond what you are aiming at. This

'biometal' you talk about is not 'the substance of life itself, shaped and formed to serve Man's every need.' The various manifestations of life always serve their *own* needs. Man only gets cooperation when a deal is struck, and then you have to make it satisfactory or the other side won't cooperate. I don't really know how to express what I am trying to say here, so I will try to make it simpler: If you've got an axe, a gun, a wrench, or a crowbar, they may not be 'the substance of life itself,' but you at least know what you've got, and you can use it. On the other hand, if you've got a cow, a dog, a cat, or a chicken, it *is* the substance of life, but again, you've got a fair idea what you've got, and, within reason, again you can use it. But just note that in this latter case, you've got, depending on the specifics, to feed it, pet it, water it, keep it from sinking its teeth into visitors, and shovel out its trough. Now, either category of thing is all right, within its limits, but *you are mixing the categories*. Do you appreciate what you are doing? Do we honestly want the equivalent of meowing crowbars and guns that can fire themselves? Never mind how sophisticated it all is, and what a tribute to Science that we can make them. Of course, it's wonderful. But do we *want* it?"

That is the greatly condensed summary of my past correspondence. There is no point trying to summarize the flood of material, all beside the point, that you have sent in return.

What is important is what I have been trying to get through to you, and unfortunately I now have a much clearer idea of that than I did the last time I wrote. I no longer have to try to get it across philosophically. Now I can give you examples.

This new Superbiometal Powercat of yours was no sooner in its shed than it gave a noise like a foghorn, and we discovered in the owner's manual that this 'serves as a reminder to load the tank feed.' It gave this 'reminder' at six that night, at ten, at around twenty minutes after midnight, at quarter of three a.m., and then again right on the dot at six the next morning.

It took us most of the next day to cut and weld new rails and push rods for the tank feed mechanism, so that it would be possible to make it hold feed enough to take this monster through the night. In the hope of getting a little peace and quiet, we were loading up this bigger feed rack when there came a thud and a clang, a noise like thirty pounds of muck squelching onto the ground, and a second clang followed by the sound of a latch clicking into place. There was a strong chemical odor, and there on the floor of the shed sat a steaming gob of what looked like lithium gun grease, with odd bits and remnants of straw, corn stalks, and so on sticking out. Excuse me for mentioning it, but this is a complication I don't need from a tractor. I know what to do with cow manure, but what do we do with this stuff?

Searching through the owner's manual, we found that, "the Powercat not only makes its own fuel from ordinary organic farm wastes, but its high-efficiency processing unit is biomechanically scavenged at regular intervals to eliminate the tedious task of cleansing the conversion tank."

Now, putting this description together with what had actually happened, it began to dawn on us that we were in worse trouble than we'd realized. The most innocuous-seeming passages in this manual could cover who-knew-what actual reality? There was, for instance, on page sixteen, the following:

"To maintain operative functioning efficiency, the Superbiometal Powercat must be maintained with adequate in-tank fuel level at all times."

On glancing over this owner's manual, I had supposed that this meant that you couldn't use the thing without putting fuel in it. But that was obvious to begin with. Moreover, the foghorn reminder was there for what purpose? What did "operative functioning efficiency" *mean?*

Could it be that this tractor would *die* if it wasn't fueled?

Just so that you'll have a fair idea what the background was like as we studied this owner's manual, I suppose I should mention that your dealer here took in around twenty of your worthless Servall models, in trade, all in the same week as he sold these Superbiometal Powercats for replacements. So there must have been about twenty new Powercats sold around here.

So, from the distance, as we were reading your manual, we could hear hootings, fire-siren howlings, low keenings and moanings—all these things have "individualized aural recognition coding for owner convenience"—and there must have been around a dozen different kinds of this noise to add to the way we felt ourselves.

Well, we finished the manual finally, and we were in none too sweet a mood as we went back to the shed amidst the moanings, hootings, and howlings from the distance, moved the Powercat to the barn and got it positioned so the glop from the conversion tank could at least land in the trough, made sure there was plenty of hay and corn stalks in the tank feed, and then we went to bed still trying in the backs of our minds to work out some of the passages in this owner's manual.

I realize you have to sell your products to keep from going broke. But would it be too much to ask that you put the Biotank model back in production and sell *it?* Progress isn't necessarily making things more complicated, and Progress isn't everything, anyway. If the only way forward is to progress downhill into a swamp, you may be a lot better off to stay where you are, or even back up. The "Tank" model we could *understand*, at least.

Anyway, around two in the morning, there was a noise outside, and a frantic barking from the dog—not a warning, and not a threatening bark at an intruder, but the kind of desperate bark that signifies some kind of disaster that scares the dog himself.

Outside, we could see a kind of vague unrecognizable huge moving shape in the very faint moonlight, with low dark clouds passing across the sky so that, from time to time, it was impossible to see anything at all.

Our car was parked beside the house, and our daughter-in-law's car was parked beside it. Our car is a standard model, four years old. Our daughter-in-law drives one of your new "Biostreaks." This huge shape, whatever it was, was moving toward the cars.

About the time this much was clear, the dog let out a frantic yelp in a higher pitch, there came a rumbling from back toward the barns, and a sort of low hoot from around the cars at the side of the house, and then a threatening foghorn rumble from beside the big barn. I say "threatening" because that was what it was.

Thanks to the noise, we were all up by this time, and things happened so fast it's hard to say what came first.

Someone turned on the outside light by the house, the phone rang, a shot went off somewhere, a horn beeped, and the looming shape by the cars turned out to be one of your competitors' "Nucleogenic Workhog" tractors, with no one driving it. This monstrosity was wheeling itself around the Biostreak car, which was no longer beside our car, but about fourteen or fifteen feet away. From the direction of the barn came the Powercat, which was now emitting a noise like a fire siren on the prowl, and if that isn't clear to you, come on out here and we'll do our best to clear it up.

The Powercat now went for the Workhog, the Biostreak coyly went *beep-beep*, our dog decided which side was which and got the Workhog by the tire, and Ed Cox asked me over the phone if I'd seen his Workhog tractor, which he said had a tendency to "start up and wander off at night."

It's to your credit, at least, that the Powercat ran the Workhog off the place, but what this necessarily involved was that this expensive piece of biomachinery was now running around loose, at night, on what errand we didn't know, and for all we could tell, it might end up wrecked. Naturally, we had to go hunt for it.—Besides, the Workhog could have been laying for it somewhere along the road, and the Workhog is a vicious-looking piece of machinery if we ever saw one, and we didn't care to have that thing win the fight.

Naturally enough, considering the circumstances, we saw no sign of the Powercat, got back worn out, and finally found the Powercat back in the barn contentedly connected up to its feed mechanism; the Biostreak car was demurely parked where it had started the night, and the whole shambles obviously was a figment of our imagination— if it hadn't been for the tracks all over the ground.

Now, that was some time ago, and since then we have kept our eyes and ears open, examined these biogenetically engineered machines, further studied the owners' and so-called "shop" manuals, and come to certain conclusions.

First, we don't think you know what you're actually doing.

Second, you may *think* you've got "the substance of Life itself" warped into the "Service of man," but we think the "substance of Life" is using *you*, not the other way around.

Third, we think we can live with this present generation of Powercats, etc., but there are plenty of disadvantages to a tractor that gives a noise like a foghorn when it's hungry, tomcats all night, and, last but not least, chooses a *car* to mate with.

Fourth, kindly do not tell us there is no possible way a farm tractor can mate with a sports car, as we are bringing several dozen reporters out here tomorrow to see what results. And we further want to advise you that neither we nor anyone we have talked to can think of any use for a low-slung streamlined tractor with four bucket seats and a power take-off.

Fifth, we want to advise you to kindly watch out in your gene-splicing-and-altering to keep your civilian and military applications separate, as, between the lot of us out here, we have had to have no less than six different military tank, groundcrawler, and doomsday-type hybrids "humanely put to sleep" shortly after "birth" (what else can we call it?) because there was no possible way we could let these things grow to full size. And I might mention that these are not exactly the easiest kinds of things to "humanely put to sleep," either.

Lastly, let me once again ask you to kindly inquire of yourselves, do we really *want* all this wonderful progress?

Faithfully, but frankly worn-out,

J. J. Wildner
Riveracre Farms

Speed-Up

Dave Martinson eased shut the door of the magnetics lab, and stood still, listening.

In the shadowy silence, with the engineers and technicians gone home, the lab was an unearthly place. Its concrete floor stretched dimly out to the distant walls, making Dave feel like a fly standing on the corner of a table. Overhead, thick loops of heavy black cable branched and rejoined, like the web of a spider woven between the looming bulks of silent equipment.

In the daytime, with the lab blazing with light, and with the cheerful greetings of friends, Dave hardly noticed the strangeness. It was no worse, certainly, than his own lab, where he worked as a cryogenics engineer. But it wasn't just the silence, the darkness, or the strangeness of the lab at night that bothered him.

What really bothered Dave was that, despite the air of emptiness and silence, he knew he was *not* alone.

Somewhere in the dimness, there was someone else.

And, remembering his conversation several days ago with Sam Bardeen, Dave knew the reason—Sabotage. What Bardeen had said had made that clear.

Bardeen, president of the research corporation, was a mysterious figure. Unknown ten years ago, he and his advisor, Richard Barrow, had risen till they headed one of the biggest, and most successful, private research outfits in the country. Bardeen made it a point to meet everyone who worked for him, and several days ago, he'd sent for Dave. He shook hands with a firm grip, then motioned Dave to a chair. They talked about the research center, and Bardeen asked, "How much do you know about Project 'S'?"

Project "S" involved the most secret work in the research center, and Dave wasn't supposed to know a thing about it.

He said, "I know it's secret. I know a great amount of material has been brought in there, but I have no idea what it was. Naturally, I've wondered about Project 'S'. I suppose we all have. I've heard it said, on good authority, that it's a new process for the purification of sea-water. All I'm really sure of is that it's *not* 'for the purification of sea-water'."

"Why do you say that?"

"To begin with, the security precautions are too tight. We already have a lighted, well-guarded fence completely around the whole research center, which itself is far out of town, isolated, and set well back from the road. But in addition, there's the so-called 'inner security compound,' with its own gate, guardhouse, and lighted fence, around the Project 'S' building, the cryogenics and magnetics labs. The people in those labs can't go into the Project 'S' building, but Project 'S' people can go into the labs. Everyone who works on Project 'S' lives here with his family, goes to the doctor kept here especially for him, goes to the dentist here, and goes to the movies here. He does his work in the *inner* compound, yet it's necessary to go through four gates and past three guardposts merely to get into the *outer* compound."

Bardeen laughed, but said nothing.

Dave said, "With due respect to the people who say they're purifying sea-water in there, I just don't believe it."

"Well," said Bardeen, "you have to remember, there's a severe water shortage developing in this country. Whoever can develop a fast, cheap process for purifying sea water can expect to make a sizeable profit. Naturally, we'd want to keep our process secret."

"If there were need for *that* much security, the words 'sea-water' would never be mentioned around here. As it is, it's the quasi-official explanation. But I've hardly begun to mention what's wrong with it. For instance, there's the fact that the cryogenics and magnetics labs obviously tie in with Project 'S,' since they too are in the inner security compound. And in the cryogenics lab, we've been doing a great deal of work close to absolute zero. Now, on the everyday Fahrenheit temperature scale, that's around four hundred and ninety degrees below the freezing point of water. At these temperatures, sea-water would long since have been frozen into one solid chunk."

"New processes—" said Bardeen.

Dave nodded. "Granted. But there are other things wrong with the sea-water idea. For instance, the superconductivity work that's been done? Where does that fit in? And the magnetics lab's work to produce powerful magnetic fields of large cross-sections? And the fact that the cryogenics lab is turning out volumes of low-temperature liquids and slushes, which are piped next door to the magnetics lab and run through huge units called 'Blocks,' which obviously are a part of Project 'S'?"

"How do you know?"

"The magnetics lab uses cryogenics products and equipment, and naturally they need our help from time to time. It's impossible to work on that equipment without noticing things. For instance, that the Blocks in the magnetics lab are shaped as parts of some larger structure. But there's no provision to join them or even get them out of the lab, so it follows that they're full-scale models, with the unified, finished device—which would be very large—somewhere else. The Project 'S' building is huge, and it's right next door. The connection is obvious."

Bardeen looked at Dave wonderingly. "I had no idea our cover was as thin as that."

"It might not be to an outsider."

Bardeen thoughtfully massaged his chin.

"What *is* Project 'S'?"

"In my opinion, it's a thermonuclear reactor."

Bardeen glanced out the window. His hands lay calmly on the desk, but for an instant he was biting his lip. Then he shrugged, and he turned to face Dave frankly.

"You're close enough. I can't tell you just *how* close, but it's enough to explain the security precautions we're taking. I'm concerned about the security aspect myself, and my partner, Mr. Barrow, thinks there may be trouble with saboteurs or industrial spies." Bardeen looked at Dave as if making some point, then he smiled and said, "Now I wonder if you'd tell me about your work. I understand you've developed a highly effective new cryostat. How did you lick the problem of conduction losses?"

And the rest of the conversation had been technical. But the idea had been firmly planted in Dave's mind that what was going on in the Project 'S' building was something that might readily attract industrial spies, eager to seek out the secrets of a competitor—and it might even attract saboteurs.

It was this thought that had made Dave glance more sharply at the dimly-seen movement near the magnetics lab tonight, when ordinarily he was not at all security-minded. That he should see anything was sheer chance. The three buildings in the inner security compound happened to lie in a straight line from north to south. The cryogenics lab, where Dave worked, was farthest north, connected by an enclosed walkway with the magnetics lab in the middle, which was connected by another enclosed walk to the overshadowing bulk of the Project 'S' building. The labs had their own individual parking lots, separated only by a swath of green grass, and it had been from the northernmost parking lot that Dave, just driving out after working late in the cryogenics lab, had seen the intruder.

The sun by then had gone down, and the deep shadow of the magnetics lab was thrown across its empty parking lot. It was the time of evening when it wasn't daylight, and it wasn't yet dark. It was impossible to see clearly, but it was still light enough so that headlights were not much help, either. When Dave saw the blur of motion, he thought at first it was a trick of the eye. But remembering Bardeen's comment, he slowed his car to a stop, and rolled down the window to watch.

From the front of the magnetics lab, about where the door should be, came a large dull flash of light, seen for a moment, then gone.

Dave glanced around. At the end of the drive, several hundred feet in front of him, was a small guardhouse by the gate in the fence of the inner security compound. Tall lightpoles lit the cars that stopped near the gate, and lit the fence that stretched due north along the edge of the compound. The guardhouse itself was dazzlingly bathed in light. One quick glance was enough to show Dave what must have happened.

The door of the magnetics lab was highly polished. The lab,

Dave's car, and the guardhouse were on about the same level, with the lab set off to one side. If the door were opened at a slight angle, its polished surface would reflect the brilliant light from the guardhouse. If the door were swinging shut, it would reflect it only briefly.

The question was—Had the door opened when someone came out—Or had someone gone in?

Dave frowned briefly, puzzled that the built-in, photoelectric switch hadn't yet turned on the lights in front of the lab. Then he snapped on his headlights, and swung the car so that their lights rapidly swept over the front of the lab from one end to the other. There, at least, it was dark enough so that the headlights helped, and he could see that there was nothing there but the wide cement walk in front of the lab, the flat outjutting roof, and the empty asphalt of the vacant parking lot.

No-one had come out. —Therefore someone had gone in.

Dave cast a quick glance at the guardhouse down the drive, set the parking brake, got out and locked the car door.

The prudent thing, he knew, was to go down to the guardhouse and tell what he had seen. But the guards, from their position, would have seen nothing. To explain his reasoning would take five minutes at least, and one of the guards might think Dave hadn't seen what he *had* seen. There usually were only two men on duty in the guardhouse, and they might well have to call up and get permission before either of them could leave. The possibilities of delay stretched out, and Dave decided not to do what he was supposed to do, but instead to do something that ought to bring action in a hurry. Leaving the car with its lights shining on the door of the lab, he turned directly into his headlight beams, ran to the door, and gripped the knob to try it. He found to his surprise that while the door was *locked*—so that he couldn't turn the knob—it wasn't *latched*. The catch had not snapped into its slot. As he tugged at it, the door pulled open.

Dave looked quickly around, and saw someone standing in front of the guardhouse, looking his way. He yanked the door wide open, and went inside.

He was immediately rewarded by the blare of a siren.

Once, twice, three, four times it sounded, in short blasts, signaling the need for immediate help at guardhouse number four.

Guardhouse number four was right there at the end of the drive, and the need must seem urgent to them to use the siren. That would bring the reinforcements on the run.

Dave let the heavy door swing almost shut, cutting the siren down to a distant wail. He made sure the door didn't latch, and looked around in the dim light at the closed doors of several offices, the two washrooms, and the lab itself. There was no sound of movement anywhere, and he paused to swiftly think things over. The car lights were directly on the front door, and the two men at the guardhouse would be watching it closely. In perhaps five minutes, the guards from the security building would be here, and any intruder in the offices would be trapped. But from the lab, the two covered walkways led to the cryogenics and Project 'S' buildings. And in the lab itself, a saboteur could make a nightmarish mess. Dave cautiously eased open the lab door, and slid inside.

And found himself listening, in the shadowy silence, with the concrete floor stretching dimly out to the distant walls, and the thick loops of cable like a web joining the looming bulks of equipment.

Then he heard the faint scrape from across the lab to his left.

In the gloom, hoping his eyes would accommodate to the dimness, Dave moved forward. His blood pounded in his ears, and he could hear the sound of his own breathing. The guards by now should be pouring out of the security building into their Jeeps. They would be here in three or four minutes. Their first move on arrival would naturally be to snap on the lights of the lab. It wasn't smart, but it was their only chance to end things fast. The trouble was, whoever was in here would be well-armed. In the exchange of gunfire, a bullet might plow through a surface designed to resist changes of temperature, not impact. One of the pipes might be cut, sending out a spray that would crystallize air in an instant. Worse yet, the liquefied gas in a big damaged cryostat might vaporize, building up enough pressure to burst the cryostat and release a blast of liquid and vapor that would freeze a man solid on contact. Dave abruptly found himself up against a large, gently-corrugated, curving surface. He reached out cautiously across it, and realized it was one of the branching coolant lines leading to the magnetic Block that loomed up over his right shoulder. The gently corrugated surface was a thin sheet of aluminum over the underlying insulation. If he tried to climb over it, it might buckle, with a noise that could bring a fusillade of bullets in his direction. He reached down, and found the space beneath it too narrow to crawl under. He worked to his left, and found another magnetic Block in his way—he looked around. The lab, instead of appearing lighter as his eyes grew accustomed to the darkness, appeared darker yet as the feeble daylight coming in the few high windows faded out.

Somewhere, there was the sound of a key sliding in a lock, the faint rattle of a door, then silence.

Dave made his way around the block to his left. He could picture the intruder going down the enclosed passage to the Project 'S' building. But if Dave could reach the door before it shut—

Not four feet in front of him, there was an explosive sigh of disgust, then a soft metallic sliding sound. The door hadn't opened after all.

But Dave was close now, and moving too fast to stop.

His left foot hit a heavy solid bulk on the floor, throwing him forward off-balance.

From a darker shadow beside him, there was a quick insucking of breath. Then the back of Dave's skull seemed to explode. He was on one knee, helpless, when a heavy thud and an agonized curse told him the intruder had tried to finish him, and had hit too high.

Across the room, there was a low voice.

Abruptly, there was a blinding blaze of light.

"Don't move!"

Exactly what Dave had wanted to avoid had now happened.

And he was nicely placed to collect the bullets.

For an instant, Dave felt the edge of a shoe press against his hand as his opponent pivoted. There was the slide-snap of an automatic made ready to fire. Dave grabbed the ankle above the foot, jerked it up, wrenched the foot.

There was a deafening roar. Bits of cement spattered across his face. The room echoed to a volley of shots. He tipped forward off-balance. There was a crash, another roar, the memory of a high whining noise, and hot wind across his forehead. His left hand slid in a slippery hotness, and then there was the sound of running feet.

In half an hour, it was all over. Dave had shown passes and permits, identified himself to the guards' satisfaction as Dave Martinson, cryogenics engineer, and then they'd called up the administration building, where Sam Bardeen had left for home, but Richard Barrow was still on hand. Barrow examined the collection of burglar's tools, the small flat camera, and the little small black tubes imbedded in them. Barrow looked at Dave quizzically, then glanced questioningly at the doctor, who was bent over the motionless form lying in a pool of blood. The doctor shook his head.

Dave and Barrow exchanged a few more words, then Dave went to wash up. As Dave left the room, Barrow called, "Watch your driving. There are a lot of fools on the road."

Now that Dave was at the wheel, Barrow's comment bothered him. It was the kind of thing anyone might say, but Barrow wasn't anyone. Barrow, like Bardeen, was unpredictable and not given to platitudes.

Irritated, Dave thrust the thought out of his mind. He fingered the bump at the back of his skull. It was large, and it was tender, but at least he was all right. He still had a date tonight.

That thought put Barrow's warning out of his head.

He slowed to show his pass at the outer gate, and a few minutes later he was on the road to town, thinking of Anita Reynolds, who was a lovely girl with a sweet personality, a beautiful figure, and only one flaw.

He was thinking of her when for no reason that he knew, he felt a sense of unease that caused him to lightly press the brake pedal.

Forty feet ahead, a truck loaded with crates of chickens roared out of a side road without stopping, swung halfway across the road to straddle the white line, and then slowed down.

Dave slammed on the brakes. His car slowed so fast the steering wheel dug into his ribs. The rear end of the truck enlarged, the swaying crates rose high above him, and his radiator tried to ram itself in under the rear of the truck.

Dave pressed with all his strength on the brake pedal.

There was a grind of gears up ahead, and Dave found himself stopped dead, the truck swaying down the road in front of him with both left wheels over the white line.

His memory awoke in a rush.

"Watch your driving," Barrow had said. "There are a lot of fools on the road."

Dave swore involuntarily, and stepped on the gas.

Ahead of him, the truck accelerated to exactly thirty miles an hour, and weaved back and forth across the road, staying far to the right on sharp curves, the tops of hills, or when oncoming cars were near, and moving back across the middle when there was a clear straight stretch ahead.

No matter what Dave tried, he couldn't pass. Then from behind came a scream of brakes as some fool, doing ninety down the narrow road, abruptly closed up on Dave, who was held to thirty by the truck ahead. The lights of the car behind rapidly grew dazzling, Dave pulled as close to the truck and as far to the right as he dared. The car swung past on Dave's left, and the driver was promptly rewarded with a rear view of the truck. By some miracle, truck and car remained unhurt, and Dave found himself third in line.

In Dave's memory, Barrow's voice repeated. "Watch your driving. There are a lot of fools on the road."

It was a slow trip back to town. But, with the back of his neck still tingling, Dave made it at last.

Anita Reynolds had a clear, bell-like laugh. Her shining brown eyes lit up as Dave told the story. The laugh made the other diners turn, and the sight of Anita's smile, her face glowing as if lit from within, made them smile with her.

"What did you do?" she asked.

"What could I do?" said Dave. "I slowed down till I had a hundred feet between me and them, then I spent the rest of the trip glancing back and forth from them to the rear-view mirror. The truck slowed down to show who was boss, and we averaged twenty-five miles an hour all the way in."

The waiter discreetly laid the check face-down on the table, and Dave stood up to help Anita with her coat. He left a generous tip for the waiter, paid the cashier, and they started out. Anita glanced at Dave and smiled. "Dinner was very good. Thank you."

Dave grinned. "They have good food here. The place seems generally stuffy and behind the times, but the food is unbeatable."

Anita laughed. "What do you want, dancing girls?"

"Of course."

She was smiling at him, and Dave, smiling back, was aware of her warmth, her quick response to him, and her beauty. If only it could always be like this. He pushed open one of the double glass doors to the corridor that led out to the street, and held the door for her.

She smiled her thanks, turning slightly toward him as she walked by. She had a beautiful figure, and for one instant Dave was dizzyingly conscious of it. In that moment, he knew that everything about this girl was right.

Her voice seemed to reach him only faintly, and it took a moment to understand her words.

"Good heavens," she was saying, her voice crisp, "look at those headlines!"

The sense of bliss was gone. Dave looked around wearily, wondering what it was this time.

Nearby in the hall was a stand displaying candy, cigars, magazines and newspapers. Anita was looking at a newspaper, whose oversize headlines screamed:
PILLS KILL AGAIN!

Dave looked at her wearily. Her shining auburn hair showed glints of flame in the light, and her face and figure were beautiful. But her brows were drawn, her lips compressed, and her eyes shot sparks.

"Look at this," she said, showing Dave the paper.

Dave looked at it dully, remembering that when he'd first met Anita, he'd told his best friend of his good fortune.

"I've found a wonderful girl," he'd said.

"Good for you."

"The only trouble is, she's a follower of this—Harkman Bates, I think his name is."

"Oh, God!"

"She belongs to the—what do you call it—the—"

"Security League," said his friend promptly. "Okay. You're not engaged to her?"

"No," said Dave, startled.

"You're not married to her?"

"Of course not."

"Drop her."

"Listen—" Dave protested.

"*You* listen to *me*! Every time you think of her, hold your breath till you're dizzy, and don't breathe till you think of something else. Go join the YMCA, and work out on the dumbbells and parallel bars till you're so worn out girls are meaningless. Sink yourself in abstruse mathematics till you warp yourself around into a frame of reference where sex isn't even conceivable. Go—"

"Listen," said Dave furiously, "I didn't say I was a victim of passion! All I said—"

"Was that you're falling in love with this girl, and she belongs to the Security League."

"I just said she was a wonderful girl. Pretty. Intelligent. Good sense of humor. Nice figure. She's got everything. Only—"

"Yeah," said his friend cynically. "Well, that's all it takes. The uncontrollable passion will come later. Whether it will be love or murder I don't know."

"What do you mean?"

"You're up against something you can't lick, that's all. You can't win. You're an engineer. The motto of the Security League might as well be, 'End Science Before Science Ends Us.' And it's backed up by facts, figures, sentiment, and some kind of mystical claptrap a man can't come to grips with. Right in the focus of this stands Harkman Bates. He's handsome, he's rich, he's got stage presence, he's got a voice of silver, and he's got an organization that works for him from morning till night. You might as well argue with an earth-moving machine.

"If you go with this girl, there'll be endless conflict, because you're an engineer, and you'll represent Science to her. Your ego is going to take the bruising of a lifetime. You're going to cease to exist any time League business comes up. When Bates comes on TV, you're going to find yourself converted into a piece of furniture. Afterward you'll have to listen to how wonderful and how right he is. Get out now. Cut your losses. It's a hopeless cause."

Dave stared at him. "How can you be so sure?"

"I've been through it myself. A different girl, but the same situation. Take my word for it. You might just as well fall in love with a land mine."

And now, Anita was studying the newspaper, her face angry and indignant.

She glanced at him reproachfully, "Your scientific friends are responsible for this. Over three thousand people have died or are in the hospital thanks to those pills, and yet we can go into that drugstore over there—" She pointed across the hall to the entrance of a drugstore—"and buy a bottle right now to cure a headache. It doesn't say on the bottle that if you take too many they'll poison your liver. But—"

Dave remembered the last time he'd tried to argue with her. That had been over a magazine article to the effect that auto exhaust was connected with lung cancer and a lung condition called emphysema.

That argument had lasted three minutes by the clock, but it was three minutes packed with emotion and insult, and Dave wound up in the street, stunned.

This memory, too, passed through Dave's mind as Anita looked at him accusingly.

Then in memory Dave saw the smile on her lips and the glow in her eyes that had been there just a few minutes ago.

And Dave realized that he was *not* going to cut his losses. Somehow, there must be a way to *win*.

He'd already tried arguing it out with her, head-on. That had not worked.

He forced himself to look at the paper as if interested.

"I have to admit, you've got a point."

She frowned at him. "I expected a lecture on the virtues of science."

"Why? You're right."

This seemed to leave her totally confused. She started to speak, looked at him for a long moment, then turned away, blushing.

He didn't understand this. But it was better than fighting.

They walked outside.

She drew a deep breath. "What a lovely evening."

"Isn't it?" said Dave. The air was cool and clear, with a fresh breeze. The streets were almost empty. Sometimes there was a solid mass of cars, the combined exhausts of which, as they started up at a green light, was enough to give anyone momentary doubts about technology.

She put her hand in his.

"I'm sorry I snapped, Dave."

"I know how you feel."

"I'm so glad you do." She smiled at him warmly. "Have you ever thought of joining the League?"

"Ah—"

They turned the corner. The theater marquee spelled out in bright lights:

BOB HOPE

Dave said hastily, "We're late. We'll have to hurry."

Where the Security League wasn't involved, Anita's sense of humor was cheerful and robust. And if there was one entertainer she liked above all other, this was the one. Fortunately, she forgot her question.

Two hours later, their disagreement completely forgotten, they came up the aisle of the theater hand-in-hand, and she smiled at him with sparkling eyes. They were buffeted by the crowd, but she didn't seem to mind. When they reached the lobby, she stopped for a box of popcorn. Around them people were rushing outside, and Dave felt a vague anxiety but couldn't pin it down. On the way out, they passed the door of a soda fountain known locally for its ice cream, and its after-movie snacks.

Dave glanced at it. Something told him he should take her in there. He looked at her.

"Would you like—"

She smiled contentedly. "The air's so fresh, and it's such a nice evening. Why don't we just take a walk?"

At the same time, he knew this wasn't going to work out, and he could think of no reason why it shouldn't.

From somewhere came the rumble of a big truck, and on a building across the street the lights of cars were swinging across as the parking lot near the theater emptied itself.

Dave looked into her clear dark eyes.

He held her hand tightly.

At the corner, the traffic light turned green.

A big diesel truck gave a loud *Baarroom!* It started forward, slowed with a clash of gears, accelerated hard.

A host of cars rushed forward as their drivers, anxious to get home so they'd be wide-awake at work the next day, jammed down the gas pedals.

The traffic shot past down the street.

The wind was right in the face of Dave and Anita.

Gas fumes and diesel smoke whirled around them.

"Oh, *Dave!*" cried Anita angrily.

Once again she was a member of the Security League.

She was somber as he drove toward her apartment.

He turned the car radio on hoping to get music. Instead he got a smooth commercial voice saying:

". . . boon for allergy sufferers, and it has been scientifically tested and found perfectly harmless, so you can take it without your doctor's prescription."

"Yes," said Anita acidly. "That's what you say *now*."

"And next," said the voice, "the news."

Dave reached out to change stations, but she said, "Let's listen."

"The town of Little Falls, Kansas," said the announcer, "was wiped out this afternoon. Not by fire, not by flood, but by a man-made catastrophe. Little Falls is in farming country, and planes were spraying insecticide unaware that the spray was remaining suspended in the air, to be blown in a thick deadly smog straight through town. Scientists say that the combination of atmospheric pressure, humidity, and temperature gradient which caused this smog was so unusual that no change in spraying technique is needed. The smog was only a freak, they say. But tonight, Little Falls is a ghost town—"

Anita huddled near the door, and the announcer droned on about detection of cheating on test bans, radioactive fall-out, the kidnapping of a rocket scientist from a Middle East missile project, an investigation of an additive used in baked goods, a case of the Black Plague carried halfway around the world in an airplane—and all through this recitation Anita shrank further from Dave. To wind it up, the announcer reported an experiment to:

". . . determine, this coming Saturday, the internal structure of the earth, by explosion of nuclear missiles, fired down long shafts with powerful laser 'head-lights' intended to melt the layers of rock in front of them when, at high speeds, they reach the ends of the shafts. These missiles are designed to penetrate further and explode deeper than any other man-made device in history. The object is to set up seismic waves that can be analyzed by new equipment . . ."

Dave slowed to a stop in front of Anita's apartment house.

The news went on.

". . . despite the qualms of we uninformed laymen, scientists assure us there is no danger because the explosions are small, geologically speaking. —And that's the news. Good night."

Dave shut the radio off before it could do more damage.

Anita said, in a small voice, "You didn't answer my question, Dave?"

"When?"

"Before we went into the movie?"

Dave remembered the question "Have you ever thought of joining the League?"

He sighed.

"To be truthful, Anita I *hadn't* thought about it."

"Tonight is the first time I've even been able to talk to you about the League. Harkman Bates is going to speak on television in five minutes or so. Would you like to come up?"

"Sure," said Dave wearily, "I'll come up."

Bates's smooth deep voice rolled on. His chiseled features, cleft chin, and wavy silver hair gave him a look of distinction and power. His eyes spoke an unmistakable message of sincerity.

Anita, watching him, sighed.

Dave, contrasting the sincerity with the man's basic message, swore under his breath. Although it was unmistakable that Bates had a point.

". . . deformed children," Bates was saying, "brought into the world because scientists *did not know* the true nature of the 'harmless drug' gave another warning. But still they do not see the nature of the very thing they work with."

His eyes blazed.

"Science is unpredictable.

"Will scientists never learn that?

"The result of any new and basic experiment *is not knowable in advance.*

"As science reaches closer and closer to the heart of nature, the results of miscalculation and ignorance loom larger. Already, the womb of woman has been distorted by science, the lungs of man filled with corruption by the technology of science, the natural longings of humanity perverted by this new godless religion.

"Steadily the world becomes more strange to us, made strange by science. Already there are those who cannot make their way in such a world, and the number grows, day-by-day.

"The scientist tells us, we must study, and learn, and take up the things of science. We must all become scientists and technicians, and then we shall all be happy, well-adjusted.

"And all the time he says this, he is blinded to the flaw of his own belief:

"The results of an experiment *cannot be foreseen.*

"No-one knows where Science will lead us, or how suddenly the trail may end. Foolish men are raising this new unpredictable force to the point where we can no longer control it. *Now is the time to control it.*

"Now is the time to say—*So far and no further!*"

From somewhere, there rose an immense cheer, a thundering applause that grew and grew, and the camera shifted to show a huge audience on its feet, waving and cheering.

For just an instant, Dave remembered the blast of gas fumes on the street, the bitter expressions of boys on street corners, ready for trouble because they could find no work—machines had the jobs. He remembered the pills that were known to be harmless, and that did their damage anyway. He remembered his amazement at the list of ingredients in a package of baked goods. What were these things, anyway? He remembered the poisoned insecticide that had wiped out a town, thought of the tons of poison that were dumped on plants yearly, washed into the soil and—then what? Did the plants take up the insecticide and pass it on, little by little, to the man who ate the plant?

These and many other things flashed through his mind.

"My friends," said the voice of the handsome silver-haired man, "*Now* is the time to stop it!

"And to stop it forever!"

The cheer rose again, but Dave was out of the spell.

The speech was over.

A band was playing, and Anita, her eyes shining, turned to Dave, including him in her own world.

"Now you've heard him! *Now* will you join?"

Wearily, Dave shook his head. "For just a minute, I almost agreed. But it's no use, Anita."

She came over to sit beside him.

"Why not, Dave?"

"Because he doesn't know what he's talking about."

He might have slapped her face. "Every word he said was *true!*"

"I know. But he didn't say enough words. He overlooked a little point."

She drew away from him.

"What do you mean?"

"*How* do you stop science? *How*, Anita? And what happens if you do? Science and technology give power, and the world is split up into countries that *want* power. If one stops, another will go on, and get the power to overcome the country that stops. So no one *can* stop. But that's only part of it. We—"

"Dave," she said coldly, "don't you suppose he's thought of this? The League isn't made up of fools."

"Then what's his answer?"

"I don't know. I'm sure he has one."

"I'm satisfied there *isn't* any. We're—"

"Then you'd better go."

Dave stood up angrily. "You don't want to listen, do you?"

She held the door open.

He walked past her. "Thanks. I listened to *your* side." He turned on his heel.

Her voice was cold as ice. "Thank you for a pleasant evening."

As Dave sat in his chilly car and pressed the starter, he could hear again his friend's voice:

"You can't win . . . It's a hopeless cause . . . You might just as well fall in love with a land mine."

Wearily, Dave drove back to his apartment, and spent the night in a miserable search for sleep.

The next day, at the lab, his friend took one look, nodded wisely, and said nothing.

Around ten o'clock, word came that Bardeen wanted to see him. Barrow was in the office when Dave got there, and listened as Dave told about the intruder in the magnetics lab.

Bardeen nodded finally. "We expected it. It's too bad, but that's life."

Dave said, "Do we have any idea how he got in?"

"Under the outer and inner fences, over the walkway between the magnetics lab and Project 'S', then around to the front and through the door. He had the key, and someone had changed the filter on the control that snaps on the lights around the roof of the magnetics lab. He obviously had an accomplice, but we have no idea who."

"The intruder wasn't one of our own people?"

"No. The police have identified him. The only interesting point so far is that he was a member of the Security League."

Dave blinked.

Barrow said, "They're naturally interested in anything that tends to discredit science. A disaster in any advanced research center would back up their argument that science is unpredictable."

"Would Bates stoop to that?"

"In that outfit," said Bardeen, "the right hand doesn't know what the left is doing, and the head is ignorant of both. Do you know much about the League?"

"I know a girl," said Dave, "who has every quality a woman should have. But she's also a member of the League. I can tell you, that can ruin a date."

Bardeen smiled. "She doesn't question you about your work?"

"Never. It's a part of science, and she doesn't like science."

Barrow said, "What do you think of Bates' argument."

"He's right that the ultimate results of an experiment are unpredictable. We don't really know whether, in the long run, science will turn out to have been good or bad. But that's beside the point."

"How so?"

"We're committed. We're in the position of a man who'd decided to jump a chasm, has gone back for a start, and now, running full speed, is almost at the edge. That's no time to think, 'Maybe I won't make it. I'll stop here.' He can't stop. He's got to go faster yet, and hope and pray he makes it. We're in the same spot. Science and technology have depleted the natural resources of the earth, disturbed the balance of nature, enlarged the population. If we tried to drop science now—even if we could get everyone on earth to agree to it— we'd face a terrific explosion of hunger, disease, and misery, followed by a drop straight into barbarism. The only visible way out is to complete the jump."

Bardeen nodded. "That's the point. Exactly."

Barrow looked at Dave almost with awe. "That's a remarkable comparison."

Bardeen, too, for some reason was looking at Dave with visible respect. Then he thanked Dave for coming over, and expressed his appreciation for Dave's help in catching the intruder. When Dave was in the hall, Barrow came out.

"Excuse me," said Barrow, frowning. "You like this girl you mentioned?"

"Very much," said Dave.

Barrow paused, his eyes unfocussed. Dave waited. This was the way things often went, and the reason why Dave had been so surprised at Barrow's commonplace remark about fools on the road.

"Yes," said Barrow, "we must have an open house. Project 'S' is almost finished. That's the only way. We'll have the people here, in case—" He looked directly at Dave, and smiled. "Invite her. Show her around. Perhaps she'll see your viewpoint."

"I don't know if she'll come."

"Tell her if you can't convince her science is all right, you'll join the League. *That* will bring her." He looked Dave flatly in the eyes. "If you really like her, be sure she's here. The day after tomorrow. Before two in the afternoon."

Barrow went back into Bardeen's office.

Dave stood staring for a moment, then shook his head, and went back to the lab.

When he mentioned this to some friends, they all laughed. "That's Barrow, all right. That's our boy."

Official word soon came from Bardeen's office, and they were all excited.

"Who knows," said someone. "Maybe we'll find out what Project 'S' is."

The day of the open house saw the wives, sweethearts, and families of the men thronging the grounds. Barrow's family was there, as was Bardeen's. And for once it was possible to move freely. Even the inner security compound was opened to the visitors, though the Project "S" building remained closed.

Anita had agreed to come, and visited the lab, but Dave's explanation of his work was no great success.

"You see," he was trying to tell her, "atoms and molecules at ordinary temperatures are in a state of rapid vibration. The properties that we take for granted, as natural characteristics of matter, actually are only special characteristics, dependent on the comparatively high temperature—which to us seems normal. But at such temperatures, the atoms and molecules are in a rapid state of vibration. In cryogenics, we study matter at *low* temperatures."

"Are they going to have lunch outdoors?" said Anita. She was lovely, but her features were slightly pinched, as though she felt the intense cold of the cryogenics lab around her.

Dave, realizing the hopelessness of it, suppressed a grin. "How can you judge what you don't understand?"

"By its results," she said.

Dave said, "Unfortunately, I don't know yet just what the final result of all this is going to be."

"Then," she said, brightening, "we can't very well judge it, can we?" She was studying his face intently, and suddenly grinned. "You're teasing me, aren't you?"

Dave laughed. "At the beginning I was in earnest."

"I'm sorry. It just doesn't mean anything to me. I suppose a man would feel the same way if a woman described the fine points of sewing to him."

Dave nodded. "Let's go outside."

It was a beautiful day, with small fluffy clouds against a delicate blue sky, light at the horizon, and deep blue overhead. The sun was bright, and there was a brisk cool breeze that fluttered the women's dresses as they stood by the tables that were laden with potato salad, and steaming trays of hot dogs and hamburgers. Dave realized that he was hungry. But as he and Anita started toward the crowd, abruptly Dave stopped.

The whole scene for an instant seemed unreal to him, as if it were painted on a balloon that had been blown so tight it could almost be seen through.

Anita said, "What is it?"

He shook his head. "I don't know."

He felt a compulsion again, the same feeling that had led him to press the brake pedal the other night. But this feeling was far stronger and more urgent.

Anita was watching him. "What's wrong, Dave?"

"I don't know. But I've got to find Bardeen." At that moment, he saw Bardeen, standing with Barrow a little apart from the crowd, which was now spreading out into small groups, holding paper plates and rolls, and balancing their cups.

Anita said, "I'll get you something to eat. I'll wait over here while you talk to Mr. Bardeen."

"Yes," he said. "Thanks."

Bardeen and Barrow were standing like two statues, each of them holding a hamburger and a paper cup. Barrow had his eyes shut as Dave approached, but now he opened them.

"No chance," Barrow said. "The lasers will melt the rock in front of them and when the rocket passes, the additional heat, and the release of pressure, will cause sudden vaporization."

Bardeen said, "It *can't* be that hot."

"The rockets will be traveling at such a speed as to compress the laser beam longitudinally. Remember, the rockets won't be working *against* gravity. Gravity will be helping them."

Dave frowned. How could that be, unless a rocket were fired *down* into a hole? Suddenly he remembered the news broadcast. Geologists planned to study the structure of the earth by analyzing the shock waves from underground explosions.

Bardeen said, "The phenomenon will be evanescent, unstable. But it will travel right along with the rocket, which will be moving at too high a speed to be crushed from the sides by the pressure. Remember, the deep layers will liquefy, then vaporize, and the pressure of vaporization behind the rocket will plunge it deeper and faster. The top of that hole will be hell on earth. There'll be a column of vapor miles high and the uprush will blast away the sides of the hole, widening it as it goes."

"It will melt the rocket."

"Yes, but too late."

"Will it explode?"

"Yes. Very, very deep."

"So far, we have a geological expedition wiped out."

"Yes, but a nuclear explosion at that depth is going to find matter under higher pressure than in any previous experiment. When the particles from the explosion strike those close-packed atomic nuclei—"

Bardeen said tightly, "Chain reaction?"

"Yes."

"Self-sustaining?"

"I can't tell yet. A small error at the beginning would slowly cause the rocket to fall behind the wave front, and penetrate less deeply."

"If we could only warn—"

"How? We tried that once, remember?"

"I know. There's no reason for them to believe us."

Before he thought, Dave said, "What is this—precognition?"

Sam Bardeen's eyes were cool. Barrow glanced at Dave without expression, then nodded.

"So that's how you could warn me last night about fools on the road."

Bardeen cleared his throat.

Dave said, "I remembered after those fools almost finished me off twice."

Bardeen started to speak.

Barrow said, "Hold it, Sam." He frowned at Dave. "After they almost hit you twice, then you remembered?"

"That's right." Dave, thinking it over, was wondering again where these hunches came from. What *had* made him put his foot on the brake pedal?

Bardeen started to speak.

Barrow silenced him with a raised hand. "My department, Sam." He shut his eyes for a long moment, then looked at Bardeen with a faint grin. "*Now* the twins work."

Dave glanced from one of them to the other.

Bardeen was saying incredulously. "No waiting to match configurations?"

"They'll match on signal. This is our boy here. They'll match, if *he* gives the signal."

Bardeen glanced from Barrow to Dave, and abruptly the coldness was gone.

"You see," he said to Dave smiling, "why Dick and I have come up fast. With precognition it's possible to avoid wasted time following the wrong path."

"If," said Barrow, "the experiment first has been carefully formulated."

Dave still felt the overpowering sense of pressure.

"What are the 'twins' you spoke of?"

Barrow said, "That's Project 'S'."

Bardeen said, "Project 'S,' is a twin set of transmission stations."

"What do they transmit?"

"Matter."

"Matter?"

"That's right. The structure of the matter is sent in a code that modulates a carrier wave. The matter is picked up here, converted to energy, transmitted as a finely-focused transient beam, and reverted to matter."

"The way a radio station sends a voice? One of the 'twins' is a transmitter and the other a receiver?"

"Not quite. Either one can focus on an object close enough to be encoded, send out its focused signal, and at the focus the object sent is reconstituted."

"How far away?"

"Tens of thousands of miles. Further yet, outside the Earth's gravitational field."

"Why 'twins'? Are they the same?"

"Identical."

"Why?"

"We *need* two."

"What for?"

"Because neither one can send *itself*."

Dave looked at him blankly, then stared.

"Good Lord! The two together are a space vehicle?"

Bardeen nodded.

Barrow shut his eyes.

Dave could feel, around him, the tight-stretched balloon of the pleasant scene drawn tighter yet. The sunlight shimmered on it and it sparkled. But to Dave it seemed that any minute it might snap and be gone.

Barrow sighed. "That does it."

Bardeen said, "Self-sustaining?"

"Self-sustaining. The picture's clear now. They'll drop that rock-et with absolute precision. It's the same thing as lighting a fuse that leads straight to the dynamite shack."

Dave said, "You *see* this?"

Barrow nodded. "I shut my eyes, and it's right there, like a garden, in a way, and in another like an attic half-full of mirrors. All kinds of things are there, some clear, and some fuzzy, some already here, and mirrored as in a mirage. Those are in the future."

"How did you learn—"

"I don't know. The knack runs in my family. My mother, uncles, and children have it. It's a maddening thing, because usually you aren't interested. But there it is, the instant you shut your eyes. Mostly it's too complex to follow the interlocking chains of cause and effect. But with a scientific experiment, it's different. So far as possible, extraneous factors are ruled out, and the chains of cause and effect are simplified. To that extent, it becomes possible to predict results accurately."

"And the accident I almost had?"

"A matter of possibilities. I could see just enough to tell you'd be in danger."

Bardeen said, "How will this—" but didn't finish the question. He looked at Dave. "It's all up to you now. Come on."

Bardeen started for the Project "S" lab. Barrow waited to speak to several of the men, then followed.

The "twins" were two huge cylinders lying side-by-side, mirrored in each other's brilliant stainless surface. Above each, near the center, was an apparatus like a wide, polished hoop. Thrust out on both sides of each huge cylinder were two short wide braces, each one powerfully hinged at the outer end to a long slender arm. At the end of each arm was a thing like a smooth bright dish. The four arms were held almost vertically, prevented, by heavy coil springs on the cylinder, from touching each other.

Bardeen said, "That short cylinder, or hoop, in the center, can detect and record very complex electromagnetic forces. When the twins are in action, a housing rises up behind it and a sequence of fine penetrating beams of coding radiation reaches out to pass through every part of the object being sent. This structural information will be received in the form of faint, brief complex echoes— reflections from the atoms struck by the coding beam. These echoes will be interpreted, stored, and used to help modulate the carrier wave sent out from the ends of the four transmission arms, which will be lowered, and adjusted to focus on a distant place.

"The coding beam is of a type of radiation we discovered in studying the various forms of instability that occur in an experimental fusion reactor. We call it 'efflux radiation'."

Dave, concentrating hard under the increasing sense of pressure, nodded briefly, and Bardeen said, "Efflux radiation is to ordinary radiation much as contraterrene matter is to terrene matter."

"What does it do?"

"When an efflux ray strikes ordinary matter, that matter is converted into ordinary radiation, traveling in precisely the opposite direction. The total effect is that the atoms of the object sent, and everything in it *are converted into electromagnetic radiation, which is sent out through the focused transmitter, and reassembled far away.*"

Dave nodded slowly. "You said I was needed. Why?"

"The trouble with this process is that we have great difficulty bringing about the form of instability that generates efflux radiation. The worst of it is that the proper form of instability must occur simultaneously, in *both twins*, if the process is to be successful."

"What do you mean?"

"Both of these cylinders are fitted out as colonization spaceships. We have a whopping government contract for this work, which is certain—was certain—to put this country far ahead of any other in space. Because after one of these two ships transmits the other, that *other ship focuses on and transmits the first*. But the proper type of instability to generate efflux radiation must occur in both ships simultaneously, because if only one has it, the other may be carried out of range before it can do its part."

"What can I do about that? I never heard of efflux radiation before. I don't know the first thing about it."

Barrow smiled. "Last night you were wrestling an intruder when a volley of shots was fired at him. He was killed. You were not touched. A moment before that volley of shots, he was shooting at you himself from a distance of possibly two feet. You weren't touched. Shortly after, you were in a deadly situation on the highway, again untouched."

"Yes, but what did *I* have to do—"

"Did you ever hear the expression 'wild talents'?"

"Yes. Sure, but—"

"Within limits, I can foresee the future—that's precognition. But you have a deeper control of time and motion relationships. It may be as automatic and unconscious as the blink of an eye, but it's there. And we need it."

The crowd was coming into Project "S" building. They looked tense, white-faced, scared.

Dave could feel the pressure, all but unbearable.

"What do I *do*?"

Barrow led him inside one of the huge cylinders, and down a corridor that had wide strips of strong black mesh on both walks.

"For getting around," said Barrow, "when we're in space. You take hold of the mesh. We have no arrangement for artificial gravity on these ships."

He unlocked a door marked "No Admittance," and there before Dave was a softly-polished panel with a large black circular screen marked off in radians, and two centers of intense violet light, surrounded by an oscillating purple region, its boundary shifting irregularly from moment to moment. Just beside the panel was a lever marked "Danger—Manual Interlock." On the pale green wall nearby was an intercom unit.

Barrow said, "These two centers of light represent the ships' fusion reactors. As long as a band of purple exists around either center, conditions are wrong to move the ship. When the purple disappears, and there are only the two centers of violet light, we have simultaneous efflux instability. *Then* pull back that lever."

"We have just a few minutes," said Barrow. "When everyone's on board, I'll speak to you through that intercom."

The door clicked shut.

Dave looked at that pale-green door, then turned to urgently will the writhing purple boundary out of existence.

Unaffected, the two bright violet centers swam in a twisting pool of purple.

Dave's heart pounded, and he felt dizzy with effort. But nothing happened.

There was a click from the wall speaker.

"All right, Dave. Everyone's on board. We've opened the dome of the building. Go ahead."

Dave opened his mouth to demand more time, to insist on an explanation—and a calmness slid over him suddenly. The intensity of the pressure was suddenly gone, the writhing purple shrank into the violet centers of light.

Unhesitatingly, Dave pulled back the lever.

There was blurring of consciousness, suggesting a room seen in a rapidly flickering light.

Then Barrow's voice was saying, "Break interlock."

Dave shoved forward the lever.

Once more, consciousness was continuous. He had a strange feeling as if he had raced over the precisely-spaced railroad ties after a train, and had finally caught it and hauled himself aboard.

He glanced at the intercom.

"Will you need me right away?"

"Not where you are. Come up to the viewer. You turn to your left as you go out, and up the ladder to your right."

"Be right up."

Dave tried to turn around, and promptly drifted up from the floor. It was only then that he really believed it.

It had worked.

They were out in space.

Earth hung on the screen before them like a big blue-green basketball with a tiny incandescent plume bursting from its equator.

Anita, her face pale, was clinging to Dave as they watched the screen. The crowd around them was tense and silent, their gaze riveted on the screen.

Bardeen and Barrow were nearby. Bardeen murmured, "It's started?"

"Yes." Barrow's eyes were shut.

"Self-sustaining?"

"It must be."

On the screen, the blazing plume strengthened and grew brighter. Dave held his breath.

The single flame erupted into a blazing circle that shot around the globe.

The terrible heat flashed the nearby seas into vapor, huge cracks appeared, and the sudden violence hurled up chunks of the solid planet that were the size of mountains. Then the blinding scene was blurred by dense expanding clouds of vapor.

How long they'd watched, Dave didn't know, but he felt worn-out and sick. He held Anita, who was crying miserably and quietly.

Bardeen turned wearily from the screen. "Any chance of the fragments fusing themselves together again?"

Barrow shook his head. "Just another asteroid belt. Maybe that's what caused the first one."

Dave forced his dulled mind to assess the situation. Science had destroyed a planet. And science had enabled a few survivors to escape in ships especially equipped to colonize another planet.

Bardeen, apparently thinking along the same line, said, "At least these ships are equipped to make us self-sustaining. We have advanced equipment, and the reactors put more energy at our disposal than the whole human race had twenty years ago. We can start again."

Anita looked up. "And try *more* scientific experiments? How long before the *next* mistake?"

"Ask Dave," Bardeen said quietly, "and he'll tell you our method is different. An experiment isn't an experiment when you can foresee the result, and stop in time."

He turned to the screen where the blaze of light glowed through boiling clouds of vapor.

"That," he said, "was the last experiment."

Rags From Riches

Lost Bear Jct., Alaska 99731
Wednesday; Fog, No Snow

Mr. William T. Whittaker
626 Campus Drive
Blickweiler U.
Sandrigham, Illinois 60054

Dear Bill:

As you know, I have trouble writing letters. Why, I don't know—after all, I write stories for a living. But anyway, Margin Books just paid for that spy opus, and the bank tells me the check cleared all right, so you can count on my answering letters a little sooner.

The reason? You may not be aware, in your ivory tower, that your old roommate is up to the latest technological marvels and prepared to take full advantage of them at the first chance that offers. It takes effort, but it is worth it. What I have done is to take advantage of the current little downblip in the computer industry—sales off forty per cent, 16,000 laid off, four major manufacturers bankrupt—that sort of thing—to buy myself, at fire-sale prices, a completely new Vectrosupermax Business System, with all its bundled software (16 different programs: total value, if bought individually, $6,472.89).

As you may know, before the market took its downturn,

Vectrosupermax was probably the leading manufacturer of hardware using the KBCDOS operating system and the 99Q processor. Two years ago, Vectrosupermax was a comet lighting the sky both day and night with new sales records. Today, they're selling them out of the back of a truck down in Mosquito Forks, and very grateful for a sale. Well, that's high tech, for you.

But to get back to what this means from my viewpoint, the fact is that the Vectrosupermax may be a drag on the market, but it works as well today as it did two years ago. This calamity in the marketplace means it is possible for me to make this initial comment on the old manual typewriter, connect the Vectrosupermax plug to the outlet (I mentioned we got electricity in my last letter), hit 10 on the keyboard (a special command so it will just print what I tell it to, and not reproduce the commands themselves), and then I simply reel this length of paper into the Vectrosuperprinter's maw, and you have a vivid record of technological progress as applied to the art of letter writing:

Sdfl;ksdkasdgf;saasdfiuas8u 234]?

SYNTAX ERROR 66

Memory munged

1234567890-=º!@#$%^{2}[*()__+ QWERTYUIOP?¶qwertyuiop[]
   1234567890-=º!@#$%^{2}[*()__+ QWERTYUIOP?¶qwertyuiop[]
      1234567890-=º!@#$%^{2}[*()__+   QWERTYUIOP?¶qwer-
tyuiop[]

WARNING! DIVISION BY ZERO!

EITHER YOU OR I HAS MADE A MISTAKE. I CAN'T FILE THIS FILE.
PLEASE GO BACK TO THE BEGINNING AND TRY AGAIN.

(Buffer Overflow)

SYNTAX ERROR 96

Well, I have to admit, that was
　　　　　　　　n't much fun. I suppose I should
have read the manual, but tha
　　　　　　　　t wasn't very attractive either.
There are sixteen different man
　　　　　　　　uals, and Now, what the—

　　00001　Well, I have to admit, that was
　　00002　have reread the manual, but tha
　　00003　There are sixteen different man

*##?a. . .^{22}%!...2..C###!
. . .$.opy..E..@@#..cC..?
.X..18.p..6ro,,1982.tt.
. . ...righj..4.##..7.##.

Vectrosuperwriter is protected by a sophisticated lockup program keyed to your individual computer and its included hardware and software. If you attempt to use our proprietary DEBUGG utility to crack the copy-protection, our built-in safeguards will lock up your computer every time you use the software, and we will be automatically notified at once when you try to use the modem. Just take this as a friendly warning and GET YOUR GUMMY LITTLE FINGERS OUT OF OUR CODE BEFORE WE CHOP THEM OFF!!

(Use VDUMP for non-ASCII.)

WARNING! SQRT OF NEG NUMBER!

　　gods and little fishes!
　　this is "user friendly"?

　　re's the stuff I typed?
　　ll with all this! What
　　o now? This son-of-a-
　　ch squeezes everthing
　　o a narrow column and

nts it out with letters
sing on the left. The
trosupermax Quikcard
mand summary is around
e somewhere. Ah, yes,
e we are. "Escape-LM" .
t could be simpler?

x Error 111!

W
E
L
L
,

w
e
l
l
!

S
o

h
e
r
e

w
e

g
o

n
o

w

!

E

a

s

y

d

o

e

s

—

H

,

m

.

.

.

Vectrosupermax Elapsetime Clock
This session: 02H29M14.7S

Vectrosupermax Elapsetime Clock
This session: 14H46M11.96S

Vectrosupermax Elapsetime Clock
This session: 42H21M38.6S

Bill—As you may notice from a close inspection of the typeface and the unevenness of the print, we are back to the old manual again. It is Friday now, and there really was a pretty good length of letter there on Thursday, but it sort of disappeared when I hit the X on the keyboard instead of the S. It seems that X is the easy mnemonic for "eXpunge," and I was reaching for the S but got the X by mistake. Oh, well. My error, of course.

There's a kind of long scratch across the top of the machine, where I only just managed to catch myself in time—I all of a sudden had the axe in my hand, and must have let out a yell because it was the middle of the night and out back the rooster started to crow. I see the dog just crawling out from under the bed now, and there were two cats in the room when I started, but I haven't seen them since I read the Vectrosupermax "Easy-Does-It" manual. It has a lot of cute pictures in it. Heh-heh. And a sheet of last-minute corrections and changes that aren't noted anywhere else. Heh-heh-heh.

Well, Bill, I guess progress has its price, so it will take me maybe just a little longer than I expected. But if I have this thing really mastered before I go in for next month's groceries, count on me to add a few good long pages after this paragraph.

All the best,
Jim

Bugs

Randy Pratt, under the hanging ad lettered "Sharke Computers," looked down pityingly on the woman customer standing clench-fisted by the showroom door. Because of the glare of the morning sun on the windows of a car parked outside, he had a little trouble even seeing her. But he strained hard to be fair.

"If," he said, locating a business card in his jacket pocket, "there is anything we can realistically do for you, just get in touch with me. But what you're asking here is not realistic. Now, I hope you'll excuse me. I am speaking shortly at the seminar." Randy favored her with a conversation-closing smile, and handed her his business card.

The customer ripped the card across three times, threw the pieces on the floor, and went out. The automatic door closer shut the door gently.

Randy exhaled, murmured, "Cretin," and picked up the pieces. He went around back of a software display to the wastebasket.

Across the room, Mort, the part-time salesman, came out from behind a display of desk, portable, and lapsize computers. "What's her problem?"

"Oh, she bought a Sharke Superbyte here a few weeks ago. Now she's got a Shomizota printer with a serial interface, I suppose from Barricuda Byte Shop. Naturally, she doesn't know a bit from a detachable keyboard, so she figures it's our job to mate the printer with the Sharke."

"Stupid. But that Shomizota's a sweet little printer. You can't blame her for getting it."

"Naturally, I don't blame her. It's cheaper than ours, you don't have to be a weightlifter to move it, and people don't run for cover when it prints. The problem is, who's going to get it working for free? It's standard with the Barricuda. Of course, the Barricuda—"

Mort looked knowledgeable. "Oh, it's not so bad."

Randy stared at him. "It's got the reset button next to the left-hand shift key. And the keyboard's got an extra-light touch."

"It's a fast keyboard."

"I saw a guy demonstrate the Barricuda, with a big crowd around him, and about halfway through he accidentally bumped the reset. Everything on the screen disappeared. Then it lit up with, 'KINDLY INSERT YOUR SYSTEM DISK IN DRIVE A.' You like losing everything you've done because you bump the wrong key?"

"There are—ah—one or two bugs—" Mort glanced at the door. "I'll straighten the magazines." Randy glanced around.

Through the glare appeared an unshaven, strongly built man wearing a sweat-soaked T-shirt. His left hand flung open the door. His voice was rough.

"Somebody here named Curtis?"

Randy quickly thrust out one of his cards. "Mort, whatever became of Curtis?"

Mort's voice came from back of the magazine rack.

"Working over at Wolfe Computer, the last I heard."

Randy nodded and turned back.

"Wolfe Computer is out on Industrial Way. You take a left, just up the—"

"He was working here when he sold my kid a Gnat computer. When it quit, Curtis says you can't fix it, the company's broke."

"Well, I'm sure Curtis—"

"It's the store's guarantee. When do we bring it in?"

"Well, I—I'm not quite sure of our policy on Gnat repairs, and—"

"Don't hand me that."

"Sir, I'll tell you what. The store manager is out today. He should be in tomorrow morning around eleven."

"I'm working at eleven."

"Then I'm afraid I don't see—"

"I'm here now."

"There's—"

"The kid worked all summer to buy that Gnat. You're going to fix it."

Randy glanced at his watch. "Mort, will you take care of this? I have to get over to the seminar." Mort's disembodied voice said miserably, "What can I do?"

Their visitor glanced around. "The thing is guaranteed, Buddy. You can fix it."

Randy stepped behind the long counter with its software display, featuring dragons, dwarfs, chests of gold, spaceships belching fire, competing captains of industry shaking their fists at one another, columns of stock prices, charts, graphs, tax forms, spreadsheets— and then he was going down the hall past a door with a window beside it that looked into the repair shop, where a technician in gray laboratory-style coat beckoned urgently. Randy stepped in, closed the door tightly behind him, and nodded.

"Mike. I'm just headed for the seminar. I have to give a talk on— heh—The Future of Computing."

"Who's that out front?"

"You remember the kid that bought our last Gnat computer? The kid that knew all about processors, operating systems, machine code, assembly language, higher level languages—you name it?"

"I remember him."

"Stewart guaranteed the Gnat for ninety days. That's the kid's father out there."

"Randy, that Gnat was full of bugs!"

"I tried to tell Stew—"

"That's the sixth one to come back on us. You almost need psychic powers to even get into the case without wrecking something. Once you get inside, there's stuff labeled 'Made in Sarabanga.' I can't find anyone even knows where that is. Not to mention there's eighteen little screws that hold down the cover, and all those screws are soft."

"I guess the margin was such—Look, I've got to be going."

"Who's talking to the kid's father?"

"Mort is—ah—trying to calm the storm, and—"

"Mort? That wimp! Look, Randy, I'm better than two weeks

behind, thanks to that Gnat guarantee. I can't keep up, much less honor this 48-hour fix you guys are offering. Get rid of this guy! Three of them came in a few weeks ago, and Curtis ran them out. Randy, if you've got to sell junk, that's your business. But I can't fix all this stuff! I didn't plan on a big scene, but you've got to know there's a limit!"

"I know. I know how it is, Mike." Randy sighed. "I never dreamed—" He paused, shoved his thoughts back on the track, and groped behind him for the doorknob. "I'm sure Mort will—"

A newly familiar voice echoed down the hall: "Twenty-one day guarantee, hell! I've got a copy of your ninety-day guarantee right here. The original's in my lawyer's office! Now, you going to make this right, or—"

Randy slid out into the hall, walked fast, stepped outside, and paused as the heat of the asphalt parking lot hit him. He opened his car door, staggered in the bake-oven blast, peeled off his jacket, and began to mentally review what he would say at the seminar.

Randy, two hours later, stood, chilled by the air-conditioning, before the blank-faced attendees of the Sharke Computing Systems Biennial Free Seminar on Home, Professional, and Personal Computing. He concentrated on the speech's conclusion:

"In conclusion, as you will remember, we have discussed the factors of density of circuit elements on the chip, number of chips to the system, architecture, assembly and machine-language programming, LSI and VLSI, higher level languages, operating systems, and applications programs. The improvement in all of these factors must be understood to truly appreciate the change that is rapidly overtaking us—the change to a Fully Computerized Environment, or FCE, as we may call it."

He smiled. If anyone in the crowd smiled back, he didn't notice it.

"I am sure," he finished, speaking the hopeful lie that had the virtue of tying things up and ending on a note of optimism: "I am sure everyone in this audience today will enter the FCE willingly, and will successfully ride the wave of the future."

There was empty silence, then a thin scattering of applause. Then, as people sat up, perhaps jarring others awake, the applause briefly strengthened. Then there was a rush for the exit.

Randy looked on moodily. "If there are any questions—"

The room continued to empty. Well, now he had to get back to the store. Hopefully, Mort would have outlasted the indignant father. That was the thing, he told himself—outlast the opposition. Maybe then things will start to look up again.

Once parked behind the store, he got out onto the familiar soft asphalt, let himself in, and listened alertly. There was a murmur from somewhere. A furtive glance showed Mike, the technician, hard at work.

Up front, Mort was speaking hesitantly. "I can see this new program might be revolutionary, but I'm not quite sure we could sell it. I mean—"

"Oh," said an unfamiliar voice, "everybody will be going for it. Of course, I could take it over to the Sharke compatibles first. Or—"

Randy stepped around the counter, and held out one of his cards. Their visitor promptly held out one bearing the name of the company, "Armagast Software."

Mort looked at his watch. "Well, about time for me to go home."

Randy said, "How did it work out with the—ah—the boy's father?"

"Stew came in after you left, and agreed to fix the Gnat. Then after the kid's father left, Stew blew up and said you and I should have gotten rid of him. Then he claimed Curtis should never have sold the Gnat to the kid. Next he said it was your fault we ever stocked the Gnat in the first place."

"Me?"

"He said he relies on your technical judgment."

"I told him for bugs the Gnat was an ants' nest! He said the margin was fifteen percent higher than the competition. Now he blames me?"

"I'm just repeating what he said. I thought you'd want to know. Well, see you on Tuesday."

Randy glanced at the avidly listening salesman. "I'm not sure we need to add anything to our line. Who did you say wrote it?"

"Armagast."

"Armagast of Armagast Software, not Armagast of Future Designs?"

"Same person."

"What's the program?"

"A problem-solving program. Very unusual. I could say revolutionary. You'll understand if you've heard of Armagast."

"Have you run it?"

"I—ah—It's so new—"

"How much?"

"Only two hundred fifty. A bargain."

"I'll take one for the store, and one for me personally."

"And your personal computer?—What make?"

"Well—I have a Model 3 Cougar."

"No problem. We could supply ENIAC, if it had disk drives."

It took Randy a moment to remember that ENIAC dated from the forties. He could feel his cheeks burn, and was still mad after he was home, settling down at the Cougar's keyboard, his wife watching worriedly.

"Randy—I hope that's a disk you borrowed from the store."

"Since when did the store stock anything for Cougar?"

She hesitated. "How did the seminar go?"

"Horrible."

"Hard questions?"

"They didn't ask questions. After I got through, I guess they figured they'd never understand. And at the store—Well, we had a woman who wanted us to interface a Barricuda printer to her Sharke computer, and if my guess is right, next she'll want to run a program set up for something else. Then we had a guy whose kid bought a Gnat from us, and it's dead already, and Mike, our technician, is swamped, and then there was the lecture, and finally—let's see—" He brightened. "Then there was a software salesman, and he had this program."

"What's the program?"

"I'm not sure. It's supposed to solve problems."

She hesitated. "How much was it?"

"Two-fifty."

She looked at him.

"Two hundred and fifty dollars?"

"Plus tax. So now I'm guilty."

"You don't know what it will do, and you spent two hundred dollars for it?"

He got up carefully, stepped to a table separate from the table holding the computer, and brought his clenched fist down on the table.

"A call went out a while back, remember? It said, 'The future is computers. Anyone who wants to earn his keep should study computer science.' I don't mean to make a federal case out of it, but I did do the work and I did earn the piece of paper. And now how do I spend my time? Answering the same questions over and over, wrangling with customers, trying to suck people into buying when for all I know it will ruin them, and, to vary the monotony, I get to deliver lectures to people who think Sanskrit while I talk Greek. We were headed for the Moon! How did we end up in this swamp? Do you know how many companies are going broke, and what the rest are doing to stay afloat?"

"I just know I can't hold a job and at the same time be in the hospital with a baby. And I can't go right back afterward. If the job is even there."

"I know. But the dream is dying! Why?"

She looked at him, frowning. "At least you do have a job."

"Thanks. I know what it is."

"But, Randy, why did you spend two hundred dollars? We need it!"

He sighed. "Armagast wrote this program."

For just an instant, he thought the room wavered. She stared at him. Then, for some reason, she came over and kissed his cheek.

He looked at her blankly.

"Okay," she said. "But please, Randy, don't get another program—unless Armagast wrote it."

"I didn't know you knew about him."

"I don't."

"He wrote Control—it's the operating system for the 99000. He's one of the giants. They drove him out of business for a while. But he's still fighting. There are rumors he's coming out with a new machine that will beat them all."

"Maybe that's why the prices are being cut? And the dream—"

"No. As long as he's there, the dream's still alive. And this is his first program, so far as I know, since Control!"

She nodded uncertainly. "All right. You go ahead. When you're through, I'll get you something to eat. I hope the program won't disappoint you."

He looked after her, puzzled. The money was still spent, wasn't it? And she was right, they did need it. He turned back, frowning, to the computer, ran his thumb affectionately across the stylized chrome cougar-head design with its big curved fangs and the horrible motto: "We Byte." He slid the disk in, listened to the familiar hum-rumble-clunk, waited, and then the screen lit with a swirl of curving lines as if he were falling into a whirlpool.

SOLUTIONS
by
Armagast Software

There was a dizzying pause, and then successive lines of print flashed onto the screen:

"This is not a problem-solving program.

"This is a program to help speed your solving of problems.

"The mind is in many ways the most practical problem-solving device.

"What it needs is facts. We will assume you have the facts, though you may not be aware of it.

"What it needs is concentration. We will strengthen that concentration.

"What is needed is to see the possible combinations of facts that, as they join and rejoin in all conceivable patterns, occasionally offer practical solutions.

"The program you are about to experience makes use of certain as yet unappreciated aspects of the nature of microprocessors and of the human brain and the human mind.

"Because this program involves factors which may not be fully understood, you should, BEFORE you run this program, carefully read our Customer Agreement. This may be informally summarized as follows:

"'We are legally responsible for nothing whatever, in any way whatever, related to your running this program, or for any consequential damages resulting therefrom. You are fully and inescapably responsible, from the moment you tore the plastic wrap, for anything and everything that happens afterward, anything to the contrary notwithstanding.'

"However, please do not rely on this informal summary. Read the Agreement. It is much more detailed and restrictive.

"If you wish, you may stop here and return the program for your full purchase price, less a slight charge for repacking. To return the program, type 'R' on the keyboard. To continue, type 'C.' To think things over, or reread the Agreement, WHICH MUST BE READ FIRST, type 'P' for pause."

Randy sneered, and hit "C" on the keyboard.

Gently at first, the screen seemed to swirl. He felt a moment's dizziness, and then the words that flashed on the screen appeared to transmute into a deep thoughtful voice:

"Too often, we overlook the obvious when we try to solve a problem. We should look the problem over very carefully, note the exact details, note how the details are related, and not hesitate to use paper and pencil. Be sure you know what the problem is. Possibly there is a similar, simpler, or more familiar problem to use as a model? Can you . . ."

The voice went on, each suggestion somehow compelling a thought-out response, and the effort of each response creating a kind of mental jolt so that he felt dizzy, as if successive blows sapped his strength. He was still struggling to put his problem into words— "What's happened to the dream?" when everything seemed to fade out.

"Randy—" The feminine voice was gentle.

"Whew." He sat up dizzily. The room spun around him. "How long—"

"I just came in to tell you good-night. You were slumped over the machine."

He massaged his forehead.

"Well—If that's Armagast's latest—I hate to say it—Maybe the dream *is* dead!"

"Oh, don't say—"

"It's junk. A little advice and a feeling like some stage hypnotist just tricked you into dancing around with a broomstick."

"Maybe it will seem better in the morning."

"I'll see if I can get my money back. I'm afraid it's too late. But the store copy goes back tomorrow, as soon as I get hold of Stew."

❧ ❧ ❧

Stewart Rafer pushed up his thick-lensed glasses and eyed the package as Randy, hand pressed to forehead, described the program.

"—and you should have seen the disclaimer in the program itself—which is supposed to be just a mild summary."

Stewart was studying a large paper covered with fine print.

"I just wonder—This whole thing gives me the impulse to see if I couldn't crack their little gimmick. What are we, the auto industry?"

Randy looked blank, then went on, "What makes me sick is Armagast. I can't believe he did this."

"Well, they get zilch for this package from me, and I'll lean on them to give back what they got from you. Not that we can count on it." Stewart glanced at his watch. "Now, I've been thinking we could give better service if we could pick up machines for repair, and bring the finished job back to the customer. One of these multiformat vans might answer our needs. But I'd like your opinion."

"What's—"

"Tell Mort you and I are going out, and we'll be back about four, at the latest."

"Is Mort in today?"

"Should be. I told him to come in."

Randy stepped down the hall into the showroom, told Mort, and then stood still a moment, considering that:

a) Stewart had not exploded at the purchase of the Armagast program.

b) Stewart was going to try to get Randy's money back.

c) Stewart had hired Mort for an extra day's work, so Randy could go along to look at the new van.

Not once in the past had Stewart treated Randy so much like an equal. And here was Stewart even saying that he would like Randy's opinion.

On top of that string of impossibilities, there was what Stewart wanted Randy's opinion on—a "multiformat van." What was a "multiformat van"?

Then there had been that about "cracking the gimmick." Apparently Stewart wanted to unlock the tricky antipiracy traps in the Armagast program. When had Stewart ever shown interest or talent for that?

In short, something was wrong. If this was reality, Randy didn't recognize it.

Of course, it could be just Stewart. Maybe Stewart was coming down with a cold, and this was how it hit him?

But then he realized there was a worse inconsistency:

Armagast.

Even when the big companies drove him to the wall, Armagast had still paid off his creditors and delivered the goods to his customers. That was one reason for the fanatical loyalty the man inspired, for the users groups that stuck with outdated Armagast hardware, for the rejoicing when the Armagast updates began to come through, against all predictions stepping up the power of the Armagast machines. Even the announcement, mailed to former customers:

"Armagast Computers is happy to offer our former customers the renewal of all services we formerly provided. Effective immediately, we also renew all Armagast warranties for a period of ninety days from the date of this letter. We offer immediately a series of upgrades to make our computers fully comparable to our competitors. We thank our customers for their loyalty, and we continue to stand by our pledge: 'Solid quality at a fair price.'"

Would the individual behind that have put out a program that didn't work?

It was at that point that Randy became conscious of a ghostly wind on the back of his neck.

No, the Stewart he knew positively would not act as Stewart now was acting.

And, no, Armagast flatly would not do as Armagast apparently had done.

Therefore—

From down the hall Stewart called, "Okay, Randy, let's go."

Randy swallowed. "Coming."

Stewart held the outside door open.

Randy stepped outside, to stare at a dirt parking lot where the high wheels of parked vehicles rested in narrow concrete troughs. The troughs curved in pairs, their tops a few inches above the muck, out into a road where they alternated with mud puddles under buzzing swarms of flies.

"Merciful God," said Randy.

Stewart growled, "Which of these heaps do we take?" He pulled open the door, and leaned back into the building. "Hey! Mike?"

The technician's voice was muffled, "Stew?"

"Randy and I are going to look at a van. What's the format for Inter-Continental Motors?"

There was a click of a door opening.

"InterCon? Wide and deep. But hey, Stew, wait." Footsteps hammered down the hall, and the technician peered out into the sunlight. "The format's about sixty-by-eight, but don't take an adjustable. I've found out InterCon's latest stunt, just by accident—and I do mean accident."

"What—?"

"They've raised the roads under their overpasses."

Stewart stared.

Mike nodded. "I saw one of those adjustable vans that's supposed to fit any format start under the overpass going in on Main Street. The top of the van hit the underpass. There was glass all over the road."

"They can't do that!"

"They can if they make it legal."

"What happened to the van?"

"A big InterCon wrecker slid under the overpass with inches to spare, and hauled the wreck out. An ambulance took the driver. That was an InterCon job, too."

Stewart shook his head. "Half the outfits using InterCon's format will start to collapse when news of this gets around. But how do we know which ones?"

Mike glanced around the lot. "Yeah. We don't want to get an orphan we can't find parts for. Well, all I can offer is, drive the InterCon job. It may be slow, but you won't spend half the day dodging underpasses."

"I was thinking of looking at one of the independents first."

"Then make two trips. But I tell you, Stew, I'd hesitate to get a van that won't go into InterCon's territory. They're big and getting bigger."

"A lot of our customers don't live there."

"Do you want to be driving a competing van when they throw the next block into the competition?"

"No. But there's an InterCon price list on my desk, stuck under the appointment pad. Take a look at that."

"That's how they play it. Well, enjoy yourself out there. Happy disposition!"

Stewart nodded moodily, and glanced at Randy. "Let's see what InterCon has to offer while we're still fresh. I'm not sure I can stand their van salesman after ten in the morning. Then we can look at some independents, and if we've got any strength left, we can try Rugged Jake."

Randy drew a shaky breath, and nodded. He glanced up. The sun and clouds looked the same. The trees looked like trees he had known before. The buildings looked unchanged. Then he looked back at the mud, the curving tracks, and the clouds of flies. Only one explanation presented itself: Things had changed since he ran that program.

Why hadn't he read the whole disclaimer? And where was he now? Had he been slung into some other continuum? Or was this just a dream?

With an effort, he straightened up. He had to eat, wherever he might be. And while this might not be the best job in the world, it was a job. He started across the lot, tripped over a curving trough, and just avoided a fall onto an angle where one concrete trough merged with another in crossing. Stewart, meanwhile, stepped with easy familiarity over the troughs to a vehicle with high wheels, lots of ground clearance, and a body that reminded Randy of the front end of a fire truck joined to the back end of a hay wagon.

As Stewart heaved himself up to the driver's seat, Randy barely missed putting his foot down a trough, and then almost slipped into a deep-looking puddle that stank of horse manure. It was a relief to climb onto the running board. He was pulling a cover off the passenger's seat when Stewart said dryly, "How about some help?"

Randy looked back blankly.

"What?"

Stewart leaned forward over the windshield, which was folded down flat, and tapped the curving red hood. He cupped his hand to his ear as if listening.

Randy stared at him stupidly.

Stewart stared back.

It occurred to Randy that he could lose his job here just as well as back home. He did a fast desperate feat of mental gymnastics, but found no answer.

Stewart shook his head. "Don't stay up so late with bad programs." He pointed to the front of the car, raised his arm to shoulder level, and whipped his forearm around in a circle.

Randy didn't get it, but decided to go look. He took a step, forgetting that he was on the running board, hit the puddle with a stiff-legged splash, and felt the water pour into his shoe. With a sucking squelch, he pulled free, then a lurch and a stagger brought him to the front of the car, and now he saw the hand-crank hanging down under the radiator. Randy took hold, and whipped the crank around fast.

Stewart snarled, "Seat it, will you! All you're doing is turning the crank, not the engine!"

Randy crouched down, shoved in on the crank, rotated it part way, and it slid forward another inch or two. He gave a heave, and got nowhere.

"Hold it!" yelled Stewart. "Sorry about that! Okay, I've got the clutch in. Try her again!"

Randy gave a desperate heave on the crank, and succeeded in turning it, but nothing happened. He tried again with the same result.

Stewart snorted. "This the first time you ever cranked an engine? Keep her going!"

Randy mopped his forehead, and as he took a fresh hold he chanced to notice two battered iron posts sunk into the ground, one near either end of the badly dented front bumper. A suspicion formed in his mind, and he looked up at Stewart.

"What gear you got it in?"

Stewart looked guilty. "Ah—" He pulled on a long lever, and there was a little grating noise. "Not that it matters. It was in low. I've got it in neutral now." Stewart's tone of voice confirmed Randy's suspicion that it did matter, though he had yet to work out exactly how. He took hold of the crank, heaved up, pushed down, heaved up, got the rhythm—

BANG! BAM! BANG!

The crank whipped out of his hands, the car shook, and Stewart yelled, "That's more like it! Okay, let's go!"

Randy detoured the puddle, his foot squelching in his shoe, climbed the running board, got over a metal lip, heaved the cover off the passenger's seat, and almost went out over the windshield as Stewart shifted into reverse. Stewart, possibly in apology, shouted, "Clutch is a bitch!"

The slimy soddenness of his shoe was getting to Randy, and he took advantage of a few seconds of calm as Stewart backed out of the lot to get the shoe off, and wring out his sock. He got that back on just as Stewart speeded up.

They backed fast on some kind of sidetrack, slid to a stop, and with a sudden lunge they jolted forward, hit repeated obstructions with a series of jarring shocks, and then Stewart grabbed his end of the windshield and yelled, "Let's put her up!"

Randy, barely able to hang on, pulled up on his end, tightened the wingbolt, then grabbed for support as they bounced around an uphill curve at possibly fifteen miles an hour; and then Stewart pulled back a lever even longer than the gearshift lever, and they slid to a stop at a traffic light. A cloud of dust rolled over them from the intersection, and then they turned onto a road each side of which looked a hundred feet wide, covered with concrete troughs of all widths and spacings, with horses trotting along at the edges. Randy watched the speedometer needle crawl up, with several shifts of gears, to twenty-five miles an hour, when Stewart set the throttle, glanced around, and grinned. "Still some life in this old baby!" Then he sat back in his seat with the steering wheel wobbling on its own as they thundered through clouds of dusts and flies, their wheels locked in the concrete tracks, with Stewart intent on a shouted conversation:

"Don't repeat what Mike told us!"

"No."

"What?"

"I said NO!"

"It gives us a little advantage to know first."

"What?"

"I said, IT HELPS TO KNOW IT FIRST!"

"OKAY!"

After several interruptions when horses began to pass them on the turns, and Stewart looked askance at the speedometer and readjusted the throttle, they reached a turnoff; and after a series of jolts through interconnecting troughs, some of them partly crumbled away, they passed a huge sign lettered BRISTOL—HOME OF INTERCONTINENTAL MOTORS—ALL MOTORIZED VEHICLES USE INTERCON OFFICIAL FORMAT ONLY—HORSE-DRAWN VEHICLES TAKE ALTERNATE THOROUGHFARES—IN THIS JURISDICTION ALL NON-INTERCON FORMATS ARE ILLEGAL!

They passed through an underpass littered with broken glass, came out the other side, and Stewart hauled on the wheel as they jounced around a corner, went down through another underpass, and crawled out on the far side to see a set of big buildings and a monster sign bearing the huge letters: INTERCON.

At a junction of concrete troughs, Stewart pulled off the road by a long shed under the sign, "Official Inter-Continental Motors Van and Auto Franchised Dealer." He glanced at Randy, "Whatever you do, don't hit the bastard."

An hour or so later, they emerged from the shed with a gray-coated individual meditatively puffing a pipe, who said in the manner of someone mentioning an afterthought, "Of course, that six thousand's the price for the main frame only. If you'd like an engine, the Thunderbolt will run you another nineteen hundred ninety-nine. If the Mule Reliable will do, that will be fifteen hundred eighty-four. You'll want wheels, I imagine; they're sixty-five each. You get one free in the Magnum Package Deal. If you'd like seats, we have a selection at various prices, or you could jam a fence rail into the slots back of the instrument panel deck. The van enclosure runs another two thousand, and it's fitted for the standard interconnecting rear port. That's four hundred ninety-nine."

"What, the van enclosure?"

"No, the rear port. That's the installed price at the time of purchase. Then there are the bolts to hold the enclosure on the main frame. They're special bolts, with grapple plates fitted to keep the enclosure from shifting, and yet it's adjustable backwards, forwards, and sideways, to suit your taste. They're seventy-five apiece."

"The ports?"

"The bolts."

"How are the ports going to match up if they're shifted around to suit my taste?"

"Well, you have to configure the grapple plates to get the ports to match up with the receiver vehicle. That's the point. These are female or male ports, as you specify. Same charge, either way."

"Well—"

"Be sure to get it right the first time. Otherwise we'll have to sell you a hermaphrodite port adaptor. And you'll need a rear bracket with a hoist to get the adaptor into place. It's a very delicate piece of work, actually, because you can wreck the port *and* the adaptor."

"What's the total on all this?"

"Depends on how you want it configured, with or without maintenance contract, and whether you want a port adaptor."

"Just give me a rough estimate."

"We don't make rough estimates."

"Then—"

"It confuses the customer."

"At least the port is standard, you say."

"Oh, sure. Standard OX444, of the InterCon Series 100 Port Type, Revision 3."

Stewart spat out a bad word. "And how do I know that what I'll have to shift cargo with is going to be the same type?"

"No problem. Don't deal with anyone who doesn't use the latest InterCon standard parts throughout."

Stewart said shortly, "We'll think it over." He swung up into the driver's seat, and glanced at Randy.

Randy climbed into the passenger's seat.

Stewart looked hard at Randy.

Randy came awake, and went up front to take hold of the crank.

The salesman looked on. "I've known people to get broken arms with that crank. Our new model has an automatic disconnect that works."

Randy swore to himself and heaved on the crank. The engine caught with a roar. There was a thud as Stewart's foot slipped off the clutch. The car, evidently in first, slammed against the posts of the parking slot. This tossed Randy back into the muck and left him with an aching wrist as the engine stalled.

The salesman slapped his thigh, and disappeared into the shed.

Stewart climbed down and made clucking noises.

"It never fails. When that bird starts talking price, I get so mad I can't think. Nothing broken, I hope?"

"Just wrenched."

"Cheap at the price."

"Thanks a lot."

"Scrape the worst of the muck off, and stand on the running board on the driver's side. See if it's in neutral, and give it a shot of gas when it catches. Don't sit down in the seat."

On the way back, they were both silent as the dust and flies flew over them. Randy spent the time trying to understand how there could be mud in some places and dust in others, and decided the troughs must drain rainwater from higher ground to lower. At the end of the deafening bone-jarring trip, as Stewart stopped with a jolt against the posts in his parking lot back of the store, he said, "Well— What do you think?"

"Of what?"

"InterCon's deal."

Randy studied his fingernails. "The nouns in my answer will cost you a hundred dollars each. Verbs are eighty apiece. For another hundred, I'll throw in some adjectives and adverbs, and connect everything up. Let me know how much you're willing to pay, and I'll put together an answer."

Stewart grinned. "You should get a job at that place." He glanced at his watch. "Go home and wash off, and this afternoon we'll try the independents. At InterCon, they figure there's no competition. Well, maybe. But we'll see."

The afternoon found them examining broad vehicles with narrow wide-spaced wheels, long slender vehicles hinged in the middle to go around curves, vehicles with rubber cogwheels in place of tires, and toughs to match, so that proud salesmen could show pictures of the CogCar climbing near-vertical slopes. There was also an assortment patterned after the vehicles they'd seen that morning.

"Yes, sir," a salesman assured them. "Not only is ours compatible, it is actually superior to the InterCon Personal Car. Ours is higher. You can wear a top hat in our vehicle. We offer 20% more maximum load! Moreover, we have the InterCon standard port, male or female, plus—brace yourselves, gentlemen—THE ENGINE IS INCLUDED IN THE PRICE! Now, any questions?"

Randy hesitated. "This male or female port—How do you know in advance which kind you'll need?"

Stewart nodded.

The salesman smiled condescendingly. "You'll have to have the other kind from the kind you're going to connect with."

"How do you know, now, what kind you may need to connect with after you've made the purchase?"

The salesman favored Randy with the look usually reserved for insects in the soup.

"By that time, sir, you should know what port you can mate with, sir."

"The other vehicle may not have the right port."

"Then you won't deal with him, sir."

"Maybe you want to deal with him."

"And pay the adaptor charge? And possibly wreck both ports?"

"What do you need a 'port' for? Why not just manhandle the load from one truck to the other?"

The salesman, bowing beside Randy as if trying to get down onto Randy's level, straightened up. "You do that, then." He turned his back, and called across the showroom, "Ed, you got tickets for the Car Show next week? Save me two. Hear? Two." He strolled away.

Randy took a step after him, but felt Stewart's hand at his shoulder. "Let's go, Randy. To knock his block off wouldn't solve our problem."

Randy walked out. "Why not forget this port mess?"

"You can if your vehicle is an adjustable, and can run different wheel formats. Otherwise, you have to shift load to another truck when you come to a change in format, and on some roads that happens every time you cross a municipal boundary."

"Why the different wheel spacings?"

"Why doesn't everyone like the same food? InterCon likes one wheel width and depth, and somebody else likes a different one, so you've got two, right there."

"For the love of—"

"Sure, it complicates everything. Every so often, a local legislature gets sick of maintaining all the different formats. Then

InterCon, or whoever, will give a special deal to drivers to buy their make of vehicle, and finally the voters choose their format as the only one that's legal. That makes it simple for the local highway department. But for truckers, it's a nightmare."

"But where's the problem in swapping loads by hand? Why do you have to have a 'port'?"

Stewart glanced at the drying mud and curving troughs of the parking lot.

"You want to manhandle crates with your feet on that? You want a broken ankle or a cracked skull?"

"But this male and female business. For—"

Stewart walked behind the vehicle they'd come in, pulled on a lever, and the lower half of the rear door opened down horizontally, the upper half swung up horizontally; and, as he pulled again, inner doors swung out right and left, the four half-doors making an extension open at the rear. Several inches underneath, two steel beams slid back below the lower door.

"This is a so-called male port. The female port is wider and higher. Now, watch." He heaved on the lever, and the two steel beams slid further, to project beyond the rear of the extension. "These support the floor of the joined ports, and the ends rest in brackets underneath the other vehicle's port. That joins the vehicles, and nobody slips in the mud or drops freight overside. But, boy, if the troughs are curved, or the trucks don't match just right—"

"Why not just have a gate that drops down at the rear of the truck, with a chain on each side to keep the gate horizontal? That would work."

Stewart thought it over. "Maybe. Unfortunately, we've now got regulations that require male or female ports, made to the standard pattern. This is the standard pattern. At least it's less bad than the gas nozzles. If they come out with one more pattern—"

"What, for the gas pumps?"

"At last count, there were eighteen different designs, and they make the intake on the auto to fit the nozzle. It depends on which car company strikes what deal with which gas company. Well, let's go see Jake."

Randy, his head spinning, cranked the car and climbed in. Stewart started to pull out onto the road, then jammed on the brake.

Out in the street, a truck rumbled past pushing a row of little shovels through the concrete troughs, to leave dirt and trash in long low piles to either side.

Randy massages his temples, and watched a horse and open carriage rumble past at the corner. The horse was moving right along, and the people in the carriage grinned at Stewart and Randy waiting for the trough-cleaner. Stewart said, "Ah, nuts," and let the clutch out so fast the car bucked and stalled. This brought gales of laughter from the carriage.

Stewart snarled, "I'll crank it. You work the throttle."

Randy dragged his mind off the question why, if this were a dream, he hadn't woken up yet. He discovered that Stewart had left the car in gear just as Stewart found out, and said some words Randy hadn't heard before. Then they had the vehicle started, and jounced and slammed through the dirt piled into the junctions as the main troughs were cleaned out.

"It would all be so easy," said Stewart, fighting the wheel, "if it weren't for the details. This is obviously the transportation system of the future—and yet—look at this."

On the street in front were two long things like narrow trap doors that popped open as they crossed the intersection. It dawned on him that these were trough-covers, closed to keep the horses from falling where horse-streets and car-streets crossed on the same level. And, of course, the covers had to open for the vehicles to get through.

"Quite a thing," said Stewart cynically, "when the trough cover gets grit in its hinges. Either the horses break their legs, or the cars climb out of the troughs."

"Why not pave the whole street and have done with it?"

"We can never vote it in. The horse interests go along with whoever favors the present set-up, and together they vote down any change. To pave the street would mean cars could go near horses, and scare the daylights out of them. And it would end the set-up we've got now, when only horses can go everywhere. Naturally, the horse-freight outfits want to keep that. It makes you wish Gritz hadn't invented the security slot in the first place."

"Who?"

"Gritz. Father of the auto industry. Invented the trough-section casting machine. The idea is to avoid accidents, and be able to keep moving in mud, fog and bad weather. Have a track, like the railroads. It sounds good. But ye gods, when you have a pile-up, or get a freezing rain!"

"Speaking of inventors, weren't there some others—Henry Ford, Thomas Edison—?"

"Ford? Let's see . . . Ford . . . no, never heard of him. Edison? Sure, he invented the electric light, the phonograph, the aerabat, the vacuum tube, and the relay-computer. —Ah, here we are!"

Randy considered the fact that Henry Ford apparently hadn't lived in this universe, dream, or whatever it was. Instead of Ford's aim, "I'll belt the world with reliable motorcars," there were all these people figuring, "I'll patent a new gas nozzle and get a stranglehold on the industry." The car gave a jolt, brought his mind back to the present, and he saw a huge sign:

JAKE'S

Ahead of them, as they bounced through the trough junctions, was a fortresslike building behind a high chain link fence. Also behind the fence were separate sheds, and small lots filled with cars. Stewart hummed cheerfully as they stopped at a gate, and a guard peered out a slit.

"Password?" said the guard.

"Stewed prunes."

The guard kept his eyes on Stewart and Randy, and spoke over his shoulder. "Stewed prunes."

A man's voice answered, "Get his name."

Stewart said, "Stewart Rafer."

"Occupation?"

"Computer dealer."

The voice said, "Checks."

The guard grinned. "Go in, but drive slow. We got a new shipment and they're fighting over it."

Stewart swung the car around a big metal-sheathed shed, and jammed on the brakes. In front of the shed stood a large man in whipcord trousers and a white silk shirt, with a cigar jutting out the corner of his mouth. Opposite him, a man in a business suit pointed to a steam locomotive three hundred feet away on the far side of a barred gate.

"You'll either let that consignment in, or that's the last load you get from me!"

"You either forget that paper I'm supposed to sign, or the gate stays shut. And I want your personal guarantee on what I buy."

"I can't change a thing. That paper was drawn up by the company's lawyers. I don't guarantee anything, either. That's company policy."

"You see that row of junk parked in the lot over there? The slot-headed cretin who brought that in started out just like you, and ended up selling it two cents on the dollar and grateful for the pay. The only thing he could guarantee was that the tires were good. I'm selling the whole load in units of two pairs of tires with vehicle attached. The wheels happen to be InterCon format, so I've had a pretty fair sale."

"I can't possibly—"

"You're selling to me because you need cash. What I need is something I can sell at a fair price with a real guarantee. Take a look at that chain link fence. A while back, I unloaded some so-called bargains that strung my customers up by the ears. Now I sleep in a bombproof bunker with a forty-five under my pillow. Don't tell me about your company lawyers. They don't scare me half as much as a bankrupt customer with a gun."

"What do you suggest?"

"The first thing is get rid of this." He read aloud: " 'Purchaser by inserting the key in the doorlock of the aforesaid vehicle signifies irrevocable agreement with each and every clause, provision, and/or stipulation of this contract, without exception, he and his heirs and assigns forever.' And then this: 'User by paying the purchase price for permission to use this vehicle acquires no ownership right or interest therein, but only permission to use the vehicle under the terms of this contract.'"

"Well, that's a perfectly standard vehicle usage clause, and you get the benefit—"

"If I try to enforce it, there's only two possibilities. First, the courts throw out the whole thing. Then I look like a fool. Second, they approve it, and I have to hire more guards. No. I value what sleep I can still get."

"What—What deal do you offer?"

"What will you guarantee?"

"The engines will run."

"Are they built-in?"

"Well—heh—they just have to be adapted to fit. There are instructions included. I guess it wouldn't be impossible."

"That doesn't sound too good."

"The engines are all right. The wheels are all right, too."

"InterCon format?"

"Our own format. Exclusive. We've got the rights."

"So nobody else can use it without a special trough?"

"Exactly. We planned to get the monopoly."

"What you've got now is an orphan format."

"We'll sell you the rights!"

"That wouldn't help me any. All you've mentioned so far is the engines. What about the bodies?"

"The frame?"

"That's what I'm talking about."

"You're planning to check all this?"

"I'd be crazy if I didn't."

"The frame is a—er—an adaptation of the old standard InterCon frame. Practically indistinguishable from the Personal Car."

"What's wrong with it?"

"Well, we had them made up in a—ah—a foreign country—too assist in the industrial development of—ah—emerging—"

"Skip all that. What's wrong with it?"

"The roof leaks pretty bad in the rain. And what they used for paint—well—but you don't have to worry about that. The disclaimer covers everything."

"Except a customer with a gun. So the paint's no good and the roof sealer's worthless. How's the structure?"

"It's just as good as the InterCon job. Why not? It's a straight copy."

"What else?"

"The brakes are all right. The clutch will snap your head off."

"Now we're talking. Bear in mind who's going to demonstrate these things. You."

"I can find someone better."

"I can't. How about the literature?"

"The maps?"

"The maps and instructions. A car's no good if you can't figure where to go with it, or how to shift gears."

"We were figuring to sell the documentation separately, with the spark plugs."

"I asked what good it is."

"Some of it's copied from InterCon. That part's all right. The rest is good to give to your enemies. I don't think we've got the road to hell in there, but there's a lot of places you don't want to go."

"Doesn't matter as long as it's labeled right."

"Together with some stuff that looks great, but there isn't any place it matches up with. It's good for a demo."

"We can sell that for novelty. How about the rest of the documentation?"

"Ah—You mean the instructions?"

"What else would I mean?"

"You want the truth?"

"No good, eh?"

"We hired a guy to put together a hundred pages that would look good, and we gave him two weeks to do the job. He cobbled stuff together from copied InterCon drawings and an encyclopedia on mechanical design, and patched a pretty good introduction onto it. Not a bad job. The only problem is, it doesn't tell how to get the engine into the frame, or the wheels on the axles, or anything else you need to know. Of course, if you can read it and understand it, you already know enough to do the job without any instructions."

Beside Randy, Stewart, who had been smiling, gave a low curse, shifted into gear, and backed up. Behind them, another high-wheeled car was just coming in, but Stewart managed to get off onto a sidetrack before this second car ground past.

"Nuts," said Stewart, hauling on the wheel. "The trough's full of muck. All we need is to climb out of it."

"Then what?"

"The guide wheel, here—" he tapped the steering wheel—"is only meant to shift troughs at the junctions. It'll tear your arms out by the roots if you try steering through raw muck."

He stopped at the gate, to shout, "You're gunked up in there!"

"Trough cleaner's down!" The gate opened. The car jolted forward.

"Miracle it didn't stall," snarled Stewart. "Damn it! I've got to deliver, and I've got to pick up repairs! But how do I do it? Did you hear that S.O.B. talk?"

"The guy arguing with him seemed all right."

Stewart hauled the wheel around, and they pulled out into a steady stream of traffic.

"Jake's okay. That was all bull about the customers being out to get him. It's the dealers. Boy, there are those who hate him!"

"Why not buy from him? At least you'd know what you were getting."

"Sure, but buy what? I want something I can count on." Stewart stared ahead, and made a grab for the brake lever. "Hang on! Somebody's jumped the trough! LOOK OUT! IT'S A PILE-UP!"

There was a crash ahead. Their own vehicle slowed, then slid. There was a jolt as someone banged them from behind. A quick glance showed Randy a monster van right behind. Off to the side, teams of horses trotted, eyes front, blinders cutting off the sight of the crashing cars.

Randy glanced at Stewart. "We should have got a horse!"

Stewart gave a fleeting grin. "Why tell me now? LOOK OUT!"

The car in front slammed to a stop. There was a sledgehammer shock, a blinding whirl of dust, a crash, blackness, remoteness, and then finally, light, and a voice.

He was slumped forward, his forehead against hard metal. He tried to stand, and landed painfully on one knee. His eyes came open and he saw a dim flat surface. He stumbled to his feet, looking for wreckage from the crash. He seemed to be in a dimly lit room.

In the dimness, a reflection glinted from the chromed Cougar emblem of his computer.

His wife asked anxiously, "Are you all right?"

He put his hand on the computer. It at least felt real. "Physically," he said, "I feel horrible. But it could be worse. What time is it?"

"Almost twelve."

"You haven't been to sleep?"

"I was waiting for you."

"You haven't been in here since I started to run Armagast's program?"

"No. Randy, what is it?"

He described what had happened.

She said, "It was like a dream?—A vivid dream?"

"A vivid dream that compared the computer industry to the state the auto industry might be in if it had our problems."

"Did it help?"

"Well, my problem was, what has gone wrong? I've got plenty of answers."

"You look awfully tired."

"It wasn't restful. Wait while I put things away."

The next day found Randy peering through bloodshot eyes at a hung-over-looking Stewart Rafer.

"Pratt," said Rafer, "ah—this Armagast program—I took it home. Ah . . . Suppose the Wright Brothers—No. No, forget that. Now, about this program—I think it's salable, but—Things are tight. We can't have you making purchases for the store without confirmation from me. You understand that?"

Randy forced a nod.

Stewart—this Stewart—looked at him owlishly.

"All right. Now, there's this business of the Gnat computer. How do you explain what we're going through with all these returns?"

Randy scowled. The Gnat was Stewart's idea. Now he, Randy, was supposed to explain it?

He reminded himself that he needed this job, and groped for a courteous answer.

Out in the showroom the outer door went shut, and light footsteps approached in the hall. Stewart and Randy glanced around. There was a rap at the door. Stewart said, "Come in." Randy's woman customer of yesterday stepped inside.

"I've brought my Shomizota printer, to be—ah—configured? It's in the trunk of my car, out front."

Randy winced. "Without the Superbyte, I—"

"I brought my Superbyte."

Randy cast a look of appeal at Stewart.

Stewart turned solicitously to the customer.

"We believe in total service here. Mr. Pratt will be glad to take care of it."

Randy went out to the car, and carried in the Shomizota. As he went back for the Superbyte, a thought occurred to him.

Would Armagast's program handle customer problems?

Why not?

He lugged the Superbyte into the showroom, and the customer said sweetly, "Mr. Rafer has assured me you'll be happy to take care of this, too." She handed him a box labeled, "WordSnapper 2 for UltraByte Computers."

As Randy groped for words, she said, "Now I must run," and left.

From the repair shop down the hall came a curse from Mike the technician, who hardly ever swore.

Randy massaged his temples, opened the word processor box, and found no instructions. Where was whatever literature Snapper Software had included with this thing?

The outer door opened. The mailman tossed some bills on the counter and went out.

Randy, examining the Shomizota printer, found a big envelope, dumped the contents, and sheets of Chinese-Japanese characters looked up at him.

Randy drew a careful breath, and reminded himself that he only had to get through the rest of the day. Then it was home to his Cougar and Armagast's program.

He glanced up as the doorlatch clicked again. A well dressed man came in with a precocious-looking boy carrying a Gnat computer. Stewart emerged from his office, a crumpled bill in his fist, to whirl as a crash and a string of oaths echoed down the hall from the repair shop.

It suddenly dawned on Randy that the Computer Age's bugs weren't confined to the hardware and software. There were human-ware bugs, and he was about to see them crash the system.

He was scarcely aware of his brief silent prayer as he approached his boss. "Excuse me, Mr. Rafer. Mike mentioned something yesterday, and I should have passed it on to you. If I could see you just a moment—"

Stewart eyed the Gnat, glanced toward the repair shop, excused himself to the customer, and stepped into his office.

Randy kept his voice low. "Mike said he can't handle the Gnat repairs plus the forty-eight-hour fix we've been promising. If he decides to quit, we're sunk. Let me promise him we'll forget the 48-hour till the Gnats are out of the way."

Stewart hesitated, then nodded. "But hurry up. He's about to erupt."

Randy, moving fast, knocked on the repair shop door, and stepped inside.

"Mike, excuse me. I told Stew you needed more time, and he agreed. He says you can forget the 48-hour fix till you've had time enough to get the Gnats out of the way."

Mike looked at him wildly. "Nobody could keep up with this!"

"Don't try. Take it as slow as you have to. We appreciate your trying, but anybody can only do so much."

"Forget the 48-hour fix?"

"Till the Gnats are out of the way. I think we're almost at the end of them."

Mike blew out his breath. "Okay. I can live with that." He bent down and set a dented wastebasket upright. "Push over that stool, will you, and shut the door tight when you go out. Thanks for talking to Stew."

Randy, coming back down the hall, heard Stewart talking to the customer: ". . . any amount of trouble from these Gnats, but we'll back up the warranty as best we can. My hardware specialist warned me about the machine, but I didn't believe him."

Randy stopped in his tracks. Was he still stuck in Armagast's program? Why was Stewart being reasonable? Then it dawned on him—Stewart had used the program, too.

The customer was saying, "As long as you'll back up my son's Gnat, I'll ask you something else. What do you have that's reliable?"

"I—ah—"

"I don't need the latest electronic miracle. I need a machine I can count on."

Stewart glanced at Randy, who mentally shifted gears.

"There's the Sharke II. That's been very thoroughly debugged."

Stewart objected. "It won't run the latest software. The Superbyte is faster, has a lot more RAM, more—" He paused. With an effort, he said, "But the II is very reliable. That's true." He excused himself.

Randy spoke carefully, straining not to be like any salesman he'd met recently in Armagast's program. "Mr. Rafer is right that the Superbyte is faster, and has more capabilities. But the Sharke II is very reliable, has excellent instruction manuals, comes with a good deal of useful software, and costs a lot less."

"Okay. Let me have some literature, and I'll be back when my son's Gnat is fixed to look this machine over. And—speaking of my son, where—"

A beeping noise became evident, from the back of a post on the other side of which was the Sharke Graphics 1000. The customer smiled, took the literature, got his protesting son loose from the Graphics 1000, and went out. Randy sat down by the Shomizota printer, thinking.

Stewart came back into the showroom.

Randy looked up. "He said he'd be back to look at the II when we get the Gnat fixed. I don't think it was a stunt to hurry us up. I think he wants a reliable computer even if it's behind the time."

"No matter what you buy just now, it will be behind the times pretty quick."

"It's a point." Randy frowned. "There's something here—some—"

"New approach to the consumer market? Possibly the industry has enough wonders for now, and ought to refine them?"

"Maybe, but also, there's a—a problem with people, aside from computers. And we're all people."

Stewart nodded. "It's almost sunk us. We've got a computer/human interface problem. Plus an expert/novice interface problem. But that Armagast program, anyway, was a good buy." He went back to his office.

Randy eyed the Shomizota printer he was supposed to make work with the Sharke Superbyte. Possibly he could get it to work despite the problems. Would that make him a sucker—or would it be good salesmanship?

From some dimly remembered book or article came a quote— "Send one customer away happy or mad, and you win or lose six others." That customer would tell his friends—Was it, maybe, sixteen others? Frowning, Randy remembered an earlier thought— there are bugs in human nature. And one was to expect everything of the new, while overlooking the familiar. Since computers involved so many things that were new, had the industry junked an unusual number of reliable truths?

At that moment, Stewart came back into the room and glanced at the printer.

"Any luck?"

"The documentation seems to be in Japanese. I have a hunch she got this from some friend who stopped off in Tokyo. But I'll see if I can get it."

Stewart nodded approvingly. "I just had a thought. That Armagast program seems to induce a—ah—a problem-solving approach. Now—Why shouldn't Mort have the advantage of it? True, he's part-time, but, just between you and me—"

"Yes. Good idea. I'll mention to him how interesting the program is."

"He'll be in Tuesday. I'll bring my machine. It should be a good test for the program."

Randy grinned. "I'll still bet on Armagast."

"If it works, we'll know he's really got something."

Stewart went back to his office, and Randy pried off the cover of the printer.

From some recess of his memory came a rough rendering of another comment, and this time he remembered who had said it— "If you have trouble in your organization, it will usually be people trouble. Therefore, value those who can solve people trouble."

As Randy eyed the printer's switches, unconsciously he adapted Andrew Carnegie's thoughts to his own line of work:

"If you have trouble with bugs, they may be hardware bugs or software bugs, but almost always they're the result of people. Therefore, value what can solve the trickiest bugs of all—people bugs."

The Free Enterprise

Positive Feedback

SCHRAMM'S GARAGE

To: Jack W. Bailey
413 Crescent Drive
City

Parts: 1 set 22-638 brushes	$1.18
Labor: overhaul generator	
set regulator	
clean battery terminals	$11.00
total	$12.18

Note: Time for oil change and install new filter.
    Noticed car seemed to pull to the left when we stepped on
    the brake.
    Can take care of it Wednesday if you want.

Joe Schramm

Dear Joe:
    Check for $12.18 enclosed.
    Will see about the oil change and filter later. The kids have been
sick and we're going broke at this rate.
    Maybe it pulls to the left, but I haven't noticed it.

Jack Bailey

SUPERDEE EQUIPMENT

Mr. Joseph Schramm
Schramm's Garage
1428 West Ave.
Crescent City

Dear Mr. Schramm:

Enclosed find literature on our new Automated Car Service Handling Machine.

With this great new machine, you can service anything from a little imported car to a big truck. The Handling Machine just picks the vehicle up, and the Glider on its Universal Arm enables your mechanic to get at any part, from above or below. By just turning a few knobs, he glides right to the spot on the end of the Arm. Power grapples, twisters, engine-lifters, transmission-holders, dozen-armed grippers and wrasslers—all these make the toughest job easy.

If you've got a dozen mechanics, buy this machine and you can get along with three or four.

This machine will be the best buy of your life.

Truly yours,
G. Wrattan
Sales Manager

SCHRAMM'S GARAGE

Dear Mr. Wrattan:

This machine of yours would take up my whole shop. It's all-electric, and looks to me as if it would take the Government to pay the electric bills. Your idea that I could buy this thing and then let most of my mechanics go is a little dull. When business gets bad, I can *always* let them go. But with this monster machine of yours, I couldn't let *anybody* go, except the few guys I still had, who would be my best mechanics.

Do you know how hard it is to find a good mechanic?

Let's have the prices and information on your line of hydraulic jacks. Spare me the million-dollar-Robot-Garage stuff.

Yours truly,
J. Schramm

SUPERDEE EQUIPMENT

Mr. Joseph Schramm
Schramm's Garage
1428 West Ave.
Crescent City

Dear Mr. Schramm:

Enclosed find prices and literature on our complete line of hydraulic jacks, jack-stands, and lifts.

Mr. Schramm, we feel that you do not fully appreciate the advantages of our great new Automated Car Service Handling Machine. This machine will more than pay for itself in speed, efficiency, and economical service. In bad times you could still cut down your repair staff. Mr. Schramm, *one man* can operate this machine.

We are enclosing a new brochure on this wonderful new labor-and-expense-saving machine, which will turn your garage into an ultramodern Servicatorium.

Cordially,
G. Wrattan
Sales Manager

⸙ ⸙ ⸙

SCHRAMM'S GARAGE

Dear Mr. Wrattan:

I'm enclosing an order sheet for jack and stands.

Your new brochure on your wonderful new labor and-expense-saving machine went straight into the furnace.

I think you are going to have plenty of trouble selling this machine. The reason is, all you're doing is to think how nice it will be for you if somebody buys it, not how lousy it will be for him to have the thing.

This machine will take cable as thick as my arm for the juice to run all those motors. It's bound to break down, and while I'm repairing it, I'm out of business.

You say I can let all my mechanics go but one. You must have a loose ground somewhere. If I fire all my mechanics but one, and he runs this machine, *who's the boss then*?

I could tell you what to do with this great new machine of yours, but I don't think you would do it.

Yours truly,
J. Schramm

❄ ❄ ❄

SUPERDEE EQUIPMENT

Interoffice Memo
To: W. W. Sanson, Pres.
Dear Mr. Sanson:

I am sending up a large envelope containing sample letters, from garages all over the country.

The response we've had on Handling Machines has been unusually large and emphatic, but unfortunately it has not been favorable.

G. Wrattan

❄ ❄ ❄

SUPERDEE EQUIPMENT

Interoffice Memo
To: G. Wrattan, Sales Mgr.
Dear Wrattan:

There are going to have to be some drastic changes around here. Bring all the letters you have up to my office at once.

Sanson

❄ ❄ ❄

SUPERDEE EQUIPMENT

Mr. Joseph Schramm
Schramm's Garage
1428 West Ave.
Crescent City

Dear Mr. Schramm:

There have been big changes at Superdee! Exciting changes!

Following a complete overhaul of top engineering management personnel, things are moving again!

Superdee is on the march!

Leading the van is our revamped ultramodern Supramatic Car

Service Handling Machine, capable of repairing anything from a little foreign car to a huge truck! Fast! Economical! Efficient!

This new version embodies the most advanced methods, together with the actual suggestions of *practical automotive repairmen like yourself!*

This machine is hydraulically operated, and even has a special High Efficiency Whirlamatic Hand Pump in case of emergency power failure!

There's practicality!

There's real manufacturer co-operation!

You asked for it! *Here it is!*

Superdee is on the march!

Are you?

Cordially,
G. Wrattan
Sales Mgr.

⛃ ⛃ ⛃
SCHRAMM'S GARAGE

Dear Mr. Wrattan:

I am enclosing an order for one of your new Superdeeluxe jacks.

I have read the stuff about your new Supramatic Machine. This one doesn't take as much space, and seems to be pretty good.

But I can't afford it.

Yours truly,
J. Schramm

⛃ ⛃ ⛃
SUPERDEE EQUIPMENT

Interoffice Memo
To: W. W. Sanson, Pres.
Dear Mr. Sanson:

Well, we've sold three of them.

G. Wrattan

SUPERDEE EQUIPMENT
Interoffice Memo
To: G. Wrattan, Sales Mgr.

Dear Wrattan:

We've got to do better than this or we'll all be lined up at the employment office in just about six months.

How about a big advertising campaign?

Sanson

✹ ✹ ✹

SUPERDEE EQUIPMENT

Interoffice Memo
To: W. W. Sanson, Pres.
Dear Mr. Sanson:

It won't work. This machine would theoretically improve just about any fair-sized repair shop's efficiency, but it's still too expensive.

To judge by the response, we now have an acceptable Handler here. In time, it's bound to take hold, despite the cost, and obtain wide acceptance.

But this won't happen in six months.

G. Wrattan

✹ ✹ ✹

SUPERDEE EQUIPMENT

Interoffice Memo
To: W. Robert Schnitzer, Mgr. Special Services Dept.
Dear Schnitzer:

Since you ran the computerized market simulation, on the basis of which we made this white elephant, I suggest you now find some way to unload it.

I would hate to be the man whose recommendations, presented in the guise of scientific certainty, were so disastrous that they destroyed the company that paid his salary.

A reputation such as that could make it quite difficult to find another job.

Sanson

✹ ✹ ✹

SUPERDEE EQUIPMENT

Interoffice Memo
To: W. W. Sanson, Pres.

Dear Mr. Sanson:

I have been giving this matter a great deal of thought, and have analyzed it on the Supervac-666.

The trouble is, the average individual does not use the available automotive repair facilities to a sufficient extent to assure the garage owner of enough income to afford our machine.

This is roughly analogous to the situation in the health industries some years ago.

I believe we might find a similar solution to be useful in this case.

W. R. Schnitzer

❀ ❀ ❀

SUPERDEE EQUIPMENT

Interoffice Memo
To: W. Robert Schnitzer, Mgr. Special Services Dept.
Dear Schnitzer

I frankly don't follow what you're talking about, but I am prepared to listen.

Come on up, and let's have it.

Sanson

❀ ❀ ❀

SUPERDEE EQUIPMENT

Interoffice Memo
To: G. Wrattan, Sales Mgr.
Dear Wrattan:

Schnitzer has one of the damndest ideas I ever heard of, but it might just work.

I am getting everybody up here to meditate on this, and want to find out how it strikes you.

This *could* be a gold mine, provided we can get the insurance people interested.

Sanson

❀ ❀ ❀

SUPERDEE EQUIPMENT

Interoffice Memo

To: G. Wrattan, Sales Mgr.

Dear Wrattan:

You will be interested to know after that discussion we had about Schnitzer's idea, that the insurance people are closely studying it. I could see whirling dollar signs in their eyes as I gave them the exact pitch Schnitzer gave me.

If they *do* go ahead, the banks will take a much rosier view of our prospects. We may weather this thing yet.

Sanson

ŏ ŏ ŏ

FORESYTE INSURANCE

"In Unity, Strength"

Since 1906

Dear Car Owner:

How many times have you suffered inconvenience and delay, because of auto failures and breakdowns? Yet how often have you hesitated to have your car checked, and repairs carried out that might have prevented these delays and breakdowns—*because you were short of cash at the moment*?

You need no longer suffer this inconvenience. *Now you can prepay your car repair bills*!

We call this our Blue Wheel car repair insurance plan. We are sure it will pay you to send in the coupon below, right away.

We can afford to make this offer because many cars will need no repairs, and the premiums for *those* cars will pay *your* repair bills. Send in the coupon today!

Cordially,
P. J. Devereaux
President

Schramm's Garage
1428 West Ave.
City

Dear Joe:

About that oil change and new filter: I've got Blue Wheel insurance now, so take care of it.

While the car's in there, check that pull to the left you mentioned.

Jack Bailey

ö ö ö

SCHRAMM'S GARAGE

To: Jack W. Bailey
413 Crescent Drive
City

Parts: 6 qts oil	$3.90
#14-66 oil filter	$4.95
#6612 brake shoes,1 set	$12.98
total	$21.83

Labor: change filter
    drain oil
    put in fresh oil
    install brake shoes
    grind drums

total	$24.00
total	$45.83
Blue Wheel	$45.83

Paid-J. Schramm

Note: Your transmission needs work. I can't work on it this week, because I'm swamped. How about next Wednesday morning?

Joe Schramm

Dear Joe:
Sure. I'll have the wife leave the car early.

Jack Bailey

ö ö ö

SCHRAMM'S GARAGE

Dear Mr. Wrattan:
Please send me your latest information on your Automated Car Service Handling Machine.

I never saw so much business in my life. I am now running about a month behind.

Yours truly,
J. Schramm

✸ ✸ ✸

SUPERDEE EQUIPMENT

Interoffice Memo
To: W. Robert Schnitzer, Special Services Dept.
Dear Schnitzer:

We are now out of the woods, thanks to your stroke of genius on the prepayment plan.

Now see if you can find some way to step up production.

Sanson

✸ ✸ ✸

FORESYTE INSURANCE

Interoffice Memo
To: J. Beggs, Vice Pres. Blue Wheel Plan
Dear Beggs:

What on earth is going on here? After making money the first few months on Blue Wheel, we are now getting swamped.

What's happening?

Devereaux

✸ ✸ ✸

FORESYTE INSURANCE

Interoffice Memo
To: P. J. Devereaux, Pres.
Dear Mr. Devereaux:

I don't exactly know what's going on, but it completely obsoletes these figures of Sanson's.

We are going to have to raise our premium.

Beggs

✸ ✸ ✸

SCHRAMM'S SERVICATORIUM

Dear Wrattan:

Please put my name on the waiting list for another Handling Machine right away.

Yours truly,

J. Schramm

*   *   *

BLUE WHEEL

Prepaid Car Care

Dear Subscriber:

Owing to unexpectedly heavy use of the Blue Wheel insurance by you, the subscriber, we must raise the charge for Blue Wheel coverage to $3.75 per month, effective January 1st.

Cordially,

R. Beggs

*   *   *

SCHRAMM'S SUPER SERVICATORIUM

Dear Mr. Wrattan:

We're going to need another Handling Machine as soon as we get the new wing finished next month.

Yours truly,

J. Schramm

*   *   *

FORESYTE INSURANCE

Interoffice Memo

To: P. J. Devereaux, Pres

.Dear Mr. Devereaux:

I have to report that ordinary garages are now being replaced by "servicatoriums," "super servicatoriums," and "ultraservicatoriums."

These places charge more, which is justified by their heavier capital investment, and faster service.

Nevertheless, it now costs us more for the same job.

R. Beggs

*   *   *

BLUE WHEEL

Prepaid Car Care

Dear Subscriber:

Due to increasingly thorough car care offered by modern servicatoriums, and to continued heavy and wider use of such care, we find it necessary to increase the charge to $4.25 a month.

Cordially,
R. Beggs

* * *

SCHRAMM'S ULTRASERVICATORIUM

To: Jack W. Bailey
413 Crescent Drive
City

Parts: 1 set 22-638 brushes	$1.46
Labor: clean battery terminals	
set regulator	
overhaul generator	$21.00
total	$22.46
	PAID

Note: There's a whine from the differential we ought to take care of on the Machine. How about Friday morning? I don't see why there was more trouble with the generator and regulator. I think we ought to check everything again. Your Blue Wheel will cover it.

Joe Schramm

* * *

SCHRAMM'S ULTRASERVICATORIUM

Dear Mr. Wrattan:

I want three of your All-Purpose Diagnostic Superanalyzers, that will test batteries, generators, starters, automatic transmissions, etc., etc. Rush the order. I can't get enough good mechanics to do this work.

Yours truly,
J. Schramm

* * *

FORESYTE INSURANCE

Interoffice Memo
To: P. J. Devereaux, Pres.

Dear Mr. Devereaux:

When I was a boy, I rode a bicycle with bad brakes down a steep hill one time, and got up to around sixty miles an hour as I came to a curve with a post-and-cable guard rail at the side, and about a sixty foot drop into a ravine beyond that.

This Blue Wheel plan gives me the same no-brakes sensation.

Incidentally, have you visited a garage lately?

R. Beggs

* * *

FORESYTE INSURANCE

Interoffice Memo

To: R. Beggs, Vice-Pres. Blue Wheel

Dear Beggs:

What we seem to have here is some kind of weird mechanism that just naturally picks up speed by itself.

Without our insurance plan, the garages could never have gone up to these rates, because car owners wouldn't or couldn't have paid them. Thanks to us, the car owners themselves now couldn't care less what the bill is. In fact, the higher it is, the more the car owner thinks he's getting out of his insurance.

The effect of this on the garage owner is to go overboard on every kind of expense.

Yes, I've visited a garage lately. I got a blowout over in Bayport, bought a new front tire, and on the way back noticed a vibration in the front end. Obviously, the wheel needed balancing.

However, when I tried to explain this to the Chief Automotive Repair Technician in Stull's Superepairatorium, he wouldn't listen. Before I knew what was going on, the car was up in the air.

Here's the bill:

Parts: 4 22-612 balance weights	$1.60
Labor: Complete diagnostic	$40.00
Wheel removal	$2.00
Transport	$1.50
Superbalancomatic	$6.50
Transport	$1.50
Wheel attachment	$2.00
Car transport	$3.25

Total parts and labor $58.35
Blue Wheel $58.35
PAID—L. Gnarth, C.A.R.T.

I think you can appreciate how I felt about Stull's Superepairatorium. I shoved past the Chief Automotive Repair Technician, and got hold of Stull himself. He listened, looked sympathetic, and said, "If you want, I will pay all of this but $2.75, which is about what it should have cost. But that won't change the fact that at least half of these bills are going to be higher than they should be, and it's going to get a lot worse, not better."

"Why?"

"Do you think anybody that learns how to tell what's wrong by using one of these diagnostic machines, and that learns how to repair a car with hydraulic pressers and handlers at his elbow, is ever going to be able to figure out what's wrong on his own, or do the work with ordinary tools? All he's learned to do is *work with the machine*. He *can't* do a simple job. He's *got* to make a big job out of it, *so he can use the machine.*

"Now," Stull went on, "a good, old-style mechanic narrows the trouble down with a few simple tests. For instance, if the car won't start, he tries the lights and horn, sees how the lights dim when he works the starter, watches the ammeter needle, notices how the starter sounds, checks the battery terminals and cables, checks the spark, bypasses the solenoid and sees if that's the trouble—in fifteen minutes, a good mechanic with a few simple tools has a good idea where the trouble is, and then it's a question of putting in new points, pulling the starter to check for a short, or maybe working on the carburetor or fuel pump. To do this, *you've got to understand first-hand the things you're working with*. Then the know-how is in your brain and muscles, and you can use it anytime.

"But now, with these new machines, especially this damned Combination Handling Machine and Diagnostic Analyzer, the skill and know-how *is in the machine.*

"What kind of mechanics do you think we're going to turn out this way? How many of them will ever be able to do *anything* without using the machine? And since the machine costs so much, what is there to do but charge more?"

That was how it went at the garage. I thought that was bad

enough, but this thing is snowballing, and there's more to it. After I left the garage, I happened to take another look at the bill and noticed that this Chief Automotive Repair Technician had "C.A.R.T." after his name. This struck me as peculiar, so I stopped at a roadside phone, and called up Stull. He sounded embarrassed.

"It's his . . . well . . . degree. It used to be a mechanic would have laughed at that. He had his skill, and knew, and that was enough. But now, with these machines, a lot of these new guys don't *have* the skill. Now they've got no way to prop up their feeling of being worth something. So, we've got this NARSTA, and—"

"You've got *what*?"

"N.A.R.S.T.A.—National Automotive Repair Specialists and Technicians Association. They award what amounts to *degrees*. They limit the number of people who can be mechanics, because anybody off the street could learn to run the machines in a few weeks.

"The mechanic who writes 'C.A.R.T.' after his name? Is he your *chief* mechanic?"

"Naturally."

"Why pick him for chief mechanic?"

"Because he has a 'C.A.R.T.' degree. If I use a guy with an A.A.R.T., or an A.R.T., I get in trouble with NARSTA. NARSTA says all its people are professionals, and have to be treated according to their 'professional qualifications.'"

"That is, how good they are as mechanics?"

"Of course not. 'Professional qualifications' is whether the guy's got an A.R.T., an A.A.R.T., or a C.A.R.T. He may or may not be as good as another mechanic. What counts is that C.A.R.T. after his name. That changes his wage scale, changes his picture of himself, and makes an aristocrat out of him."

There was more to this phone conversation, but I think you get the picture.

This mess is compounding itself fast. I talked to Sanson over at Superdee about it, but Superdee is making so much money out of this that Sanson naturally won't listen to any objections. Instead, he went into a spiel about the Advance of Science. Sanson doesn't know it, but this trouble comes because there is one science, and the Master Science at that, that is being left out of this. But I think if we put it to use ourselves we can end this process before it wrecks the country.

I have hopes that you know what I am talking about, and will see how to put it to use.

Bear in mind, please, that when the rug is jerked out, we want *somebody else* to land on his head, not us.

I might mention that I have recently had cautious feelers from one Q. Snarden, who turns out to be the head of NARSTA. Snarden wants, I think, to take over Blue Wheel.

He would then, I suppose, run it as a "nonprofit" organization. Do you get the picture?

Devereaux

⛀ ⛀ ⛀

FORESYTE INSURANCE

Interoffice Memo
To: P. J. Devereaux, Pres.
Dear Mr. Devereaux:

I don't know just what you mean by the "Master Science." But I have a good idea what we ought to do with this Blue Wheel insurance.

Suppose I come up this afternoon about 1:30 to talk it over?

R. Beggs

⛀ ⛀ ⛀

FORESYTE INSURANCE

Interoffice Memo
To: R. Beggs, Vice Pres. Blue Wheel
Dear Beggs:

I have now had a chance to analyze, and mentally review, your plan for dealing with Snarden, and Blue Wheel. I think this is exactly what we should do.

We want to be sure to run out plenty of line on this.

Devereaux

⛀ ⛀ ⛀

BLUE WHEEL

A Nonprofit Organization
NARSTA-Approved
Dear Subscriber:

In these days of rising car-care costs, one of your most precious possessions is your Blue Wheel policy. To assure you the best possible service at the lowest cost, Blue Wheel is now operated under the supervision of the National Automotive Repair Specialists and Technicians Association, as a *nonprofit* organization.

Yes, Blue Wheel now gives you real peace-of-mind on the road. And your Blue Wheel card will continue to admit your car to the finest Servicatoriums, whenever it needs care.

But as costs rise, the charges we pay rise.

As we spend only 4.21% on administration expenses, you can see we are doing our best to hold prices down; but costs are, nevertheless, rising.

To meet the costs, we find it is necessary to raise our premium to $5.40 a month.

When you consider the cost of car care today, this is a real bargain.

Cordially,
Q. Snarden

ö ö ö

BLUE WHEEL

(Nonprofit)
NARSTA-Approved
Dear Subscriber:

For reasons mentioned in the enclosed brochure, we are forced to raise our premium to $6.25 a month.

Cordially,
Q. Snarden, Pres.

ö ö ö

BLUE WHEEL

Dear Subscriber:

Blue Wheel has fought hard to hold the line, but next year, rates must go up if Blue Wheel is to pay your car-care bills.

As we explain in the enclosed booklet, Blue Wheel will now cost $8.88 a month.

This is one of the greatest insurance bargains on earth, when you consider today's car-care costs.

Cordially,
Q. Snarden, Pres.

❦ ❦ ❦
BLUE WHEEL

Dear Subscriber:

Blue Wheel is going to have to raise its rates to meet its ever-increasing costs of paying *your* car-care bills.

Future rates will be only $10.25 a month.

Cordially,
Q. Snarden, Pres.

❦ ❦ ❦
BLUE WHEEL

Dear Subscriber:

Blue Wheel's new rates will be $13.40 a month.

Cordially,
Q. Snarden, Pres.

❦ ❦ ❦
BLUE WHEEL

Dear Subscriber:

Blue Wheel is going to $16.90 a month effective January 1st.
See our enclosed explanation.

Cordially,
Q. Snarden, Pres.

❦ ❦ ❦
BLUE WHEEL

Dear Subscriber:

$22.42 a month is a small price to pay to be free of car-care expense worries nowadays.

This rate becomes effective next month.

Cordially,
Q. Snarden, Pres.

❦ ❦ ❦
SCHRAMM'S SERVICATORIUM

To: Jack W. Bailey

413 Crescent Drive
City

Parts: 1 set 22-638 brushes	$2.36
Labor: Super diagnostic	$85.00
Giant Lift	$65.00
Manipulatorium	$55.00
Extraculator	$28.00
Gen. transport	$1.25
Treatment	$12.50
Checkulator	$4.50
Gen. transport	$1.25
Ultramatatoni	$5.00
Installator	$15.00
Ch. transport	$3.75
Checkulator final	$6.50
Ch. transport	$3.75
Car transport	$5.25
Total parts and labor	$291.75

Blue Wheel $291.75 PAID

❧ ❧ ❧

FORESYTE INSURANCE

Interoffice Memo
To: P. J. Devereaux, Pres.
Dear Mr. Devereaux:

The other day, the turn-signals on my car quit working, and before I got out of the garage, the bill ran up to $417.12.

In today's mail I got a notice that Blue Wheel, with Snarden at the helm, is going to raise its rates to $28.50 a month.

This notice, by the way, piously states that administrative costs now only come to 2.4% of Blue Wheel's total revenues. Naturally, if they keep raising their revenues by upping the premium, administrative costs will get progressively smaller, in proportion to the total. The percentage looks modest, but that's 2.4% of *what*?

I was talking to a physicist friend of mine the other day, and he says the trouble is, the car-repair setup now has "positive feedback," instead of "negative feedback." When the individual owner used to pay his own bills, his anger at high bills, and his reluctance or even inability to pay them, acted as negative feedback, reacting more strongly against the garage the higher the bills got. But now, not only is there none of this, but the garages are used *more* the higher the Blue Wheel premiums—because people feel that they should get *something* out of the policy. This is positive feedback, and my physicist friend says that if it continues long enough, it invariably ends by destroying the system.

Already there is talk of government regulation, and of plans to spread the burden further by taxation. This is just more of the same thing, on a wider scale. It will only delay the day of reckoning, and the trouble when the day of reckoning comes.

I think we'd better pull the plug on this pretty soon.

R. Beggs

* * *

FORESYTE INSURANCE

Interoffice Memo
To: R. Beggs, Vice-Pres. Special Project
Dear Beggs:

Snarden goes before the congressional investigating committee next week.

When he is about halfway through his testimony, and has them tied in knots with his pious airs and specious arguments, *then* we want to hit him.

Have everything ready for about the third day of the hearing.

Devereaux

* * *

FORESYTE INSURANCE

Interoffice Memo
To: R. Beggs, Vice-Pres. Special Project
Dear Beggs:

Now's the time. Snarden has pumped the hearing so full of red herrings that it looks like a fish hatchery.

Pull the plug.

Devereaux

FORESYTE INSURANCE

Interoffice Memo
To: P.J. Devereaux, Pres.
Dear Mr. Devereaux:

The first ten million circulars are in the mail.

Beggs

🐾 🐾 🐾

FORESYTE INSURANCE

"In Unity, Strength"
Since 1906
Dear Car Owner:

When car-care insurance cost two dollars a month, it was a bargain. Now it costs about fifteen times as much.

This present insurance plan is so badly set up that it *forces up car-care costs*. And when car-care cost go up, *that forces up insurance premiums*.

This is a vicious circle.

Before this bankrupts the whole country, Foresyte Insurance is determined to stop the endless climb of these premiums, by offering our *own* plan.

Possibly, after paying these present terrific bills, you will understand why we call our plan *Blue Driver*. But you won't feel blue when you learn that our monthly rates on this new insurance are as follows:

$90.00 deductible 90%	$18.50
$90.00 deductible 75%	$12.50
$90.00 deductible 50%	$5.25
$180.00 deductible 90%	$13.75
$180.00 deductible 75%	$7.95
$180.00 deductible 50%	$3.75

Compare this with what you are paying now.

We are convinced that the huge increase in car-care costs is due mainly to the fact that the system now used makes it *nobody's* business to keep costs down, and puts the ever-increasing burden just as heavily on the man who *doesn't* overuse the plan as on the man who does.

Our plan is different, and puts the burden where it belongs—*on the fellow who overuses the plan.* You don't have to pay for all *his* expenses. He can't get away *without* paying for them. This is how it should be. Moreover, this plan gives good protection, at a lower cost.

For instance, with our $90.00 deductible 90% plan, you pay the first $90.00 of the bill yourself. True, $90.00 is a lot of money, *but in less that a year's time, you save that much or more in premiums.*

The 90% of the plan means that *we pay 90% of the rest of the bill.* You only have to pay 10%. On an $825.00 bill, for instance, you pay $90.00, which you have probably already saved because our premiums are so much lower. This leaves $735.00. We pay $661.50 of this, right away. *You pay only what's left.*

This lets you pay the small bills you can afford, while we take most of the big bills that everyone is afraid of these days.

Meanwhile, the less you use the plan, *the more you save.*

The larger the share of the risk you are willing to take, *the more you save.* Our $180.00 deductible 50% plan *costs only $3.75 a month.*

Because we may be able to lower premiums still further, these rates are not final. But at these rates, you can see that this plan rewards the person who doesn't overuse it.

We are already using this plan ourselves, and saving $10.00 to $24.75 a month on it.

How about you?

> Cordially,
> R. Beggs
> Vice-Pres.

413 Crescent Drive
Crescent City
Dear Mr. Beggs:

Here is my check for $7.95. I am signing up on your $180.00 deductible 75% plan, and saving $20.55 a month.

But you better not jack the rates way up, or I will go back to Blue Wheel. If we only burn one light in the house, heat one room, and eat cornmeal mush twice a day, we can still pay *their* premium.

> Yours truly,
> Jack Bailey

SCHRAMM'S SUPER SERVICATORIUM

To: Jack W. Bailey
413 Crescent Drive
City
Note: Time for oil change, new filter. Our Automatic File Checker also says it is time your car had a Complete Super Diagnostic and Renewvational Overhaul on our special new Renewvator Machine. Your Blue Wheel will cover it.

Joe Schramm

Dear Joe:

In a pig's eye my Blue Wheel will cover it. I'm a Blue Driver now, and I get socked 180 bucks plus 25% of the rest of your bill, and it sounds to me like I will get hit for enough on this one to buy a new car.

Keep the Renewvational Overhaul. As for the Complete Super Diagnostic, I found an old guy out on a back road, and he can figure out more with a screw driver, a wrench, and a couple of meters than those stuck-up imitation mechanics of yours can find out with the whole Super Diagnostic Machine.

Don't worry about the oil change. I can unscrew the filter all by myself. I will pay myself $4.50 for the labor, and save anyway a hundred bucks on the deal.

If the transmission falls out of this thing, or the rear axle climbs up into the back seat, I'll let you know about it. But don't bother me when it's time to oil the door handles and put grease on the trunk hinges.

Jack Bailey

* * *

SCHRAMM'S SUPER SERVICATORIUM

Dear Mr. Wrattan:

I just got your monthly booklet on "New Superdee Labor-Saving Giants."

Since the paper in this fancy booklet might clog up my new oil burner, I'm afraid I don't know what to do with it.

I am enclosing half-a-dozen letters from ex-customers, and maybe they will explain to you why business is off twenty per cent this month.

Yours truly,
J. Schramm

SUPERDEE EQUIPMENT

Interoffice Memo
To: W. W. Sanson, Pres.
Dear Mr. Sanson:

I am sending up a big envelope containing letters from garage-men and their customers. These letters are representative of a flood that's coming in.

What do we do now?

G. Wrattan

* * *

SUPERDEE EQUIPMENT

Interoffice Memo
To: G. Wrattan, Sales Mgr.
Dear Wrattan:

I put this one to Schnitzer and his Supervac 666. It flattened them.

There's just one thing *to* do. We take a loss on this latest stuff, and get out while we're still ahead.

As for these questions as to how much we offer to repurchase Renewvators, Giant Lifts, et cetera, we don't want them at any price. Point out how well made they are and how much good metal is in them. That's just a hint to the customer, and if he deduces from that that the best thing to do with them is scrap them, that's *his* business.

Do you realize it cost me $214.72 to get a windshield-wiper blade changed the other day? They ran the whole car through the Super Diagnostic first to be sure the wiper blade *needed* to be changed.

As far as I'm concerned, this whole bubble can burst anytime.

Sanson

* * *

SCHRAMM'S ECONOMY GARAGE
To: Jack W. Bailey
413 Crescent Drive
City

Parts: 1 set 22-638 brushes	$1.48
Labor: overhaul generator,	
set regulator	$8.50
total	$9.98

Note: Time for oil change, new filter. We will take care of this for you next time you're in—no charge for labor on this job. Al Putz says there was a funny rumble from the transmission when he drove the car out to the lot. We better check this as soon as you can leave the car again. Once those gears in there start grinding up the oil slingers and melting down the bearings, it gets expensive fast.

Joe Schramm

Dear Joe:

Thanks for the offer, but I'll take care of the oil change myself. I want to keep in practice, just in case the country comes down with another epidemic of Super Giant Machinitis.

As for that rumble from the transmission, I jacked up a rear wheel, started the engine, and I heard it, too. It had me scared for a minute there, but I blocked the car up, crawled under, and it took about three minutes to track down the trouble. In this model, the emergency brake works off a drum back of the transmission. Since I brought the car down to your garage, one end of a spring had somehow come loose on the emergency brake, and this lets the brake chatter against the drum. It was easy to connect the spring up again. The transmission is now nice and quiet.

I am enclosing the check for $9.98.

Jack Bailey

⸚ ⸚ ⸚

FORESYTE INSURANCE

Interoffice Memo
To: P. J. Devereaux. Pres.
Dear Mr. Devereaux:

We were able to bring the rates on Blue Driver car-care down again last month. We are still making a mint from this plan, even with reduced premiums, and we are still getting enthusiastic letters.

I can see, in detail, how this works, by giving everyone involved an incentive to keep costs down. But I am still wondering about a comment you made earlier.

What is the "Master Science" you referred to, in first suggesting the idea of this plan?

R. Beggs

FORESYTE INSURANCE

Interoffice Memo
To: R. Beggs, Vice-Pres. Blue Driver
Dear Beggs:

I am delighted you were able to bring the premium down again. Maybe we will get this thing within reason yet.

What do you *suppose* the Master Science is? Isn't it true to say that Science first comes into existence when the mind intently studies actual physical phenomena? And the mind operates in this and other ways, doesn't it, when it is moved to do so by reasons arising out of *human nature*?

What is the result when the mind intently studies *human nature*?

Engineers, physical scientists, biological scientists, mathematicians, statisticians, and other highly-trained specialists do work that is useful and important. As a result, we have gradually built up what amounts to a tool kit, filled with a variety of skills and techniques.

They are all useful, but nearly every time we rely on them alone and ignore human nature, we pay for it.

All our tools are valuable.

But we can't forget the hand that holds them.

Devereaux

Two-Way Communication

Cartwright, April 16. The Cartwright Corporation, manufacturer of electrical specialties, is reported on the brink of ruin today, after a disastrous plunge into the communications field. Word is that Cartwright research scientists had developed a new type of radio receiver, that the corporation backed it heavily, and that the equipment has now proved to have a fatal flaw. It is reported that Nelson Ravagger, the well-known corporation "raider," has now seized control of the company. Ravagger is expected to oust Cyrus Cartwright, II, grandson of the corporation's founder.

Nelson Ravagger ground his cigarette into the ultramodern ash-tray and looked Cyrus Cartwright, II, in the eye.

"When," Ravagger demanded, "did it finally dawn on you that you had a mess on your hands?"

Cartwright glared at Ravagger. "When you walked in that door and told me you had control of the company."

Ravagger smiled. "I'm not talking about that. I'm talking about this Cartwright Mark I Communicator. That's the cause of this trouble."

Cartwright said uncomfortably, "Yes—the communicator."

Ravagger nodded. "I'm listening."

"It dawned on us we had a mess," said Cartwright, "when the Mark I receiver broadcast through the microphone of the local radio station. Up to that time, the thing looked perfect."

Ravagger frowned. "What was that again?"

"The Mark I receiver," said Cartwright patiently, "broadcast through the local radio station's microphone. That's when we knew we were in trouble."

"The *receiver* broadcast through the microphone of the *transmitter?*"

"That's it," said Cartwright.

Ravagger looked at him in amazement. "How did that happen?"

Cartwright spread his hands. "It's a new principle. The circuit isn't a regenerative circuit. It's not a tuned R-F circuit. It's not a superhet. It's a . . . ah—Well, they call it a Cartwright circuit."

"Did you invent it?"

"I don't know anything about it. I took the Business Course in college. You know, economics, mathematics of finance, and so on. Management is all the same after you get to the higher levels."

Ravagger smiled at him wolfishly. "Let's get back to this communicator. You don't know anything about it?"

"Not technically. I could see, from a business viewpoint, that it could be a very good thing for us."

"Why?"

"Well, we *had* been selling to manufacturers. Quality switches, circuit breakers, things like that. What we needed was a broad approach to the consumer himself. That's a much bigger and less demanding market."

Ravagger lit up another cigarette and studied Cartwright with a look of cynical disbelief. "In other words, the quality of your product had been falling off, and sales were going down, so you figured you better get into something else?"

Cartwright squirmed. "Well, competition was getting pretty stiff."

"So you decided to turn out this communicator. All right, what was *it* supposed to do?"

"It is an all-purpose communicator. You have AM, FM, short-wave, longwave—*everything*—all in one package."

Ravagger showed no enthusiasm. "In other words, a luxury receiver. I suppose it was portable?"

"Oh, yes." Cartwright got a little excited. "We were going to turn it out in a nice leather case, with three colors of trim."

"Naturally. And, of course, with an antenna you can pull out three feet long." He added sarcastically, "You were really going to skim the cream off the market with this thing. There must be a dozen different makes out right now."

Cartwright shrugged. "No antenna. It didn't need one. Besides, in a shirt-pocket radio, an antenna that pulls out seems to me to be a nuisance. If you've *got* to have it, then you're stuck with it, of course. But we were going to advertise that ours didn't *need* an external antenna."

Ravagger blinked. "Shirt-pocket size, eh? And it worked?"

"Except for the little shortcoming I just mentioned."

"This thing was to be called a Cartwright Mark I *Communicator*. Why not just Mark I *radio*, or *receiver*? Why *communicator*? Just because the name sounded good?"

"It sounded good to us at first. That was our original reason. Then we got a bright idea. Why not build it so it could really *be* a communicator? You know, two-way. Then we could turn out a citizen's band set, and a walkie-talkie. It could be everything. An all-purpose communicator. If it's broadcast, this could pick it up. Longwave, shortwave, amateur, police, the sound from TV programs, AM, FM, foreign, domestic—" Cartwright ran out of words, and took a deep breath. "It was an all-purpose, universal communicator that would—"

"Wait a minute." Ravagger was staring at him. "All this in a *shirt-pocket radio?*"

"Yes. Oh, there's no problem there. It's just a question of build-ing it differently. If you consider it, it's *obvious* that eventually we'll have sets as small as that on the consumer market. Take a look inside the average portable receiver these days. Compare it with the size of the sets ten years ago, twenty years ago, thirty years ago. We're moving toward very small sets. We—here at Cartwright, I mean—happened to get the principle for the next advance first, that's all. Now, to make a transmitter is admittedly more of a size problem, even with our new manufacturing process. But there was enough room in the case, and it could be done. So we thought, why not do it?"

"All right," said Ravagger, scowling. "Now, if I understand this correctly, what you're saying is that you had a shirt-pocket set that could receive AM, FM, and shortwave broadcasts, could transmit and receive on citizen's band, and—"

"No. It had the *potentiality*, if we chose to make the necessary connections, to use citizen's band. But we'd have to make connections to the right points on the unit crystal. This initial set was to be purely a receiver. Later, we'd bring out the Mark II, Mark III, and so on, which would be transmitter-receivers. And *still* shirt-pocket size. The point was, that for a few thousand bucks more on the fabricating equipment, and a few cents more on each unit crystal, we could have the potential to raise the price twenty to forty dollars a set later on, and *still* give the customer a break."

Ravagger frowned at him. "What's this 'unit crystal'?"

Cartwright pulled open a drawer on his modernistic desk, and took out a small portable radio in dark-blue leather with gold trim, with a line of gold knobs down one side, and a tuning dial with so many bands that it covered the entire face of the radio. He unsnapped the back, took out the solitary penlight battery, pulled the little speaker out of the way, and exposed an olive-colored metal can.

"Inside that," said Cartwright, "is the crystal."

Ravagger squinted at it. "Where's the rest of the circuit?"

"That's it."

"The whole thing is in one crystal?"

"Sure. That's the point."

Ravagger scowled at the radio through a haze of cigarette smoke. "Let's hear it."

"All right." Cartwright snapped the set together again. "But don't say anything out loud, or we may get in trouble with the FCC."

Ravagger nodded, and Cartwright turned the radio on. A girl with a voice that was not improved by the small speaker, was singing a popular song. Both men winced, and Cartwright quickly tuned in a recorded dance band, a news report, a voice talking rapidly in French, and then an amateur who was saying, ". . . Coming in very clear, but I didn't quite get your handle there . . ."

Ravagger said, "Do you mean to tell me—"

Cartwright said angrily, "Quiet!"

The radio said, "Wyatt? *Wait a minute!* I could have sworn—"

Cartwright snapped off the set. "I *told* you not to say anything!"

Ravagger stared at him. "You mean to say, this set will let you *talk to any station you can receive?*"

Cartwright took a deep breath, nodded glumly, and shoved the set back in the drawer. "The trouble is, we should have been content with the receiver circuit. We should never have built up the circuits for the transmitter. It was a big mistake to combine the two in the same crystal. They interact."

"There's no way to . . . say . . . break off the part of the crystal that has the transmitter in it?"

"It's not that simple. You can't separate them that easily. You need a whole new crystal."

"Well—Suppose you build a new crystal?"

"The fabricating equipment to mass-produce the crystals costs a mint, and our equipment will only turn out the one crystal it was built to make. It will do that with great precision, but that's *all* it will do."

"And you're already spread so thin you can't afford to buy new equipment?"

"That's it."

"Hm-m-m." Ravagger leaned back. After contemplating the ceiling for a while, he sat up again with a bang. "Now, as I under-stand this, Cartwright, the broadcast . . . ah . . . the transmission *you* send out turns up at the broadcaster's *microphone*. Is that right?"

"That's right."

"How could *that* happen?"

Cartwright squirmed uneasily. "The boys in the Research Department have an explanation for it. It has something to do with the 'carrier wave.' Let's see, the crystal is energized by the carrier wave, resonates, transmits in precise congruity with the carrier wave, and then the mike at the transmitting station 'telephones' and the sound comes out. If you want me to get them up here—"

Ravagger waved his hand. "They know *why and how it happens.* But what I'm interested in is *what we can do with it.*"

Cartwright said drearily, "I haven't thought of anything."

"It would make a good walkie-talkie."

"Only if it were a transmitter, too. To make it a transmitter would require another stage in the manufacturing process. As it is, it's *not* a transmitter—except in this one freakish way."

Ravagger frowned. "How many of these sets have you got?"

"We've got a warehouse full of them. Naturally, when we first tried them out, this never entered our heads. We only stumbled onto it by accident."

"Hm-m-m." Ravagger leaned back and looked thoughtfully at Cartwright. "If it hadn't been for this thing, you'd have been raking it in by the barrelful."

Cartwright brightened. "By the truckload. We could eventually get the cost of the whole set down to about nine dollars a unit. We could charge any price within reason."

"And nobody could have predicted this trouble?"

"At least, nobody *did* predict it."

"Yes, I see." Ravagger knocked the ash off the end of his cigarette, ground out the butt, and looked at Cartwright. Ravagger's expression was a peculiar blend of calculation and benevolence. "As long as I'm cleaning out fools who should never have been in charge of companies anyway, what do I care if they say I'm a pirate and pronounce my name 'ravager'? I'm performing a useful function. If I start cleaning out *first*-raters, I'm not doing any good. Now, you had a good setup here. You *should* have made money. You were smart to switch over to this portable set. No one could blame you. You made the right moves."

Cartwright looked dazed.

Ravagger leaned forward. "I'm not going to take over this company. I'm going to get you off the hook. I aim to see to it that every one of these sets *and the fabricating equipment* are bought at your cost."

Cartwright was dumbfounded. "But—"

Ravagger waved his hand. "No buts. My job here is to get you off the hook. I'll profit, you'll profit, the stockholders will profit, and the whole country will profit. This situation has possibilities."

For an instant, Cartwright seemed to see a halo around the financial pirate's head.

"Anything you say," said Cartwright gratefully.

❧ ❧ ❧

Cartwright, May 5. Cyrus Cartwright, II, president of the Cartwright Corporation and grandson of the corporation's founder, today beat off a formidable attempt by business buccaneer Nelson Ravagger to gain control of the company.

The Corporation had been rumored to be in serious difficulties, due to failure of a revolutionary manufacturing process. But Cyrus Cartwright today revealed the sale of the entire stock of merchandise and related manufacturing equipment to Hyperdynamic Specialty Products, a recently-formed distributing firm.

* * *

New York, June 2. Trading on the Big Board was heavy today. Among the most active stocks was the Cartwright Corporation.

* * *

New York, June 4. An astonishing advertisement has been running for the past week in several leading New York papers.

This reporter visited the showroom mentioned in the ad yesterday, picked up one of the devices advertised, and spent a truly delightful evening at home.

The advertisement is as follows:

**ARE YOU
SICK
OF
DULL
COMMERCIALS
?**

Strike back at silly announcers with revolutionary device that enables *you* to talk to *them!* Introductory price of $29.99 for new Electronic Miracle. You can set it beside your radio or TV and blast moronic announcers and admaniacs to your heart's content. THEY WILL HEAR YOU! Haven't you suffered in silence long enough? Call at Hyperdynamic Showroom today!

* * *

New York, June 10. Rumors current for the past week were confirmed today by Harmon Lobcaw, president of NBS Radio, who admitted that "a serious situation has arisen in the broadcasting industry."

Mr. Lobcaw stated that voices have been heard, coming from microphones, accusing announcers of "stupidity, bad taste and a number of other things I don't care to repeat."

Mr. Lobcaw was unable to explain how this could be, but insisted that "It is a fact. Government action," he said, "is imperative."

* * *

New York, June 11. Saralee Boondog, popular singer, was removed from the NBS studio by ambulance today, and rushed to the hospital for treatment of shock. Cause of Miss Boondog's illness was "loud hisses and boos coming from the microphone" while she was singing the popular favorite, "Love You, Love You, Love You, Honey." Miss Boondog's manager has threatened to sue the person or persons responsible."

* * *

New York, June 11. The Nodor Antiperspirant Spray Co., Inc., has temporarily suspended its radio and TV commercials due to "abusive comments from the microphone, threatening the persons of the actors." A spokesman for the company warns that the company will seek damages.

* * *

New York, June 12. Attempts to locate the whereabouts of a concern called Hyperdynamic Specialty Products, rumored to be distributing radio sets of unusual properties, have so far proved futile. The firm's showroom was vacated before police arrived.

* * *

Havana, June 14. Julio Del Barbe, Special Communications Commissar, today blasted "Yankee imperialism" in a lengthy speech, interrupted a number of times as Mr. Del Barbe smashed his microphone. Mr. Del Barbe, among other things, angrily accused "a cutthroat Yankee CIA cover agency called Hyperdynamic Specialty Products" of selling his organization a case of expensive "special electronics equipment," which blew up on arrival.

* * *

Moscow, June 18. The Soviet Government has delivered a stiff protest to Washington, charging that "voices with American accents" are interrupting Soviet news and cultural broadcasters, with comments from the microphone such as "Lies, all lies," and "Communism is the bunk." Moscow demands that these "crude provocations" cease at once.

* * *

Washington, June 19. At the same time as the Russian note was received here, word got around that an official of the Russian embassy here recently paid $2,500.00 for a portable back-talk radio set such as is sold on the black market here for about $50.00. The back-talker was reportedly flown to Moscow on the very fastest jet transportation available.

❦ ❦ ❦

Washington, June 20. The President was interrupted several times last night by caustic comments from the microphone. The Russians are believed responsible.

❦ ❦ ❦

New York, August 1. Harmon Lobcaw, president of NBS Radio, announced today the installation of a system of "remote live broadcasting" which "strains out" microphone back talk before it reaches the announcer. Mr. Lobcaw also said that there is now a "crying need for announcers," as an estimated four hundred have recently quit their jobs. Asked why they quit, Mr. Lobcaw said, "Their self-confidence was shattered."

❦ ❦ ❦

Washington, August 2. Following several nasty comments from the microphone, Senator William Becker has summoned Cyrus Cartwright, II, to testify before his committee regarding the Cartwright Corporation's connection with the mushrooming sales of back-talk radio and TV devices. Mr. Cartwright has stated that he will appear, and has nothing to hide.

❦ ❦ ❦

New York, August 3. The price of Cartwright Corporation stock plummeted today, as rumors spread that the Government is determined to punish the company.

❦ ❦ ❦

Washington, August 8. Cyrus Cartwright, II, today won a clean bill of health from Senator William Becker's investigating committee. The committee is now looking for Nelson Ravagger, the well-known speculator and corporation-raider.

❦ ❦ ❦

New York, August 9. Cartwright Corporation stock rose sharply today.

❦ ❦ ❦

Washington, August 11. In a stormy, shouting session financier Nelson Ravagger defended himself against charges of Senator William Becker's committee that Ravagger is responsible for distributing radio-TV back-talk devices. Mr. Ravagger asserted that he had not purchased the devices, but that they had been sold to a firm run by his business associate, Skybo Halante. Mr. Halante is now being sought.

* * *

New York, August 11. Cartwright Corporation climbed to a new high as it was learned today that the corporation developed and is now selling the cheapest and most effective system for "filtering" back talk and "sorting and storing" it for program-improvement purposes. Development of this device was reportedly instigated by financier Nelson Ravagger, who has emerged as apparently the major Cartwright stockholder following a series of complex market operations reported to have netted him millions.

* * *

Washington, August 16. In a furious session before the Becker Backtalk-Investigating Committee, businessman Cyrus Cartwright, II, and speculator Nelson Ravagger defended themselves against renewed charged of "mulcting the public, deceiving this committee, and attempting to destroy the communications industry in this country." Skybo Halante, Mr. Ravagger's long-sought business associate, appears to have evaporated into thin air. Grilled about this, Mr. Ravagger replied, "How should I know where he is? I'm not his chaperon." The search for Mr. Halante is continuing.

* * *

New York, August 17. Price of Cartwright Corporation stock fell sharply today as it was learned that damage suits totaling upwards of one billion dollars are to be brought against the corporation.

* * *

New York, August 19. Price of Cartwright Corporation stock rose sharply today as word was received of a fantastically cheap and effective Cartwright portable radio entirely free of back talk.

* * *

New York, August 22. The bottom fell out of Cartwright Corporation stock today as the rumor spread that the new-model portable radio produces back talk.

* * *

New York, August 24. Cartwright Corporation stock made a dramatic recovery and rose to an unprecedented high as the first of the new

Cartwright portable receivers found their way into circulation today. The portables, extremely attractive and entirely free from back talk, are made to sell at a very reasonable price.

*   *   *

New York, August 25. Trading in Cartwright Corporation stock has been suspended, pending completion of an investigation to determine whether the recent sharp rises and falls have been due to behind-the-scenes manipulations. It has been rumored that speculator Nelson Ravagger and a small group of associates have made enormous profits from Cartwright's erratic behavior.

*   *   *

Washington, August 26. Cyrus Cartwright, II, was again called to the stand as the Becker Committee attempts to unravel the facts concerning the reported transfer of a huge quantity of back-talk radio sets from Cartwright Corporation, by way of Nelson Ravagger, to the still missing Skybo Halante. In a savage exchange, Senator Becker today called Mr. Cartwright a "bold-faced liar." Mr. Cartwright had just described the alleged circumstances surrounding the original sale of the back-talkers.

*   *   *

New York, September 25. Cartwright Corporation stock, following completion of the investigation into price-manipulation by insiders, continued to rise sharply this week, despite sporadic rumors that Nelson Ravagger and associates are now unloading most—if not all—their holdings.

*   *   *

Washington, September 29. The Becker Committee has closed its investigation into the Cartwright Corporation back-talkers. Cyrus Cartwright, II, pale and drawn, grimly told reporters, "The last few months have been the most terrific experience in my life." Asked what he intended to do now that the investigation was over, Mr. Cartwright said, "Sleep."

*   *   *

Budapest, October 2. Officials here have admitted for the first time that back-talkers are in fairly common use. They refuse to call their use a problem, however, saying that, thanks to the devices, people "let off steam," and "sometimes we get good suggestions." Several announcers have been sacked because of pointed back-talk comments.

❦ ❦ ❦

New York, October 4. Cyrus Cartwright, II, today announced that he was stepping down as active head of the Cartwright Corporation, though he will remain on the Board of Directors. Mr. Cartwright said he wished to "sort things over in my mind. I have the sensation that I have just stepped off a combined merry-go-round and Ferris wheel." Mr. Cartwright refused to criticize Mr. Ravagger, who is reputed to have effective control of the corporation.

❦ ❦ ❦

New York, October 5. Wall Street opinion is divided as to whether Nelson Ravagger actually controls large holdings of Cartwright stock at the moment. "It depends," a well-known speculator is reported to have said, "on whether the stock goes up or down. If it skyrockets, it will turn out that Ravagger has a big chunk of it. If it falls through the floor, we'll know for sure that he dumped it some time ago. You can't keep up with that guy. You can only reconstruct things afterward." Trading in the stock continues at a high level.

❦ ❦ ❦

Washington October 6. A broadcast lecture by political economist Sero Kulf, on the "continuing iniquitous aspects of an unsocialized philosophy" was interrupted today by comments, getting through the filtered microphone, of "Crank," "Cretin," "What do *you* know about it?" and by Dr. Kulf's own replies, which unfortunately got through before the program was cut off the air. Stronger filtering systems are reported to be in production against bootleg backtalkers.

❦ ❦ ❦

Washington, October 12. The uproar about back-talk radio sets seems to be gradually starting to die down. Senator William Becker remarked to reporters that "for the first time in fifteen years," he had listened to the radio the other day, and found it enjoyable. Mr. Becker feels that manufacturers are now getting the word about the more offensive commercials, and that the new system of filtering and registering complaints has led many stations to cut down on too frequent advertising. "This mess may," said the senator, "prove to have its compensations."

❦ ❦ ❦

New York, October 24. At a meeting of the Better Radio and TV

Association, president Jack M. Straub today awarded the association's Distinguished Service Plaque to Cyrus Cartwright, II, and Nelson Ravagger, for "distinguished efforts which have resulted in vastly improving the dismal standard of radio and television broadcasting, by enabling listeners and viewers to record their actual feelings spontaneously and directly, rather than through the doubtful intermediary of sampling procedures."

Mr. Straub said that he will give an even bigger and better plaque to missing financier and reputed boot-leg-manufacturer Skybo Halante, "if someone will locate him for us."

"Communication," Mr. Straub added, "generally needs to be two-way to be effective."

High G

James M. Heyden, head of the Advanced Research Projects Division of the Continental Multitechnikon Corporation, blew his breath out exasperatedly, sat back in the expensive aggregation of pads and springs that served as his desk chair, and read the hand-written note again:

Jim

Pat tells me we are now so far ahead of the international competition, defensewise, that no large new government orders can be expected. Introduction of any new and revolutionary gimcrack at this time would, therefore, be most unwelcome and inexpedient. So put the new gimmicks on the back burner, and get going full blast on that Kiddie Kit Science Series. We'll expect rapid progress, as we want the first three Kits on the market at least ninety days before Christmas. Naturally the Moon Krawler should be one of these first Kits.

Any suggestions you may have for utilizing our now top-heavy staff of technicians and engineers would be appreciated. We assume you will cull the deadwood. Remember that in pruning, you want to cut pretty close into sound wood, as this actually promotes rapid healing and leaves no dead stump to fester.

Also, you will of course bear in mind that we have a

little different approach, expensewise, on items for the general public, as opposed to rush government orders. The Krawler should retail at not over $13.95, according to market simulation on our big new MIMIC computer. The Krawler, remember, does not have to fit into a cramped space, or endure high acceleration, vacuum, or a lunar landing. It won't break our hearts if the thing fails to last long enough for our great-grandchildren to play with it on Mars; of course, it shouldn't fall apart before the holidays are over, either.

I know I don't have to spell this out for you, Jim. Ed and I are going to be out on the coast for a couple of weeks, enjoying the California smog, and trying out those twelve-lane, six-deck highways they brag about. If the merger goes through, we'll be gone another week, anyway, but that won't matter. We'll be so diversified then that nothing but another 1929 could really put us under.

So, bear down hard on the reconversion, streamlining, and rationalization of your operation. Incidentally, the MIMIC simulator indicates that the other two kits should sell, respectively, at $8.95 and $29.95. Obviously, you can shoot the works on the later model, though we'll expect a more generous profit, too.

Just what these other two kits should be, we don't know, as our programmer was evidently unable to figure out just how to put the question to the computer. The computer gave out nothing but gibberish on the subject. So we'll leave that up to you.

This is, of course, all *your* responsibility, Jim, but I hope you'll be generally guided by the spirit of these few suggestions.

We'll look forward to seeing things well along when we get back from Cal.

Stu

Heyden sat up straight, and swore. He hit the intercom button. "Nell!"

There was a startled feminine squeak, "Sir?"

"Dig up that note from Stu Grossrad—the one he sent about eighteen months ago—the one that said 'full speed ahead, damn the torpedoes,' and so on."

"That was longer ago than eighteen months. I think"

"Never mind that. Dig it up. And the one before that—that one about blasting out a foxhole and hiding in it. And the one before that, too—I think there was one before that."

Heyden sat back and looked over the note. A fresh burst of profanity escaped him just as his secretary came in with several sheets of paper, and then, blushing bright pink, turned to leave.

"Hold on," said Heyden. He looked over the previous notes, and glanced up at her. "Listen to this: '. . . the sky's no limit, boy. With this monster government program shaping up, we can carve off any size chunk we can eat. So beef up your technical staff, get that wild blue yonder stuff out of the deep freeze, shove this low-key junk we're working on onto a back burner, and set your sights on Arcturus . . .'"

Heyden looked up in angry indignation. "There's three pages like that."

"Yes, sir." His secretary looked baffled for a moment, then struggled to match his look of indignation.

"And," said Heyden, reaching for an earlier note, "before that, we had *this* business:

"'. . . too bad, but the bottom has gone out the way it can only go out when Uncle pulls the plug, and now instead of cruising along in ten fathoms of deep green sea, all of a sudden we're grinding on the rocks. We're going to have to shorten sail and throw the ballast overboard, or we're ended right here. We're top heavy with hypertechnical stuff that nobody wants but Uncle—when he wants it. And now he doesn't want it. So get rid of it. Junk the heavy projects. What we need is a money-maker, fast . . .'"

Heyden shoved that aside, glared up at his secretary, who swallowed nervously, and then he reached for the earliest sheet of paper, settled back, and read aloud:

"'. . . the opportunity of the century, boy. We can get in there on the ground floor. The public is screaming for action. Congress is boiling over with urgency. It's "Get results! Damn the expense!" I don't need to tell you that in an atmosphere like this, the streets are paved with golden opportunity. Now's the time to beef up your technical staff, build for the future, get in on the ground floor, and . . .'"

Heyden slapped the papers down. "And so on, for pages. Well, there we are. Just what do you think of that?"

His secretary scanned his face quickly and looked indignant again.

"You see," said Heyden angrily, "just what happens here. We're like a damn-fool rocket that wastes half its thrust decelerating. Now we're supposed to unload people we pirated away from other outfits six months ago. Twelve to eighteen months from now, we'll be scrambling to get these very same people back again. We set up a winning team, then when we get a few points ahead in the international game, we have to disband it. The other team, over across the ocean, keeps on playing, and all of a sudden there comes a howl from the fans. The opposition is wiping us all over the field. Then, *quick*, we've got to put together a winning team again. And then, again, when we get a few points ahead—" His face changed expression, and for a moment he looked boiling mad. Then he blew out his breath, and shrugged. "It's like a manic-depressive psychosis. The wasted energy is terrific. And when we're on the 'down' half of the cycle, if the other side should just get far enough ahead—"

"Yes, sir," said his secretary agreeably. "That's just what you said the last time, sir. Did you want to see Mr. Benning, or should I—"

Heyden scowled. "What does Benning want?"

"He says it's about that advanced 'High-G' project. I knew you'd be busy reading Mr. Grossrad's letter, so I had Mr. Benning wait."

Heyden shrugged. "It's all academic now. But send him in."

"Yes, sir." She went out. A moment later, a tall intense man with blue eyes that seemed to be lit from within walked through the doorway, carrying under one arm a bundle wrapped in dark green paper. He shut the door, walked directly to Heyden's desk and set the bundle down. There was a faint light crackle of paper, and then the bundle tipped lightly back and forth, resting on the desk with all the solidity of a piece of hollow balsa wood.

Having set the bundle down, Benning now glanced all around furtively, then nodded to Heyden. "Well," he said, in a low secretive voice, "we got it."

Heyden was glancing from the bundle to Benning. He'd never seen Benning like this before.

Benning, blue eyes glowing, repeated, "We *got* it." He turned, glanced around the room, put his finger to his lips, and reached across the stupefied Heyden's desk to pick up a scratch pad. He scribbled rapidly as Heyden, with fast-growing uneasiness, moved his chair back so he'd have freedom of action if it suddenly developed that Benning had gone off the deep end.

Benning sat down across the desk, and slid the pad to Heyden. Heyden read:

High-G total success. Working model right there across the desk from you. Don't talk about it out loud. Have reason to think your office here is bugged.

II

Heyden glanced rapidly from the pad to Benning to the green-wrapped package. For a moment he considered what it would mean if Benning was telling the truth. The package immediately looked like a huge bundle of big green banknotes. He came back to earth and reminded himself that Benning might be out of his head. He wrote rapidly on the pad: *Bugged by who, the Russians?* and said aloud. "When you come in here with that pretentious look, Ben, you better have something to back it up. You say you 'got it.' Don't just sit there looking happy. You got *what*?"

Benning could now do any of a number of things, and Heyden sat on the edge of his chair, watching intently to see what came next.

Benning looked at the pad, glanced at places where a "bug" might be hidden, and crossed his fingers to show he spoke for the benefit of uninvited listeners. "What we've got is a damn good gimmick to get us a government contract on this, boy. We've run into a little glimmer of pay dirt on this one. I can see just how to start the golden flood pouring in, and keep it flowing for years."

He wrote rapidly on the pad, and shoved it across the desk. Heyden read:

Not the Russians. I. I.

Heyden winced and glanced around. "M'm," he said aloud. "Well, I don't know. I got quite a note from Stu Grossrad."

Benning sat up. "No kidding."

"No kidding."

"What did Stu say?"

"What does he ever say. It's either 'Full speed ahead!' or 'Emergency reverse!' The last time we were supposed to go all out, shoot the works. Naturally, this time we're supposed to chop off all the deadwood, shove everything we're working on now onto the back burner, and pull that toy kit idea off the back burner and put it onto the front burner. Whenever we're eager to do something, we're supposed to let it congeal on the back burner. When we couldn't care less about the thing, *then* we're supposed to work on it. How does this fit in with your bright new idea?"

"Not so hot. What toy kit is that?"

Heyden wrote *I. I. You mean Interdisciplinary Intellectronetics? Or Interspatial Ionics?*

He shoved the pad across the desk, then handed over the note from Grossrad. "Read it. You'll remember."

Benning crackled the paper, glanced at the pad, wrote briefly, looked back at the note, wrote some more, glanced at the note and groaned.

"Ye gods. Hasn't somebody else got a Moon Krawler out by now? This thing was a bright idea when we thought of it. It's stale now." He slid the pad across, and Heyden read:

I mean Interdis-, etc.-Jawbreaker Electronics, Inc.

Heyden wrote, *Where did you learn this?* Aloud, he said, "Naturally, we'll be supposed to gimmick it up with flashing lights, clicking noises, and a recorded voice like a talking doll, only more mechanical. No doubt the thing should have claws that open and shut, a power scoop for, quote, taking samples of the lunar surface, end-quote, and maybe a guide-wire to control it with as it crawls across the living-room rug waving its claws."

"Boy," said Benning. "From the sublime to the ridiculous in one easy jump." He shoved the pad back. "What's this business about the $29.95 item? What toy could we make that anyone would be crazy enough to buy at that price?"

Heyden was reading: *Right from the horse's mouth. Their Industrial Intelligence chief. They're in some kind of financial cramp, want to cut his salary and slash his staff, "temporarily."*

Heyden said, "Take a look through some recent toy catalog. You'll get a shock." He wrote, *Is he reliable?*

Benning had been rapidly scanning Grossrad's note, but was now reading it more carefully. He glanced up in exasperation. "Listen to this: '. . . of course, it shouldn't fall apart before the holidays are over . . .' Isn't *that* nice?" He glanced at the pad, wrote rapidly, and said, "What kind of sleezy junk are we supposed to turn out, anyway?"

"Just so it sells," grunted Heyden. He took the pad, and read: *That guy is as reliable as a rusted-out two-buck hair-trigger Spanish automatic. He just figures I. I. is double-crossing him, and he never lets anybody get ahead of him in that game.*

"You realize," said Heyden, frowning, "we're going to have to let some people go and that we'll wish we'd kept them about eighteen months from now."

"Agh," growled Benning, still reading the note. "Listen to this: 'Introduction of any new and revolutionary gimcrack at this time would, therefore, be most unwelcome and inexpedient.' Just suppose we *should* hit on something new and revolutionary?" He tipped his head toward the green-wrapped bundle. "Then what? Are we supposed to think you can actually put it in cold storage, and keep it like frozen fish? Suppose somebody else gets it? What's the *point* of this whole thing, anyway?"

Heyden wrote: *What's in that bundle?* He slid the pad across the desk, and said, "Let's get back to the question of those people we're going to have to let go."

Benning wrote on the pad, then said aloud, "This is crazy."

"Do you think," said Heyden dryly, "that you're telling *me* something?" He glanced at the pad: *Lift off the paper and see.*

Heyden felt a tightness in his chest. He said, "Let's have that note from Grossrad. I've been reading some of his previous stuff here—" He stood up, gently pulled off the green paper—"and nobody can tell me anything new about how crazy—" He stared at the short length of board with square box attached, and slide-wire rheostat beside the box. Beneath the rheostat was a penciled arrow pointing to the right, and marked "Up".

Heyden felt a brief spasm of irritation. What was this supposed to be? Antigravity? He felt a brief wave of dizziness as he thought, Ye gods, what if it *is*?

Belatedly, he finished his sentence: "—how crazy a thing like this really is."

"But," said Benning sourly, "we're stuck with it? Is that what you mean?"

"Yeah." Heyden pulled the board toward him, noting its weird lightness, despite the fact that it felt solid enough to the fingers. "We're stuck with it, and we better figure out who to let go."

"I should think," said Benning, "that would be *your* job."

Heyden shoved the rheostat slider in the direction of the arrow. The board drifted up out of his hands, and started accelerating toward the ceiling. A hasty grab brought it down, but it continued to tug toward the sky.

"My *responsibility*," said Heyden, eyeing the board, "but I need *your* suggestions."

"As to who to fire?"

"Say, as to who to *keep*." He slid the rheostat slider in the opposite direction, and the board sagged so heavily that it seemed to Heyden that it must be made out of solid lead. Frowning, he said, "Take Magnusson, for instance. We could unload him to start with, I suppose."

"He's had a lot of expenses. His bank balance is pretty feeble."

Heyden was experimenting with the slider. He got the impression that as he approached either end, the weight or lift of the concealed device went off toward infinity. He paused to glance at the connections to the rheostat.

"Not our fault," he grunted.

"No, but—"

"The point is, that's *his* worry."

The board was headed for the ceiling again, and it felt as if it would tear Heyden's arm out by the roots. Scowling, he pulled the slider back toward the center.

Benning said, "I think we ought to be decent enough to give Magnusson enough time to get back on his feet."

"How about Simms?"

The board was so heavy Heyden had to rest it on the corner of his desk. As he pushed the slider further, the board settled immovably in place, as if spiked down.

"Well," said Benning evasively, "Simms has had a little streak of bad luck, too."

"What have we got," said Heyden, carefully pulling the slider back, "nothing but hard-luck cases?"

"Well, you know how it is"

"We've got to start *somewhere*."

"Sure, but poor Simms."

"We aren't going to get anywhere this way. Make out a list of the people you think are essential. I want them in groups, the most essential at the top of the list." He wrote on the pad: *Did I. I.'s spy-chief say there was a visual pickup anywhere in here?*

Benning glanced at the pad. "What the heck, Jim. I can't *know* which men are essential till I know what we'll have to do later."

"Just assume it's the usual thing, Ben. We've been through this before." He pulled the pad over, and read:

He didn't say. Personally, I doubt it.

Heyden wrote: *We better explain this package, in case there's something outside.*

Benning read it, and nodded.

Heyden said, "Well, forget that for now. What have you got over there in that paper?"

Benning shrugged. "A little promotion gizmo." He rattled the paper. "See, you look in these portholes, and you're inside the space-ship. Shows our control panel, amongst other things, for the Genie Project."

"Cute," conceded Heyden, smiling wryly. "Well that's down the drain now. Wrap it up and forget it."

"Based on the old-time stereoscope," said Benning, putting the actual board with its box and rheostat inside the paper wrapper. "Too bad. It seemed like a good—"

Heyden wrote on the pad, *Let's go somewhere where we can talk.* Aloud, he said sourly, "Put it on the back burner. Now, I've had enough of this for a while. Where are you headed?"

Benning glanced at the pad. "Back to my lab. You want to come along?"

Heyden put Grossrad's latest note in his pocket. "Sure."

III

They went out, walked down a lengthy corridor, went into a big airy structure built on the general lines of a hangar for dirigibles, walked along the wall to the right, and finally arrived at a door marked, "Private—Danger—Keep Out."

Heyden followed Benning inside, and down a short hall. Benning did something complicated at the door, then they stepped in. Benning snapped on the lights, then flipped another switch, and the room filled with sounds of laughing voices, the clink of glasses, cars starting up somewhere in the background, and a close-at-hand murmur and mumble that seemed to include every tone of voice conceivable.

"Okay," murmured Benning, "I think this room is safe enough, but if they *have* got anything in here, they're welcome to try and filter it out from this mess. You did see what we've got, plainly enough, back in your office?"

"I saw it. But did you see what we're going to run into when we try to convince Grossrad?"

"He couldn't be so stupid he wouldn't catch on to this."

"That's not the point. He says new gadgets aren't *wanted*. This means somebody higher up figures we've now settled down to a nice international stalemate, with us ahead of the opposition. This device, it strikes me, is going to make a lot of expensive equipment obsolete in a hurry."

"You're not just kidding. With this, we could put a man on the moon in a few weeks, not years from now. And that's just the start."

"What the Sam Hill is it, anyway?"

Benning frowned. "Did you ever hear the comparison of gravitational fields with the bending of frictionless surfaces?"

"I think I know what you mean. If you had a flat frictionless surface, flexible enough to bend when objects were placed on it, and if this whole frictionless surface were accelerating uniformly at right angles to the plane of the surface—"

Benning nodded. "That's it."

Heyden went on. "If you had such a frictionless surface, an object would slide across it in a straight line until it neared another object, when the dip in the surface caused by these objects would pull them toward each other. There would be, apparently, a 'gravitational field' around each object, the strength of the 'field' depending on the mass of the object."

"Exactly. This would cause the effect of attraction. Now, how would you create *repulsion*?"

"Well—" Heyden frowned. "There would have to be a hill—a ridge, or rise, in the frictionless surface. You could do it only if the surface had some other property—if it were made of the right metal, for instance, you could position magnets toward the stern of a properly shaped object resting on the surface, and this might create enough slope to cause the object to slide forward."

Benning was nodding and smiling broadly. "That's one idea. And how much power would it take?"

"It would depend on the properties of the surface."

"Yes. Well, we started this project without much hope that there was any physical counterpart to this comparison. But after tracking down some previously unexplained discrepancies, we found it. The effect can be made comparatively large, the power consumption is small, and by proper manipulation, we can create either a positive or negative deflection of the 'surface'. The result is, we've got a space drive."

Heyden sat back, and thought it over. "This just *could* be a nightmare. How complicated is it?"

"Mathematically, it's very complicated. Physically, it's not bad."

"This might make life very exasperating for everybody concerned with it."

Benning frowned. "Of course, it's bound to be highly classified. They'll doubtless bury it under a ton of regulations, but—Oh." Benning was silent. "Naturally, *we* discovered it. We shouldn't be running around at loose ends, ready to spill the works in the nearest bar."

"Naturally. That's one aspect. But there are others. Now, how much leverage do you get with this thing? How much advantage over a rocket, for instance?"

"Agh. Ye gods, a rocket."

"Could it beat a rocket for *speed*?"

"Easy. Weight for weight—I mean weight at rest with the device turned off—there's no comparison."

"How about for lifting a payload?"

"There's still no comparison. You don't have to lift a lot of cargo you're just going to fire out the tail end anyway."

"Could you put a warhead in one of these and hit within five miles a thousand miles away?"

Benning hesitated. "Not yet."

"But eventually?"

After a long silence, Benning said, "For accuracy, used as a missile power source, I fail to see any advantage in this. But you could knock one of your opponent's missiles off course with it. You might even smash it up in mid-air."

"How would you do that?"

"Make one big enough, with enough power back of it, make a strong enough mount and screw the thing down to a solid base— What do you think you've got? It's a tractor-repulsor unit. You can make a steep 'hill' in the 'frictionless surface' the missile is sliding along. What does that interpret as in physical reality? A violent repulsion. Then you can make a trough. Subject anything to sudden yanks and shoves, and what happens to it?"

Heyden nodded slowly.

Benning said, "Didn't I see you pick up Grossrad's note before we left?"

"Yes, you want it?"

"I'd like to look it over again."

Heyden felt through his pockets, and handed the note to Benning. Benning read the note amidst gales of hurrying girlish laughter that grew loud and faded, with male curses, mumbling, a variety of audible conversations, and a weird varying note in the background.

Benning grunted and looked up. "He sure doesn't leave any doubt about this 'no new advances wanted at this time'."

Heyden nodded. "That's what bothers me."

"But," said Benning, "Any good business man can see the potential in this."

"What potential? Where's the profit in something you can never put on the market because it's sure to be classified?"

"Well, the defense contracts, then."

Heyden shook his head gloomily. "Remember: 'we are now so far ahead of the international competition, defensewise, that no large new government orders can be expected.'"

Benning said angrily, "Can't you convince that guy—"

"Probably, but so what? Grossrad doesn't write contracts with himself. Suppose I convince him? Then he's got to convince somebody else. That guy has to convince the next one. At some point in there, someone conceivably may have to convince the defense secretary, and *he* may have to convince Congress. This is assuming it goes through all those offices and ever comes out again. Each of those guys is going to be hard to convince, precisely because he knows how hard it's going to be to convince the next man. Meanwhile, all we can do is chew our nails and wait for their decision."

Benning said, "While we're waiting, what if somebody else, say in some foreign laboratory, maybe even where they've got pictures of Big Brother hanging on the wall—What if they should come up with this?"

"Is that conceivable?"

"Sure, it's conceivable. I told you, physically, this thing is not too bad." He frowned. "Well, what then?"

Heyden frowned. "As soon as they make it public, count on us to get a contract so big we couldn't fill it if we were General Motors, U.S. Steel, and A.T. and T. combined. We'll have to kidnap every scientist and technician we can lay our hands on."

Benning said angrily, "We're missing something here. What if they don't make it public? What if they quietly build up a fleet of these things while we're sitting around waiting for the go-ahead? They could seal off outer space so tight we'd never get out there." An intense look appeared on Benning's face. "Think, Jim—what if they're building them *right now*?"

Heyden blinked, gave an irritated wave of his hand as if to dismiss the thought, then frowned. "How hard is it to make these things?"

"I've *told* you. The actual physical construction isn't too bad, once you know what to do."

There was a long period in which neither man said anything. Then Heyden said slowly, "You said, 'With this, we could put a man on the moon *in a few weeks.*' Did you mean that literally?"

Benning nodded. "Remember all the research that's already been done. Think of the problems we *don't* have, because the drive is no worry. Think how we're set up here. Sure, in three weeks, we could put a man on the moon."

"Could you mount the drive so it could also be used as a weapon?"

"Yes. And, for that matter, a smaller one could serve as an auxiliary weapon in flight, if you wanted. But it would take money."

Heyden thought it over, then grinned. "If Grossrad's going to have his Kiddie Kits ready in time, he's going to have to give us money."

"Are you serious?"

"Yes, I'm serious. This is the biggest technological advance in history."

Benning was wide eyed. "And what you're thinking of making is a full-size spaceship—good enough for an *actual expedition*?"

"That's exactly what I want—if we can make such a thing. No trim. No flimflam. Just let it work."

Benning seemed to lose some enthusiasm. "This is risky."

Heyden nodded. "You bet your life, it's risky. If Grossrad gets wind of it I'll be hung from the rafters. But never mind that. Are you sure you can *do* it?"

"Of course I'm sure." Benning frowned. "Right now we can do this better than Kiddie Kits. A month from now, if we follow Grossrad's letter, it'll be a different story. But—"

"Then this may be the only chance our side gets. We'd better take it."

Benning drew a deep shaky breath. "Okay."

IV

The next two weeks passed in a blur of desperate activity that left Heyden no time to think of anything but the problem immediately in front of him. Benning's remark that a man could be put on the moon in a few weeks turned out to be a little optimistic.

Benning said exasperatedly, "I didn't figure in all that life-support stuff. So far as the drive is concerned, that's what I meant."

Heyden said angrily, "We could have put a corpse on the moon a long time ago."

"I'm sorry," said Benning. "We're coming fast, anyway. Thank heaven the thing is basically simple."

Before them loomed a big black shape like an overgrown boiler. It had all the sophistication of a sledge-hammer, but Benning insisted it could take off inside a week.

"You see," he said, "the only real problem with the drive is durability under stress. Theoretically, we could use that demonstration model I showed you. The trouble is that in practice if the drive-unit is too small, it will crush."

"That's nice. But we've got around that, have we?"

"Yes."

Heyden eyed the looming black boiler shape. "We don't want to get out there and get cooked."

"The other side shades from black into a pure reflective coating."

"How do we see out of it? In addition to the radar, which may fail on us?"

"There's a window in the end. Also, we're practicing with a light-weight kind of drive-unit. We figure we can use that as a sort of detector."

"How does it work?"

"To create a given negative bending or warping where there's a physical object present takes more power than where there isn't. Set things up right, and you can read the mass of the given object off a meter."

"How about the distance?"

"The reading drops in front and behind the object. There's no problem there."

Heyden stared at the looming shape and nodded slowly. He had no clear idea *why* there was no problem there; but there was nothing to do but take Benning's word for it, and hope things would turn out. He turned to make a final comment, then paused.

A bulky overalled form had just ducked out the door of the boiler-shape, and now, scowling deeply, pushed through a knot of people standing just outside. Carrying a flimsy sheet of yellow paper, he headed straight for Benning, and immediately got down to brass tacks.

"That inside-drive idea won't work. If we try that, we're going to swivel that drive around, stress the walls, and crack the window on the end. That leaves us with an air-leak. That drive has to go *outside*."

"That's insane," said Benning angrily. "With that size unit, the whole ship's inside the distortion."

"Maybe, but there's a fringe effect."

"We're inside it."

"We are? Look at this."

Benning took the paper. "Well . . . this is just a freakish—"

"Maybe it doesn't last long, but what's it going to do to that window?"

"Yes, but if we put it outside, it will *still*—"

"Not if we have it on a boom. That puts us outside that gradient."

Benning stared at him. "How long a boom?"

"About two hundred feet should do it."

"Two *hundred*—"

"Unless you can breathe vacuum, that's where it's got to go, if we make it that size."

Benning was staring at the flimsy sheet of paper as there came the sound of a feminine throat-clearing to Heyden's right. He glanced around to see his secretary holding out a special-delivery letter. Leaving Benning to deal with the technical problem, Heyden headed back to his office, and read the handwritten letter:

Jim—

Well, boy, we've got the merger, but doing business with this outfit really puts your wallet through the wringer. I hope you're coming along fine with the Kiddie Kits. We'll need every cent we can scrape up, so pare expenses to the bone, and shave everything just as fine as you can. We're going to have to cut down more than I expected on the scientific talent, and I just hope we can pick them up again when we need them.

I know how this Kiddie Kit business must strike you after the stuff we've been working on, but when the oasis gets this dry, there's nothing to do but fold your tents and move on. Nothing we could produce, no matter how advanced, would get a really sympathetic hearing right now.

I don't mean to dwell on this, Jim. I know we can count on you all the way, even if it is a let-down. I keep harping on it because I think this toy business is going to make the difference, one way or the other. It's hard to believe, I know, but there it is.

Ed and I are both totally worn out. There are some things that you have to do in business that aren't very business-like, but there's no time to argue about that. You either do them or get kicked in the head, and somebody else walks off with the prize.

I must be more worn-out than I realized to go on like this. Well, here's to the merger, and stick to those Kiddie Kits. You don't know what it means to know we've got somebody back there we can count on.

We'll see you in a week, Jim.

Stu

Heyden swallowed and sat back dizzily.

When his vision cleared, there stood, across the desk, an apologetic individual from Purchasing. "Sorry, sir, but it seems we have to have your signature on this."

Heyden took it, and scowled at the figures. "Are you sure the addition is right?"

"Yes, sir. That special silver wire is expensive stuff."

Heyden sat still for a moment, then scratched out his name. The paper was briskly whisked away.

"Thank you, sir." The door shut, and the incident was gone beyond recall. Heyden picked up the note, read it through again, and shook his head. He started to get up, then changed his mind. He sat still a minute, then drew in a deep breath and let it out in a rough sigh. The realization went though him with inescapable finality that in seven days the ship would be ready or not ready.

And then something else, that he'd been vaguely aware of theoretically took on a sudden solidness and reality.

In seven days, he would be either a hero of broad vision, or a fool and a traitor.

And there was not a thing he could do about it.

He had made his move, and if it didn't work out, he could never, never explain it.

The first four or five days after that crawled past with Heyden almost in a daze. Time and again, between emergencies, he dredged up memories, trying to discover exactly how he had gotten into this. The astonishing thing was that, in retrospect the decision seemed to have been so easy. Blandly, calmly, he had given the decision that might wreck the corporation, and land him, personally, in the worst mess he'd ever been in.

His meditations were enlivened, toward the end of the week, by a telephone call from the comptroller.

"Hello, Jim?"

"Right here, Sam." Heyden tried without success to inject a little warmth into his voice. His voice retained a calm unconcerned coolness.

There was a hesitant cough over the phone. "Say, no offense, Jim, but what the devil is going on there?"

"Business as usual," came Heyden's voice, cool and totally assured. "Granted the changes that I'm sure Stu must have told you about."

"Well, Stu told me—" There was a brief pause. "Do you know something I don't know? Is that it?"

Heyden laughed. The sound was that of a man without a worry in the world. "Sam," his voice said cheerfully, "before I know if I know anything you don't know, I know you know I have to know what *you* know, otherwise I won't know, you know, if what I know is something you *don't* know."

"Ah, for—" Over the phone, the cautious voice sounded irritated but relieved. "Listen, we can kid all we want, but this is serious business."

"It *is*," said Heyden emphatically. After a moment, he added, "Thank heaven."

"What do you mean? Wait a minute, now, do you mean—" There was a long silence. "I know of course, that the merger went through, but I didn't realize—Do you mean that we're frying *their* fish?"

"All I can say is, this here is *serious* business. If Stu didn't tell you, I'm not going into it over the phone."

"What if I come down there?"

"Glad to see you anytime, Sam. But I can't mention it if Stu didn't."

"Did Stu say, specifically, *not* to tell me?"

"No. Of course not."

"Then why can't you—"

"Because he didn't tell me *to* mention it."

"Maybe I better call *him* up."

"No harm in it. Just don't give anything away over the phone."

"Then how the devil am I—"

Heyden said irritatedly, "Look, Sam, I'm sure it was an oversight on his part. Stu doesn't make a practice of leaving anyone in the dark. But he was worn out. I don't know what he had to do to put the merger across, but he seemed pretty thoroughly wrung out to me. Now, you can either try to locate him now, or you can wait a couple of days till he can tell you himself."

"All right. But meanwhile we're spending—"

Heyden exploded. "What do I have to do, spell it out? For Pete's sake, Sam! Look, do you think Stuart Grossrad is a commercial moron? With things the way they are now, would he deliberately stretch us out as thin as a rubber band? This merger wasn't a cheap proposition, you know."

"Well—the point of the merger was that, ultimately we'd reap the advantages of diversification."

"How would that get us through the next six months?"

There was a lengthy silence. Finally there was a long sigh over the telephone. "Did Stu tell you this beforehand?"

"Beforehand, all he told me was such a tale of misery I almost drowned in my own tears. No. He didn't tell me a thing, *beforehand*. What I couldn't figure out was why he was so eager for this merger, if there wasn't more in it than what he mentioned."

"He's smooth, all right. He wanted us psychologically set up to take full advantage of this. Or, if the merger fell through, he didn't want us moping around, thinking we'd lost our last chance. Either way it went, he was ready."

"I suppose that must have been it."

"Well—I just had to find out. No hard feelings, Jim?"

"Of course not, Sam. Any time."

"See you, boy."

"So long, Sam."

Heyden put the phone in its cradle, and mopped his forehead. He had, if Sam remained convinced, succeeded in hanging on to two more days. If, that is, Grossrad didn't decide to come back early. If there were no other catastrophes. Heyden glanced at his watch, and decided to go take a look and see how Benning was coming along.

It took Heyden some time to walk down the long corridor, but only a few moments more to find his answer. The big boiler shape stood in solitary glory in the hangar-like building, apparently forgotten. Everyone was fifty feet away, crowded around a smoldering mess about a foot-and-a-half long and eight inches in diameter, and that had, apparently, once been something useable. Benning had his hand at his chin, staring at this ruin. He, and the rest of the men, all looked so dazed and tired that Heyden didn't have the heart to ask what had happened. Wearily, he shut the door, went back to his office, and sat down.

"Well, Stu," he said mentally, "you see I thought we could make it to the moon . . . Yes, the *moon* . . . Yes, I know the thing doesn't work, Stu . . . That's where all the money went, Stu . . . That's right . . . Yes, Stu . . . Sorry . . . Yes . . . That's right, Stu—I mean Mr. Grossrad . . . Yes, Mr. Grossrad, I did it on my own responsibility . . . Yes, sir, I know, but—You see, sir, if somebody else had got it— And if it *had* worked, Mr. Grossrad, then . . . I know it didn't sir, but—"

Heyden abruptly sat up, and smashed his fist on the desk. "Damn it," he said savagely, "it's *got* to work!"

By the time he got to Benning again, Benning looked glassy-eyed with pure stupefaction, and the others had expressions that varied from ordinary gloom to total defeatist resignation.

Heyden told himself that he would have to keep himself under tight control.

"What's this?" he said abruptly, and a good deal louder than he'd intended.

Instantly, every eye in the room was focused on him. They watched him with the alert attention a man gets when he breaks the silence by cracking a bullwhip.

Benning turned around, his expression that of bafflement and disbelief. "This size builds up heat faster than we imagined. It's got to have a cooling system."

"Is that the drive-unit for the ship?"

"No, this is the forward unit. The ship drive-unit is bound to be worse yet."

"How long to rig up a cooling system?"

"Too long. We've not only got to cool the drive-unit itself, we've then got to unload all the heat from the cooling system. The stupefying thing is, we tested for this with smaller units, and the heat build-up was gradual and well within bounds. We've apparently run into some effect that increases exponentially with mass, while thrust—"

"Can you get the same thrust with a group of small units as with one large one?"

Benning blinked. "It wouldn't be as *efficient*, but yes, we *could* do that."

"Any drawbacks to having a bunch of them?"

"Yes. All the mounts have to be duplicated."

"Why not mount them together?"

"If they're too close, we've discovered they interact."

"Can you mount them far enough apart so they don't interact, but not so far apart as to make control impossible?"

"Yes, but the expense—"

"Damn the expense," said Heyden savagely. "How long will it take?"

Benning mopped his forehead. "If we work straight through without a break we can have it ready the day after tomorrow."

"All right. Starting now, everyone who volunteers to work straight through, and who sticks with it, gets quadruple pay, and a thousand-dollar bonus after taxes, if the job's done on time."

There was a brief sudden burst of excitement.

"My God!" blurted Benning.

"Look what's at stake!" said Heyden angrily. "Control of space! A drive that can reach the planets! All the high-grade ore in the asteroid belt! Are we going to fold up, or are we going to get it?" He paused just long enough to see the glint in their eyes, then turned to Benning. "What do you need?"

Benning said soberly, "A list as long as your arm."

"Let's have it."

Benning got him off away from the others. "Listen, do you know what's going to happen to you if—"

"It's too late for that."

"I wish I'd never brought that damned thing to your office."

"We've taken a flying jump, and we're now halfway out over the crevasse. There's no point wishing we'd never jumped. We've got to go the rest of the way and put our mind on grabbing any bush or clump of grass that will get us over the lip of that drop."

Benning swallowed. "Okay."

"Now listen," said Heyden. "You're going to need plenty of hot coffee in here, and I don't know if you can literally keep going without *any* break. We don't want a bunch of zombies staggering around in here holding the wrong end of the wrench."

"You're right. Could we have some rough army blankets and some narrow folding cots? That's heaven for an exhausted man, but he shouldn't be too reluctant to get up."

"Good idea. Now *can* you finish it by the day after tomorrow?"

Benning nodded. "If, God willing, nothing *else* goes wrong."

V

The next day was a nightmare. Suppliers were beginning to need reassurance about pay. A weird rumor was making the rounds, to the effect that Grossrad had stripped the corporation treasury and was now settled down in Brazil with a nicely tanned blonde mistress, the two of them living cozily in a mansion with an Olympic-sized swimming pool outdoors, and gold-plated faucets indoors.

Heyden put the rumor down temporarily by showing the two hand-addressed envelopes from Grossrad, with their recent postmarks, but the rumor failed to *stay* down. It popped up again with new refinements. Someone who looked just like Grossrad had been seen in Brazil by Milton Sharpbinder, vice-president of Interdisciplinary Intellectronics, and Milton had immediately called back to sell his holdings in Continental Multitechnikon before the bottom fell out. Somebody else had actually been out near Grossrad's Brazilian mansion, and had seen him lolling with a bottle in a deck chair while the blonde did laps in the Olympic-sized pool.

The details mounted up fantastically. Grossrad had been seen wheeling around the streets of Rio driving a Mercedes-Benz roadster. Later information had it that it was a 1959 300SL Mercedes-Benz with removable hardtop, and Grossrad was gripping a long thin cigar between his teeth, and had one arm casually around the blonde. Somehow, the burgeoning details added further solidity to the rumor, which grew yet more solid as Grossrad moved on and was seen with the blonde at Copacabana.

That this was not just a local rumor developed as Continental Multitechnikon began to slide on the stock market while other space stocks were creeping upward. This, in turn, seemed to support the rumor. In the midst of this, with suppliers demanding payment, the phone rang, and a familiar voice jumped out:

"Say, Heyden, what the hell is going on out there? I just got a phone call from Sam, and he's—"

"Stu?" shouted Heyden, his voice filled with synthetic delight. "Hello? Is that you?"

"Is it me? Who the—"

"Hold on! Listen, we've got a bunch of guys here who think—wait a minute. Where are you calling from?"

"Where am I calling from? Santa Barbara. What about it? Listen, what—"

"Where have you been the last week?"

"I've been holed up, getting over what we had to go through to get that merger across, what do you think? Didn't you get my letter? Listen, what the—"

"We've got a bunch of guys here that claim they won't supply us, because you're down in Brazil with a blonde, rolling around in a Mercedes 300SL."

"I'm what?"

Before Heyden could say anything, one of the men in the room said nervously, "Is that him? How do we know—"

Heyden said, "I don't know if you heard that, Stu. They think maybe this isn't you. Could you talk to a few of these—"

"Wait a minute now. What is this? I don't get this."

"Brace yourself. There's a rumor afloat that you've disappeared, vanished completely, and someone like you has been seen in Rio by—get this, Stu—by Milton Sharpbinder, who immediately dumped all his holdings in Continental before the news of what had happened got out."

"Sharpbinder, eh?"

"Yes, and someone else definitely saw you living in a mansion down there with gold plumbing and a big swimming pool. It seems you were outside by the pool, taking the sun, watching this blonde plow back and forth."

Grossrad laughed.

Heyden said, "Before you laugh this off have you taken a look at the financial page lately?"

On the other end of the line, Grossrad was starting to have hysteria, but that brought him around.

"No," he said, "that's one thing I *haven't* been doing. I've been trying to get a rest. Is this stupid play by Sharpbinder actually—"

"We're going down. Everybody else is going up."

"That boob is just one week too late to hurt us. If this drop had come *last* week, without our having any idea what was wrong—"

"Just the same, I still don't think it would hurt if you showed yourself out there."

"I will. Now, let me speak to a few of these boys that think I'm in Brazil."

Heyden said, "Okay," and held out the phone.

A few minutes later, Grossrad was saying to Heyden, "I had no idea this was the trouble. Sam went through all kinds of verbal contortions trying to tell me something without giving away anything. The impression I got was that *you* were making off with the treasury, not me." He laughed. "I was relieved to even hear your voice."

Heyden laughed. "*I* was relieved to hear *you*. I was starting to believe this business about the blonde."

Grossrad laughed so hard Heyden had to hold the phone out away from his ear. Then Grossrad, half-choked, said, "Say, Jim, you won't skip out now? You *will* be there when I get back?"

"Either here, or halfway to the moon."

"I know what you mean." Grossrad burst out laughing again. "I was in orbit myself for a little bit there. Well, so long, Jim. I'm going out and make myself public."

Heyden felt like a hollow shell as he put the phone back in its cradle. But, with an effort of will, he looked deliberately around the room, and studied the shamefaced glances that looked back at him.

"Now," he said, with forced calm, "can we go back to doing business on a normal basis?"

No one offered any objection.

The needed supplies came in, but the tension failed to ease. The final day was the worst. The comptroller came to Heyden's office while Heyden was on pins and needles to go see Benning, and it was a precious half-hour before Heyden could get free. Then, just as he was leaving his office, a telegram arrived from Grossrad telling when he would be back. Heyden glanced at his watch and saw with a shock that he had only two hours and fifteen minutes left. If he wasn't at the airport, Grossrad would be puzzled, and then curious. If he was at the airport, Grossrad would be bound to question him about the Kiddie Kits, and the lack of work he had done on them would show up quickly. Either way, the lid would be off inside an hour more at the longest. That gave him three hours and fifteen minutes.

Heyden sucked in a deep breath, forced himself to look brisk and confident, and went to see Benning.

He found Benning slumped on a bench with his head in his hands.

Heyden stared around. A number of men were asleep on cots, or rolled up in a blanket on the floor. Several were at the big coffee boiler filling their cups.

Heyden looked at the spaceship. Despite what he'd said about forgetting appearance, the overgrown-boiler look had been softened, at least from this angle. There was a shining silvery surface, that shaded off to one side. Heyden blinked, and glanced at Benning.

"Say, you've moved this?"

Benning looked up drearily.

Heyden glanced uneasily back at the spaceship, with its radiating arms holding what must be the drive-units.

"Ben" he said. "It's all right, isn't it?"

Benning looked down at the ground. "It doesn't work."

Heyden shut his eyes.

Benning's voice reached him. "I'm so tired I can't think. It worked once. We rotated the ship on minimum power. It was smooth—perfect. And it apparently burned something out. We're all half-dead. We've checked and checked."

Heyden forced himself to be sympathetic. "You've been working overtime for three weeks." He sucked in a long breath. "Is everything on board that I had on that list?"

"Everything. But it doesn't work. There's no response at all."

"How long to fix it?"

"We'll have to tear it down completely."

"How long?"

"Another three weeks."

Heyden sank down onto the bench beside Benning.

"Oh, God," said Benning miserably. "Jim, I'm so sorry I got you into this."

"Yeah," said Heyden.

"It's a flop," said Benning. "We should have taken more time to test it. We ran off half-cocked."

Heyden didn't say anything.

Benning said, "All that *money*. I'm so sorry, Jim. What will Grossrad do?"

Heyden shut his eyes.

Benning's voice came through. "We must have been crazy. That's the only explanation. No one ever does anything like this. Well, now we pay the piper."

Heyden dizzily looked up to see the big shiny boiler through a haze. Someone was leaning out the door, and put his hands to his mouth like a megaphone.

"Hey, Chief. The trouble is, somebody left this master switch open, back of the control panel."

Benning sat paralyzed for an instant, then sprang from the bench. He was across the floor and inside the ship before Heyden realized what had happened.

Slowly, the meaning seeped through to Heyden. He watched.

The big silver form lifted, hovered, and then smoothly rotated, the radiating arms swinging around like the spokes of a giant wheel, the central hub shading from silver to gray to black, then back to silver again. Smoothly it settled down, with a faint grating crunch.

Heyden stood up. Across the room, the sound of that faint crunch turned men around at the coffee boiler. An instant later, they recognized the ship's changed position, set their cups down with a bang, let out a wild yell, and ran to wake up the men on the cots and stretched out on the floor.

Heyden was still fervently thanking God when the men burst into cheers. Then Benning was wringing him by the hand. All around the huge room, it seemed that people were banging each other on the back.

Heyden sucked in a deep breath. "Listen, when can we take off?"

"Take off?" Benning looked blank. "We're finished. The thing's ready. It's completed, and it works."

Heyden stared at him. "Do we talk different languages? What do you think we're going to do now?"

Benning stared at him. "Show it to Grossrad. It's finished. It works. He'll see"

Heyden opened his mouth and shut it with a click. "You remember what I said we wanted? A full-size actual spaceship, so far as we could make such a thing. Now that we've *got* it, you think we're going to just *show it to Grossrad*? What good would *that* do? Outer space is in our hands, *now*, if that ship will do what we think it will do. And yet, what can Grossrad do with it but use it as a working model? What good does that do?"

Benning swallowed. "You mean, *we*—"

"Who else? Have we gone through all this to quit now? We have to carry this through all the way to the finish."

Benning paled. "I though we were going to make a demonstration."

"We are. When can we take off?"

"I thought all that food and the cargo and that other gear was just to make it look good. More realistic. More—"

"The idea is to keep us from starving out there, and to fix it so we can get some use out of this. Will that radio work?"

"Everything should work."

"Then," said Heyden, "let's get a crew and get out of here before something else goes wrong. It shouldn't be hard to get volunteers, should it? Can you pick the men who'll be most help to us?"

Benning grinned suddenly. "We're going to try to do this like Lindbergh?"

"Why not?"

"What about germs on the moon? What about—"

Heyden said brutally, "If you don't want to go, say so now."

Benning paused. "I want to go."

"Then pick the crew while I write a note to Grossrad."

Benning nodded, and started over toward the coffee boiler. Heyden whirled, and went back to his office. He yanked out a sheet of paper, and wrote fast:

Stu—
When you receive this, we should be, as I jokingly said earlier, on our way to the moon. Only, this is real.

Now, this is the first commercial venture into space, and no doubt the Government will blow all its fuses. Nevertheless, it is up to us to make it pay. First, I'm afraid that at the moment we're in something of a hole, financially; but we have powerful radios, along with enough lights and selected chemicals to make ourselves seen, and it seems to me there are a few commercial outfits around that ought to be happy to pay through the nose to have a commercial beamed toward earth from the moon.

Charge more for the visual stuff, Stu. When the Government screams, point out that they will get their cut of the profits in due time.

There is doubtless a whole lot of rock and dust on the moon that it wouldn't break our backs to load into the ship, and that would sell for a price per pound to rival solid platinum, but I'm sure there will be objections to that.

As the next best thing, I've gotten a large quantity of thin sheet metal and loaded it on board. While we're out there, we will orbit the moon. When we come back, we can stamp out millions of little flat space-ship models, which can be colored suitably and molded in plastic for souvenirs. Bear in mind, each one of these will have been around the moon and back.

Next, we have a large cargo of fabric, Stu, which will also go around the moon, and can be cut up into moon scarves and moon dresses when we get back.

Figure out what you can make on this, without having to charge anybody more than he will cheerfully pay for the vicarious pleasure of taking part in this trip. If this doesn't cover expenses, and leave enough over for handsome bonuses all around, I'll be surprised.

Incidentally, you might put some of this money into a special fund—I may need it for bail bond.

Jim

Heyden put the letter in an envelope, wrote Grossrad's name on the outside, and gave it to his secretary to deliver.

He went back down the corridor, found Benning waiting with his chosen crew, and climbed on board. The ship slid smoothly and easily out the big opened doors, paused momentarily, and the ground began to fall away.

Heyden was beginning to have doubts. He stepped back as Benning shut the door, and said, "How are the odds on our getting out there and having some little thing strand us a hundred thousand miles from home?"

"Surprisingly poor," said Benning, "assuming we can count on odds at all when we're dealing with something this new."

"Why? I mean, why are the odds against us poor?"

"The amount of weight we can lift with this drive. Suppose just half the weight that goes into the lower stages of a chemical rocket could be added to the payload. Think of the added space, stronger materials, spares, and general increased margin of safety. After you work on stuff to be lifted by rocket, this is a dream."

Heyden relaxed and glanced around. They were standing in a small chamber with a second door partly open behind them. He became conscious of a continued sensation like that of rising in a very fast elevator.

Benning said, "All the same, this is incredible, in a way."

"That—we hope—we're going to the moon?"

"No, we're used to that idea, fantastic as it would have seemed a few years ago." He frowned. "No, it's—it's—"

Heyden suddenly caught the thought. "That we're just *doing* it?"

Benning sighed. "Yes. Without filling out forms in quintuplicate. Without stewing over it. Without a hundred changes of direction and reevaluations."

Heyden nodded. "But that's supposed to be more 'scientific'."

"It's more bureaucratic, anyway. But even if a method *is* more scientific, that's beside the point. The point is *to get the job done*," said Benning.

He stood thinking back to that endless interval when the ship sat dead on the ground and Benning told him the whole thing was a failure, and when the weight of failure crushed him down. Then he'd learned in his bones the penalty of following one's own judgment against the shrewd decisions of superiors—when one's own judgment turns out to be wrong.

But now, beneath his feet he could feel the solid unvarying

thrust, lifting them up at constant acceleration and steadily increasing speed.

Down far below now were the nations of the earth, run by monster bureaucracies made up of many people who hesitated—partly because they sensed the awful penalty for failure—to take the risk of questioning even the most self-defeating procedures.

And yet, here were Heyden and Benning and their men, high above the bureaucrats, and rising higher fast, because they *had* risked disgrace and disaster. They were only here by the skin of their teeth, and Heyden was beginning to realize from his reaction just how long he would think before taking a risk like *that* again.

But, all the same, they were *here*.

"Come on," said Heyden, walking a little heavily under the steadily maintained thrust. "Let's either get to a place where we can sit down, or get up front to that window. *Maybe* we could see the moon."

Doc's Legacy

Felix N. Muir, A.S., forgot the beautiful summer morning outside as he glanced from James Allen, Director of Research, to the gadget that Allen with studied casualness was unloading onto Muir's desk.

At first sight, the device looked like a pocket calculator. But where the display should be, there was a meter; and where there should be rows of push buttons, there were just two grey buttons, with an additional black button around on the side. Connected by a thick electric cord was a small megaphone-shaped apparatus of slender copper rod.

As Muir came to his feet, Allen gave a genial nod, then reached back for the knob of the hall door. Plainly enough, the Director of Research was about to toss Muir a few words of instruction, and depart.

Muir, though still new at this job, moved fast, and pulled over a chair.

"Have a seat, Dr. Allen."

"Oh," said Allen, "I don't have time—"

"And what is this?"

Allen favored Muir with a friendly man-to-man smile.

"It's just a little—you know, a—ah—toy—of Doc's. I want you to—"

Muir blinked. In this company, "Doc" meant just one person.

"Toy? Of Dr. Griswell?"

Allen got his hand on the knob. "Yes. Now, I want you—"

The words were out before Muir had time to think: "If this belonged to Dr. Griswell, I don't touch it without an explanation."

Allen's face lost its friendly smile. "See here, Muir—"

Muir's thoughts caught up with his reactions, and he added persuasively, "Suppose someone gave you a bottle of yellowish oily liquid, Dr. Allen? Wouldn't you be uneasy if it turned out to be nitroglycerine?"

"Glyceryl trinitrate. Well, that is a—h'm—mistaken comparison." Allen hesitated, cast a penetrating glance at Muir, and added, "But I see your point." He pulled over the chair, and uneasily moved the little megaphone-shaped device so it aimed elsewhere than at him. "You're comparatively new here, Muir. What do you know about Doc Griswell?"

"Well—He invented the asterator."

"Do you understand the asterator?"

"As far as the mechanism is concerned, I don't remotely understand it. As for the effect, I know what's common knowledge."

"Namely?"

"The asterator has a number of reaction chambers. Each chamber emits a narrow beam. Just as glass is transparent to light, ordinary matter is transparent to the asterator beam. The beams can focus on a common target. In a target containing unstable nuclei, the nuclei decompose."

"The significance of this—?"

"Nuclear weapons and reactors contain a lot of unstable nuclei. If an asterator focuses on them, the weapon or reactor blows up."

Allen nodded. "And the political effect?"

"Not long ago, the major powers had arsenals of nuclear weapons. Then Doc Griswell invented the asterator. Suddenly a nuclear weapon was more dangerous to its possessor than to anyone else. The result was rapid voluntary nuclear disarmament, which is still going on."

"And Dr. Griswell?"

"Dr. Griswell's car crashed into a stone wall before the facts came out."

Allen nodded soberly. "The asterator was a work of extraordinary genius, or a remarkable accidental discovery—Or, perhaps, both. But for Doc Griswell it was a tragedy. Doc wanted safe, trouble-free nuclear power. The wave of accidents, when the asterator was first tested, was completely unexpected. And, of course, no one realized at first that the asterator was the cause. Doc evidently blamed himself, and—" Allen's voice briefly choked.

Muir said sympathetically, "Well—They said it was suicide. But who knows? Where his car went off the road, there's a sharp curve. If he was distracted—"

"You're familiar with the spot?"

"I drove out there one night. There are big evergreens that cast dense shadows in the moonlight. With the wall and the curve hidden in the shadows, that spot looks like two or three perfectly harmless places on the road."

"But Doc's headlights—"

"On high beam, on the rise just before the curve, the lights lift up off the road. The danger isn't clear."

Allen stared across the room. "Beasley and I blamed ourselves, and felt guilty. You see, we worked very closely with Doc, but he didn't trust us enough to take us into his confidence when things went wrong."

"That's assuming he deliberately drove into that wall. But suppose, as he neared the curve, that a thought occurred to him about the asterator? All it takes there is night, a fast car, the moon in a part of the sky to cast the right shadows, and one second's distraction. He knew the road; but he may not have had that combination before."

Allen sat silent for a moment, then cleared his throat. "Gloria Griswell brought the touchstone in yesterday."

Muir looked blank.

Allen said, "Gloria is Doc's widow. The device I just put on your desk is what Doc called his 'touchstone.'"

Muir looked at the meter, push buttons, and electric cord with its small cone-shaped apparatus. "A 'touchstone' is used to test whether something is genuine. What kind of—"

"Exactly the sort of question I'd like you to investigate, Muir."

Muir cast him a fishy look. "And Mrs. Griswell?"

"What about her?"

"Dr. Griswell died almost two years ago, didn't he? Why did his widow only bring this in yesterday?"

"Roughly two years ago. Yes. I was surprised to see her."

"Why did she bring it in now?"

"She wanted it out of the house."

"Why, after having it around that long, did she only now want it out of the house?"

Allen looked at Muir approvingly. "You're quick, Muir. You really should try for a higher degree."

"Not with my temperament. Why did Mrs. Griswell suddenly want to get rid of this device?"

"What does your temperament have to do with it?"

"There are times when I think I'm leaning over backward, and everyone else thinks I'm spoiling for a fight. It doesn't go down well against an academic background."

"With a little tact, people would soon realize that they were mistaken."

Muir looked faintly embarrassed. "The trouble is, they're not always mistaken."

"Ah," said Allen, smiling, "that's different."

"Why did Mrs. Griswell suddenly want this device out of the house?"

"Her fiancé objected to it."

"Fiancé?"

"Well, she—you see, she—" Allen paused, then tried again. "She intends to remarry, and, of course, no one can criticize her for that. She's certainly waited long enough to show respect for Doc's memory. Especially as things are these days. And no one could ask—"

Muir squinted as if trying to get Allen back into focus. "I had the impression Dr. Griswell was quite elderly when he died."

"Yes. He was an elder brother to us. He had not only an exceptional and vigorous originality, but a long experience in the field."

"How old is Gloria Griswell?"

"Oh, quite young. Everyone was stunned when she and Doc got married. Two people more completely different . . . But they understood each other, and got along wonderfully."

"You're saying Gloria Griswell is young, is getting remarried, and her boob of a fiancé doesn't want this 'touchstone' in the house?"

Allen stared at Muir, then nodded.

Muir said shortly, "Did she just let him into her bedroom, or what?"

Allen's head jerked as if he had been slapped. He began to speak angrily, then stopped with an odd listening look. "You reason that she would probably have kept the touchstone near her as a kind of memento? And that her fiancé would only have come in contact with it when he—er—experienced a—ah—considerable degree of intimacy?"

"If this fiancé didn't object before, why now? Something must have changed."

"That reasoning does seem valid."

"What doesn't the cretin like about it?"

"How—"

Muir leaned across the desk. "You're holding something back, Dr. Allen. And incidentally, is he marrying her for money, or what?"

Allen stared at him. "Muir, you have a habit—Not that I object, of course—Doc used to do the same thing—"

"What?"

"You don't respond to what's said, you respond to what you deduce from what's said. And I fail to grasp your reasoning. For instance, you've referred to Gloria Griswell's fiancé as a 'boob,' a 'cretin'—"

"Isn't he?"

"Oh, most assuredly. A more conceited, theatrical, self-seeking . . . But the question is, how do you know? Have you met him?"

"No. And I'm not eager to."

"And now, you ask, is he marrying her for money? Where did you get that idea?"

"Don't you agree?"

"Of course I agree! Though, really, she's attractive enough. Beautiful, actually. But the question is, how do you now deduce, rightly or wrongly, that he's marrying her for money?"

"What you said implied it."

"I didn't imply it. You inferred it. How?"

"There was something in what you said—"

"What?"

"H'm . . . I don't know . . . But now you're saying that there is some serious drawback—some reason a man wouldn't want to marry her. Even though she's beautiful."

Allen nodded wonderingly. "Exactly the kind of answer I used to get from Doc. That is, no answer at all, and very possibly a new deduction, equally unexplained."

"It's there in what you said."

"How?"

"Well—if there was no reason to think this fiancé naturally would not marry her, then how can you be sure he's marrying her for money? If she's young, rich, and beautiful, how do you know he's only thinking of the 'rich,' and not the 'young and beautiful'?" Muir paused, frowning. "And incidentally, why is she marrying him?"

Allen looked momentarily disoriented. "I don't know. But she's very vulnerable."

"A young rich widow?"

"It's worse than that. She admired Doc greatly. You could see the affection and the pride in her eyes. I'm afraid that her admiration for Doc led her to admire genius in general. Then, too—" He paused suddenly.

Muir was frowning at Allen. "You mean, she takes this fake for a genius?"

Allen sat back, staring at Muir. "Precisely. And—" He caught himself.

"And what?"

"Oh, nothing specific. We've gotten off the track. What I need done is to have the properties of this device very carefully investigated."

Muir looked at him skeptically. "You worked with Dr. Griswell. You must know the answers already."

"Well, but . . . You see, Beasley and I couldn't be sure . . . and . . . You could say Doc was much closer to Beasley . . . And of course to Gloria . . . Yes, I'm sure he explained to Gloria. —And then, his sense of humor. Was he serious, or . . . His scientific reputation could be badly damaged if . . . No. I can't do it. But . . ."

Muir nodded. "In short, whatever the thing does, there are theoretical objections. So you are tossing me the hot potato."

"Well, I—ah—" Allen smiled. "Yes. Precisely."

"At least we understand each other. Now, what if there should turn out to be some credit in it?"

" 'You do the work, you get the reward.' That was Doc's policy. But be careful, Muir. I doubt there is anything in this theoretically but trouble. And you have to remember, it's Doc's device. However, aside from all that, if it makes you rich and famous, well . . . just add a footnote that I put it on your desk."

Muir smiled. "It's a nice dream."

"Possibly more than that. I'd better mention what Doc said about it: 'If the human race survives the nuclear mess, the principle behind this may keep us out of the next hole.' He wouldn't have said that lightly."

"But you don't want to say anything more about it?"

"No."

"Where is Dr. Beasley now?"

"As nearly as I can recall, he was going to take a long vacation as far from the lab as he could get. I think that would put him somewhere in the South Pacific. I'm afraid he's out of reach."

"I see. Well, if you should happen to remember anything about this device . . ."

Allen gave a sort of half-nod and half-shake of the head, along with an uninterpretable wave of the hand. He came to his feet, and reached for the doorknob. For an instant, he seemed about to say more. Then he smiled, and went out.

Muir sat for a moment looking at the closed door. Then he carefully picked up the device, turned it in his hands, and considered the black button on the side. Then he looked thoughtfully at the two grey buttons.

He sat frowning for a moment, then went to the back of the room, and bent to a large old-fashioned safe. He straightened up holding a scuffed attaché case, crumpled up a newspaper for padding, and carefully put the "touchstone" in the case. A few minutes later, he was in the sunlit parking lot, getting into a small beat-up blue car that sat in the shade of the building. Despite its appearance, the car started at once, and he pulled out onto the road.

If he remembered correctly, it should be seven or eight miles to the Griswell place.

Eli Kenzie, president of the company, stood at his office window, and watched the battered blue car glide swiftly out of the lot and down the road. He turned at a knock on a door that led, not to his outer office, but to a short hall giving access to a washroom, a small elevator, and the stairs down to his parking slot.

Kenzie unlatched the door, and Allen stepped in, looking bemused. "I gave Muir the touchstone. But it cost some information to get him to work on it."

Kenzie closed and locked the door.

"Why not just tell him to do it?"

"He wouldn't touch it without an explanation. He compared it to 'nitroglycerine.'"

"He did? Well, he's got a point. By the way, he just came out the north door carrying a briefcase, got in his car, and left in a streak."

"Already? Which way?"

"Away from the highway. Toward Doc's place."

"Then there's a good chance he went to ask Gloria about the touchstone."

Kenzie sat down on the edge of his desk. "I'm surprised he's so independent. From what you'd said, I'd gathered that his qualifications were few and far between."

Allen looked uncomfortable. "He has few formal qualifications; but he was on that list Doc made out, of individuals whose work he wanted followed. When we needed someone, I sent a query to everyone on the list. Muir was the only one still low enough on the totem pole to be interested."

"Which, by itself, suggests he's no hotshot."

"No hotshot at getting ahead in the world."

Kenzie shrugged. "Cream rises to the top."

"There are times when you want to check the bottom. Gold is pretty heavy."

"Name an instance."

"Well, Galileo wound up imprisoned. If I'm not mistaken, Archimedes was very unpopular for a while. First-rate minds have passed unrecognized simply because they didn't seek recognition, antagonized people, published in the wrong journal, or their methods just weren't in style."

"What's the explanation for Muir? He's old enough to be a lot further ahead."

"I don't know. But for just an instant, I would cheerfully have fired him myself."

Kenzie looked interested. "Why?"

"He told me flatly he wouldn't work on the touchstone without an explanation."

"He did, eh? He's lucky to have the job, and he's being paid for it. And if it weren't for Doc's interest, whatever the reason, he wouldn't have it."

"All that was in the back of my mind. It boiled down to: 'Who is he to use that tone?'"

"What did you do?"

"Before I got started, he explained his reasons."

"That took the edge off it?"

"Yes. And incidentally left the impression that he had just recently discovered tact, and was determined to give it a fair try."

Kenzie laughed. "That could explain quite a lot."

Allen nodded. "In some ways, Muir reminds me of Doc. He has Doc's trick of answering not what you say but what he deduces from what you say. I'm just wondering if he also has Doc's quirk of assuming anyone who misunderstands him does it on purpose. It made trouble enough with Doc, as you remember."

Kenzie winced. "Let's hope not. At any rate, he has the touch-stone?"

"Right."

"Then, for now, that gets the impossible damned thing off our necks. There isn't another invention of Doc's lying around, is there?"

"Not that I know of. Anyway, one mess at a time."

"That leaves Gloria herself. Even if it isn't any of our business."

Allen said exasperatedly, "But what can we do?"

"Well, the touchstone's apparently on its way back out there. That should confuse matters a little."

"I tried to argue with her yesterday. She thinks that bearded fake is a genius."

"Genius? That confidence artist!"

"But what can we—?"

"If it weren't for Doc, I'd say, forget it! A woman can fall in love with any slick conceited fraud."

"I don't think," said Allen, frowning, "that it's actually love."

"She's going to marry him, isn't she?"

"I think it's a sense of duty. Remember, she has some serious little problems."

Kenzie nodded moodily. "True enough." He walked around the desk and sat down in his chair. "If it's not love, then, at least, if she should fall in love with someone else—"

"With Gloria, who knows? She may even feel it's her duty to Doc. After all, she can't handle the situation alone. And, just incidentally, who but a confidence artist would stick around?"

Kenzie shook his head. "We shouldn't be spending our time on this. But, damn it, the company was built on Doc's ideas! We can't just toss his widow to the wolves!"

Allen said exasperatedly, "The fellow uses the situation to present himself in a favorable light. But you'd think even he would have his limits."

Kenzie sighed.

"Well, let's hope Muir makes some progress with the touch-stone."

Muir slowed, rounded the remembered sharp turn, and soon was looking at Doc Griswell's colonial house set back in the shade of big maples. To the left of the house, a shiny black Cadillac was parked in the graveled drive. Muir pulled in behind it, got out, and closed the car door loudly. He stood still, to listen.

In the warm sunlight, there was a sigh of wind in the trees, and a buzz of insects—but no sound of people. Leaving his attaché case locked in the car, Muir followed a shaded walk of flat stones toward the front of the house. The only new sound was the whine of a passing mosquito that came back for a closer look.

Muir paused opposite the front door, heard no one inside, stayed a moment to settle with the mosquito, then followed the walk to the side of the house. From somewhere in back came sounds of an argument, then of running feet. Muir paused, to cough loudly.

A small boy burst around the rear corner of the house, sobbing, and raced along the walk toward the front.

Muir stepped aside. The boy stubbed his toe, tripped, and Muir, moving fast, caught him before he hit the stones.

The boy, sobbing desperately, threw his arms around Muir's neck.

Beside the rear corner of the house appeared a young auburn-haired woman who called angrily, "Marius!"

"No!" cried the boy, his face buried in Muir's shoulder.

Just behind the woman strode a man with a black mustache and beard, wearing a black suit, black shoes, a black cape lined in red, and carrying a black attaché case and a straight black cane with a shiny metal tip. He spotted Muir, and stepped in front of the woman, as if to shield her from contamination.

Muir grunted. "Now what? Count Dracula?"

The boy twisted around, looked at the black-caped figure, glanced at Muir's expression, and grinned. He murmured, "Mommy's would-be inamorata."

"Wrong gender."

"No, it's an insult."

After a moment glaring at Muir, the caped figure came striding up the walk, the metal tip of the cane striking the stones rhythmically.

The boy kept a tight grip around Muir's neck. "Watch out for the cane. He's tricky."

The approaching figure studied Muir with distaste. "And just what do you flatter yourself that you're doing here?"

"I'd like to talk to Mrs. Griswell."

"Mrs. Griswell isn't free to talk to you."

"I'll ask Mrs. Griswell, if you don't mind."

"I do mind. My name is Vandenpeer. You are asking to speak to the future Mrs. Vandenpeer. I refuse permission."

The boy said, "Mom won't marry you! I'll die if she marries you!"

Down the walk, the woman put her hand to her forehead.

Muir said politely, "I appreciate your feelings, Mr. Van Damper, but I'll ask Mrs. Griswell herself."

"Vandenpeer." He pointed the cane at Muir, then flicked it toward the driveway.

"Get out."

Muir turned toward Gloria Griswell, as she wearily brushed back her hair, looked in faint puzzlement at Muir, and turned to approach. As Dr. Allen had told him, she was beautiful. Muir had seen beautiful women before, but this was the first time he found himself unable to look away. The sun, shining at intervals through the trees, lit her auburn hair with a warm glow, and Muir suddenly realized how much he liked auburn hair. Her movements, too, though slow and weary, were indescribably graceful.

Vandenpeer's voice pierced Muir's trance.

"Set that boy down and get out!"

Muir tore his gaze from Gloria Griswell. The boy tightened his armhold on Muir's neck. Muir said, "I came to ask Mrs. Griswell about something important—"

"Important to my fiancée or important to you?"

"I won't know until I've had a chance to speak to Mrs. Griswell."

"Then my advice is, get out. You aren't going to get a chance."

"I don't mean to be disagreeable," snarled Muir, "but I didn't ask your advice. And keep that stick out of my face."

Vandenpeer smiled contemptuously, and swung the cane so that he was holding it against his thighs, horizontally, apparently negligently, in widely spaced hands. He was holding it, Muir realized, in such a position that if he, Muir, were to step forward, Vandenpeer could hit him across the midsection with the end, and move on from there.

Muir tried to set the boy down. The boy clung tight. "No. He'll get you with the cane."

"Has he used that thing on you?"

"Not yet. He wants to marry Mommy first. Then he'll have the right. He'll call it 'good discipline.' He's already stolen my magic carpet. He calls that 'good psychology.'"

Muir turned to speak to Gloria Griswell. He looked at her, but immediately forgot what he was going to say.

Vandenpeer straightened menacingly.

From down near the corner of the house, there came a high-pitched scream, a sob, and the rapid patter of small feet.

Vandenpeer turned furiously. "I told you she'd get out, Gloria! You've got to put something over the top of her playpen!"

A small girl burst around the corner of the house, sobbing hysterically, "Mommy! Mommy! Don't leave me! I'm afraid!"

The boy leaned away from Muir's ear, to shout, "Watch the stones, Mom! I'd have broken my neck, but the man caught me!"

Vandenpeer cast the boy a venomous look.

The girl stumbled, and Gloria Griswell caught her, and the girl threw her arms around her mother's neck and sobbed. As her mother picked her up, she stopped crying to glare over her mother's shoulder at Vandenpeer; after a truly nasty look, she went back to sobbing hysterically.

It occurred to Muir that there was something here he didn't understand; but as he glanced at Gloria Griswell, the thought evaporated.

Vandenpeer stared at his fiancée's small daughter, shook his head, reached for a handkerchief, and mopped his brow.

Muir said in a polite voice, "I don't mean to intrude, Mr. Vandenpeer, but—"

Vandenpeer stared at him incredulously.

Muir went on, "but I'm curious about the boy's 'flying carpet.' Did you really take it?"

"By what right—"

"There!" cried the boy. "It's sticking out of his case!"

Muir noted an edge of worn blue cloth protruding from the attaché case. "It might be a good idea to just open up that case and show what you've got there."

"Oh, for—Why, you impudent pipsqueak! If you don't want to intrude, get out! Set the boy down, get back in your car, and go!"

The boy tightened his arm around Muir's neck. "He's got more right here than you have! All you do is threaten me and steal my things! Daddy gave me that magic carpet! You've got no right to it! Give it back to me!"

Gloria Griswell, holding her daughter, was looking with an unreadable expression at her son clinging tightly to Muir.

Muir said to Vandenpeer, "I don't claim it's any of my business. But since you are neither the boy's father nor his stepfather, whatever your intentions, it strikes me you have no right to his things. Suppose you just hand over what belongs to him, and I'll leave for now. But . . ."

The boy said, "He'd just take it back as soon as you left."

"But," said Muir, unaware that his manner suggested a gun turret turning toward a target, "unless Mrs. Griswell says no, I aim to be back later today, or tomorrow, or just as soon as she will speak with me."

Vandenpeer studied Muir alertly, then shrugged. "Get it over with now. Speak your piece, and get out."

"What I have to say," said Muir, looking at Gloria Griswell, and he was again struck dumb. After a stretch of time somewhere between a few seconds and eternity, he recovered enough to finish, "could only be said privately."

She looked back at him, and he didn't think to look away. Time drifted pleasantly past.

It dawned on Muir that the boy had dropped free, grabbed the attaché case, and was now yanking out what looked like a worn pale-blue blanket.

Vandenpeer, clearly surprised, made a grab at the boy, missed, and snarled, "You damned little sneak!"

Gloria Griswell looked around in astonishment.

Vandenpeer noted the look. "That blanket has to be gotten away from him, Gloria! He's dependent on it!"

Muir said, "What of it?"

Vandenpeer snarled, "Who spoke to you? What do you know about it? Are you a psychologist?"

"Are you?"

The boy had returned to Muir, who absently picked him up, and then felt the blanket pressed hard against his fingers. Embedded in the cloth were what felt like fine wires.

Gloria Griswell said angrily, "I don't see why Marius can't keep his blanket!"

"We won't discuss it now."

"Oh, yes," she said, "we *will* discuss it now!"

"Not in front of outsiders."

"Will you stop telling me what to do! And how dare you call Marius a sneak!"

The little girl twisted around in Gloria Griswell's arms, and favored Vandenpeer with a sickeningly sweet smile. The face of the boy was invisible to Muir, but not to Vandenpeer, who looked jarred, and suddenly said, "Now I will leave!"

Muir said helpfully, "I'll move my car."

As they walked around to the front of the house, Vandenpeer cast a murderous look at the boy, then glanced curiously at Muir. "I hope, for your sake, that you know what you're getting into."

"Frankly, no. But if you feel that way, shouldn't you be glad to get out?"

Vandenpeer began to speak sharply, then scowled. "As a matter of fact, that is a damned good point. There's a limit to the price any-thing is worth!"

Muir got into his car, and backed onto the grass beside the drive.

Out on the road, a car accelerated past, followed a moment later by another.

Vandenpeer started to back his car down the drive, then paused opposite Muir, and his window slid down. Vandenpeer raised his left hand, and peeled back a flesh-covered bandage. He said, man-to-man, "Watch out for Sally. She bites."

Muir blinked. "Thanks." He hesitated. "Careful on the way out. Some of those cars speed up going by."

Vandenpeer nodded. "They come fast." He backed out, and left with a roar.

Muir parked, and glanced sharply at the boy. "What did you do to yourself?"

"Rubbed spit on my face."

"Why?"

"It makes him sick. I almost made him throw up once."

Muir handed over his handkerchief. "*Does* Sally bite?"

Marius wiped off his face. "Well, she's just a girl. There isn't much she can do. But it helps. He can't suck around Mommy when he's in the emergency room."

"H'm." Muir got out, and started down the walk. The something here that he didn't grasp plainly related to Marius and little Sally. Could it just be Doc Griswell? Doc had been regarded as a genius, but a curmudgeonly genius capable of defying authority and standing opinion on its head. Possibly the children took after their father?

This train of thought was interrupted as Muir discovered he was again carrying the boy. They went to the corner of the house, saw no one, then, from inside, came a sound of quick footsteps. Muir turned toward the front door.

Gloria Griswell looked out. "Won't you come in, Mr.—"

Muir's pulse speeded up. "Muir," he said. "My first name, I'm afraid, is Felix." He started to let the boy down, but the boy declined to get down, so he went up the steps carrying him, and stepped through a hall into a large cool living room. The boy said, matter-of-factly, "You can't make anything good out of 'Marius,' either." He dropped to the floor, and looked at his mother. "I'll go watch Sally while you talk to Felix, Mom."

Gloria Griswell turned to stare after her son as he ran, clutching his blanket, out of the room. She turned back toward Muir, who now experienced the pleasant illusion that the room was far from any-where else, with just the two of them there, alone. After basking in this illusion for a lengthy stretch of time, he recovered the use of his voice.

"I'm afraid I've interrupted your whole day. What I started out to ask about was one of Dr. Griswell's inventions."

She smiled, and time stopped again.

Muir finally recovered enough to glance at a clock on the mantle. "It's after one. I know you won't want to leave Sally and Marius, but I think there's a fast food place down the road. If you don't mind the menu, I could bring back something for lunch."

Before she could say anything, Marius stepped back into the room. "Mom, Dad's touchstone is gone. It was always in the hall cupboard, outside your door, and it isn't there now."

Muir said, "That's what I came about. Dr. Allen put it on my desk this morning, and I've brought it with me."

The boy, startled, looked at Muir.

Gloria Griswell shook her head. "My crimes are catching up with me." She looked back at her son. "I took it in to Dr. Allen, because I thought your father would want him to have it if we didn't. And I knew Van didn't want to see it again. You used it on his plans, remember?"

"Him," sneered the boy. He glanced at Muir. "He brought his plans for the house he was going to put up here after he tore this house down. You should have heard the touchstone."

Muir shook his head. "I don't know much about it. Dr. Allen wanted me to look into it, and I came out here to ask for advice."

Marius beamed. "I'll show you how it works. Or Mom can." He looked back at his mother. "But, Mom, I'm hungry, and Sally says she's hungry. Did I just hear Felix say he'd get us something to eat?"

"Just before you came in. But—"

"You better go with him, Mom. He might get lost." The boy glanced apologetically at Muir. "It can be kind of complicated."

Gloria Griswell looked hard at her son.

Muir nodded. "A good idea." He glanced at her. "But if you'd rather not leave them alone—"

Her voice had a somewhat strangled sound. "I think they can

take care of themselves." She took another look at young Marius. "It should only take us a few minutes."

"If," said Marius, "you don't get lost. I want a double cheeseburger and a chocolate milkshake. Sally wants a hamburger and orange juice. We both want French fries. We could use a blueberry pie and an apple pie, and we'll fight that out after we've got them."

Muir dutifully repeated the order, led the way outside, and held the car door open.

"Did you," she said, on the way down the road, "have the impression of being manipulated?"

He laughed. "How could you think it?"

"Look there."

Straight ahead was the local franchise of a worldwide fast-food chain. So far, they had passed no intersection or side road.

She said, "Did you need my help to get here?"

"Of course. I could have turned the wrong way, coming out the drive."

"For weeks, nearly every time I've tried to go out, something would happen, and usually Marius or Sally was responsible. Now they all but push me out."

"Sally, too?"

"Sally, too. Though he's the ringleader."

They stopped in the line of cars at the drive-in. He turned to her, and she looked back and smiled. The car ahead moved on. The car behind gave a blast of the horn.

A few minutes later, they were back on the road, with their order in several large bags. As they got out of the car, Marius ran out, studied their expressions anxiously, then looked relieved. He took the bags, methodically selected his share and Sally's, and said, "I cleared off the table out by the sandbox, Mom. You and Felix can eat there."

Gloria Griswell stared after him as he went into the house, then bit her lip.

Muir said, "What's wrong with the spot?"

"Let me show you."

They went down the walk, over a little footbridge across a brook that now in the summer was reduced to a trickle, and then along a narrow path through thick young pines to a little sunny clearing containing a small very clean table, two benches, and a sandbox.

"For the children's picnics," she said.

In the warm stillness, he looked around at the dense pines. "It does look unusually private."

She divided the various burgers and drinks. "Marius has a maze of tunnels through the lower branches."

"He could pop through anytime?"

"And will."

They ate in silence, then he said, "I'm not usually tongue-tied. But—"

A trapped look momentarily crossed her face, and he glanced around. "But I haven't wanted to ask about the device Dr. Allen showed me until there was more time to talk." She flashed him a grateful look as young Marius popped out from the pines.

"Mom, is the ice-cream in the freezer?"

"Why don't you look?"

"Because you left the wash on the freezer in a clothes basket."

"Can't you—"

"It's wet. You didn't put it in the dryer."

"Then—"

"I could get it off, but it's heavy, and it might spill. And the floor's filthy . . . Because, remember, you forgot—"

"Never mind," she said.

Muir thought that he could now guess what Allen had been thinking when he implied that Gloria Griswell was handicapped in the marriage market. He said, "I'll be glad to move the clothes basket, Mrs. Griswell."

Marius said, "Mom's name is—"

She said, "Will you get out of here, Marius?"

"Why can't Felix—"

Muir turned to her. "May I call you Gloria?"

"Yes!"

Marius grinned. "You sound—"

"For heaven's sake! Marius—"

Muir smiled. "I'll help Marius look for the ice cream. After all, no one can talk and eat at the same time."

She said, "I'm not sure of that, but it's worth a try. If you'll move the basket, I'll see if I can find the ice cream. Maybe we could even have some ourselves."

Marius said shyly. "There might be a little left."

Muir had expected to leave in an hour or two, but found himself, toward four o'clock, putting Sally in her crib. Sally, who had her mother's enchanting smile, clung to Muir's hand, smiled up at him, then put her head on her pillow, sighed sweetly, and shut her eyes.

Gloria Griswell looked down unbelievingly into the crib, glanced at Muir, and bit her lip. Muir followed Gloria out of the room, glanced back at Marius standing with innocent satisfaction beside the crib, and murmured, "Is Marius staying with Sally?"

"Evidently," said Gloria.

As they started down the stairs, Muir kept his voice low, "Could we talk about the touchstone?"

"All right."

"It's in my car."

"I'll go with you. There's something I have to say."

He led the way outdoors. "Did you want to get in?"

"I . . . Yes."

He held the door for her, then got in the other side.

She sat looking at her hands. "I'm willing to help you learn about the touchstone. But I—" She paused, and turned to him in silence.

He studied her look of bleak determination, and said carefully, "If you are trying to tell me not to presume on any momentary sympathy between us, or not to imagine that Marius selects your friends for you, you'll have to say it. I'm short on tact, and make it up in stubbornness."

She looked at him in silence, then her eyes went shut, she looked away, and tears ran down her cheeks. Her voice was a whisper. "I'm trying to—to keep you from being entangled in a—fate worse then death, by Marius."

"You think Marius . . ."

"He's afraid his blockheaded mother will attract some unsympathetic fellow that he and Sally will then be stuck with. He likes you, so he's doing everything he can to throw us together. He knows Sally is a little demon when she gets mad, and he doesn't want you to see that. He's been so busy driving men away that it took a while to grasp his latest tactics."

"I liked you before he had a chance to do a thing."

She blushed, then said stubbornly, "At the risk of sounding even more silly than I must already, you don't want to get entangled with a widow with two children."

He nodded. "In principle, that's true. And you don't want to get mixed up with someone too dull to understand tact. Still, on the other hand, a lot depends on specifics. Which two children? Which woman? You can't deal with these questions in generalities. Have you considered the details?"

She said, "I'm beginning to be sorry I tried to save you."

"That's all right. I appreciate the gesture."

After a moment, she sighed. "Where were we?"

"You were going to tell me about the touchstone."

She nodded, and he got the briefcase, and they went back into the house.

She led the way down the hall, to a paneled white door with a brass knob.

"Marius's father used this room as a study."

Muir looked into a large dim room with book-lined walls, comfortable chairs and sofa, and a closed rolltop desk.

She turned on a floor lamp, and pushed up the curving slide of the desk, to reveal numerous pigeonholes and shelves. On two shelves lay a pair of books, which she placed, face-down, on the writing surface of the desk. She took the touchstone, aimed its little cone at the first book, and pressed the right-hand grey button. There was a singing melodious note.

She turned the cone toward the second book. The touchstone gave a sickly groan.

Muir picked up the first book, to recognize a chemistry text of the early 1900s. The author had used care to distinguish fact from the theories of his day, so the book was still useful. Muir picked up the second book, didn't recognize it, and read:

". . . is 'at random.' Like when you're shooting craps you don't know what numbers will turn up. Or when somebody gets high, you don't know what he or she will do. This is at random.

"When these mollies bounce off each other, and hit the wall, it is at random. But when they hit the wall, their push makes a pressure. You can measure the pressure.

"CHEMFACT: Maybe you can tell what will happen even when the thing that makes it happen is at random.

"NEWWORD: Mollie. Mollie-cule. Mol-e-cule. Molecule. See?

"CHEMQUIZ: 'When people get beered up, is it at random?'"

Muir flipped to the front of the book, to learn that "this is the first in a new series of science texts designed to relate intimately to today's more demanding student."

Gloria Griswell watched the expressions that crossed his face, and smiled. "The left button gives a reading on the meter. The right button gives a tone. The meter can measure small differences. The tone can differentiate all sorts of things."

"It's a touchstone for quality of workmanship?"

"As nearly as I can judge."

"It will work on what?"

"Anything man-made."

He let his breath out carefully. "No wonder Allen wouldn't give details. All right if I try it?"

She handed the device to him.

Muir aimed the cone at the desk itself, and pushed the right-hand button. A singing note sounded.

He tried the left-hand button. This time there was silence, but the needle swung far across the dial from left to right.

Muir glanced around the bookshelves, to a green plastic hand that held aloft a pot metal ashtray. He aimed, pushed the right-hand button. The touchstone emitted a croak.

Muir went methodically around the room. Usually the device gave a pleasant tone. But it made no response to the potted plants that sat on a window sill, and it made groaning, croaking, or bleating noises for a stoneware spider with nine legs and a built-in clock that didn't run, for a small doll in a bikini that shot from its mouth a cigarette-lighting flame, and for a printed invitation, preserved in plastic:

"Congratulations! Our sophisticated computer analysis has revealed a small select group of individuals who capably manage their own affairs. You are one of this select group! Now, for a limited time, we invite you to place at your disposal the limitless credit and extensive financial resources of our prestigious exclusive organization . . ."

Muir turned the plastic over, to find on the back a lengthy questionnaire in fine print, along with a little notice:

"DO NOT apply for Credit Approval if your income is below $39,000. Return the enclosed Card AT ONCE by Registered Mail!"

Like an insect preserved in amber, the credit card itself was embedded in the plastic, made out to "Marius Gristmill, Sr."

Muir aimed the cone-shaped coil at the card; the touchstone emitted a sickly bleating noise, several times repeated.

He looked up. "I have to agree with its sentiments. But I don't begin to understand it."

"I didn't mention understanding. I only said I would show you."

"Do you understand it?"

"I know what it will do. That's all."

"It won't work on people?"

"It will respond to clothing or accessories. There's no response to an individual, as far as I know."

"Did Dr. Griswell ever explain this?"

She nodded ruefully. "More than once."

"What—"

"The explanations varied."

"Why so?"

She shook her head. "His sense of humor. He said once that the lab had deciphered the genetic codes of the nose of a cat and the vocal organs of a goat, translated them into machine language, and burned the result into an EPROM installed in the touchstone."

As Muir grappled with this, she added, "So they had a program that could smell a rat, and say what it thought of it in sounds anyone could appreciate."

Muir became aware of a catch in her voice, and stopped asking questions. He sat down on the couch, and set the device carefully on a low table nearby.

She blew her nose, and after a moment's silence, said, "Does the touchstone make problems?"

"Unless there are circuits inside that are complicated beyond belief, and sensors to match, I'm afraid the touchstone is 'scientifically impossible'—unless Dr. Griswell made it as a joke."

"A joke?"

"Well, he could have embedded, in items around this room, tiny devices—like what's detected when a book is taken out of a library without having been checked out. The touchstone would give the reading, or the kind of sound, that had been encoded in advance."

She shook her head. "It will work on things that are brand-new as of now. How can you say it is 'scientifically impossible'?"

"If it works, of course it's scientifically possible. I mean that it looks incompatible with present-day scientific assumptions."

"But it does work. And it's useful. Yet Mr. Kenzie and Dr. Allen seem embarrassed by its existence."

"A genuine touchstone is something some people—I'm not thinking of Mr. Kenzie or Dr. Allen—might not want around."

"Does that matter?"

"Say we have a text written by Bungle, Murk, and Damnation, and published by Confusion Booksmiths. The school board runs a touchstone over this text, and never wants to see the book again. Confusion Booksmiths rises up a hundred feet tall in the law courts to demand proof from whoever made the touchstone that it is scientifically valid. We then have the problem of proving the scientific validity of something that does not conform to present-day scientific theories."

"To sell it would bring about situations in which an explanation will be demanded?"

"It seems so to me. And then what?"

"What *is* the explanation?"

"That's a question I've been trying to answer." Muir turned the device over in his hands. "Is it all right to open this?"

"As far as I know."

He got out an all-purpose Swiss pocket knife, and carefully undid four screws. Very cautiously, he lifted off the back of the case. After a lengthy silence, he looked up.

"However this device may judge quality, it doesn't use any method humans would use. I have the impression I'm looking at some variation on the Geiger counter."

"How—"

"Conceivably it counts something emitted from the object the coil is aimed at."

"Is that bad?"

"For whoever has to explain it. What does it count?"

She nodded. "I see."

"What is it again that this works on?"

"Anything man-made."

"But not on anything that's not man-made?"

"I don't think so. Marius would know better than I. But that's my—"

The door opened, and Marius looked in. "The touchstone only works on man-made objects. Dad showed me. Mom, I wanted to tell you Sally wants to get up. But I didn't want to interrupt when I heard you and Felix talking."

Muir listened with conflicting emotions as Marius went on: "I can show Felix more about how the touchstone works. But it's getting late, so maybe you could make supper. And we've got the extra room, so if Felix wants to stay overnight—"

Muir glanced at Gloria Griswell, who stared for an instant at her son, then turned to Muir, who said, "I appreciate the suggestion, but I think I should get back."

Marius said, still speaking to his mother, "You remember what happened the night before last, Mom? It wouldn't hurt to have a man around the house."

Muir started to speak, paused, then said, "What happened the night before last?"

Marius said, "Someone broke in."

"Marius," said Gloria, "we aren't sure—"

"You heard it, Mom. And the window was unlocked the next morning. And someone had gone through the desk. Sally was scared to death, and so was I."

Muir said sharply, "What desk?"

Marius pointed silently to the rolltop desk.

Muir said, "Was anything taken?"

"We don't think so," said Gloria.

Marius said, "Whoever did it might be back."

Muir said, "In that case . . ."

The sun was low in the sky next morning as Muir pulled into the company lot, parked, and went inside. He had just locked his attaché case in the old-fashioned safe when there was a knock, and Dr. Allen looked in.

"Muir, Mr. Kenzie and I would like to talk to you."

Muir followed Allen down the hallway, through an unmarked door, and up in a small elevator. They crossed a short hall, to an office where Kenzie, his suitcoat over the back of a chair, tie half-undone, prowled like a caged panther. Kenzie paused at the window to glance out, then turned to Muir.

"What do you make of the touchstone?"

"A useful device."

"Which does what?"

"Measure the quality of human workmanship."

Kenzie glanced at Allen.

"That's where we got stuck."

Allen nodded soberly.

Kenzie looked back at Muir. "We have got to get moving on this. You've had little enough time, but let's hear your impressions."

"At first, I thought the touchstone might be a joke, detecting something Dr. Griswell had already put in the objects it judges. But Gloria said it works on things made recently, and it does."

Kenzie looked at him sharply.

"Mrs. Griswell helped show you how it works."

"Yes."

"She has a fiancé. Did you meet the—"

"He was there when I got there."

"You met her family? A son and daughter?"

Dr. Allen said dryly, "Both delightful."

Muir smiled, and nodded. "Nice kids."

Allen stared. Kenzie looked momentarily blank, then said, "Do you see any way yet to market or even explain the touchstone?"

"To explain it, yes. But I'm not sure . . ."

Allen said, "Namely?"

"Well . . . People judge workmanship by appearance, performance, and comparison with some standard. This device does it some other way; the works suggest a radiation counter. But what's counted? Could there be a form of radiation that gives a measure of quality of workmanship?"

Allen said, "If so, where would you go from there?"

"Then the operation of the device would be possible to work out. But first there are some trifling little problems in identifying this radiation."

Allen nodded. "Not least of which is that 'quality' and 'workmanship' relate to subjective human judgments, and they are being measured objectively by an instrument. The explanation will blow up in your face."

"Unfortunately, there so far seems to be no alternative. For the sake of argument, why should that create an explosion?"

"Science," said Allen, "is based on objective repeatable experiments. The judgment of quality rests on what is essentially a subjective sense of esthetics, combined with various aspects of experience. There's no connection."

"The touchstone works. Therefore there must be a connection."

"There can't be."

Kenzie straightened his tie. "There's no connection between 'objective experiments' and 'various aspects of experience'?"

"No relevant connection. Quality of workmanship involves human esthetics; human esthetics is not an objectively measurable quality."

Muir nodded. "Obviously, that's true. But we're up against something still more basic than that, and that has been shown over and over again. It's why there's a bloodbath every now and then between science and philosophy."

Allen looked at Muir in foreboding. "What?"

"Argument doesn't refute facts. Facts dominate. An argument only interprets facts."

"But what—"

"The touchstone exists. It is a device based on science. It accurately judges the quality of workmanship. Therefore workmanship must be objectively measurable."

Kenzie glanced at Allen.

Allen exhaled slowly, and nodded. "It's arguable in the case of a structure or a machine. There esthetics may depend on function. But what about modern art?"

Kenzie nodded. "Doc had two touchstones, Muir. One he kept at home, one in a safe in his office. We tried out the one he kept in his office. Among other things, we took it to a museum, to see if it would judge art."

Muir remembered the green plastic hand and pot-metal ashtray. "And it did?"

Kenzie nodded. "And it actively disliked most modern art."

"What did it—"

Allen shook his head. "You can't imagine. The noises it made brought a guard on the run. He thought we were sick."

Kenzie said, "The only way we see to market this thing is as what it seems to be . . . a detector of quality workmanship. But how do we prove it? And what happens when the museum, for instance, discovers that most of the exhibits in that priceless collection have been 'scientifically' graded as junk?"

Muir thought it over. "The touchstone could be right."

Kenzie nodded. "Ninety percent of those expensive exhibits could be the worst kind of artistic trash. But how does that help us? Whoever the touchstone damages financially may try to recover. He may very naturally try to recover by means of a lawsuit. If we claim that the touchstone is what it seems to be, we have to be able to prove it."

"Where it judges technology," said Allen, "at least we can argue the case; but it will judge any kind of workmanship. Outside the museum, there's a pedestal that holds up a thing like a—ah—like a—"

Kenzie said, "Like an oversize bronze pretzel with its hands in its pockets."

Allen nodded. "Exactly. You don't dare get anywhere near that piece of statuary till you've shut off the touchstone."

Muir laughed. "That's a reason to question its judgment?"

"Legally," said Kenzie, "yes, it is. That bronze pretzel cost the museum sixty thousand dollars. Just suppose our device should knock the market price down to the scrap value of the bronze? The museum will naturally think they've been damaged by false claims. How do you defend a thing like this in court?"

"I don't know."

"Doc was a genius. My impression is that the touchstone sees through slipshod work and confidence stunts, artistic or otherwise, as an x-ray sees through tissue paper. But we may have to prove it. How?"

Muir said, "Gloria would like to see the touchstone produced and sold. She thinks it could do a lot of good."

Kenzie nodded. "We all have to rely on specialists; and it's all but impossible to judge their work except by results, and then it's too late. The touchstone could help. Suppose you need a car. You aim the touchstone, push the button, and if there's a groaning noise, you walk off the lot. That's better than buying a lemon. But again, if this happens often enough, what's the manufacturer likely to do? Attack the touchstone. How do we defend it?"

"Maybe we're approaching this from the wrong direction."

"It could be," said Kenzie exasperatedly. "The whole thing is skewed, off-center, and hard to grasp. What's your thought?"

"The better we prove the touchstone is right, the worse it makes the problem. We've vouching for the truth of what the victim sees as slander."

"The touchstone unmistakably detects quality workmanship. That's a slap in the face to the sellers of all the inferior goods on the market, but it's true. To compound the problem, the touchstone is scientific, but sounds like a joke. If Doc hadn't invented it, I wouldn't touch it."

Muir said, "But that may be the answer!"

"What?"

"That Doc Griswell invented it!"

Kenzie shook his head. "The whole problem is that Doc isn't here and can't explain it. Believe me, when Doc got on the witness stand, the opposition had troubles. But he's not here. How do we explain what only he, if anyone, understood?"

"But since he isn't here, how does it help to argue that the touchstone's judgment is scientifically accurate? It's better the other way around."

"How . . ."

"Why not call this 'Doc's Legacy,' say that Doc left this behind, you don't want to withhold it, because it seems useful; but you don't know for sure just what it does. You think Doc used it as a touchstone for good workmanship; but does it give exact truth, or a curmudgeon's viewpoint, or the facts as Doc saw them, or what? Anyone can try it, and see for himself. It would still be just as useful. But you would have sold it as an intriguing puzzle, not as an infallible electronic judge."

Kenzie looked thoughtful, and glanced at Allen.

Allen rubbed his chin. "It might work. Would Gloria be agreeable to this?"

Muir said, "I expect to see her tonight. I can ask."

Kenzie nodded absently, then joined Allen in a close look at Muir, who missed the look, as he said, "Incidentally, what you would be saying would be the strict truth. Who can say what Doc Griswell was trying for, or for sure that he got it?"

Another look passed between Kenzie and Allen. Muir, who saw this one, was reminded of parents debating whether to reveal some jarring fact of life to their offspring.

Allen gave an embarrassed cough. "Well, Muir, that question involves something I—ah—hadn't mentioned to you as yet. There was a discarded first draft of a patent application in Doc's desk. It includes a theory to the effect that the human mind, in a particular creative state, produces 'alpha-psychons,' which, impinging upon matter, in turn cause certain changes, such as the radiation of what are tentatively called 'qualitons.' There is a large faint X penciled across the cover page of this mind-boggling document, along with a big question mark. What the theory hypothesizes is nothing less than interaction between mind and matter, with the touchstone detecting 'qualitons,' to prove the theory. Of course, it is in this creative state that high-quality workmanship is achieved, and the touchstone judges it by the qualitons emitted."

Muir tried to speak, but words wouldn't come.

Kenzie said dryly, "Doc had these inspirations from time to time."

Allen said, "But usually he took care of them himself. This is the first one we've had to contend with on our own."

Muir exhaled carefully. "Is the theory comprehensible?"

Allen thought the question over. "Well—"

Kenzie said, "Not to ordinary human beings."

"Doc," said Allen judiciously, "usually made considerable use of mathematics. The problem is that there were times when no one else could follow his math. That's not to say that the math isn't valid. But there is that problem of following it in this case. Much worse is that there are parts that are not mathematical and that will be automatically rejected."

Kenzie sighed. "In addition to which, he uses a theory of atomic structure—"

"Subatomic structure," said Allen.

"Atomic substructure," said Kenzie. "If an atom were a house,

Doc would be talking about the composition of the bricks the house is built of. You not only have the complications of Doc's math, but also the complications of this theory to which Doc was applying his math. Plus the alpha-psychons. Taken all together . . ."

Muir kept a firm grip on his choice of words. "Does the part of this theory that is comprehensible seem self-consistent, assuming you don't automatically reject it?"

Kenzie glanced at Allen. Allen looked thoughtful, hesitated, then finally nodded. "I suppose in that respect it's a little like the quantum theory, when it was first proposed. You have to accept certain assumptions you don't want to accept; but if you do that, the rest becomes reasonably clear—except that in this case we have the theory without the theorist, so it is not easy to follow the details."

"But the details you can follow?"

"Well—it depends. There is one aspect of this, Doc called it 'the remote resonance force' I think, that could make special trouble. You see, the touchstone not only reacts to the original inspired plans for a device, but to later reproductions of the device, very possibly made by not especially inspired people routinely following the plan. How do the alpha-psychons radiated in March of one year, in Boston, create qualitons in Savannah, Georgia, two years later, when the blueprints are turned into reality? There's a problem there. Doc may have four pages of mathematics and two special theories between Boston and Savannah; but there are going to be people who skip all that, and intuitively reject the idea."

"The 'remote resonance force,'" said Muir, "explains how this could happen?"

Allen glanced helplessly at Kenzie. Kenzie smiled. "With Doc on the other end of the theory, the 'remote resonance force' is like a six-teen-inch gun aimed at the critics. Most of them wouldn't want to face the monster projectiles Doc could fire from that cannon. Unfortunately, we don't know how to load the thing."

Allen said exasperatedly, "And Doc very evidently was dissatisfied with something about the theory."

"Yes," said Kenzie, "or he wouldn't have put an 'X' across it and tossed it in his bottom drawer."

Muir said, "But, the touchstone works."

Allen nodded. "All told, the mathematics is baffling but very possibly valid; the theory of matter to which the math is applied is anyone's guess; the device itself works. But the idea behind it all is going to be just as nice to put across as Galileo's original argument."

"Yes," said Muir. "I can see that."

Kenzie said, "But your suggestion about marketing the touch-stone is a help, Muir. We're going to have to think that through. It's the first progress we've made with this thing in quite a while."

"But how does it fit in with that patent application?"

"As far as I can see, it doesn't. But don't worry about it. Ah—You said you were going to see Gloria Griswell—?"

"Yes, for dinner tonight. And I'll ask if she's agreeable to marketing it that way. But—" He paused, baffled at Kenzie's wistfully hopeful expression.

"Don't worry," said Allen, following Kenzie's thoughts easily enough. "It's like a jigsaw puzzle, Muir, and you've just given us a good-sized piece. You've had very little time to work on it, but it's a pleasure to see how you've taken hold of the problem. It's a relief to see this . . . ah . . . this last work of Doc's moving again."

Late that day, with the sun at the horizon, Muir was in the little clearing with Gloria when Marius spoke:

"Felix?"

Muir looked blankly around.

Overhead, something moved against the deep-red sky. Muir glanced up, to see Marius, apparently floating face-down by the tops of the evergreens. Marius said, "Why don't we write out our ideas about the touchstone, then use the touchstone to judge them?"

Muir heard the words, but didn't answer as he stepped aside, eyes narrowed, to look up at Marius from a different angle. Muir had the impression of looking up from the bottom of a pool at a swimmer on the surface. Obviously there had to be something holding Marius up, but so far all Muir could see was the thin pale-blue thing Marius was lying on, and it appeared to be unsupported from any angle.

The slender tops of the evergreens moved in a light breeze, and Marius, looking down at Muir's face, grinned suddenly and slid side-wise in the air, gathered speed, and shot off to the side out of sight, streaked back from a different angle, much higher, then dropped like a rock to brake to a stop, and hover motionless, overhead.

Muir, looking at the pale-blue something Marius was lying on, belatedly recognized Marius's "flying carpet," a gift from his father, Doc Griswell. Next he remembered the feel of fine wires when Marius had pressed the "blanket" to his fingers.

It dawned on Muir with a shock that the idea of taking care of 'Doc's last work' was premature. Here was another of Doc's working models. Like the others, it came with no warning, with no one knew what complications to follow.

For the first time, Muir felt sympathy for people who had bet against the incandescent light and snorted at the thought of a carriage with no horse. Progress was fine, but the touchstone had yet to be worked out, no one dared say whether Doc's asterator would save humanity or wreck it, and here was this thing.

And why would Doc Griswell make a toy of an invention that, on a large scale, could lift man off the earth and truly begin the Age of Space? Why, for that matter, had Doc just used the touchstone himself, when he could have got it into production? Legal uncertainty might stop Kenzie and Allen, aware they didn't understand Doc's device; but would it stop Doc?

It was then that Muir thought of the patent application with the question mark and the X across it.

What if Doc didn't understand it, either?

From time to time, someone uncovered something really new, perhaps just as everything seemed finally explained and systematized. The results could turn civilization on its head. To most of the survivors, it might some day seem perfectly clear, one of life's familiar certainties. But those who had known other certainties tended to be more cautious.

Now, looking up from below at something really new and revolutionary, Muir winced.

Looking down from atop it, Marius grinned.

Negative Feedback

Julia Ravagger watched her husband, Nelson Ravagger, pay off the deliverymen. Nelson's somewhat predatory profile, the workmen's uneasy glances at the chandelier, marble floor, sunlit conservatory, and other details of the lavishly furnished apartment, taken together with the aggressively prosaic look of the object they had just delivered, all added up to something Julia had felt too often since marrying the famous—or infamous—stock speculator.

"Ummm, Nels—" she said, as the door closed, leaving them alone, "why do I again have this feeling of total perplexity? What, precisely, is that thing?"

Ravagger grinned, creating an unfortunate effect like the surfacing of a shark that is in the process of eating a swimmer. He patted the curving metal top of the object, which was enameled a sickly shade suggestive of dog droppings.

"This, my dear, is a product of the Cartwright Corporation's Fuels Sciences Division. This is the 'business opportunity of a lifetime.' Specifically, this is a 'solid-fuel converter, designed to eliminate the dependence of our nation on foreign oil producers, and thereby return control of our fuel destiny to these shores.'"

She stared. "That's a quote?"

He nodded. "From one of the company's brochures."

"Is it true?"

"If you strain out the high-tech wordage, this is a coal stove. And if it's the kind of coal stove I think it is, it's a bomb."

"Meaning—"

"That after you install it and use it, it won't be long before you'll do almost anything to never have to use it again."

"Then, why are you putting it in our living room?"

He opened a large cardboard box near an elaborately simple white sofa, and pulled out a quivering rectangle of curving black metal—a section of stovepipe not yet locked into a cylinder. He smiled at her.

"Remember the wood-stove craze?"

She glanced covertly at her left wrist, where the burn scar had almost disappeared.

"I couldn't forget that."

Nelson delivered himself of a grisly chuckle.

"No. Me, either. But it was educational."

She glanced up at a small decorative snow scene nearly hidden behind a spray of imitation pussy willows in a tall pearl-colored vase. The snow scene was painted on a circular brass flue cover; the flue openings in the old building had been unplastered and put to use during the time of the Oil Embargo, then thankfully covered up again afterward.

"Well," she said, "but what connection—"

"I'm not sure," said Ravagger, "but we just might have a coal-stove craze next. Cartwright is convinced of it. And as it happens, I'm on their board, and the management has a tiny little flaw that we will have to live through somehow, preferably without bankrupting the company in the process."

Cyrus Cartwright II, at the head of the long table, winced as Nelson Ravagger settled into his chair near the far end. Beside Cartwright, W. W. Sanson of the Machines Division—former head of Superdee Equipment before its near-bankruptcy and merger with Cartwright—growled, "Ravagger doesn't look too cheerful."

"No," said Cartwright uneasily. "It's nicer when he's just bored."

"Damn it, he's got that blowtorch look." Sanson dropped his voice to a murmur. "Remember, you're the chairman."

Cartwright squinted at him side-wise. "What's that supposed to mean?"

"Keep him in line. Use your authority."

"I'm chairman because he doesn't want to be stuck with the job. If he wanted it, he could take it any time."

"It's your name on the door. Remember, your granddad founded the company."

"Granddad isn't here. And just incidentally, which one would be worse to get along with, I don't know." He glanced at his watch. "Well, time to get started."

The meeting commenced with boring routine, and proceeded in its accustomed groove until, just as Cartwright had almost forgotten Ravagger, the speculator's voice reached across the table. This voice had a peculiar resonance, 10 percent of it made up by the construction of Ravagger's chest and voicebox, and 90 percent by the listeners' awareness of the number of shares of the company the voice represented.

Ravagger said, "We haven't heard from the head of our new Fuels Division yet."

On Cartwright's left, R. J. Schwenk of the Fuels Sciences Division said cheerfully, "Nothing to report, Mr. Ravagger. No problems. Everything proceeding according to plan."

Cartwright smiled. "Nels, Schwenkie is a source of real comfort, but demand for our solid-fuel products, as yet, is just starting to perk up."

On the other side of Cartwright, W. W. Sanson cleared his throat. "As vice-chairman, Mr. Ravagger, I have made it my job to follow the progress of our new Fuels Sciences Division with particular care. Our statistical analysis shows everything on plot."

" 'On plot'?"

"Everything proceeding according to plan."

"Meaning what?"

"Aah—meaning that the—ah—that expenses are under control, sales are about where we expected, the market for our products is developing as forecast, we have the appropriate number of dealers signing up. Everything is fine."

"How about quality?"

Sanson chuckled. "Well, you know our slogan: 'Quality First, Quality Last—Our Name Is Quality.'"

"OK, you've made a special study of the Fuels Division's products, then?"

"Yes, precisely. Ah, no, wait a minute."

"Of course, you haven't had time to do everything."

A soothing purr was suddenly present in Ravagger's voice, and Sanson broke out in a sweat. "What I'm saying is, I've studied the results. That's what counts. I haven't examined each individual product. We have quality control experts, inspectors—I wouldn't intrude that far down the ladder. Our people do their jobs."

Cartwright spoke up hastily. "Nels, if you're thinking of checking up on our workers, the union wouldn't like that."

Ravagger glanced at Sanson. "Which products have you studied, then?"

"Well, as I said, it's the *overall* results that count."

"You haven't examined *any* of the products?"

Sanson said, "What difference—"

"None *at all?* Even though you're making it your job to follow the division's progress 'with particular care'?"

Cartwright stared down the table at Ravagger, then glanced to his left at R. J. Schwenck.

Schwenck said at once, "That's my job, Mr. Ravagger. I'd be offended if Mr. Sanson felt it necessary to check me up on that."

"Oh, I see." Ravagger looked back at Sanson. "You were scared to check any products for fear Schwenck might get mad at you?"

Sanson blew out his breath. "No, I just trust him to do his job."

"All right. Now, Mr. Schwenck—"

"Yes, Mr. Ravagger."

"You've just heard our vice-chairman say he's not afraid of your taking offense. Naturally, I'm not afraid either. As a matter of fact, I don't think there's anyone here who would hesitate to check on anything because someone might take offense."

"Well, all I meant—" Schwenck hesitated. Before he could find some way around his own comment, Ravagger's words trod on his heels:

"You meant what?"

"Oh, we don't want to interfere further down in the hierarchy, or in each other's territory. It's bad manners. It assumes the other man doesn't do his job. An organization is built on mutual trust."

Ravagger purred, "An excellent defense of your comment, Mr. Schwenck."

Schwenck looked relieved. Sanson looked alarmed.

Ravagger said, "So *you* have checked the products in your own division, then?"

"No, that's what I just—"

Ravagger glanced around. "Then who does check on them? Are we selling stuff we don't know anything about?"

Schwenck said, "As we've said, Mr. Ravagger, we have quality-control inspectors to see to that. Really, you shouldn't criticize what you don't understand."

Ravagger slowly turned his head to look directly at Schwenck. The effect on Schwenck was like having a machine gun take aim at him. Schwenck began to perspire, but kept his mouth shut.

Ravagger said quietly, "In the final analysis, Mr. Schwenck, who is the ultimate authority in this company?"

Schwenck said carefully, "I guess you are, Mr. Ravagger. But that doesn't mean you necessarily understand it."

Cartwright said nervously, "Gentlemen—"

Ravagger shook his head. "I'm not the final authority. What I have to do is make you aware who is. And if I have to smash heads or look like a jackass to do it, I will do it anyway. Now, just consider— Who is not in the company, but controls the destiny of the company— any company? Who, because he can make the company succeed or fail, influences the destiny of everyone in it? Who is below the bottom of the organization and above the chief executive at the top? Whose opinion is often ignored or unknown, and whose favor is almost universally courted?"

Schwenck stared. "You can only mean the customer."

"Right. Now, anyone that important is going to have his interests looked after. And since this is your division, you will look after those interests! What do you mean, the quality-control inspector will do it? The quality-control inspector may check the thickness of metal or the finish on the enamel, but there's more to satisfying a customer than that! You can't delegate that job! That job is the most important job you've got! It is your personal responsibility to check that those products are right! The only way you can do that is to become a customer yourself! Mr. Chairman, I move that a special allowance be made to Mr. R. J. Schwenck, head of our Fuels Sciences Division, to enable him to immediately purchase, as a customer, one of our

Superheat Solid-Fuel Converters—colloquially known as a 'stove,' preferably Model J616 or J617—and report to us at the next meeting on his personal installation and use of this device."

Madeleine Schwenck looked on in bafflement as her husband paid the deliverymen and eyed the massive bright-red object they had left. "Richie, what, pray tell, is that?"

Schwenck exhaled carefully.

"It's a—it's a stove, Hon."

"Where are you planning to put it?"

"Right here. Where I had them leave it."

"There?"

"Remember, we had the wood stove here."

"Richie, look, we agreed to get rid of the wood stove. And the chainsaw. And the pick-up truck. If you had to get another wood stove—"

"This is not a wood stove."

"That's true, you only said it's a stove. Well, then, what kind of stove is it?"

"It's a—ah—a solid-fuels converter. Of—h'm—fossil fuels."

"It's a what?"

"It's a coal stove."

She took a fresh look at him, then at the stove. Then she looked at him again.

He stood frowning at the curving bulk, and asked himself, exactly why did this thing look like a cross between an old-style fire truck and a juke box when the sketches and presentations had shown it as modern and cheerful. A 1930s aura radiated from it, along with a sense of stubborn intractability.

She said carefully, "Richie—"

He said, "Look, Madeleine, this is not necessarily permanent. I—uh—you might look on it as a sort of, well, company homework."

"Rich, please, I don't know what you have in mind, but please remember that I'm a lawyer, and we don't want another of those arguments where we both forget ourselves. And I can feel it starting to build up already. I do pay part of the costs—a good part of the costs—of this house, and I don't mind it, it's fair, but I like to be consulted about what we do and what we don't do. Now—"

He groaned, and told her about the directors' meeting.

"Well," she said, frowning, "I hear it, but I don't understand it. This was the idea of this stock swindler?"

"Hon," said Schwenck, "I may have put it too strong. This guy cuts things pretty close to the line, but it's not that line he cuts close to. He's opinionated, overbearing, and damned tricky; but he's not a swindler."

"Then you're saying he's a stock *operator?*"

"He sure is. The problem is, for some reason, he's down on this stove; but my whole division is set up to take advantage of an inevitable disruption in the oil industry—this business of upheavals in the Middle East gives us a chance to see what is bound to happen eventually. Now, we are presenting a whole line of these—these solid-fossil-fuel converters, based on products a branch of Superdee Equipment used to make—"

She said, "So what it boils down to is that the biggest shareholder in the company is on the board of directors, and everybody is afraid of him, and he is making you personally try out one of the products you're planning to sell?"

He said, "Yeah. I guess that is it."

She grinned.

He said aggrievedly, "Damn it, it all makes perfectly good sense! As a country, we're well supplied with coal. Oil, comparatively speaking, is scarce. If there should be a break in the oil supply, the demand for some other source of energy would be fierce. Natural gas can take up part of the slack, but not all. There's going to be a hole there, and something has to fill it. Now, wood stoves produce a lot of smoke; they don't generally burn very long before you have to reload them; there are complicated pollution-control requirements; wood is not a predictable fuel unless you make it into pellets, which costs money; there are environmental objections to the burning of wood on a really large scale; meantime, you have problems storing wood.

"The obvious answer is coal! There are only a comparatively few companies set up to produce coal stoves on anywhere near the basis that we are. And the others, as far as I know, are all asleep at the switch. And we've got our Combuster, a really effective pollution control device, which is a step ahead of everyone else in this business. If something unexpected happened to oil, we could make a mint!

And don't tell me nothing could happen! We import a lot of our oil from a place that's a powder keg!"

His wife nodded. "OK, you go ahead and get it ready. Are the stovepipes black, like for our wood stove?"

"They're enameled red. A red stove with black pipes—our market research indicated people wouldn't go for that."

"Richie, that is quite a vivid shade of red."

"Yeah, I know. I just noticed that. The color in the sketches looked darker. And the first stoves we made didn't look like this to me. This has an electric effect."

"It jumps back and forth when you look at it."

He swallowed, and said nothing. He had just noticed that the stove was not properly centered in front of the flue opening. It would have to be moved, or the stovepipe would be crooked. And the thing weighed, at a conservative estimate, around four hundred pounds, since the dealer had conned him into getting the big model while he was at it.

His wife sighed.

"I'll put the frozen glop in the microwave. You set up the fossil-fuel converter. That doesn't have an oven in it?"

"No, it's got a HydraFlame Combuster to, among other things, fully burn the gases given off in initial combustion of the solid hydro-carbons."

She said irreverently, "You can't eat that," and went out to the kitchen. He stood, eyes squinted against the electric effect of the red outer metal jacket seen against the pale-green walls of the room. Damn it, how was he going to move this thing?

W. W. Sanson eyed the trio of blocky-looking objects, and silently asked himself, "These slabs are what we saw the sketches of? What the hell happened?" Aloud, he said, "These are the Cartwright stoves I phoned about?"

The salesman said, "Yes, sir. As a matter of fact, these are a lot like the standard old Superdee coal stoves we used to carry. Only this model has a tricky gimmick in it that's supposed to turn the coal into gas, and burn it up atomically, with nuclear destruction of the pollution."

Sanson got a feeling of chills and fever. With that description, the customer could get nervous and look around for another make.

"H'm, yes," he said, peering into the dark interior.

The salesman said, "Run you about three thousand for the biggest model. You could heat a church with that one."

"I wasn't thinking I needed anything that big." Sanson reminded himself he was, after all, paying for the thing, out of a totally natural irritation with Ravagger. Damn it, he asked himself, why should we go out and buy these things when the market research people had handed in their assessment, and everything was going according to plan? On the other hand, he had already discovered that the design, in reality, had all the appeal of a claw-foot bathtub turned inside-out and stood on end. The price, met in reality, not in a report on paper, gave him a fiercely possessive grip on his checkbook. If it did that to him, it was going to hit other customers the same way. And the pale-blue enamel on this batch of stoves was way too light, as if he were looking at several monster chunks of blue cheese.

The salesman was saying, "The middle-sized one is $2,200. The little one is $1,600. You can knock half-a-buck or so off all these prices."

Sanson moodily considered that there went all the crafty calculation of laying out a price line-up of $2998.49, $2198.59, and $1598.69.

"I'll take the small one," he said.

The salesman shook his head. "I wouldn't. That spare buoy they stuck in the center to eat the pollution takes too much space. Even in the old Superdees, that little model wouldn't hold a fire overnight unless you damped it way down. Then the fire stays warm, but you freeze. What's the point?"

Sanson stared at him. If the damned thing wouldn't hold a fire overnight, what was the point? Why sell it? He said, "The little Superdee wouldn't hold a fire? Since when?"

"Not if you wanted heat out of it on a cold night, it wouldn't. What you had to do was get up in the middle of the night and load her up again."

Sanson grunted. "You ever tell the company about that?"

"Why waste breath? They were happy. It sold because it was cheap. They were well made, those old Superdees."

"How about this job? What is it for quality?"

"Same as the old Superdees. I'll give them that. They didn't skimp on the metal. —As you'll find when you come to move it."

Sanson squinted at the salesman. "I'll take the midsize one."

"Good choice. You just give me your address, and we'll send her around. You pick out where you want it put, and get it right the first time. You don't want to have to move it. Now, you're going to want some other stuff to go with it, and we have to work out the details. Where's the flue opening? How much pipe you want? How far from the wall? What—"

Sanson gave a grunt of disgust. He had come in here out of a sense of defiance. After all, what could be wrong? And before the stove had even been delivered, he was already fed up with it. Who approved this guy to be a dealer, anyway?

Cyrus Cartwright II looked thoughtfully at the display. Well, there they were. Of course, there was no sense of urgency, no crowd around, no background of an oil crisis. What stood out now was the dowdy style and the price. But why had the style seemed attractive and the price reasonable in the plans?

A salesman materialized at Cartwright's elbow. "Interested in a stove, sir?"

The board of directors settled grumpily into their seats, and under the wary guidance of Cyrus Cartwright II, who held one hand in his lap while he kept a cautious eye on Ravagger, the meeting proceeded in routine boredom until Cartwright glanced coolly at Schwenck.

"Mr. Schwenck, I believe you have a report on one of our—ah—solid-fuels converters?"

Schwenck, a strip of woven cotton protruding from under the cuff of his left sleeve, growled, "Yes, I do, Mr. Cartwright."

"Perhaps," said Cartwright, his own bandaged right hand, clenched into a fist, coming briefly into view, "you will be kind enough to briefly summarize for us your personal impressions regarding this solid-fuels converter?"

Schwenck clamped his jaw. "Yes, I will."

"Please do," said Cartwright.

Down the table, Ravagger, glancing at Schwenck's wrist and Cartwright's hand, for the first time showed a perceptible facial expression—a quickly suppressed grin.

Schwenck took a deep breath.

"The stove stinks. That's as brief as I can summarize it."

A murmur went around the table. Schwenck said angrily, "If we have another oil shortage, we'll be able to sell these damned things to a lot of people, because it will be either that or freeze to death. But as it stands right now, nobody in his right mind will ever buy a second one."

Cartwright let his breath out in a hiss, and nodded agreeably. "All right. Now perhaps you could give the board, and Mr. Ravagger in particular, since checking on this was his idea, a few of the more specific details."

"The stove," said Schwenck, "to start with, is too heavy; if you need to move it, you're up the creek without a seven-foot crowbar. Even then, it's damned near impossible to insinuate the end of the bar between the floor and the lower extension of the sheet-metal outer jacket. Worse yet, there isn't enough room between the inner stove itself, and this enameled metal jacket. If the fire overheats, the jacket can give you a nasty burn. A child could get seared on the part of the jacket near the firepot. Just incidentally, you can see what that means in terms of liability.

"Then, the feed door doesn't open wide enough; when you try to load the stove, the door swings shut on you. The feed door, by the way, is hot. You can get burned on it, too.

"The ash pit is too small, so you are everlastingly carrying out the ash pan, which is likely to be overfull and ready to dump. The ash shaker gets stuck when coal or clinkers jam in the grate, so to get it free you have to push hard on the handle; the handle then gives way all of a sudden and your knuckles slam into the knife-edged frame of the ash door.

"All this is bad enough, but for irritation, the worst is the so-called Combuster. This chunk of metal takes up space, and gets in the way every time you try to put a shovel of coal in.

"Finally, for good measure, the mount for the optional fan vibrates inside the sheet-metal lining of the stove so that the fan itself rattles and clanks against the cast-iron inner body of the stove. It doesn't always do this. It does it now and then, in certain unpredictable, non-reproducible-at-will conditions of heat and related stress possibly determined by the phases of the Moon.

"In the small model, which I tried out after using the big one, this list of defects makes the stove frankly worthless. As a matter of fact, we ought to pay the customers to take it off our hands."

Schwenck's recital, delivered with venomous conviction, left a stunned silence. Finally, Grissom, the treasurer, sat up, and said, "Frankness is a virtue, Mr. Schwenck, but hasn't our solid-fuel converter got any good features at all?"

Schwenck looked as if he were thinking earnestly. "If it has one, I can't think of it."

"But wasn't this device your responsibility?"

"It was, Mr. Grissom, and if you are suggesting I ought to be fired for that reason—"

Grissom looked startled. "No. But either you're overstating the criticisms—"

"—You may just be right, at that," said Schwenck.

"—Or we've got a real mess on our hands," said Grissom.

There was a little silence as Grissom, Schwenck, and everybody else in the room, put the pieces of sentences together, to work out who had just said what. Then Schwenck cleared his throat.

"I'm not overstating the objections. I haven't even finished with them. The shape—the style—of this trap is straight out of the Great Depression. The colors—in the catalog, the one that's called 'Cherryapple'—in reality it's an off-shade of red that clashes with more backgrounds than anything I ever saw before. We have succeeded in getting dozens of these stoves into the hands of the dealers, and the one thing I'm grateful for is that it's dozens and not hundreds."

The silence following Schwenck's last remark was broken by a faint rustling and creaking of chairs as people shifted position uneasily, then Schwenck shook his head.

"Last night I dreamt some fanatical gang blew up half the oil industry in the Middle East, and everyone was buying our stoves. They were selling like hotcakes. The president himself bought one. I woke up in a cold sweat. All I could think of was the shock in store for all these customers."

Halfway down the long table, a pretty woman with dark-blonde hair said, "Do our stoves *work*, Mr. Schwenck?"

Schwenck reminded himself that the name and seeming mildness of this director—descended from a manager of the company named John J. Phyllis—could both be deceptive.

"They work," he said finally, "but to keep warm on a really cold night you pay a small fortune for one of the larger versions, or get up twice to reload the little one."

"Does what you've mentioned conclude the list of defects? Or are there more?"

Schwenck opened his mouth, but didn't get a chance to speak. Sanson, apparently out of an impulse to protect his subordinate, put in, "You have to remember, Miss Leslie, it's the small model Mr. Schwenck is really unhappy with."

The pretty blonde looked at Sanson coolly.

Sanson looked briefly puzzled, then winced. "Excuse me. I mean, Miss Phyllis."

She glanced back at Schwenck, who said, "It doesn't conclude the list of defects, though it's all I can think of at the moment. It's all but impossible to remember all the things that are wrong with this stove."

"But does it work?"

"It does give heat."

"And that is what it is supposed to do, isn't it?"

"Yes, but the problem is the way it does it. It's a very wearing way to try to stay warm."

"But if there were a fuel shortage, it would help solve the problem, wouldn't it?"

"Yes, it would. But if we ever want to sell two of these stoves to the same customer, or to sell one by word of mouth to anyone, we have a lot of improvements to make."

"What are you doing to correct the problem?"

"I've got everyone I can working on it. It looks to me as if we need a complete redesign."

"And how long will that take?"

"If things don't go just right, it could take a year-and-a-half. I never knew things to go just right yet."

"When this 'solid-fuel converter' was first suggested as a fit source of investment for us," said Leslie Phyllis sweetly, "it seems to me we were told it already had a long successful history behind it."

Schwenck opened his mouth, and shut it again without saying anything. Involuntarily, he glanced at Sanson.

Sanson cleared his throat. "That was my responsibility, Miss Phyllis."

She turned to look at Sanson.

Sanson said, "At Superdee, we sold a lot of these stoves, including the small model. So far as I know, no one ever complained."

"Then you disagree with Mr. Schwenck?"

"I wish I did. No, he's right. This stove is a real bomb, and that's leaning over backwards to be polite."

"But it's the same stove you sold before, isn't it?"

"In most ways, yes, it is."

"Well, how can that be?"

"Two things have changed. We've added the Combuster. That takes up space, and gets in the way, particularly in the small model. Then, too, we're planning to sell these stoves in great numbers, to new customers—customers used to oil heat. At Superdee, we sold them to rural families who had been using wood or coal stoves for a long time. These present models are still solid, well built, long-lasting stoves that will do a good heating job for people who need a reliable coal stove, and are used to them—or for people who are upgrading from wood stoves. For someone used to an oil burner, it's a different matter entirely."

"Why?"

"For someone who learned to drive in a car with a stick shift, changing gears is no problem. It's a different matter if you've always driven an automatic, and suddenly you've got to drive a stick shift. The market we are aiming these stoves at now will respond to them the same way. These are people used to automatic heat—to thermostats."

"Yes . . . but if there's an actual fuel emergency?"

"People will buy them if they have to. But everyone will make stoves once it's clear there's a need. What we can naturally expect is a big demand, which we can't possibly keep up with. Then, after we increase production, demand for our models will drop like a rock— because word will get around about the defects in this stove. Then our competitors will skim the cream."

Cartwright said, "I have to agree with Mr. Sanson and Mr. Schwenck. The fact remains, we at least have a stove—which is more than most of our potential competitors can say. And now we see what the problems are. If we can clean up the problems, we'll have the advantage we've been aiming at since the beginning."

"Does the combuster work?"

Cartwright nodded, and glanced at Schwenck.

Schwenck said, "It works, but the fifteenth time you bang into that brace when you put in a shovel of coal—"

"But, look here, Mr. Schwenck, didn't you know where the combuster was going to be when you authorized production? How is it that it ended up in the wrong place?"

"I've asked myself the same question. In the original computer design, we allowed room for the shovel to enter the feed-door opening and deposit the coal in the combustion zone. We even checked out the measurements on a full-scale hand-assembled model to be sure. And it is possible, if you have someone open the door and hold it open, to carefully put a normal-sized fire shovel into the firebox and not bang into anything."

"Then what's the problem?"

"There's a difference between loading the stove in a laboratory-type setting, and actually using it. This Combuster is held in place by braces—three of them reach down into the firebox. It's perfectly possible to miss all three. But the feed door tends to swing shut; to avoid the door, you move the shovel a little, and then you hit the left-hand brace. That never happened when we checked it out, because we were crowded around the stove, and someone held the door open."

Leslie Phyllis looked at him thoughtfully. "But now that you're actually using it, you run into these difficulties?"

Schwenck nodded.

"Are there any further defects?"

Sanson shook his head. "Mr. Schwenck hasn't yet mentioned one of the worst. For years, at Superdee, we routinely put a black protective coating on the body of the stove inside the enameled outer shell, to protect the metal from rust, and improve its looks." He gave a little laugh.

Schwenck looked at Sanson. "I never heard a complaint."

"No," said Sanson aggrievedly. "Me either."

"Now what?" said Leslie Phyllis.

Cartwright said sparely, "Fumes. Every time the fire gets hot, some of this protective coating boils off."

Grissom, the treasurer, glanced from Sanson to Schwenck. "Well, you weren't the only people to use that coating. I bought a wood stove during the fuel shortage, and the first good fire I lit the stuff boiled off in clouds. It stank up the house, and a fine oily dust settled over everything."

Sanson and Schwenck studied the tabletop. Cartwright looked mad, but kept his mouth shut. Down the table, Nelson Ravagger was elaborately expressionless.

Cartwright sucked in a deep breath. "Well, we now know first-hand exactly what our customers are going to run into. We have to clean up these things." He glanced at Schwenck.

"We're counting on you, Schwenckie."

Schwenck settled visibly under the burden, then nodded.

"There's got to be some way around all these problems. If we just have time enough, we'll find it."

Nelson Ravagger was wearing a blue bathrobe with an elaborately patterned red-clawed dragon on it as he opened his front door some twenty-two months later, picked up the Sunday paper, and padded back to the bedroom with it.

Julia Ravagger yawned as her husband settled into his side of the bed, noisily unfolded the first section of the paper, then gave a sharp grunt, as if he had been hit.

She sat up. "What's wrong?"

He passed over the front page, where big black headlines screamed:

BLASTS IN MIDEAST
PIPELINES HIT
LOSSES HEAVY

Julia Ravagger stared at the paper, then handed it back without a word to her husband.

He read aloud, ". . . It is believed that the powerful weapons used were originally smuggled out of the Soviet Union at the time of its political collapse . . . nightmare of the U. S. Administration come true . . . terrorists reportedly demanded five hundred billion dollars not to use atomic bombs against the refineries and pumping stations . . . authorities are now convinced that atomic weapons have not in fact yet been used although . . . at 2:00 A.M. the first heavy rocket attacks were made, cutting oil shipments, and creating fires which rival in intensity the conflagration in Kuwait at the end of the Gulf War. More explosions soon followed . . . A quick-reaction strike-force is already on the scene, and troops are in motion halfway around the world. But nothing can now be done to prevent serious energy short-ages. It is not known at the present time if. . . ."

Ravagger took a second careful look at the papers, then reached around and plugged in the phone that sat on the night table. He dialed a number.

Madeleine Schwenck's voice replied sleepily. "Hello?"

"Nelson Ravagger, Mrs. Schwenck. May I speak to your husband?"

R. J. Schwenck sounded even sleepier than his wife. "No, no, Mr. Ravagger, I haven't seen the paper yet. What's up?"

Ravagger methodically read the headlines, and as Schwenck exclaimed in horror, Ravagger read aloud the first part of the article, which reduced Schwenck to silence. Ravagger said, "How close to ready is our improved coal heater?"

"We tested it last week at the lab. I've been using one in my office for several weeks. Mr. Sanson has had an early version at home since around New Year's. The small model can't cut it till we find some way to shrink the Combuster, but the other two are not bad at all. Compared to the first version, they're straight from heaven."

"You see what we're going to have to do."

"We've already got a moderate production going. There's no reason we can't step it up. By next fall we can flood the market with this improved version. I'll call Mr. Sanson right away."

"Good. I'll get hold of Cartwright."

Julia Ravagger had turned on the bedside clock-radio, where an announcer was saying ". . . Inevitable that gasoline supplies will be affected. Heating oil prices will skyrocket. By next winter, a severe worldwide fuel shortage will be in place. There is already no way to prevent the most severe hardships in the depths of the coming winter. . ."

She glanced at Nelson Ravagger, who was hunting through the phone book. She said, "You actually have an improved version of that monstrosity in the living room?"

"Yes. That monstrosity's just a prototype. The problem was, they didn't know it."

Ravagger dialed a number.

Julia Ravagger said, "Was that the 'tiny little flaw' you said the management had?"

"The flaw was the company actually didn't have any negative feedback worth mentioning on some of its products, including that stove."

" 'Negative—' Oh, yes, negative feedback is the signal that tells which way a robot arm is off-course as it reaches out to take hold of something? A correction factor that puts things back on course."

"Right. And one way to get useful negative feedback is to have the exact people who can end a problem be the ones to get kicked in the face by it."

There was a click in the receiver, and Cartwright's voice said, "That you, Nels?"

"Right here."

"Thought it was you. I've heard, and I'm on the way in."

"Good work." Ravagger hung up the phone, and warily unfolded the paper. As he settled back, Julia Ravagger was favored with a fresh view of his combative profile. As one of her old friends had said on hearing of her marriage, "Well, Jule, now you've really done it. How are you going to domesticate that throwback to the Age of the Robber Barons?"

Julia glanced at the screaming headlines, and exhaled carefully.

Considering what the world was like, possibly the country could use a robber baron or two.

Crime and Punishment

The New Way

The night was dark, with a fog that blurred vision despite brilliant lights spaced along the road curving through the park. Traffic had thinned out, and only an occasional car glided past. Then from the distance came the harsh rhythmic sound of approaching heels.

A solitary figure came into view, indistinct in the fog. As the figure approached, it resolved into a well-dressed man of about sixty. He strode with an athletic pace along the sidewalk and past a low spreading tree growing to one side.

As he passed the tree, three figures rushed out behind him. There was a blur of motion, a sharp flash of reflected light, and a brief struggle. The three knelt for a moment over the fallen figure, then dragged it back into the shadows.

A car, wet and gleaming, slid past with a hiss of tires on the wet pavement.

Burr Macon, Chief of Criminal Documents, snapped off the screen and glanced at Hostetter, who was in charge of Apprehension and Arrests.

Macon said, "There you are, Stet. Time of Crime, 2:46 a.m., yesterday. Place, Central Park, within twenty feet of Criminal Activities Documentor #18,769,483 (fixed.)

Hostetter nodded. "Any previews or follow-ups?"

"Just a matter of patience and routine," said Macon. He picked up a sheet of paper. "The criminals entered the park together at 12:09 a.m. They passed, respectively, Documentors (fixed) #18,442,612,

#18,696,381, #18,512,397, and fourteen others before they arrived at the scene of the crime. They also passed through the range of Documentor (mobile) #146,987, but that merely duplicates information we already have. After the crime, the criminals, still moving in a group, passed six fixed documentors, left the park, split up, and made their way separately past various other documentors to a rooming house. They went inside and came out separately after about two hours. Right now, mobile documentors are with each of them, wherever they go. When you want to pick them up, it will be a routine matter."

Hostetter nodded approvingly. "How about the victim?"

"We've traced him back, too. He was apparently just out for a walk."

"At a quarter to three in the morning?"

Macon shrugged. "We don't have all the information on him, yet. But maybe he was a night-owl. Who knows?"

Hostetter nodded. "Well, I'll let you know what turns up. Thanks for the information."

"Glad to help," said Macon. He watched Hostetter go out with the folder, then sat down thoughtfully at his desk.

"What," he asked himself, "would it be like to live in a world where there were no crime documentors?" The thought made him uneasy, because he knew that until a few years ago, people *had* lived in a world where there were no crime documentors. But then the techniques of miniaturization had developed into techniques of microminiaturization, and these in turn into techniques of sub-microminiaturization, and now as a result hosts of tiny inexpensive devices watched the public streets, subways, and parks of the whole city.

They hadn't, Macon admitted, prevented crime. But they had certainly made it hard to commit a crime without being caught and punished.

He was uneasy as he thought of the punishment.

Burr Macon spent the rest of the morning in desk work, and in supervising the test of a new type of mobile documentor. Later, returning from lunch, he found a note from Hostetter:

Burr—
I picked up the three who killed the man in the park,

and they broke down under questioning. Their purpose was simple robbery, but one of them got too enthusiastic with his knife. The victim was a diplomat newly returned from a long stay in Turkey. That accounts for his restlessness, by the way. While it was the dead of the night here, it was late morning in Turkey, and he wasn't readjusted yet to our time.

We've checked the criminals for everything, including indications of deep hypnosis, and are clearing the business with the State Department, and the F.B.I. So far as we can tell so far this is a plain case of ignorance combined with an urge for unearned money. But the crime has to be punished.

Since the Farr Bill was passed, punishment by directed union is optional in the State of New York. All three have chosen this. I don't know if you would like to witness this punishment, but if you would I can save you a ringside seat. It promises to be something special.

Let me know if you want to be present.

Stet

Macon read the note over twice, noting especially the phrase "I can save you a ringside seat." From what Macon knew of directed union, a "ringside seat" at the place of punishment was like a choice spot near the electric chair at an execution. However, he decided that he should go, if only to find out for himself what it was really like.

Late that night, Macon found himself in a room about fifteen feet wide by twenty feet long. The room was, for some reason, painted a light green. Not only were the walls painted this color, but also the floor and ceiling. There was one door that opened into the room, and this too was painted light green. The door knob, and the hinges of the door were painted light green. There were no windows, the room being lighted by a bulb in a pale green globe overhead. At Macon's end of the room was a row of oak benches, shellacked but otherwise left their natural color. Before the benches was a long table, painted light green. On the light green table lay eight sets of what appeared to be headphones. With each set of headphones was a flat box with a pointer on a numbered dial.

At the other end of the room were two wheeled stretchers. One was covered with a sheet that outlined a body. The other stretcher was empty, but was equipped with four sets of broad straps. At the head of this empty stretcher lay what looked like a set of headphones, their cord neatly coiled.

Macon took his seat beside Hostetter, who sat at the extreme right of the bench. Several other men sat down to Macon's left. All looked uneasily at the headphones before them, then at the sheet draped over the stretcher at the far end of the room. Macon found himself glancing uneasily from the headphones before him to the headphones lying on the empty stretcher across the room. They appeared to be identical.

To Macon's left, someone cleared his throat. Macon glanced at Hostetter, and saw that he was sitting with his eyes tightly shut, and his clenched hands resting on the light green table.

The door opened, and a male attendant wearing a light green smock came into the room, walked to the empty stretcher, picked up the headphones and put them on the floor. He then rolled the empty stretcher out the door. The door closed behind him.

There was an intense quiet in the room, in which Macon could hear someone to his left breathing with a faint wheeze.

Macon looked around the room, and everywhere he looked, he was confronted with the same unvarying shade of light green. His gaze was drawn to the one differently-colored object at the far end of the room. He found himself staring at the stretcher covered with a sheet. The sheet was plainly lying across a human body.

The door opened, and the other stretcher was wheeled in. This stretcher, too, now had a human form lying face-up on it, and covered with a sheet. But here, the sheet reached only to the neck, and the face, pale and grinning nervously, was visible above the sheet.

Two attendants, both green-smocked, wheeled the stretcher so that it lay side-by-side close to the other stretcher. The head of the prisoner twisted to look at the covered form on the stretcher lying close beside him, and the grin vanished. His eyes widened. He glanced around, and swallowed.

One of the attendants picked up the headphones and their cord, and set them on the prisoner's stretcher, close to his head.

The prisoner twisted to look at the phones.

The door opened again, and a man in a plain business suit walked into the room, glanced at his wristwatch, and closed the door behind him. He stood about six feet from the door, with his back toward the door, and waited.

One of the attendants smoothed the sheet over the prisoner, then smoothed the sheet over the other stretcher. The attendants took their places, one at the head of the prisoner's stretcher, one at the head of the other stretcher.

The room became very quiet.

The prisoner on the stretcher swallowed again, looked around the room, then twisted his head to look at the stretcher beside him. He tried to glance back at the attendants behind him.

The man in the business suit by the door glanced again at his wristwatch, and nodded slightly to one of the attendants. Then he reached into an inside coat pocket, and drew out a sheet of paper. The paper crackled loudly in the quiet room. In a low monotonous voice, he began to read:

"The penalty for murder in the State Of New York normally is prolonged imprisonment, or death by electrocution. Owing to the advancement of technology, however, a more enlightened method of dealing with lawbreakers has been devised and is legally applicable in the State of New York. This method is known as 'Directed Union.' You, the confessed prisoner, have chosen this alternative. In the course of the next ten minutes, you will undergo the experience of directed union, and it is to be hoped that from this experience you will derive a new and firm appreciation of the inadvisability of causing injury to others.

"To the spectators witnessing the re-education of the prisoner, it is only necessary to state that the dial before you, numbered from one to ten, indicates the degree of conformity of your experience with that of the prisoner. 'Ten' is the setting corresponding to a full identity of experience. For reasons of mental hygiene the dial is pegged at the numeral 'five', which is roughly one-half the intensity experienced by the prisoner.

"Bear in mind that this particular prisoner *killed* a fellow human. If the experience becomes too intense, turn the pointer to zero on the dial. If you become sick, please leave the room quietly. The attendants will be fully occupied, and cannot assist you.

"At the beginning of the directed union, place the headphones on your head, as if they were ordinary listening devices. Remove the headphones at any time, but first reset the pointer to zero. Failure to do this may cause a violent and prolonged headache.

"The Directed Union will now begin, by authority of the State of New York, and by the choice and consent of the prisoner, feely given.

"Proceed."

At the far end of the room, one attendant put the headphones on the head of the prisoner.

The other attendant turned back the sheet on the other stretcher, to show the pale lifeless head of a man about sixty, a set of headphones in place on his head.

The prisoner jerked his head around suddenly, and shouted, "No!"

The headphones twisted off onto the stretcher.

The attendant behind him opened a long black leather-bound case, and took out a hypodermic.

"No!" screamed the prisoner. He twisted violently against the straps.

The attendant turned down the sheet on one side of the stretcher, inserted the hypodermic needle, and pressed the plunger.

"No!" screamed the prisoner. "No! No!"

Macon swallowed and looked down at the green-colored table.

The screams of the prisoner died away into a moan.

Macon looked up.

The prisoner was lying still, a blank expression on his face. The attendant was putting the hypodermic back in the case. He put the case away, drew the sheet up again, and waited.

A look of conscious horror replaced the vacant expression on the face of the prisoner.

The attendant placed the headphones on the head of the prisoner.

At Macon's right, Hostetter nudged him. "Phones," Hostetter whispered. "You'll miss it all."

Macon drew a slow breath and put on the phones. He adjusted the pointer to "five."

For a moment, nothing happened. Then he became aware of a grayness. Then there was a bright light that gradually died away. Then another light. Macon closed his eyes. Before him, he could see fog, and a highway. A car glided past. Just ahead was another dazzling light above the highway.

"Odd thing," he was thinking. "Here it is, the pit of the night in New York, and it's morning in Istanbul. It seems strange to be back. Lord, the air is fresh. It does a man good to get out, move around. Trouble with our generation is, we don't get enough exercise."

Somewhere, a peculiar high-pitched keening sound began, but the thoughts went on unruffled. "It's just like Benita to say, 'Don't go out, Ted. It's late, and you don't know who may be out. You could get mugged, or beaten up, or anything.'" He laughed to himself, and thought, "It may be night, but it's certainly a well-lighted night. Cars going by. The whole place filled with spy devices. Any criminal should know he'd be caught. Odd, though. There's an unpleasant sensation—a sort of—grimness up ahead there. Not grimness. A sort of grisly feeling. Maybe Benita—No, I can't permit myself to go psychic at my age. —I'll laugh about this later tonight."

There was a steady rhythmic sound of footsteps in his ears, and he realized that these were the sounds of his own heels striking the cement pavement. Certainly, he thought, no-one hearing that hard regular beat would think that he was uneasy.

Ahead, to his left, he could see a sort of low tree to one side of the sidewalk. He felt an increased uneasiness, stiffened his jaw, and strode on toward the tree.

"No!" screamed a voice somewhere. "No! No!"

He opened his eyes. For an instant, he was confused. Then he saw the two bodies, under their sheets, at the opposite end of the pale green room.

Abruptly, Macon remembered where he was—And who he was. He shut his eyes.

Something—He was aware of a swaying of branches. There was a scruff of leather close behind him. A feeling of dread gripped him, and he struggled like a man in a nightmare to force his body to run. Something smashed at the back of his knees, buckling them under him. There was a sudden brief pain at his back, then a sense of weakness.

Abruptly, rage flowed through him. While he was still falling, he jerked both arms forward. His right arm twisted free. He reached up to grip the little finger of the arm around his throat. Again there was a brief pain at his back.

And again, and again.

His right hand slipped, and fell away.

The bright light began to dim.

"No," he thought desperately. "*I don't want—*"

The grayness faded. There was a sense of distance. Then a sort of snap, as if whatever Macon had been in contact with was gone.

Macon opened his eyes. The room was intently quiet. But, he thought, I'm still in contact with *something*. But *what?*

He closed his eyes. There was a peculiar sensation, as of stiffness, dullness, a feeling such as one might have in a deserted house filled with a lifetime's treasures, but with the roof fallen in, the boards rotting, the plaster falling from the ceiling, and a must and mold taking hold everywhere.

A sense of horror began to grip him.

He opened his eyes.

His left hand, resting on the green table by the dial, twisted the pointer back to zero.

All along the green table, hands were twisting at the pointers.

Macon tore off the headphones.

A horrible scream gurgled up from the stretcher and filled the room.

Macon shut his eyes.

There was the sound of a body hitting the floor across the room. Then there was a floundering, flopping sound, as of a caught fish in the bottom of a boat.

The scream went on. Then words could be made out, as if spoken with a thick tongue. At first the words weren't clear. Then there was a vivid, clearly spoken cry:

"Oh, my God! Oh, help me! *Please help me!*"

There was a sudden, total silence.

Macon, both hands gripping the edge of the green table, stayed still for a long time, then forced open his eyes.

One of the attendants was wheeling the prisoner, white-faced and unconscious, toward the door. The other attendant was drawing the cover back over the lifeless face on the other stretcher. On the floor beside the stretcher lay the headset, and its cord neatly coiled.

The official in street clothes glanced at Macon and the others on the bench. "We anticipate that this form of punishment will cut the rate of certain categories of crime considerably. If any of you would like to stay, several other prisoners are scheduled for similar treatment. It will only be a comparatively short wait."

"Thank you," said Macon. There was a mumble of voices around him.

Hastily, they all made for the hall.

Identification

Mike Carstairs rose to shake hands with his latest client, a tall, expensively-dressed man with a streak of silver at his temples. The client reached into his coat pocket as he sat down, and handed Mike a small newspaper clipping.

"This is yours, Mr. Carstairs. Do you mean it seriously?"

Mike glanced at the clipping, which was a small ad reading:

"Law enforcement agencies punish crime. Criminal syndicates *commit* crime. We *prevent* crime. Call Carstairs Consultants . . ."

Mike nodded, and handed the clipping back. "That's the service we offer, Mr. Johnston."

Johnston said hesitantly, "I am in a very serious position, Mr. Carstairs. This is a matter of life and death."

"We'll do everything we can for you," said Mike.

Johnston glanced first around the office, which was furnished with expensive simplicity, then at a framed drawing on the wall, behind Mike's desk. The drawing was an artist's sketch of the Carstairs Building, and showed it rising impressively in a stretch of flat land well outside the city. Mike, who considered the building to be ugly but functional, had put the drawing where he wouldn't have to look at it, but where it would intimidate the type of client who otherwise might have a thousand questions as to Mike's ability to perform the service he offered.

Johnston said hesitantly, "I understand your principal interest, Mr. Carstairs, is in manufacturing electronic components."

Mike said, "Was that your purpose in coming here, Mr. Johnston?"

Johnston started to answer, hesitated, glanced again at the sketch of the building they were in, and shifted his position uneasily in the chair. He leaned forward, and said, "As a matter of fact Mr. Carstairs, I'm here because of a very ugly personal situation. Now, I hope you'll excuse me if I ask a little further as to the service you offer. You say you can *prevent* crime?"

"We can prevent certain crimes, including generally, the more serious crimes of passion."

Johnston said tensely, "Can you prevent murder?"

"Generally."

"Will the potential murderer, when he has been stopped, try again to commit murder?"

"No. Once we stop him, he has usually had enough for a long time."

"Will he be injured mentally?"

"He may suffer something similar to the dread, anguish, and remorse he might have felt after he had committed the crime."

"But this isn't anything similar to . . . say . . . prefrontal lobotomy?"

"No."

"I see." Johnston hesitated, then said tensely, "Mr. Carstairs, three years ago, my wife died. Some time after her death, my son and I had a serious disagreement, and I was forced to discharge him from my firm. There were some pretty harsh words spoken. Then last year, I remarried. My wife is considerably younger than I. Last night, I came home from the office somewhat earlier than usual, and overheard my wife crying, and being comforted by my son." Johnston hesitated.

Mike said, "Your son had a key to the house?"

Johnston shook his head. "I haven't got the picture across, Mr. Carstairs. My house is a very large one, really much larger than I need. When I discharged my son, for business reasons, I saw no reason to throw him out of his home. We don't get along. But the house, as I say, is a very large one. He has his room in another wing, and takes his meals in the kitchen. Our paths seldom cross. For some reason, it never entered my head that he and my young wife would do more than nod in passing if they chanced to meet. I realize now that this was extremely stupid."

"What did you do when you overheard them?"

"I stood stock-still for the moment, and listened. My wife's voice, between sobs, was very low. My son was saying, rather briskly, "Don't worry. I'll take care of him for you. There won't be anything left when I get through with him.""

"Did you *see* them?"

"No. I just heard them. The conversation seemed rather out-of-focus to me. It was a great deal clearer to me this morning, when my brakes failed in heavy traffic, and I narrowly escaped a serious accident. The brake line had been cut."

"What did you do?"

"I'd seen your ad in the paper a week or two ago, and been curious about it. I immediately bought a paper and turned to the classified section. You see, I don't want the police or private detectives in this. There is too much possibility of scandal. I want you to find out what is going on, and if my son *is* behind this, stop him. It seems clear enough that the situation is very bad. But it may be possible to save something out of the wreckage."

Mike leaned back and carefully thought over what Johnston had told him. Then Mike said, "Would you mind repeating what you heard your son say?"

"He said, 'Don't worry. I'll take care of him for you. There won't be anything left when I get through with him.'"

"How did he say it?"

Johnston frowned. "He said it briskly, as if he were about to squash a spider."

"Then what?"

"My wife was crying, and saying 'Don't. You can't do it,' or words to that effect."

"What did you do?"

"Well, I was furious. To tell the truth, it didn't *all* add up to me until my brakes failed this morning. But I had a perfectly plain impression that *something* was going on behind my back. I was home early, you see, or I wouldn't have come across this. For just an instant, I considered walking in on them. Then, instead, I went back outside and closed the door heavily as I came in. Sure enough, my wife acted odd when I got there. My son had gotten away, and I didn't see him till this morning."

"How did he act?"

"Perfectly cool, as usual."

Mike thought for a few moments, then said, "How did you get here? Did you come in a taxi, or did you drive out yourself?"

"I drove myself."

"Did you, by any chance, notice a car that stayed behind you for some time?"

Johnston looked at Mike sharply. "How did you know that?"

"It seemed a reasonable inference, in the circumstances."

"Yes, there was a blue sedan about three years old, that I noticed several times in the rear-view mirror. Sometimes it was one car behind, and sometimes two. I was suspicious because of the accident. I slowed down, and the car slowed down with me. When I speeded up, it dropped several cars back. But when I pulled into the parking lot here, it went on past."

"Did you happen to notice this car when your brakes gave out?"

"Mr. Carstairs, I didn't notice anything."

Mike laughed, then said, "When did you plan to go home tonight?"

"Not till around eight. There's some work I have to finish up at the office."

"Good. We'll be on the job by then. I think we can protect you, but chance can always enter into the things, so be on your guard."

Johnston nodded. "It will be worth a great deal to me, if you can take care of this."

"We'll do our best."

The two men shook hands, and Johnston went out.

Mike leaned back in his chair, shut his eyes, and thought it over carefully. Then he snapped on the intercom.

A few minutes later, Sue Lathrop came in.

Mike took the sheet she handed him, glanced at the background information Johnston had filled in while waiting for his appointment, and noted the type of car Johnston drove and its license number. Mike picked up the phone, and asked his man on parking-lot duty if the car was there.

"It's right here, Mr. Carstairs, parked near the west wall of the building."

"Has anyone been near it since it was parked?"

There was a pause of about thirty seconds. "No, sir. Ten minutes ago, a man walked past the car . . . oh, about twelve feet away . . . and got into his own car. That's all."

"Have we a blue car in the lot? One about three years old?"

"N-No. We haven't. But one drove through the lot slowly about half-an-hour ago, and went out again."

"Drove in, didn't park, and drove out again?"

"That's right. As if it were looking for someone."

"Did it pass near the car we're interested in?"

"Yes, sir, it drove right past it."

"Good. Get the license number from the films, and see if you can find a decent shot of the driver. Have it blown up and sent up to me."

"Yes, sir. I'll get right at it."

"Fine." Mike hung up and glanced at Sue. "How much did Johnston give you as a retainer?"

"Five thousand. He said money was no object, and not to hesitate if we thought we needed more."

Mike nodded and picked up the phone again. Looking at the addresses on the data sheet Sue had given him he said, "Hello, Martin?"

"Right here, Chief."

"Send one of our special cars out by 1430 Ridgewood Drive, and another to 1112 Main Avenue." Mike read off Johnston's name, gave a description of him, of his car, and briefly described the trouble he was having. "You might put one of our own cars out to follow him when he leaves here, and have the driver keep his eye open for a blue car about three years old. You can get what is probably a good picture of that car from the lot."

"O.K., Chief. You'll want us to have a couple guys in the tank, too, won't you?"

"Yes, I don't think we can afford to waste any time."

"O.K. We'll get right to work. Good-by."

"Good-by."

Mike hung up and glanced at Sue. "How did you know to send Johnston in to me, instead of one of our interviewers."

"I can usually tell when it's serious."

The phone rang, and Mike picked it up to hear the man on duty in the lot say, "Mr. Carstairs?"

"Right here."

"We've run into something a little peculiar."

"What's that?"

"The license plate on the front of the blue car we want to trace is splashed with mud, as if the car had gone through a puddle."

"Does that obscure the number?"

"Well, no. But there's a blob of mud that partially covers that last numeral in the date of the plate."

"This is in front?"

"Yes, sir. And, strange to say, there's a blob just about the same shape over the same numeral in back."

"You think the plates are old ones?"

"Yes, sir. It looks as if the plates are old, and probably the numerals of the date are retouched."

"What about the driver of the car?"

"He's got a hat on, and he's wearing a big set of dark glasses. Aside from that, we've got a good picture of him."

"Well, send it up, and send pictures of the man and the car to Mr. Martin, too."

"Yes, sir."

Mike set the phone back in its cradle, glanced at Sue, and said, "You heard me describe this to Martin. How does it seem to you?"

Sue frowned. "A little out-of-focus."

Mike smiled. "It could be. Or it could fit the pattern of a slightly careless murderer. He has a plan that strikes him as brilliant. It *is* brilliant. But he's afraid that if he waits, something about the situation will change. Therefore, he puts the plan into effect, right away, and drives it hard to finish things off fast before they get out of control. From the look of things, I think this might come to its conclusion pretty fast. How would you like to be in on the end of it?"

"I'd like to. I could have one of the other girls take over for me here."

He smiled. "Care to go in the tank?"

She shivered. "I'll watch at a screen if you don't mind."

Mike laughed, and glanced at his watch. "I don't think anything will happen till Johnston reaches either his home or his office. That gives us an hour, and probably a lot longer. It might be a good idea to have a light lunch first, then go on down to the tanks. We may be there for a while."

She nodded. "Good idea."

Sue and Mike had lunch in the dining room at the top of the Carstairs Building. Mike, having had the building constructed well out of town, had also provided a place to eat. The dining room he'd had built was quiet, modern, and pleasant, but the view from it was terrible. He looked out the window and groaned.

Sue followed his gaze, and laughed. Directly below was the black-topped parking lot. Then came a tall wire mesh fence. Beyond that stretched the railroad track, a mathematically straight strip of cinders dividing the scrubby vegetation into two halves. In the distance, the city hunched on the horizon, its manufacturing district contributing a pall of smoke to the general desolation.

Sue said, "It's no worse now than when the Indians were here. It only seems bad by contrast."

"The taxes aren't bad," he growled. "And it gives us room for expansion. That's about all you can say."

The waitress brought their order, then moved quietly away.

Sue said, "Yet, five years ago, I wouldn't have thought this was possible. I was still your combined stenographer, receptionist, confidential secretary, and laboratory assistant. When the bills came, I'd divide then into three classes. Those without threats or pleading went into the wastebasket. Those that tried to appeal to our better nature and sense of fair play went into the wastebasket. The ones that threatened us with lawyers, I passed on to you."

He laughed, "Yes, and I could always reduce that bunch by three-quarters, at least."

"And we ate lunch in terrible places, or brought it in with us."

"True," he said, "and what is this leading up to?"

"We're here," she said.

A messenger threaded his way among the tables to Mike's place at the window, apologized for interrupting, and handed him a brown envelope about twelve inches by eight. Mike opened it up, and took out two large photographs, one of a blue sedan, and one of a pale man wearing dark glasses and a gray felt hat. Two smaller photos showed the mud-splashed license plates. Mike studied them carefully, then slid them across to Sue.

"Not much," he said. "That's a popular car, and those license plates are probably inside the car trunk by now."

"If we ever see this man," said Sue exasperatedly, "we can recognize him by the nondescript appearance of the lower half of his face. Plus that mole just to the left of his nose."

"I know. The mole is the only distinguishing feature. And it could possibly be a fake."

They ate in silence for a moment, then Mike said, "What did you mean when you said, 'We're here'?"

"I mean, we've arrived. You've done it, and we've reached the goal." She glanced at him with a trace of exasperation. "What I'm try-ing to say is, here you are, a success. We are now eating in a dining room *that you own*, rather than in a scrubby joint. But somehow, I don't think it really means anything to you."

He looked at her earnest expression and laughed suddenly.

"Why is it funny?" she said. "What I said is true. Not one man out of a hundred thousand has done what you've done in so short a time. And what do you do? You don't like the view." For an instant, she looked as if she might cry.

"The view," said Mike quietly, "stinks. Now let me tell you some-thing. I am very grateful that things have worked out as they have, because it gives me a limited power to do things the way they ought to be done. There's nothing I know of that's much more painful, mentally, then to know what's the right thing to do, and to have to stand by powerlessly while some self-assured fool does things in exactly the wrong way. But you have to be careful, because the odds are good that this self-assured fool wasn't always a fool. He got there by a natural process. And one of the steps in that process can be what people call 'success'."

"What do you mean?"

"There are two ways to look at success. One is to look at the outward result, an accumulation of goods and power. The other is to consider the cause, the combination of work, thought, and good fortune that brings about the outer success. The outward things are subject to loss anytime. A war, a change in business conditions, or a natural disaster, can wipe them out, either in a flash or by slow stages. A new technological innovation could make this place, for instance, as obsolete as the four-horse chariot.

"Put your faith in outward signs of success, and you're in about the position of the owner of a sand dune. It may last quite a while, or it may blow away, and leave you with nothing but a gritty taste in your mouth. The man who achieves success is confronted with this problem. What will he do? If he doesn't see the problem at all, he is likely to get a rude shock. If he sees it and tries to ignore it, he has the mental strain this creates in his own thinking. If he sees it and recognizes it, he may fall into the trap of thinking, 'All things are impermanent. So what's the use?' Or, on the other hand, he may decide to *not* put his faith in outward signs of success, and then the whole problem vanishes. Instead of priding himself on something out of his control, he is free to concentrate on the attitudes of thought and work that he *can* largely control, and that helped bring success in the first place."

Another messenger was at Mike's elbow, and apologetically handed him a small envelope. Mike thanked him, opened it up, and pulled out a slip of paper. He read the message, wrote briefly on the margin, and sent it back.

"The license plates," he said, "are a blind alley." He glanced at Sue, who was looking at him with an unreadable expression. He decided that she thought she had been lectured. He said defensively, "Well, you brought up a philosophical point. I say outward success can be a trap, if you forget the part that inner attitudes and the Grace of God play in bringing it about. There are a lot of people with one foot in this trap wondering what it is that hurts."

Sue laughed. "I wasn't criticizing you. Do you remember what we used to talk about over day-old doughnuts and tap water?"

"Well," he said, "I guess a lot of things."

"Yes," she said, "and this very thing was one of them. I thought at the time that you had that idea because of circumstances. Certain ideas, you know, naturally go with day-old doughnuts out of a bag, and others with cake on a tray."

"True," he said, "but those ideas are moochers, not friends. When you need them, they're just on their way out. It's better to have ideas that stick with you when things got rough."

She looked thoughtfully out the window for a moment, and then said, "You know, as a matter of fact that view *does* stink."

"It sure does," said Mike, "and there's no escaping it. Well, suppose we go on down and take a look in at the tanks."

"You go ahead," she said. "I'll be down in a few minutes—if I don't lose my courage."

"Still uneasy about it?" he said. "Why?"

"I don't know," she said, as they stood up to leave. "Somehow, there seems to be something horribly fundamental about it. But I can't say what."

The "tanks" were located in the subbasement of the building, and even though Mike had planned the layout, he was always surprised when he saw it at close range. He had started out in three rooms, after a blowup with stubborn-minded superiors in a giant corporation. It now struck him as a sort of grim poetic justice that his own business had flourished and as a result was coming to take on some of the characteristics of the monster corporation he had detested. The only compensating features were that *he* owned this business, and he had such a long technical lead that there was comparatively little sense of the competition breathing down his neck. This might change overnight. But until it changed, he was able to run things as he thought they ought to be run.

He stepped around a raised, heavy glass tank about eight feet long by four wide, with a framework of rods and levers above it, and clusters of waterproof wires and hoses growing out of it like the roots and stems of some ominous jungle plant. He glanced up, to note where the wires and hoses were gathered into clusters, then spread out again to lead into massive white boxes in the ceiling overhead. On the floors above, he knew, were labyrinths of complex equipment, arranged by types in separate layers one above the other, with specialized technicians working at each level of the central core of the building. But down here was where it all added up. He glanced around at the blocks of tanks, with an intent technician seated at the head end of each tank in use and alternating his gaze between a monitor screen and a bank of gauges.

Sue Lathrop, wearing the white smock that was customary down here, threaded her way through a block of tanks, then walked swiftly down the aisle toward him. She looked a little pale, and shivered as she reached him.

"This place," she said, in a low voice, "gives me the creeps. Take my hand, will you?"

He took her hand, which felt very small in his, and looked at her quizzically.

She said, "I just want a little human contact. This place is so horribly impersonal."

"It's functional," said Mike smiling. "Or would you like us to paint everything pink, put murals on the walls, and pipe music in through loudspeakers?"

"No matter what you did, it would still be like having a morgue in the basement."

Mike laughed. Then he took another look around, and he wasn't so sure.

They were walking down the aisle toward a block of twelve tanks with a large placard suspended overhead, and numbered "1". This was the set of tanks Mike intended to use for Johnston's case, and he was glad to see that Martin, the chunky man in charge, was already well along with the work. Four of the tanks were horizontal, with the yellow lights lit that signaled that they were in use. Two other tanks were slowly lowering from vertical to horizontal, and two of the remaining tanks were hidden by the circular white screens that were put in place as the operators got into their suits.

Sue's hand tightened in Mike's. Then she took a deep breath and released her hand.

"Can't go walking around holding hands with the boss," she said. "It just isn't done."

They had reached the No. 1 block of tanks, and Martin looked up to nod to Mike and grin as he saw Sue. "Worked up your courage, again?"

"No," she said, "I just had the silly idea I wanted to see how this case worked out. Now I'm here, I know I'll have nightmare material for a month."

Martin said cheerfully, "There's nothing nightmarish here. Everything just looks like what it is."

"I think that's the trouble."

Mike said, "Maybe if we'd do the place over in Early American, and stick a few fireplaces around here and there—"

"Just the thing," said Martin. "We could have special workmen to trundle in the cherry logs, and we could hide the tanks here in secret passages."

"Just like the House of Seven Gables," said Sue, shivering. "Well, I don't mean to get in the way of business. After all, no one dragged me here."

Mike glanced at Martin. "Where's Johnston now?"

"In his office," said Martin.

"Any trouble on the way back?"

"No. The only unusual feature was that he slowed down well in advance for every stoplight. That brake failure must have made him uneasy."

"Any signs of that blue car?"

"None at all."

"How are things going out at his house?"

"Nothing unusual as yet. We're just getting started out there." He glanced around. "Here, it's just coming onto the big screen."

Mike glanced at the composite screen, that reproduced the scenes of each tank's monitor screen. A section of the composite screen showed a big white villa-type house, set in a broad lawn planted with many shrubs and trees. The screen showed it as from a slowly-moving camera about forty feet above the ground. There was noticeable fuzziness, particularly of distant objects, but aside from that the view was satisfactory. Mike was studying this scene, noting the drive that curved back past the house, and trees along the drive, when he overheard Martin saying to Sue, "Here's something pretty for you. How do you like this?"

Mike glanced around to see Martin holding out what appeared to be a hummingbird moth. Sue took it, and smiled. "It's awfully pretty. Is that a receptor?"

"One of the newest," said Martin. "Here's one that looks like a bumblebee."

Mike turned back to the view on the composite screen. The house was much closer now, and as Mike looked at it, he saw a man come around the side of the house carrying a set of electric hedge shears. The man's face had a slightly odd look, and after a moment, Mike realized what it was.

"Mart," said Mike.

Martin was saying, "Got them down to the size of large mosquitoes now, but below that, we're licked. There must be some way—" He stopped abruptly, "Yes, Chief?"

"Look at this man."

Martin came over. After a moment, he said, "I don't see any-thing."

Sue said suddenly, "I do. Look at the left side of his face."

Just before the man passed out of sight at the lower edge of the screen, it was possible to see that the left side of the man's face was a little pinker than his right. And the pinkness was in the form of an outline around a paler area that ringed his eye. There was a small mole just to the left of his nose.

Martin said, "I see it. He's been wearing sunglasses. And he's driven around long enough to get a little sunburn. The left side of his face, on the driver's side of the car, is more exposed to the sun than his right."

Mike said, "I'd like to get a closer look at that house."

"We've got a spare tank with a suit your size, if you'd like to use it."

"Yes, I think I would." He glanced at Sue. "Care to monitor for me?"

"Just like old times," she said with a smile. "Yes, I'll monitor. As long as I don't have to get in it."

Mike pulled a screen around an unused tank, stepped inside, stripped, put on a clear suit liner Martin handed in to him, and then stepped over to the black suit with its color-coded wires and hoses sprouting from it like limbs from an untrimmed tree. The suit hung inside the uptilted tank, and, as usual, Mike had great difficulty getting into it. When he had it on, he could neither see nor hear, and he still had the supreme awkwardness of making sure that it was properly fastened. The multiple cables that branched from the suit dragged at his every movement, and the sense of confinement brought on a claustrophobic sensation he had forgotten about. But he went through the necessary motions without help, because if trouble ever developed inside the suit, he wanted to be able to get out of it without waiting for help.

When he was satisfied, he said, "Sue?"

"Right here," came a voice at his ears.

"Tilt the tank up, check the fastening, and then we can start."

He felt himself slowly shifted backward, then his weight and the weight of the suit came to rest heavily on his back and shoulder blades. After a moment, Sue's voice said "Fastenings checked. I'm going to flood the tank and lower the control frame."

"Ready."

Gradually, the pressure on his shoulder blades eased. He heard a very faint rumble, groped with his hands and feet, slipped his hands into two sets of grips, one at each side, and raised his legs so that the slots in the bootheels of the suit slid down over the studs of the control levers.

"O.K." he said.

"Ready for test?"

"Ready."

A vague brightness appeared before his eyes, seemed to move closer like two separate movie screens approaching on trolleys, then merged, and after an instant of painful disorientation, formed into a faintly fuzzy view of the tank room. He could see Martin looking at the composite screen, and slipping on a headset. Sue was seated at a monitor screen, glancing from the screen to a set of gauges.

"Clear now," said Mike.

"Right," she said. Sue turned on her stool, and looked down into the tank, then looked up in the direction from which Mike was now watching.

Aware of a split in his sense of location, Mike pulled his left hand back slowly. The hand control moved back against a noticeable resistance, then the resistance gave way completely, only to reappear as Mike continued to draw back.

Sue said, "First detent. Wing covers open—Second. Wings spread."

Once more the resistance built up and gave way. Mike felt a throb at his shoulders, from the rhythmic pulsation in an hydraulic tube.

"Wings moving. Slow beat," said Sue.

Mike drew back farther, moved his heels by reflex action, and the scene around him shifted, began to fall way, and stabilized. He moved forward, till he was looking at Sue from less than a yard away.

She smiled. "It's the strangest thing to see you moving in that tank, and this little bug obeying your slightest move."

"You could appreciate it better if you tried it," he said. "There's a sense of identification I don't think you can appreciate without experiencing it." He was hanging now about a foot in front of her nose, moving the controls automatically, without conscious awareness.

She shook her head. "No. I'm content to remain ignorant. Incidentally, this receptor looks a lot like a big June bug, and I hope you won't want to come any closer with it."

"Test for hearing," he said. "I'm not sure how I'm getting this."

She swung the microphone away from her lips. "Hear me now?" The sound came from directly in front of him.

"Yes," he said, and swung back to land neatly on the narrow stand near the tank. "O.K. Switch over to a receptor near Johnston's house."

"Right," she said.

A minute or so later, the large white, villa-type house, was in front of him, and he was using one of the receptors from the specially-equipped car parked up the road by a big, over-spreading tree.

The first part of the check of the house went normally, with Mike and other operators switching control back and forth as they flew the receptors to trees around the house, and left them clamped in place, to give a view that covered the house, and the four-car garage behind it, from every angle.

Martin's voice cut in to say, "Composite screens II and III on. We now have complete coverage of the outside of the house and grounds. Better plant one or two inside the garage, Aldo, and bring in a sleeper."

"I got one, Mart. In the willow tree just outside."

"Not good enough. If they close those garage doors, you could be shut out in no time, and then all we could do would be to look."

"O.K. I'll fly one in, and clamp it overhead."

"Good boy. Now how about the inside? Terry?"

"Right here, Mart. I've checked the house pretty carefully. It's completely screened in, doors and windows. The chimney looks good, but there's a steel plate blocking the flues to each fireplace, and the only other flue winds up inside an oil burner. It's not very promising, if you see what I mean."

"Have to cut then," said Martin.

"I've got a cutter clamped to an oak tree outside an upstairs window. The tree screens the window from outside, and the room seems to be vacant."

"The window open?"

"Halfway. From the bottom. Third window at the side from the right front corner of the house."

"Oh, I see. Yes, cut the screen there. We have to get in somehow. O.K., get at it." He hesitated, then said, "Mike?"

"Right here," said Mike, aware that Mart, who had the whole picture on the composite screens, had to run this.

"Better fly up some gp's, sleepers, and grips, so we'll be ready to go in."

"How about the finalists. Do we want any inside?"

"Not yet. They're a little too bulky, and I don't want to commit them yet. Watch out when you bring up the others that you vary your route and cover yourself as much as possible. We don't want any hornet's nest effect around that car."

Mike grinned. "Right, Mart. I'll watch it."

A few minutes later, Aldo's voice said, "Garage's all set, Mart. Want me to scout around the outside of the house?"

"Good idea. I haven't seen any sign of life in that place yet. Buzz along near the windows, and see if you can see or hear anything."

Several minutes passed, with Terry slowly cutting the strands of the screen, and Mike bringing fresh receptors from the car to the oak by varied routes. Aldo said, "I've got something, Mart. I'm back of the kitchen. I think this is the servant's quarters. There's some kind of argument going on here. I don't know what because they're talking too low. Seems to be a man and a woman."

"What are you using?"

"A cutter."

"See if you can get through the screen, and up against the crack where the upper and lower halves of the window join."

"I'm in view through the trees from the next house. Is that all right?"

"It's about eighty feet away, isn't it?"

"Yeah."

"It's worth the risk. We've got to find out what's going on in there."

Gradually, the afternoon wore on. Mike brought up more receptors, and Terry began flying them in.

"Unoccupied room, all right," said Terry. "Empty closet, no shoes under the bed, nothing on the dresser but a white cloth, a comb, and a hairbrush."

"Good start," said Martin, then asked, "You getting through, Aldo?"

"Gradually. It's slow work."

"They still talking?"

"Yeah. The man sounds as if he's trying to convince the woman of something. Better hook into the recorder."

"It's in. There's nothing much coming through with that cutter on."

"Can't get through without the cutter. Can't do too well with it, for that matter. We're going to have to step up the power of these things."

Martin growled, "What do you think we can fit in a bee-size receptor? If you guys had your way, they'd be giant condors and we'd be out of business."

"Then we need something small enough to slip through."

"We've got prototypes, but for now, you're just going to have to sweat it out with what you've got."

"You can believe it or not," said Aldo, "but I feel like I *am* sweating it out. How do you get tired using a receptor's energy?"

"Nerve strain. And you unconsciously tense your muscles."

Terry's voice cut in. "Something funny here. There's a corridor with—to the right—an empty room, a bath, another empty room and a staircase to the floor below. But to the left, there's a room with the door shut, and a key turned in the lock."

"That's to the left of the room you went into first?"

"Correct."

"On the composite, it looks like that's a corner room with three windows. All the windows are shut, and all the shades are drawn. Mike?"

"Right here."

"Better go in with a grab, and see if you can wrestle that key out of the lock."

Mike dropped in through the cut screen, went through the first room, and approached the door. As he came close, it loomed before him like the side of a thirty-story building. The key looked like an iron bar a third of a foot thick. Mike hovered to one side of the key, and maneuvered up and down to see how it was turned in the lock. He flew up to slide a light-alloy rod, actually thinner than a knitting needle, but that seemed to him the size of an overgrown crowbar, through the metal ring at the end of the key. Then he pulled with all the strength of the receptor's powerful wings. The key resisted, then turned with a scrape in the lock. Mike dropped to the floor, let go the bar, flew up, took hold of the key, drew it carefully out of the lock, and lowered it heavily to the floor.

There was a whir above him. "There's a guy on the bed here, Mart. I can see his chest, and his head. He's gagged, wrapped up in a strait jacket, and strapped by the neck to the bedpost. He's got his eyes open, but he's not moving."

"How old is he?"

"Early or middle twenties, I'd say."

"Mike, maybe you could take a look."

Mike hovered, and looked in. He studied the brow and eyes of the man on the bed. "I'd guess that was Johnston's son. There's a strong family resemblance."

"That knocks the old man's theory to pieces. Aldo, are you through yet?"

"Just. If I can bend this back. There."

"Get next to the crack. If we're lucky, we can get a line on this thing. Terry and Mike, get that key back, then start moving in. Sleepers first. This is getting tough faster than we expected."

Mike said, "You want finalists?"

"After you've got everything else in first. Right now we want power on tap. We want a receptor behind every drape and picture frame, and crouched on every molding in the house."

The next twenty minutes went by as they brought in one receptor after another. The only spoken comments from the three operators came from Aldo. "You getting all this?"

"Yeah," said Martin. "But it's a little sketchy. They seem to have settled everything that counts before we got there."

Another quarter hour went past. Mike said, "We've got enough stuff in here to knock out a platoon. Except for the cellar. You've got all this on the composites. Do you see any way down there?"

"There's a dumb-waiter shaft, but all the upstairs dumb-waiter doors are shut. You'll have to get in at the top from the attic."

"Is it worth it?"

"The way this is breaking, I don't think we can overlook it. It'll take a trip up and down through half the house, and the door of the shaft may be shut at the bottom. But we'll have to try it."

"O.K."

They found the door open, and moved into the cellar.

Finally, Terry said, "Now what? We're loaded for bear on all floors of the house."

Martin said, "Aldo's left his receptor clamped to the window, and he's getting the finalists in place. Let me just play back a strip of recording so you'll get the full picture. Listen:"

There was a faint hiss, then a woman's voice said tensely, "I don't *like* it, that's all. We didn't plan it this way."

A man's low voice said angrily, "It doesn't *matter*. Nobody will *believe* him. We set it up last night, and the old man fell for it. He's gone out to a private detective outfit outside the city. We *know*, because I followed him. He'll have told them everything. That will back us up when we hang it on the kid. But we've got to do it tonight, before they move in."

"One thing's already gone wrong. If Roger should find out—"

"He can't. The kid's laid out and can't tell him. The rest doesn't matter. When the neighbors hear the fight, rush in, see the old man lying there, and the kid, still on his feet, it will be open and shut. He won't have a chance."

The woman murmured, "Everybody *does* know how they fight."

The man said in a low voice, "It's now or never. All or nothing."

Martin said, as he cut off the recording. "That's the way it's been going. There are all variations on that."

Terry said, "Do we know who the guy tied up upstairs is? *Is* that Johnston's son?"

"Yes," said Martin. "That's the 'kid' they're talking about."

Aldo said, "How did he wind up strapped to the bed? I don't get that."

Mart said, "I've only heard it half a dozen times. Listen:"

The woman's low voice said venomously, "Yes, you've got it all figured out! How come it's gone sour already?"

The man's voice said tightly, "The kid came home early. So what? Is that going to do him any good?"

"He knows."

"He knows what we're going to do. But not *how*. That's all that counts."

Martin said, "The son apparently walked in unexpectedly, overheard them, and got laid out for his pains."

Aldo said, "Could you figure out for me who this man and woman are?"

"That's easy enough," said Martin. "She's Johnston's charming new wife. She speaks of him as 'Roger'. And you notice the man has to get her to go along with him or it's all off. Here and there, there are some sloppy scenes where he tells her how crazy he is about her. Naturally, when she's going to inherit all of Johnston's money."

"What about his son?"

"How's he going to get it? That's why they're hanging the murder on him. The law won't let a criminal profit by his crime. Johnston's *wife* will inherit the money, and his son will go to the deathhouse. That ties it all up neatly."

Mike said impatiently, "But *how*, Mart? How do they plan to do it?"

"I can't say. They're going to do it tonight. But *how* I don't know. They've apparently got the mechanics of the thing rehearsed so well they just take that for granted."

"Well, we better figure it out, or they're likely to get away with it right under our noses."

Aldo said, "Mart, what about this in the basement under the cellar window at the side of the house?"

"I see it," said Martin, "but it just looks like a cot with a portable phonograph on it to me."

"What's it doing there?"

Martin hesitated. "Well, why not? You know how people dump stuff in the cellar and the attic."

Mike switched his viewpoint to a receptor in the basement. The cot was like that he'd seen in army camps, with a steel head and foot, flat springs, and a bare mattress. What looked roughly like a portable phonograph sat at the center of the mattress, directly under the cellar window, with a coiled extension cord beside it. Several pillows were piled at the head of the cot, and at the foot. On the ceiling of the cellar, about ten feet from the windows, Mike noticed a bare electric bulb in a socket.

Mike swung the receptor over to look out the cellar window. Directly outside was a large evergreen with low spreading branches, and just beyond that was the graveled driveway, curving to the garage past more trees and shrubs. About thirty feet back from this window, and around a corner, was the rear door of the house, with a flight of steps leading down to the cellar.

Terry said, "This looks like some kind of a setup, to me."

"Yeah," said Aldo. "But what?"

Martin said, "We'll find out before long. The woman's let herself be persuaded. You guys better practice switching back and forth from one receptor to another. Get the finalist in the trees along the drive, and a get a couple in the garage. Something tells me we're only going to have one chance to do this right."

By eight o'clock, Mike, Aldo, and Terry, had rehearsed so many possible maneuvers that all three were worn out. Martin had relief operators on tap, but was afraid to bring them in for fear they wouldn't have time to understand the situation and would just get in the way. The evening began to reach that stage of dimness where nothing is distinct, and Mike was hoping that Johnston would delay a little longer so that they could use the receptors with more freedom in the gloom. But at that moment, his long shiny car swung into the drive, and rolled back toward the garage.

Terry, watching Johnston's wife, said, "Here she goes, like clockwork, out the front door and across the grass toward the neighbor's house."

Aldo, watching the man, said, "He's at the upstairs window. There, he clipped Johnston's son over the head—not too hard—and now he's getting him off the bed. He's rolled him onto the floor. The belt, strait jacket and gag go into a laundry bag. He straightens the bed up, and tears out into the hall and down the stairs to the first floor carrying the laundry bag. Now he's in the kitchen. He's rushing down the cellar steps. He opens the door of the dumb-waiter shaft, pulls the dumb-waiter up about six feet, leans into the shaft, and stuffs the sack under something at the bottom of the shaft. He looks in with a pocket flash to check it. Now he lowers the dumb-waiter to the bottom."

Mike, watching Johnston, said, "Johnston's car is approaching the garage. Two doors are up, with cars in them, and two down. Johnston apparently wants the left-hand garage door, which is down. He thumbs a button on the dash. The garage door starts up—evidently a radio-controlled electric door. Wait a minute, the door's going shut again. Johnston stops the car and thumbs the button. The door goes up, and comes down again. Johnston's getting out to look at it."

Terry said, "The wife's ringing the bell of the house next door.

She glances at her watch, tries to look through the shrubs and trees that separate the two lawns. Now she's ringing the bell again."

Aldo said, "He's through at the elevator shaft now. He shuts the door, runs down to the cot, opens the cellar window, picks up the record player, takes off the cover, and shoves it out the window under the evergreen. Wait a minute, that's no record player. It's a tape recorder."

"What the hell," growled Martin.

Mike said, "Johnston's wrestling with the garage door. He isn't having much luck."

Terry said, "The wife's telling the neighbors how Johnston's son is in a rage at his father, and she's afraid there's going to be a terrible argument. Won't they come over? These arguments the father and son have are just awful and she doesn't know how this one will end. But she thinks if someone else is there, they'll stop, so please, *please*, they've got to help her."

Aldo said, "The man is putting some kind of thin rubber gloves in his pocket. He spreads the pillows on the cot under the window and puts a couple on the floor nearby. He unwinds the extension cord to the recorder, and plugs it in the light socket. Now he's going out the back door."

The man had now come into Mike's range of vision. "Johnston," said Mike, "is still wrestling with the door. The man comes out onto the drive. 'Let me help you with that, sir.' Johnston turns around. 'I'd appreciate it if you'd put the car away. And see about that door-opener. Nothing at all would be better than this.' 'Certainly, sir.' Johnston takes a brief case from the car, and starts up the drive. The man gets in and starts the motor."

Terry said, "The woman's leading half a dozen people from the next house. One of them starts to run ahead. She grabs him. 'Don't,' she says. 'I'm afraid he's dangerous. We must all get there together. He won't do anything with so many people around.'"

Martin said, "The son is just getting to his feet upstairs. He looks around wildly, yanks the door open and stumbles out into the corridor. He goes back into the room, pulls open the bottom drawer of his dresser, and yanks out a Marine belt. He staggers out into the corridor, puts one hand on the wall, and runs for the staircase."

Aldo said, "The man's started the car engine. Now he's backing the car. He stops and glances back at Johnston."

Mike said, "Johnston has his back to him, walking up the driveway."

Terry said, "The wife is leading the crowd of neighbors through the trees toward the drive near the front of the house—What's that?"

Mike heard it, too. A loud voice burst out from the direction of the evergreen beside the drive. "You can't treat me this way, Father!"

"You good-for-nothing!" shouted Johnston's voice. "If you can't do decent work, you don't deserve a decent wage!"

"You know that's not what I'm talking about!"

Johnston had stopped dead-still, looking around. For an instant, there was the faint whispering sound of a recorder's tape unwinding, then the son's voice came, very loud. "You can't treat me this way, Father!" There was a pause, and then an incoherent shout: "Take that!"

Aldo said, "He's out of the car! He's got a knife!"

There was the sound of scattering gravel, and Johnston whirled, off-balance.

Martin snapped: "Final it!"

Instantly Mike switched his attention. He rose, then dropped, feeling the spasmodic guiding pulsations of powerful wings as he dove for the figure springing forward in the shadows.

"Got him!" said Aldo. There was a faint glimpse of something small and solid that rebounded like a rubber ball to pass Mike with a whir.

From well up the driveway came a woman's scream. The voice of Johnston's wife carried down the drive, "Oh, I hope we're not too late!"

Johnston's assailant landed on his face in the drive as Mike swerved away. Johnston bent to look at him closely, glanced around, and stepped to one side of the drive, behind a tall shrub.

Terry said, "Don't hit her with the sleeper till she's committed herself, Al."

"Don't worry," said Aldo. "Mike, is he out?"

"Out good," said Mike. He'd landed his sleeper again, switched viewpoint to another receptor, a "finalist" this time, and now hovered behind a certain spot on Johnston's head. He triggered a weak signal on a particular frequency, and an instant later the response came, to be stored in the complex microminiaturized circuits of the receptor.

"Final it," growled Martin tensely. "Johnston's son is running for the side door of the house. There's no telling what will happen when he gets out."

Mike dropped the receptor, to hover over the fallen assailant. He again sent out the signal, but this time when the response came, he didn't store it, but instead transmitted the signal received from Johnston.

From up the driveway, there was a crunch of gravel, and Johnston's wife screamed, "Oh, we're too late."

She came running down the drive.

Johnston stepped further back behind the shrub, and watched.

Mike was now well overhead.

In the gloom, Johnston's wife bent briefly at the fallen figure, then screamed, "He's killed Roger! Oh he's killed Roger!" She ran back towards the little crowd, advancing none too eagerly down the driveway, with their flashlights swinging around over the numerous shadowy shrubs to either side.

Just then the side door of the house came open, and Johnston's son, the thick belt in his hand, came out. The crowd was by now opposite the side door.

Johnston's wife screamed, "You murderer! You killed him!"

Martin growled, "Aldo. Get that woman."

The son was looking around in the gloom. He said in a low furious voice, "Give me that light," and taking the flashlight from one of the unresisting crowd, started down the drive with it.

There was brief whir, and Mrs. Johnston was falling. While the crowd was still paralyzed by the sight of Johnston's son, Mike dropped his receptor by the wife, and repeated the process he'd used on the man who'd attacked Johnston.

Martin said, "Aldo. He's coming out of it. Just in case, get a sleeper ready."

The would-be assailant came to his feet, still holding the knife, and blinking in the glare from the son's flashlight.

In the darkness, there was only the steady crunch of gravel, and then the low voice of Johnston's son as he came forward with the belt:

"Now, we'll even things up a little."

"Aldo," snapped Martin. "Hit the son!"

"Not on your life," said Aldo.

"Mike," said Martin.

"I've got a malfunction," said Mike.

Terry said, "That one tried to kill the guy's father, and frame him into the deathhouse as a murderer. Don't ask me to interrupt."

Some moments later, the voice of Johnston shouted, "Don't kill him, Boy! Stop!"

The wail of a police siren traveled down the street and there was a crunch of gravel as the headlights swung in the drive.

Martin growled, "You fools. This muddies it up so the police won't know who to drag in."

Mike said, "Don't jump to conclusions. Watch."

The police, four of them, were springing out of the car, demanding to know what was going on. Johnston's voice rose over the clamor with the ring of authority.

"Officers! Down here!" Taking his son's flashlight, he flashed it around till he found what he wanted, then angrily pointed out the recorder, still unreeling its tape under the tree. "This thing," he said, "had recorded snatches of argument my son and I have had together. As my second wife here brought neighbors in to hear it, my handyman came at me from behind with a knife. They were going to hang this on my son, who was no doubt tied up inside, but he got free and came out just in time."

Martin growled, "That isn't exactly what happened."

"No," said Mike, "but don't worry. They'll work out an explanation."

One of the policeman growled, "Guy had a knife all right. Look here. And look at these rubber gloves he's wearing."

Another said, "You know how to run this recorder? I'm afraid I'll erase it."

"I'll show you," said Johnston. A few moments later the recorded argument was playing back.

At this point, Johnston's wife revived, and came down the drive weeping and crying, "Oh, I'm sorry, Roger. I shouldn't have done it!"

Martin grunted, "Well, that ties it up. Start working the receptors back to the car. Watch out as you bring them by the house lights, and hurry it up."

Mike was grateful it was over. He felt totally worn out. But there was the advantage that now the cellar door was open, apparently so that Johnston's assailant could get back through it quickly after murdering him. This would enable him to yank the recorder back in, quietly shut the window, erase the recording, and then rush out to join in accusing Johnston's son. As it was, the pillows were still spread out, to muffle the sound of a crash, if the recorder had to be shoved through the window hurriedly. But what was now of most interest to Mike was that the back door was still open, which made removal of the receptors from the cellar much easier.

Outside, Johnston's revived and bloody assailant was remorsefully telling his story to the police.

"All in a day's work," grunted Martin. "Next get the receptors out of that garage. We want to be sure they don't get locked in. Then it's home for a hot toddy and a good night's sleep."

A huge dim shape flashed toward and over Mike, swung back, came closer and darted away. Mike dove for the nearest shrubbery.

Aldo's voice growled, "The hell you say, Mart. There are bats cruising around here."

Terry said, "Now, what do we do?"

"Wait," said Martin disgustedly. "You'll have to go back in short sprints or we'll lose a hundred thousand dollars worth of equipment, and a lot of bats will have bellyaches tomorrow."

"Tough on the bats," snarled Terry. "It'll be black as pitch in another hour."

The job dragged on till about three in the morning when it was over, and Mike had never felt gladder to get out of the tank.

The next day, Sue brought the newspaper in to him, as he and Mart were discussing equipment modifications at No. 1 block of tanks in the subbasement. Sue held up the newspaper to show the big black headlines:

EX-MARINE BEATS KILLER!

"You boys don't get much credit," she said.

Mike said, "Well, we have Johnston's five thousand advance to split with the government, and maybe we ought to bill him for more. I think we earned it."

"More headlines," said Sue, giggling, "CARSTAIRS CLOBBERS CLIENT! —WANTS CASH!"

Martin stared at her, then glanced with a smile at Mike. "I haven't seen her in this mood before, Chief. You think it's safe to let this girl monitor for us? It seems to hit her like drink."

"I think she needs some work in the bookkeeping department," said Mike. "Long columns of figures ought to quiet her down."

"You know you wouldn't trust me with long columns of figures," she said, grinning. "Besides, what did you get all those computers for?"

Martin said, "What gets me is, how does she get the courage to come down here? Yesterday, the place made her shiver."

Mike said dryly, "Women are changeable."

"No," she said. "I'm curious. You've made some changes in things, and I want to know about them. What's a 'finalist', for instance. I take it a 'sleeper' is a receptor fitted with a small hypodermic. But what's a 'finalist'? And exactly why did Johnston's wife and his handyman break down? According to this paper, they've told all and seem filled with remorse."

Mike nodded. "As I told Johnston, once we take care of the attempted murderer, he has had enough to last him for a while."

"But what's the process?"

"Well," said Mike, "the basis of our process is the biophysical method we use in constructing and improving these receptors. But once you have one basic technical advance, you're likely to stumble over others accidentally, and that happened with us. We know, you see, that in some way the brain stores impressions of past events. But these impressions aren't always available on demand. There is a scanning process by which the memory is obtained from the stored record of events."

"Yes, I understand that."

"Well, we've found purely by accident that a particular signal serves to trigger the remembrance of very recent events. This signal is apparently much stronger than that occurring naturally in the brain itself, as the memory is close to complete. It is possible to detect and amplify the complex signal that accompanies this vivid memory, provided you have sufficiently sensitive equipment."

"A sort of electronic telepathy?" she said.

"Not exactly," said Mike, "because no one else is aware of the thought as yet. The signal accompanying the thought has only been recorded. But it can be transferred provided a second person's recent memory is first triggered, and then while that small section of the brain is sensitized, the stored signal previously taken from another brain is transmitted to it. It's a clumsy procedure, but it works."

"But what happens?" asked Sue. "Does the second person seem to receive a thought from the first person?"

"Oh, no. The second person finds himself suddenly with *two complete sets* of memories. He has his own memories as he plans the other man's death. He has also the memories of the other man, as he approaches the spot, as he hears the footsteps behind him, as he turns, as he sees the knife, as suddenly he realizes he hasn't time to get out of the way—it's all there in full detail, *just as clearly as if he lived it himself.*"

"Oh," said Sue, her eyes widening.

"You know," said Mike, "the impression a narrow escape will make. The man, for instance, who jams his car to a halt at the cliff-edge, to admire the view, and who suddenly feels the brake pedal go all the way to the floor. That man can get the parking brake on before the car starts to roll, but when he steps out of the car, looks at the pool of brake fluid underneath, then looks down over the edge of the cliff, something happens inside of him. His mind can't help putting that brake fluid and the cliff-edge together. He is likely to wake up in a sweat for some time afterward. It's much the same thing with the would-be killer, who also puts two and two together. The victim's memory is now his own, seen from within, and experienced just as the victim experienced it. When he thinks of the incident, the murderer can't help identifying with the victim."

Sue shivered, "I don't believe I want to try any murders."

"No," said Mike.

He glanced at the front page photographs in the newspaper she was holding, and pointed out the horror-struck face of Johnston's wife.

"It makes quite a difference," he said, "if the victim turns out to be yourself."

The Golden Years

The three tough youthful figures rose intently from the shrubbery, to watch the elderly man stroll through the sunlit park toward the lake. Briefly they studied his neatly pressed expensive blue suit, his stylish black cane, and his air of peaceful assurance. Then the tallest of the three jerked his head, and they were out from behind the brush.

They crossed the grass swiftly, almost silently.

Eric Morgan felt the warmth of the sun through his suit, breathed the comparative freshness of the air, enjoyed the park's varied shades of green and brown, and light and shadow. Ahead, still out of sight, was the lake. Today, the lake should be calm, reflecting the trees along the shore, though on a more breezy day the waves would sparkle, and—

His thoughts were interrupted by a sharp buzz—a sound that seemed right in his head.

There was an instant before Morgan's nearly automatic reaction could operate. In that instant, his attention was drawn to the chain of associations roused by the buzz, and, for a moment, he seemed to be back there at the beginning, two years ago, looking at the small white card, like a business card, that Ben Stevenson had handed him:

Benjamin L. Stevenson
Associate
The Prudent Assurance Co.

Morgan blinked at the card, then looked at Stevenson.

"What's this, Ben? I thought you'd retired, too."

Stevenson grinned.

"I *have* retired."

There was something carefree about Stevenson that puzzled Morgan.

"Retired from W-S," said Morgan, referring to Stevenson's old company, "and working for this Prudent Assurance outfit?"

Stevenson continued to smile.

"Not working *for* them. Working *with* them."

Morgan, faintly irritated, glanced back at the card, and on impulse turned it over. The reverse side bore an address and phone number in Stevenson's handwriting. Morgan started to hand it back, but Stevenson stopped him.

"I wrote that down for you. Listen, Eric, how does retirement hit *you.*"

"You want a frank answer?"

"That's why I asked."

"I figure everybody dies sometime. I also figure everybody *retires* sometime. Retirement is like death and taxes. And old age. You're stuck with it. That's how I feel about retirement."

Stevenson nodded. "My own feelings exactly."

"But, what good—"

"That's why I gave *you* the card. I have to pass that card to someone. It's a condition of association with Prudent."

"Wait a minute. 'Association' means employment? Or *what*?"

"Go to that address and they'll tell you."

"Generous of them." Morgan's eyes narrowed. "What's their line of business?"

"Assurance company."

"They're insurers?"

"Not in the usual sense. If you have an automobile accident insurance policy, then you're insured against auto accidents, right?"

Morgan frowned. "Go on."

"But," said Stevenson, "you can wrap the car around a light pole any time. All your insurance means is—you or your heirs will receive a certain amount of reimbursement—a cash payment, or protection against being forced to pay damages—in case of an auto accident. Prudent is different."

"How?"

"Its policy aims to protect you against *the actual situation specified*."

There was a silence as Morgan stared at Stevenson.

Stevenson smiled, and raised his hand.

"If you're interested, they'll tell you about it. I have to go now. See you."

Morgan blankly raised his hand in good-bye, then, during his solitary lunch, he glanced again at the card, looked up at the phone booth in the back of the restaurant, then glanced at his watch. Like a blow at the back of the head, it came to him again that he had *nothing to do* this afternoon. A succession of empty days stretched out before him like vacant subway platforms in a deserted city. He got up, paid his check, and went outside, calculating the shortest route to the Prudent office.

Twenty-five minutes later, he stood before a tall narrow marble-faced building, and read its discreet bronze plaque:

THE
PRUDENT
ASSURANCE
COMPANY

He crossed the marble pavement, pushed open one of the short row of polished glass doors, and went in. A line in the building directory caught his attention:

Prudent Assurance, Information 401

Morgan stepped into the nearest elevator, and punched the button for the fourth floor. 401 proved to be a large room divided into cubicles. A pretty girl flashed a smiled at him, and directed him to a Mr. Benvenuto.

Morgan, unable to fit the arrangement into his experience, shook hands with Benvenuto, and held out Stevenson's card.

"A business acquaintance of mine recommended Prudent. He said you don't *reimburse*—say—accident victims who have one of your policies. You provide *against the accident's happening in the first place.*"

Benvenuto studied the card briefly, and smiled.

"Did Mr. Stevenson draw a distinction between the approach of an insurer and *our* approach, so far as policies are concerned?"

"He drew the distinction I've just mentioned."

Benvenuto returned the card, and sat back.

"The usual insurance company policy is based on probabilities. *Our* policies are based on probabilities. But there is a difference. We attempt to *alter the probabilities* in our policy-holders' favor. What do you consider to be the usual basis of an insurance company's operations?"

Morgan, frowning, settled back.

"The idea is that there are *bound* to be a certain number of accidents. Other things being equal, the cost of these accidents will naturally fall on those who *have* the accidents. These costs will often be so heavy as to ruin people financially. But—by spreading the costs over a great number of individuals, each individual has to bear only a small share of the total expense, whether he had an accident or not. And he *can* bear that share of the expense. The underlying principle insurance companies are based on is—'Many hands make light labor.'"

Benvenuto nodded. "The drawback is that many hands make light labor *only* if the burden stays below a certain limit."

Morgan thought a moment, nodded, and spoke dryly.

"Yes, the idea doesn't work too well if the many hands are carrying a stock tank—open at the top and they have to pass under a waterfall while they're carrying it."

"No. And that, in principle, is almost exactly what *has* happened. Someone hit lightly by a car used to be embarrassed. How clumsy to get in the way! A jury asked to award a verdict against an honest man who had accidentally bumped someone else was likely to award just enough to cover the actual real visible damage. But the existence of the insurance company has changed all that. Now the jury may well decide to wring a big award from the insurance company. And a person only lightly damaged, knowing the jury may so decide, sees the chance to get a big award, and acts accordingly. The same general principle holds to one degree or another in hospital insurance, fire insurance, malpractice insurance, and what-have-you. The many hands pick up the open-topped water tank, and, lo! the burden is light! Then they pass under the waterfall of public attitudes and stagger out on the other side scarcely able to bear the burden. Hospital *insurance* now costs, just for the premiums, what a considerable stay in the hospital used to cost. A year's car insurance can cost more now than the car itself once cost."

Morgan nodded. "But what can you do about it?"

"There are other ways to make light labor."

"Such as?"

"Stronger individuals, a lighter burden, a better handle on the load, some way to permit those who want to bear part of the burden to *not* be forced to let go. Different applications of the same underlying principle, which is *to lower the ratio of load to strength applied.*"

Morgan looked at Benvenuto intently. "The principle is clear enough. But how do you *apply* it!"

Benvenuto smiled. "Our approach is the by-product of an unexpected discovery. I'm sure you're familiar with some variation of the parlor game played by one person studying cards and 'sending' a mental image of what he sees, while another person 'receives'—or tries to receive—what is sent?"

"Yes."

"And are you also aware that TV sets can be built at home, as part of various correspondence-school courses of instruction?"

"Yes—I've gotten a few ads for them in the mail—'Make Big Money In TV Repair.' What's the connection?"

Benvenuto leaned forward.

"Suppose, Mr. Morgan, that you were constructing one of those TV sets—incidentally one with a digital clock display in the corner of the screen—and in the same room someone else was 'sending' the mental image of a card, and suddenly as you worked on the TV *you saw the card.*"

Morgan blinked.

"If you could repeat it—"

"Yes."

"Then you have what? Some form of telepathic signal amplifier?"

Benvenuto nodded. "Close enough."

Morgan frowned. "But—this seems a long way from an *insurance* policy."

"You have, perhaps, the suspicion of having wandered into a nest of crackpots."

"Not yet. Your come-on isn't slanted to take advantage of gullibility. But I still don't see the connection."

"You grant the possibility?"

"Why not? After men have walked around on the Moon, why should I claim *this* is impossible? Grant it, and say you *have* a form of telepathic signal amplifier. Still—aside from settling the argument whether there is such a thing as telepathy, where are you? Is this amplifier small, compact, easily used?"

"In its enormously improved and precisely accurate form, it is large, bulky, quite heavy, complex, and requires a moderate amount of electrical power to use it effectively."

"In short, it's a white elephant?"

Benvenuto smiled. "It certainly won't enable us to compete with the Bell System or Western Union."

"Then—"

"It is, however, our principal tool in backing up *assurance* policies."

Morgan, frowning, sat back and considered Benvenuto. "You're giving me a good deal of information. How do you know you can trust me with it?"

"In the first place, who would believe you? In the second place, how can you be sure I've told you the actual undisguised truth? In the third place, I *know* how sick you are of retirement. I also know that you were retired because of an arbitrary company rule having nothing to do with any actual inability. You are perfectly able to work, yet you have nothing to do. A succession of meaningless days stretches out before you like empty subway platforms. You—"

"Now you're repeating my own mental images!"

"You aren't likely to use what I'm telling you against *us*, because we represent a way *out of retirement* and back to the top."

Morgan was unaware that, briefly, his eyes blazed. He sat back, and spoke carefully.

"What is *Prudent's* retirement policy?"

"We retire employees and deactivate associations only because of what we believe to be a lack of capability. The recovery of capability means rehiring or renewed association."

"All right, I'm interested. What's your offer?"

Benvenuto's eyes glinted. He leaned forward.

"Prepare yourself, Mr. Morgan. I am a fanatic on this subject. Western civilization is sinking—and it is sinking largely because of a lack of *insight and self-discipline.* We have the physical means necessary to pull ourselves out of this ruck. We lack only the insight and the *will.* With such means, plus the drive to achieve, where is the limit? Very well. I am an enterpriser. And I possess a telepathic signal amplifier. Is it wrong for me to receive a financial reward for reversing the decline of the West? Not if I do a good job. Here, Mr. Morgan, is a sample of one type of Prudent's assurance policies."

Morgan took the crisp slip of paper, glanced over the policyholder's name and the policy number, and read:

"The aforenamed policyholder is hereby *guaranteed* against failure in his *effort to secure the degree of M.S. in physics.*"

Morgan turned over the crisp pale-green paper with its interwoven design of eagles and starbursts. The back was blank.

Benvenuto leaned forward.

"Here is another."

Morgan read:

"The aforenamed policyholder is hereby *guaranteed* against loss of nerve if detected by the government involved, while engaged in espionage for the purpose of *locating and if possible freeing prisoners of war still held contrary to treaty obligations.*"

Morgan stared at the name on this second policy.

"Is this real?"

"Absolutely."

"But—"

Benvenuto nodded. "There is no credential so convincing in some places as treason in another place. It follows that to be accepted *there,* one should appear a traitor here . . . Here is another of our policies."

Morgan didn't take it. "You're showing me too much. I don't have any need to know this."

"There is no possible harm in your seeing this. This is a somewhat different type of policy."

Morgan read:

"The aforenamed policyholder is hereby *assured* that he will effectively *defend himself if attacked by a street gang while carrying out his duties in or about the above-named address.*"

"How," said Morgan, "could you possibly assure *that*?"

"By the same means," said Benvenuto, "that we can prevent a failure of nerve under torture, or any weakening of determination in the pursuit of any reasonable goal. We gather to ourselves *every unoccupied but capable man and woman* we can lay our hands on, and we use our receiving and transmitting equipment to stay in close touch with our policyholders. Our associates' skills and nerve are constantly on call, and they reach the policyholder by a route that no merely human opponent has yet shown any means to block."

Morgan stared. For an instant the possibilities dazzled him. Then abruptly he came back to earth.

"Wait, now—a fight against a *street gang*—"

"We have," said Benvenuto, "some combat veterans of unusual skill among our retirees. Are you aware that some organizations forcibly retire their men at *fifty*? Yet there are those in their fifties who can demolish the average thug of whatever age, and never breathe hard in the process."

"Some of this must be going over my head. How does *their* skill help your *policyholder*?"

"Why, Mr. Morgan," said Benvenuto, "*everyone* has at least a slight telepathic ability—and when that telepathic ability is sufficiently amplified by the apparatus that takes up most of this building, what do you suppose might happen then?"

The buzz was still in Eric Morgan's head as he turned, to see the three grinning tightly, coming for him. He had a brief sharp memory of the gym in the Prudent building, of the white-jacketed doctors and instructors, and of the exercise period imposed daily on every Prudent staff member, employee, or associate, and then that memory vanished as his hand automatically swung the cane up, and his other hand casually gripped the cane, near its lower end.

The voice, offhand and familiar, seemed to speak inside his head:

"*Jim here, Eric. Hyperventilate.*"

Eric Morgan breathed deeply.

The voice spoke again, louder and closer, deeply content:

"*Just relax. It's all mine now!*"

Morgan suddenly felt a transformation—like a sudden change in body tone. For a glaring instant, he was a tiger, a killing machine, trained for one purpose.

The cane snapped upward, the edge striking under the nearest chin, erasing the grin, then it came down again, partially deflected by the upflung arm of the second assailant, and Morgan could feel the tight grin on his own face as the tip of the cane scraped down across the partly exposed flesh, and then he turned to ram the end of the cane into the third attacker's midsection.

Inside his head, the same voice murmured, *"Okay, Ito, it's your turn."*

"Ah, so," came the pleasant reply.

Eric Morgan, suddenly gasping for breath, could see in one swift glance the look of stunned shock on his attackers' faces. The first one to have reached him was in the process of being thrown back by a brutal blow under the chin. His fellow thug was bent nearly double by the vicious jab in the midsection. It was number three who now represented danger. His face blank with shock, he nevertheless had a tight grip on Eric's sleeve, just at the elbow.

Eric Morgan was conscious of a faint hiss, of the letting go of the cane, and then his arm swung up and back and down, and, as he felt his assailant's grip tighten, he brought his forearm up, pressing up against the caught elbow, and his assailant sucked in his breath and went over backwards.

Breathing deeply, Morgan studied the three dazed figures on the ground. The third, the least injured, was the first to try to rise. Suddenly there was the glint of a knife.

Inside Morgan's head, there was an indrawn hiss.

Morgan turned partly sideways.

His assailant yelled and lunged.

Morgan's right heel smashed against his opponent's knee. The knife whirled through the air. Morgan picked up the cane.

The voice spoke politely in Morgan's head:

"Ricardo?"

"Thank you, Ito . . . H'm . . . Interesting . . ."

Morgan's assailant screamed as the cane flashed out, striking to the groin, the chin, the abdomen, the neck, the side of the head—to display in quick succession the vulnerable points of a man.

On the ground, the second attacker rolled over to partly rise, looked with dazed eyes at Morgan, then sunk back down again. The first assailant hadn't moved since he'd hit the ground.

Morgan, breathing deeply, walked toward the lake.

In the *Times-News* building, a man in a striped pink shirt, sporting a handlebar moustache, shook his head glumly and spoke into the phone.

"It isn't *news* . . . I know . . . 'Elderly Woman Breaks Mugger's Arm'—that would have been great stuff a few years ago. But it's going on all over, now . . . No, no, . . . Would *you* buy the paper because of that headline? . . . See? . . . How would *I* know what's behind it? But it isn't *news* . . . Okay, thanks, anyway . . ."

At the police station, a bored patrolman jerked his thumb toward the door.

"Sarge, there's another three cases out here for the bandage man. They claim an old guy with a cane went for them in the park."

"What's the matter? Couldn't they run fast enough to get away?"

"The story is they were just running up the walk *past* him, and suddenly without warning he went berserk. You know how these misunderstandings will happen."

"H'm. You know the latest crime statistics show a *drop*? We got help from *somewhere*."

Popov mopped his forehead and sank into the soft leather chair.

"One more day like this, and I defect to Albania!"

Andrei Sakharov stolidly emptied the last of the bottle into the shot glass, and loosened his collar. He glanced at Popov and raised his eyebrows.

"What now?"

Popov banged his fist on the table.

"This bargaining is supposed to wear *them* down! I am dealing with one man only—and yet I have the impression I am contending with relays of them!"

Premier Alexis de Toqueville blinked in surprise, took a second look at the rough-hewn, reputedly uncultured Ambassador Griscom, and ran the ambassador's beautifully spoken phrases over in his mind.

"But," said the premier, in his own tongue, "you—euh—you speak French?"

Ambassador Griscom beamed, and innocently spread his hands.

"Et pourquoi pas?"

The premier glanced at his aide, Jacques Belfort. Belfort was already mentally groping through his dossier on Griscom, Arthur P., retired, former president the Griscom Bolt and Spring Co., born Springville, Iowa, educated the Springville Public School System, summoned from retirement by President Curtis, who had himself come out of retirement to upset three front runners of formidable reputation—all of them destroyed in those famous face-to-face debates.

Where, Belfort demanded of himself, *had Griscom picked up that flawless freedom from accent?*

Burton Rainey could feel the discouragement build up as he thought of anatomy, physiology, dissection, internship—the whole combined into one long grind stretching out into the distant future. How he wanted the *goal!* But—the process of reaching the goal—*that* was another thing! Would he be able to persist? Would he fold up under the pressure? *Could* he—?

Almost guiltily, he slid the little pale-green paper from his pocket, and partially unfolded it:

"The aforenamed policyholder is hereby *guaranteed* . . ."

Ahh, that was reassuring! And it had worked so far. But was it real? Was it *really* real? Was it *really* real? In the long run, could it—?

The familiar growl sounded in his ear. But possibly he imagined it. Perhaps it was only a sublimated materialization of his desire. Possibly, by a process of autohypnosis, he himself could succeed—

"*Enough of that,*" growled the mental voice. "*Let's hear those nerves again.*"

"M'm," thought Rainey, "olfactory, optic, oculomotor, trochlear, trigeminal, abducent, facial, acoustic, glossopharyngeal, vagus, ah . . . accessory, hypoglossal."

"*Again. You hesitated.*"

"Olfactory, optic, oculomotor, trochlear, trigeminal, abducent, facial, acoustic, glossopharyngeal, vagus, accessory, hypoglossal."

"That's better. Keep at it."

In the big building, its numerous rooms filled with capable people unobtrusively—*undetectably*—helping other able people elsewhere, Eric Morgan settled into the booth in the lunchroom, and gave his order. The waitress wrote rapidly and hurried off.

On the other side of the table, Benvenuto smiled and settled back.

"What do you think of the assurance business?"

"Well—for a strictly impartial judgment, the dollar is rising against the Swiss franc. That's good."

"But you have reservations?"

"When I hear," said Morgan, "that the dollar is rising against hospital insurance premiums, dentists' bills, and a bag of groceries, *then* I'll think we have a grip on the thing."

"M'm. Everything takes time. But, we have the right principle. You see, it is all embodied in those few short words you mentioned: 'Many hands make light labor.' But the youth is no longer expected to labor—he is too young. And the adult is forcibly retired. He is too old. And as the age of leaving school is raised, the retirement age is further lowered, so that between the increased burden and the decreased hands, the weight to be borne gets heavier, not lighter.

"And this," continued Benvenuto, "results from *not* following perfectly simply general principles. Unknown to itself, our civilization has been throwing away a large part of its own assets—the energy of its most unwearied people, and the insight of its most experienced people. We can—as an assurance company—strengthen the individual hands involved by reinforcing the individual's determination, lighten the weight of the burden by giving pause to our opponents and encouragement to our friends, and indirectly increase the number of hands that are permitted *to* bear the burden."

Eric Morgan smiled. "By enabling people to *un*retire?"

"If it is a waste to throw away an aluminum can with perfectly good metal in it, what sort of a waste is it to throw away the tempered will and insight of a lifetime's experience? No, if employers can be so foolish as that, *we* are not. We—"

The two men sat back as the waitress brought the order. As she left, Morgan smiled.

"They save metal, but *we*—"

Benvenuto nodded, and beamed.

"*We* save ability."

Of Other Worlds

No Small Enemy

James Cardan saw the flash as he rounded the last horseshoe curve of his short cut on the way to the company plant near Milford.

Ahead of him, the gray morning sky lit up in a blue-white glare that outlined the bare trees of the forest, and reflected dazzlingly from the snowbanks melting by the roadside.

Cardan brought the car to a quick stop, set the parking brake, and glanced at his watch. He rapped the button that in this car rolled down the windows, then reached forward to snap on the radio. As the windows slid down, he could hear the diffuse roar of snow water rushing down a nearby ravine.

Ahead of him, the glow faded, to reveal a bright, slightly jagged line, like a stationary lightning bolt. Cardan located the bright center of the glow in the same direction as a large oak and a tall slender maple. Then the glow faded out, and abruptly the bright line was gone. Cardan glanced again at his watch, then turned down the radio, which had come on loudly and with a crackling of static. He twisted in his seat to see no other part of the sky lit by a glow like that he'd seen ahead.

There was a crash, as of heavy distant thunder, and Cardan looked at his watch. A little over thirty-one seconds had passed. Whatever had happened, it must have happened about six miles away.

The radio was now free of static, and playing dance music. Cardan switched from station to station, to find only music, local news, and road and weather reports. He frowned, shoved in the cigar lighter, and glanced out to study the oak and maple he'd lined up in the direction of the brightest part of the glow. What he wanted now was a compass, to find the direction of the bright glow.

The lighter popped out, and Cardan thoughtfully puffed his cigar alight. In his own car, he carried a compass and some other emergency supplies that he'd found useful on hunting trips. Unfortunately, this wasn't his own car, but an experimental car converted to steam propulsion by several enthusiasts among his men. Cardan had driven it home over the weekend to see how it worked, and had put in chains and a few tools, but nothing else. He glanced in the glove compartment, saw a collection of odd nuts, fittings, and lock washers, shut the compartment, and got out of the car.

Overhead, the sky was gray, but in one part of the sky, a relatively bright spot offered hope that the sun would come out. Cardan broke a thin straight stick off a fallen branch, lined up the oak and maple he'd used to fix the direction of the flash, and traced their direction on the muddy road. He glanced up the see the sun fade out, then start to rapidly grow brighter. He held the stick vertically, traced the direction of its momentary shadow, and held his watch so that the hour hand was lined up in the same direction, its point toward the place where the stick had stood to cast the shadow. Cardan considered his location within the time zone, decided he could neglect the difference between standard time and local sun time, and took half the angle between the hour hand and the numeral twelve on his watch as the direction of south. That meant the flash had taken place roughly to the northeast.

Cardan frowned and straightened up. If he was right, the flash had happened on or over a stretch of low-lying farmland about two miles to the right of the highway, on his way into town. He shifted his cigar as he mentally checked his calculations. Then he cleaned the worst of the mud off his shoes with the stick, and got back into the car. He released the parking brake, and changed stations on the radio as he guided the car around a slight curve. The radio switched from dance music to an announcer's voice:

". . . Widespread calls from rural families. No, folks, there has been no plane crash, to the best of our knowledge, and authorities contacted by this station assure us that the 'light in the sky' was just a momentary bright reflection of the sun on the snow. It's a dark day, and when the sun does come out, it can be unusually dazzling. Now, we have a popular ballad by . . ."

Cardan tried a variety of other stations, one after the other, found nothing about the flash, and switched back to the local station. He turned down the volume, and drove swiftly but carefully toward the highway.

He puffed his cigar alight once more as the car came down the last steep hill toward the highway. He judged the speed of the oncoming cars, swung out into the traffic, and settled down for the run to Milford, keeping to the right-hand lane so he could pull over to the side if he saw anything unusual near the site of the flash.

Soon the hum of the tires, and the soft *whoosh* of traffic passing to his left, formed a background to Cardan's thoughts, and for a moment the cars gliding smoothly by made him think of all the changes that had come about in the past fifty years. This in turn led him to wonder briefly about the coming fifty years. Then he puffed thoughtfully on his cigar, and he was thinking of that last meeting at the plant, and of what was waiting for him there today. As Donovan had remarked at the end of that last meeting, while squinting over Cardan's shoulder, "You know, Chief, if you rush too fast into untraveled country, you're likely to wind up all of a sudden at the bottom of a sinkhole, or inside a bear's den."

"Sure," said Cardan. "If your legs outrun your eyes and your mind, that may happen. But," he added, studying the layout of wires, resistors, condensers, and other circuit elements mounted on a board, "if you refuse to travel unfamiliar country, you aren't likely to find anything new."

"You won't be so likely to break a leg. Or to electrocute yourself, either."

Maclane, a sharp-featured, slender man sitting on the other side of the table, said, "Nobody is going to electrocute himself with this, Don. That's the whole business, right on that board."

"No power source?" said Donovan. He walked around the table, a tall, athletic, blond-haired man, and stood looking down at the circuit.

"Nothing but what you see," said Maclane.

Cardan said, "And you got the diagram for this by sending for a patent?"

Maclane shook his head. "I got the *idea* there. It struck me that if I made a change here and a change there, the circuit would look better. It would be . . . well, better balanced. So I made the changes. And there's the result."

"Let's see if I understand you," said Cardan. "You say that if you put your hands on these contacts, and adjust this variable condenser, you get a *sensation*?"

"Right. In the original, I understand it was a tactual sensation. With this adaptation, it's visual."

Donovan said roughly, "In my opinion, this sounds like a lot of bunk."

Maclane looked up sharply. "Why?"

"Because, with no power source, there's no current flow, and with no current flow, the circuit can't operate. Therefore, you can't feel anything, or have any other effect."

"There's no power source in a crystal radio set, either," said Maclane. "Are you going to say that there is, therefore, no current flow in the circuit, and therefore you can't hear anything, or have any other effect?"

"Well, that's different. The crystal set picks up man-made signals sent out to it on purpose."

"You think it won't pick up *natural* signals that aren't sent out to it on purpose? How about a flash of lightning? The crystal set has no optical components to pick up the flash. It has no megaphone device to magnify the sound of the thunder. Therefore, how could it possibly detect a flash of lightning? The idea is too ridiculous to consider, isn't it?"

Donovan frowned. "What you're saying is, we've got something new here, and we're in about the same position as the original experimenters with static electricity?"

"I touch those contacts, and I get a visual impression. That's all I say. But I *do* say that."

"How could you explain a thing like that?"

"Let's work the textbook out later," said Maclane. "Right now all I want anyone to do is to touch these contacts."

Cardan said, "Turn it over and let's see the other side."

Maclane picked up the board and held it up. There was nothing on the back but a faint smear of what looked like grease.

"All right," said Cardan, putting his cigar in a tray. "The worst we should get out of this is a jolt from a charged condenser."

"Let me do this first, Chief," said Donovan.

"Go ahead," said Cardan.

Donovan put his hands on the contacts. Maclane turned the variable condenser. Donovan said, "Heck, Mac, I don't get any effect at all. I might as well—" Abruptly he cut off, and frowned.

"Well?" said Maclane.

"Go back a little. Do that over again."

Maclane eased back on the variable condenser.

Donovan said sharply, "Hold it. Right around there. Stop. That's it."

"What is it?"

"I don't know." Donovan had his eyes shut tightly. "I don't know what it is. But I see *something*."

Maclane nodded. "In color?"

"No. There's no color. For that matter, there's no form." Donovan scowled. "I mean, the form doesn't—" His voice trailed off.

Maclane said, "It's not in focus?"

"I guess that's it. It's not in focus."

Cardan glanced at Maclane, then at Donovan. Donovan let go of the contacts, turned the condenser a trifle, took hold, and let go again. He shook his head, and glanced at Cardan. "It's a funny effect."

Cardan got up, slid the device over, and took hold. He had no more awareness of any unusual sensation from it than if he had just taken hold of a doorknob.

Maclane turned the knob of the variable condenser. Cardan, his eyes shut, suddenly seemed to be looking at a light through a gray blanket. He raised his hands as if to brush away an obstruction. The sensation was gone instantly. He took hold of the contacts again and now there was nothing unusual.

"Go back," said Cardan. "Try that once more."

Abruptly he had the sensation again. He seemed to be looking through a gray blanket, or through an unfocused microscope in a bad light.

Cardan let go of the contacts and opened his eyes. "You've got something."

Maclane smiled. "Thanks."

Donovan said, "What are you going to do now, Mac?"

Maclane said, "I'm going to get a record of the temperature, humidity, weather conditions, and everything else I can think of. This may not work tomorrow."

Cardan puffed his cigar alight. "Suppose you were to replace a few more constants in that circuit with variables? Now here, for instance, you've got a resistor. Suppose you put in a rheostat? Why not use this circuit as a model, and build another like it with more variable circuit elements? It might not work, but then again—"

Maclane nodded. "It's worth a try, all right. I can do that over the weekend."

"Good idea."

The three men looked at each other.

"Well," said Maclane with a grin. "I have to get home on time for dinner tonight, or my wife will have a fit. But I don't think I'll be there a heck of a long time."

Now, as Cardan sped along the highway on Monday morning, he was wondering what Maclane had done over the weekend. Ahead, he saw he was coming to a spot on the highway about opposite the site of the flash. A quick glance showed him nothing unusual. Then he was swinging around a wide, well-banked curve to the left, and abruptly he slammed on the brakes.

Straight ahead was a massive pile-up of traffic. One State police car was pulled off on the shoulder of the road, and two more were parked on the partly snow-covered grassy strip in the center. A patrolman was on the road ahead of Cardan, waving the oncoming traffic across the grass and back into the southbound lanes on the other side. The stopped cars in the traffic jam ahead of Cardan were unlike cars he'd seen in traffic jams before; a great number of these cars had their hoods up. At some of the cars, the owners were bent down looking into the engine compartment. Other cars were apparently deserted, the owners trying for rides in the cars now being sent back toward the south.

Directly in front of Cardan, the State policeman thrust his right arm out to his side, gesturing urgently for Cardan to cross the mall and head back. Cardan obediently crossed the grass, then swung over onto the shoulder of the southbound side of the road, stopped, backed out of the stream of traffic crossing the grass, and swung the car around so it was headed north.

A shout, followed by the blast of a whistle, reached him, and he glanced around to see a police officer striding toward him angrily from the right. Cardan glanced at the other cars, all apparently stalled, thrust his cigar at a belligerent angle, set the brake, slid under the wheel and was out of the car on the right-hand side, pointing angrily at the stalled cars, before the policeman had time to reach him.

The officer was shouting and pointing at the southbound lanes. At the fender of a parked police car, several other patrolmen turned around, and looked on alertly.

Cardan ignored the others, and concentrated on the patrolman before him. Some switch in Cardan's brain seemed to mute the function of hearing, so that he was aware only of a generalized noise. With his mind concentrated on the other man's eyes, Cardan hurled words at him like a warship slamming rockets and shells at its target. As the police officer angrily gestured to the south, Cardan remorselessly pointed to the stalled cars. There was an interval like a combined earthquake and hurricane, and at the end of it Cardan was still pointing at the cars. The policeman, looking dazed, glanced over his shoulder for support. The other officers had moved off to help direct traffic.

"Now," Cardan demanded, "what is this? Why are these cars stuck? How long has this been going on? And wasn't there a bright flash about two miles to the northeast, in that direction?"

The policeman said uncertainly, "Are you investigating that?"

"That's right. I want to know if there's any connection between that flash and this tie-up. How long have these cars been here?"

"It started about fifteen minutes ago. One of our cars was in the middle of it and radioed the news. We were already on the way, so we managed to straighten things out and get traffic turned around and moving south."

"These cars with the hoods up are stalled?"

"That's right, sir. They're *all* stalled."

"What happened?"

"Their engines just sputtered and quit."

"They can't be started again?"

"No, sir. The starting motors will turn the engines over, but the engines won't fire."

"How about that flash? Wasn't that right over there?"

"I've heard about that, but I don't know anything about it. Anyway, that was before this happened."

"But it was near here?"

"Yes, it was. It was out on the flats there, somewhere. But I don't know where."

"What's at the north end of this jam? Are there police there, turning the southbound traffic around heading it back north?"

"Yes, sir. Just the same as we're doing here."

Cardan nodded. He looked at the stalled cars, glanced out over the low flat land to the right of the road, then looked back at his car.

The police officer said, "If I were you, sir, I'd investigate this on foot. If you go in there, you're likely to get stranded."

"The engine would sputter and then quit?"

"That's right. If you were going slowly enough, you could probably back up and get out. But if you roll too far, you're stuck, and we'd have to use a tow cable to get you out."

Cardan thought a moment, then said, "I'll go slowly. This car has an experimental engine, and it may be important to know if it can get through."

The patrolman's eyes widened.

Cardan got back into the car, leaving the door open. "You want to ride down with me?"

"I'd better stay here. Thanks, anyway."

"Thanks for your help."

"That's all right, sir. I hope you get through." The policeman shut the door, and Cardan drove the car slowly ahead. When he'd gone about a hundred feet, Cardan stopped and called back, "Am I in it, yet?"

"You're right in it! Your engine should have stalled by now!"

"It's O.K., so far!" Cardan waved, and started ahead. Gliding steadily up the grass, Cardan rolled along between cars stalled on both sides, with people thronging back along the sides of the road and up the mall in the center. He tapped his horn gently, and they jumped out of the way, staring and shouting questions. The pile-up lasted for a good half mile. Somewhere in the middle of it, Cardan spotted a young woman in a little red sports car, a look of furious determination on her face, her hands gripping the wheel as she went nowhere. At this point, most of the cars were deserted. Cardan stopped, and rolled down a window.

"Are you planning to stay here?"

"I've just finished paying for this car, and if I leave it, I don't know *what* will happen to it." She stared at him. "Your car's moving!"

Cardan nodded. "I'd pull you if I had a chain."

"I've got a tow strap."

"Fine. Now, tell me what happened. I take it you've been in this from the beginning."

She nodded. "I was going about fifty when the engine coughed and quit. I put on the brake, then for just an instant I thought I must be mistaken about the engine, because I wasn't falling behind the rest of the traffic. We all rolled to a stop more or less at the same time. I tried to start the car, but I couldn't do it."

"Did you see a flash?"

"Not then. Earlier."

"About how much earlier?"

"Oh, I'd say five to ten minutes."

Cardan nodded. He got out of the car and looked thoughtfully in the direction from which he thought the flash had come. He could see nothing unusual but only flat land with brown strips where the ground showed through a layer of snow. To the other side of the road here, the ground rose in a long hill that grew steep and was cut away by the road ahead. But nowhere did he see anything unusual.

"O.K.," he said. "Let's have that tow strap."

He towed the girl out, and down a slight downgrade at the head of the traffic jam, then watched as the engine of her little sports car caught with a bang. She jumped out, ran back, threw her arms around him and gave him a big hug and a kiss. The police grinned as Cardan wiped off the lipstick, and the sports car buzzed off into the northbound traffic. A few minutes later, Cardan followed, having parried questions as to whether he was working for the Defense Department or the Atomic Energy Commission. When he pulled into the parking lot of the Milford plant, he noticed that it was less than half-full.

He parked, went up to his office, and found a small crowd packed around Donovan and Maclane, who were seated at the long table, wearing headsets with one wire at each earphone cut, bent back, and taped. Somebody glanced up, and murmured, "Morning, Chief," and Cardan grunted a greeting. The crowd momentarily broke into individuals, who looked around to say a brief "good morning," and then went back to watching Maclane and Donovan, both of whom were leaning forward, their elbows on the table, their hands at their temples and their eyes tightly shut.

Cardan looked at the crowd, and wondered exactly what Maclane and Donovan had found. No one seemed anxious to let him in on it, but Cardan, studying their tense expressions, felt an uneasy premonition.

"Gray," said Maclane in a low voice. "Taller and more strongly built then usual. Dressed in a kind of coverall, with what I guess are insignia pinned on the chest. They're apparently working some kind of launcher. There goes another one. Can't judge direction at all because the sun isn't visible, and I'm not familiar with the place."

Cardan scowled, took out a fresh cigar, and worked his way around behind his desk. He pulled open a drawer, got out a match, and puffed the cigar alight.

"Listen," said somebody in the crowd around Maclane. "I don't quite get that. Does it slide on rails, or what? Is there a rocket blast? Is it catapulted out by steam? How *is* the thing launched?"

Donovan said, "When the thing—missile—whatever you want to call it—is dropped into the launcher, it travels up a half-cylinder shaped like a . . . oh . . . a piece of half-round guttering about a foot across at the top."

"You mean, this launcher is like half of a cylinder that's a foot in diameter?"

"Yes. A cylinder split lengthwise, so as to form a sort of trough. The whole thing looks about six feet long, and it's mounted on a tripod. There are a couple of wheels on the side, I suppose to set azimuth and elevation, there's a set of graduated scales, and several locking levers. The missile is set in at the lower end, and slides up the cylinder with no means of propulsion *I* can see."

Maclane said, "You may think I'm nuts, Don, but I can influence this picture."

A plaintive voice said, "How about another look, Don?"

"It's Mike's turn," said Donovan.

Maclane said, "If you think I'm going to let go of it at this point after two days and a night wrestling with the circuit, you're crazy."

Cardan, his curiosity growing by the minute, stepped forward, said "Excuse me," and "Let me through, please," and got no result from the tier of intent backs between him and the table. He grunted, puffed his cigar to a red glow, and angled it so that it heated the back of first one neck and then another. In a few seconds he was at Maclane's shoulder. He studied what was visible of the circuit, and noted that the modified headphones had wires that ran to two contacts like those he'd touched when Maclane had demonstrated the device on Saturday. Cautiously Cardan touched the contacts.

His view of the room vanished, and he was looking at the back of what seemed to be a powerfully-built man in coveralls, who bent at a kind of half-round guide tube mounted on a heavy tripod. The man spun two small wheels on the mount, yanked a cylinder about a foot long out of an almost empty case, nearby, and put the cylinder down at the base of the guide tube. The cylinder slid up the tube, picked up speed like a falling stone, and streaked out into the distance. Cardan tried to follow its path over the snow-covered lowland, but without success. Then the man was again spinning the wheel on the side of the tripod, and someone else came over carrying a fresh case of cylinders. When this second individual set the case down, Cardan's gaze was riveted on his face.

Two eyes, a nose, and a mouth were present on this face, but the overall effect was that of a bobcat. The face seemed to be no shade of brown, tan, or pink, but a dull gray.

Cardan shifted his cigar in his mouth, and Maclane sucked in his breath.

"Chief," said Maclane, "look out with the torch, will you?"

"What have we got here?" growled Cardan.

"That's what I'm trying to figure out."

"Somebody get me a chair. Then I won't be dropping ashes down anybody's neck."

There was the sound of a chair being slid around, and Cardan, watching the two muscular figures drop another cylinder onto the guide tube, felt the edge of the chair press against his legs. He sat down, slid the chair closer to the table, and saw another cylinder streak out over the snow.

"Where is this place?"

"I don't know. I worked all day Sunday on the circuit, and part of last night. I thought I hadn't gotten anywhere, because I couldn't see a thing. When I touched the contacts, they just cut off my vision. This morning, I came in, tried it, shifted some of the settings, and got a flash that blinded me, as if I'd looked into a searchlight. I waited a few minutes, tried again, and got blinded again, though the light didn't seem quite so intense. I tried again, and this time all I saw was a thick dazzling line in the foreground. That faded out, and—"

"Where was this dazzling line?"

"It seemed to hang right in the air in front of me—like an incandescent rope or hose."

"It faded out?"

"No, it was just—it was *gone* all of a sudden."

"Was there any noise—a sound like an explosion?"

"Sorry, Chief, there's no sound with this thing."

"I mean, did you hear any explosion later—as you hear me talking now?"

"Oh, I see what you mean. Did I see it with the circuit, then hear it independently of the circuit? No, I—Now, wait a minute. I think I did hear a sort of low roar some time afterwards. But that could have been anything."

"Then what?"

"Nothing particular. At first I thought the flash was some fault in the circuit. Then I wrestled with the focus a little, got it clearer, and noticed that some of the snow in front of me had a glazed look, as if the top layers had melted and settled to form a shallow trough. But I didn't know what to make of it. Then something blurred across my field of vision from left to right. A little later it happened again. I changed the focus on this thing, and after backing and filling for quite a while I got this scene you see now."

"Is it hard to change the focus?"

"It's an awful job. It isn't enough to just . . . say . . . change the resistance in one branch of the circuit. You've got to change inductance and capacitance, too. And then if you don't change them just right you get some kind of fantastic picture like a surrealist's nightmare. The patterns are almost familiar and three-dimensional, but they just don't add up. Then when you've almost got the scene, everything's fuzzy, and it slops back and forth between the scene you're after, and this other scene I mention, and it's enough to drive you nuts. The actual scene is unstable unless everything is just right. That's why you don't see me trying to change the focus to find out where this scene is located. In the process, we'd miss whatever is going on here. I think what we've got here is the filming of some kind of monster picture, but I don't see how those things get slung out of that half-cylinder."

Cardan, his hands still on the contacts, watched the powerfully-built figure in coveralls shoot out another cylinder. Cardan grunted, let go of the contacts and looked up at his men crowded around the table.

Cardan puffed his cigar back to life, and said, "Smitty, go out and see if you can get any news. Try all the stations, and listen particularly for anything about highway trouble, big traffic jams, car engines quitting, lights in the sky, or unidentified flying objects being sighted."

Smitty, a wiry figure with black hair combed straight back, nodded and went out.

Cardan glanced at a pugnacious-looking towheaded six-footer, noted his habitual combative look, and grinned. The towhead hesitated, then grinned back. Cardan said, "Consider the mess you got into this morning. You were taking a trip south to finish up a business deal. You tried to drive out on Route 27 and the State police turned you back. You've been thinking it over, and you want to know how there could be a traffic jam on a weekday on both sides of a four-lane highway. You've got a right to know. You're a taxpayer. And if they tell you the cars all stalled, you tell them you know that's not so because you saw a late-model car drive up the mall towing a sports car. How come *that* car could run if the others couldn't. Give 'em hell. And then demand to know just how you *can* get out of this place before the middle of next week."

The towhead grinned and went out.

Cardan said, "Now, as long as we're dependent on just one of these circuits, we never dare vary the focus, because we'll miss what's going on while we fight with the various adjustments. Mac, why don't we make up a batch of these circuits?"

Maclane nodded. "Good idea."

"O.K." said Cardan. Half-a-dozen of the men around the table eagerly volunteered for this job, and Cardan was sending them out when the door opened and a shapely brunette stepped in. "Mr. Cardan, there's a General Whitely on the line. I told him you were in conference, but he insists he has to speak to you right away. And Dr. Crawford was due to get here early this afternoon. He called up and said all flights coming into Milford have been cancelled. I came in to tell you about Dr. Crawford a minute ago, but you were busy and I didn't want to interrupt."

Cardan nodded. "Put Whitely on the line. If Crawford calls back, tell him to keep out of here till things clear up. He'd particularly better not come by car unless he's got a Stanley Steamer or the equivalent."

Cardan's secretary looked perplexed. But she nodded. "Yes, sir, I'll tell him that. And I'll put General Whitely on right away."

"Good."

Someone handed Cardan a phone, and he heard a voice say loudly, "Hello, Bugs?"

Cardan winced. He and Whitely had been boyhood friends, but Cardan didn't care for this nickname.

"*Bugs?*" The voice jumped out at him.

Out of the corner of his eye, Cardan could see several of his men glance at each other. Cardan blew out a cloud of smoke, set his cigar on the edge of the table, and growled, "Right here, Tarface. What do you want?"

"Listen," said the voice loudly, "what's going on up your way? Fill me in."

Cardan squinted at the phone. "I thought you had an Intelligence section."

"Never mind all that secondhand stuff, Bugs. I've got an idea you know what's going on. You're right in the middle of it."

"All right," said Cardan, "I'll trade you item-for-item. About an hour ago, Route 27 was blocked with half-a-mile of cars stalled on the curve about four-and-a-half miles toward Milford from the shortcut over the ridge. You remember how I drove you out last time?"

"I remember. Now I'll tell you something. About three quarters of an hour ago, a man in a late-model car drove smack through the middle of that jam. The police in charge think he was an official of the Atomic Energy Commission, driving a car with a nuclear engine. I notice, Bugs, their description is such that he was about your height and build, conservatively dressed, smoked a cigar, and had your manner. Also, he looked a little younger than you are, but you look a little young for your age, so I suppose that's natural. Now what is going on up there?"

Whitely's voice jumped out of the phone like a whiplash, and Cardan grinned. "What you just told me is something I already know, Tarface, so it doesn't count. Now I believe there were one or two trucks stuck in that traffic jam, but I have no way to be sure whether their engines stopped, or they just got trapped amongst all the stalled cars and couldn't get out. Now some trucks have gas engines and some trucks have Diesel engines. You see what I'm getting at?"

"It hits gas and Diesel engines both. But there's a kind of engine it doesn't hit, and I want to know about it."

"There are at least *two* other kinds of engines it doesn't hit. The starters in the cars worked, so low-voltage electrical motors aren't stopped."

"That's right. What's the other kind?"

"My turn, Tarface. Is Route 27 the only place this has happened?"

"Until about an hour ago, yes. But this thing, whatever it is, has also begun moving out along an arc, like a crayon on the end of a forty-mile string. Rail, truck, and highway travel are stopped dead, along a quarter-circle with this forty-mile radius, and the arc is still spreading out with mathematical accuracy. We've had three plane crashes so far, but some planes at high altitudes have gotten over all right."

"O.K. Where's this forty-mile string centered?"

"Wait a minute. How about that nuclear car?"

"Not nuclear. Steam."

"Steam-propelled, eh? What heats the boiler?"

"A main burner fired by kerosene, and pilot burner run on gasoline. Where's the center of this forty-mile arc?"

"Smack in the middle of the industrial district north of Milford."

Cardan stiffened.

Whitely said, "You hear me, Bugs?"

"Yes, and I think that's a blind. Take a look at the low land opposite that traffic jam I mentioned on Route 27."

Cardan could hear faint voices as if someone had covered the mouthpiece. "All right, Bugs," came Whitely's voice suddenly. "You got anything more? I'm in a rush here."

"Nothing more yet," said Cardan.

"O.K. You know how to reach me. Keep away from that traffic jam on 27."

Cardan heard a click, and he was holding a dead phone.

Smitty was standing on the other side of the desk, and the belligerent towhead was just coming in the door.

Cardan glanced at Smitty. "What did you find out?"

Smitty said, "Pretty straightforward coverage on radio and TV. Motorists are warned to keep off the out-of-town highways, because some unknown effect causes car engines to stall. Travel within town, and between specified points on a map shown on TV, is O.K. The airport is closed, but travel out-of-town by train is all right for now, and emergency travel on Route 34 is permitted, subject to cancellation any time if the trouble spreads. They call it the 'stalling effect.'"

"What explanation do they give?"

"They've got some professor from the local college at a blackboard showing how ionized air around the spark plugs can short a high-voltage spark from the plug to the cylinder head. The professor has a very cultured voice, and treats the whole thing as if it were a trivial matter."

"What causes the ionized air around the spark plugs?"

"He's a little vague about the exact connection, but bears down heavy on the fact that cosmic rays cause ionization in a cloud chamber. When I left he was saying something about sunspots."

"What's the conclusion?"

Smitty grinned, "It would be premature at this time to attempt a definitive characterization of the precise nature of this disturbance. There is, however, no cause for alarm. This is nothing more serious than the slightly irritating situation encountered when the porcelain insulating material of the automobile's spark plugs becomes moist due to fog or mist."

One of the men at the table snorted. "Some of those spark plugs are buried under valve covers bolted down on waterproof gaskets. You could run those engines under Niagara Falls if you had the air intakes clear."

"Well," said Smitty, "it's an explanation, anyway, and to see this authority sneer at the whole business certainly has a calming effect."

Donovan said, "I heard you ask about Diesel trucks, Chief. Any information on that?"

"They got stopped, too."

"Then there goes the spark-plug argument. A Diesel fires by compression, not by spark plugs."

Cardan glanced at the towhead, who shook his head, and said, "All I could get was the same stuff. The police say they aren't responsible for sunspots and to keep off the highways except in case of emergency. Apparently the trains are still running, and Route 34 is still clear. About the car that went through the traffic jam, they say they're sorry, but for security reasons, they can't give any information on it. The government is investigating the tie-up, and that was a new experimental kind of car. I'm not supposed to repeat that, and if anybody asks me about seeing the car, I'm supposed to say 'no comment,' or deny any knowledge of it."

Cardan laughed.

Somebody said, "What's this about a secret governmental car?"

Cardan said, "I had to give some explanation for that steam car. I didn't *say* it was a secret government car. But if they want to think so, that's *their* business."

Maclane said, "Excuse me, Chief. I'd better see how those circuits are coming along. You want to watch this?"

Cardan said, "Sure," and Maclane handed him the headset. Maclane went out, and Cardan sent everyone but Donovan out of the room to keep watch on the radio and TV news coverage, to go down to the local supermarkets and bring back some meat and fresh grocery orders, and to drop in at nearby sporting goods and Army-Navy stores to pick up weapons and ammunition.

Cardan put on the headset for a moment to study the tripod, then took the headset off, and, frowning, fired up his cigar.

Donovan said, "I wish we could change the focus on this thing. I'm sitting here watching nothing while there's no telling what may be going on just twenty feet away."

"When Mac gets the other sets ready," said Cardan, "we ought to be a lot better off."

"I keep hoping that when we can see more of this, we'll find out it's just a big flap over nothing. Maybe, say, the filming of a motion picture. But this trough on a tripod just isn't dramatic enough for that. And they acted too casual when they used it."

"It's no flap over nothing," said Cardan. He described his phone conversation with Whitely.

Donovan shook his head. "You'd think a race that *could* do this would have gotten past the point where it *would* do it."

"Why?"

"It seems to me to be a basic truth that when you set out to injure someone else, you may succeed. But, in due time, the thing will curve around in such a way that you get your own teeth rammed down your throat. I'd think an interstellar race would have had enough experience to have learned that."

Cardan blew out a cloud of smoke. "You're talking about how it *ought* to be. But what if this interstellar race isn't perfect? What if they have competition from *another* interstellar race? For that matter, by the time *we* can travel from star to star, will the whole human race have turned into saints?"

Donovan hesitated. "Maybe not the *whole* human race."

"There's another catch."

"Why?" Donovan asked abruptly.

"The bulk of our own people are law-abiding. But how does that help you if you run into a gang of murderers? How do we know your wise interstellar race won't have a band of fanatics, or frustrated adventurers, who will get a ship, go off to some planet out in the hinterlands, take the planet over and run things *their* way?"

Donovan frowned. "Kind of a rough situation. They'd have the advanced technology, but not the restraints that went with it."

"Which would be our tough luck."

"Yeah."

A cold, hard expression passed over Donovan's face, then he said, "I don't know if you're watching this or not, Chief. If you aren't, you'd better take a look"

Cardan put on the headset. Directly before him sat the tripod, still deserted, and with its half-cylinder pointed at the horizon. For a moment there was nothing else nearby but tracks in the snow. Then a thing like a huge, pale gray oil drum rolled from the left into

Cardan's field of view, wheeled, and swung back in the opposite direction, the long snout of a gun showing momentarily in outline against the sky.

Cardan looked at the snow, where there were two broad tracks, each of which appeared to be about four feet wide, with roughly a two-and-a-half foot space between them.

A moment later, another of the gray drums rolled into view, and Cardan glanced rapidly from point-to-point on this drum, noting the non-rotating central part, the wide treads turning on either end, the slit between these two treads, and the long gun that thrust out, canted slightly skyward, below the right end of the slit.

Then the vehicle wheeled, and Cardan had a brief glimpse of a tube like a short length of fifty caliber machine gun, thrust out the rear of the cylinder and aimed straight at him. Then the thing was out of his range of vision.

Cardan slipped off the headset, and snapped on the intercom. "Miss Bowen, see if you can get General Whitely for me."

"Yes, Mr. Cardan."

Donovan said, "Those guns *could* be for self-defense."

"Sure. Which is why they try to paralyze traffic along a circle eighty miles across."

"Yeah," said Donovan slowly.

"A circle eighty miles across takes in about five thousand square miles," said Cardan. "That's about the size of the state of Connecticut. What's going to happen to all the people inside the circle when neither trucks nor trains can get through with food?"

"They'll have to get out."

"How? On foot?"

"They'll drive to the place where their cars stall. Then they'll walk."

"What happens to the cars they leave behind when they get out to walk?"

"They—" Donovan stopped.

"Say the cars average sixteen feet in length," said Cardan. "If half a dozen drivers, with or without their families, just stop their cars one behind the other, there's a hundred feet of road blocked up. Five hundred and twenty of these cars will block a mile of a single-lane road. If you stand on a highway, with the cars going past fifty feet apart and at sixty miles an hour, it will only take about four minutes for that number of cars to go by."

"But can't the police—"

Cardan snorted. "The police can operate for two reasons. First, their own organization and discipline. Second, the fact that the great bulk of the people are on their side, actively or passively. Now, what's going to happen when everybody, including the police, realizes that the only way to get food for themselves and their families is to get on the other side of this eighty-mile circle?"

Donovan was silently thinking that over when the door opened up and Maclane stepped in. He grinned at Cardan, and said, "Anything new?"

Cardan described the cylindrical vehicles, with their guns fore and aft.

Maclane whistled and put on the headset. "Nothing in sight now but the tripod and a lot of packed snow. What do you mean, this vehicle is like a big thick axle with a wheel on each end?"

"More like an overgrown oil drum, with broad treads turning on each end."

"Does the drum itself rotate?"

"Not while I was looking at it. How about you, Don?"

"The drum rotates a little, but not much, just the way a car dips a little in the front when you stop suddenly."

Maclane said, "How much clearance between the underside of this drum and the ground?"

"Oh, I'd guess about a foot."

The door opened, and Cardan's secretary said, "I have General Whitely on the phone, sir. And Mr. Farrell—he's working on the circuits—said to tell Mr. Maclane they're having an 'h' of a time focusing the circuits."

Cardan grinned. "You'd better get back down there, Mac. When you get them focused, send one up here, and take another down to the subbasement and see if it works down there."

Maclane nodded and went out.

Cardan picked up the phone, and held it cautiously a little way from his ear. The general's voice jumped out at him. "What are we up against here, Bugs? Have you got any inside dope on this?"

Cardan said cautiously, "I've got a kind of long-range viewer with a very narrow fixed field of view, overlooking what I think is the spot where the trouble is. How about you?"

"I've got aerial TV and blown-up aerial photographs."

"What do you see?"

The general snorted. "There's a big cylinder piled into the snow, with one end open, and things like pale blue fuel drums dropping out and rolling away."

"Rolling away toward what?"

"The highway. Where that traffic jam is, on the curve south of Milford."

"What are you doing about it?"

"I managed to get a couple of helicopters around this arc of interference to take a close look. Their engines quit before they could get close. I've got some special jets high overhead."

"How about their engines?"

"They give out, too. Whether because of what hits the others, or because of a kind of drifting fluff or fuzz we've run into, I don't know."

"What does the fuzz do?"

"It gets sucked into the air intakes, and apparently knocks out the engines. I've told you something. How about something in return?"

"Well," said Cardan, "this thing I'm looking through has a narrow fixed field of view, but I'm trying to get that fixed. Meantime, those drums you saw are a pale blue, is that right?"

"Right. What about them?"

"I got a close view of them but without color, and it didn't last very long. The drums seem to be about twelve feet long, the center section fitted with a view slit and a gun in front, a gun behind, and broad treads mounted on either side of the center with about a foot ground clearance. The treads look about four feet wide. They may actually be several treads mounted side-by-side. The whole drum doesn't roll over, but just the treads. Directly in my field of view, there's a heavy tripod mounting a half-cylinder that looks about a foot through and six feet long. This half-cylinder is something like a big bazooka split lengthwise, and mounted on a tripod with two adjusting wheels, graduated circles—apparently for elevation and azimuth, and several locking levers. About an hour ago, a big brawny individual in coveralls was dropping cylinders a foot or so long in his end of this split bazooka, and the cylinders streaked up the trough and shot out for the horizon. I don't know what the means of propulsion is."

The general said tensely, "See the face of the individual, Bugs?"

Cardan hesitated.

Whitely's voice sprang out at him. "Did this individual look human, Bugs?"

Cardan said, "Depends on what you mean by human. All the features were there, and the body looked human, but the overall effect was that of a lynx or a bobcat. Why?"

"You know why. Either this is Orson Welles' shocker come to life, or it all started out on Earth. If so, I think we know the foreign power responsible."

Cardan thought of the vivid streak across the sky, the intense bluish glare of the explosion, the tripod with its half-cylindrical launcher, and the drum-shaped vehicles churning toward the highway jammed with stalled cars. Cardan tossed his dead cigar into the ashtray. "Nuts," he said irritatedly. "If the Russians had this stuff, they could put it into production and crowd us right off the map into the Pacific Ocean. They wouldn't tip their hand like this. You're going off the deep end, Tarface."

"Hell, it could be a test. To see if we've got the stuff ourselves. *Then* they spring the main attack."

"And what if we happen to be jumpy and the minute this 'test' of theirs starts, we hit them with everything we've got?"

Whitely was silent a moment, then he laughed. "I just wanted to see how it sounded to you."

"It sounds lousy. Suppose in the course of this test we should turn out to have the devices ourselves. Then we overpower the 'aliens,' tear off their Halloween masks, and they turn out to talk Russian. Next we put on a big propaganda exhibition featuring the 'alien spaceship,' plus vehicles, guns, and alien invaders complete with masks. The Russians would look foolish for the next five years."

"It doesn't sound too good, does it?"

"They just aren't stupid, that's all. They'd have their neck stuck out a mile, and no way to pull it in."

"You got any more information?"

"Not yet. Maybe later."

"O.K., Bugs. If you can get any more close views, it will be a big help. Keep me in touch. And keep away from the highway."

Cardan frowned at the dead phone. That was the second time Whitely had told him to stay away from the road. He put the phone on its cradle, and looked up to see Maclane holding another circuit, and looking serious. "Was that the general?"

Cardan nodded.

Maclane said, "You don't look too disturbed, Chief."

Cardan frowned. "Why? Have you got a better view on that set?"

"We've got a ringside seat."

"Let's see."

Cardan put the headset on, and got a view across the northern end of the traffic jam out over the lowland to the east, and to the southeast along the bend of the highway. Several of the big cylindrical vehicles were on the highway above the traffic jam, and others were spread out, approaching across the low snow-covered ground. About five hundred feet from the highway a helicopter was burning. Another plane was burning about a thousand yards away. Still further back, he could see a line of towers that carried power lines across the low-lying farmland. In the foreground, a parachute was caught in some brush, billowing in the wind near the foot of the embankment below the highway.

Cardan glanced at the stalled and deserted cars, then back at the big cylindrical drums, rolling northward on the road. They seemed to be moving only about fifteen or twenty miles an hour, but they were moving steadily. More of them were working along a slanting cable up the bank and onto the road. As Cardan watched, one of the cylinders wheeled toward the jammed cars. There was a blur at the forward gun of the vehicle, and a puff of rolling black smoke burst amongst the nearest cars which lifted up and smashed heavily back and sidewise. There was another blast. A figure in airman's uniform jumped up to dart back amongst the cars. There was a third puff of smoke and the figure disintegrated.

The cylinder rolled down the grass strip toward the south, followed by another cylinder, and then another. Far out across the lowland, a blast of smoke billowed at the base of a tower supporting the power lines. The tower tilted and leaned out. There was a dazzling display of arcing sparks, then the power line came down.

Nearby, several of the cylinders crossed the highway, spread out, and started up the hill on the other side, passing out of Cardan's field of vision.

Several powerfully-built figures, carrying crates, walked onto the shoulder of the northbound side of this highway, and began setting up a half-cylinder on a tripod.

Maclane's voice reached Cardan. "I'm watching this thing, Chief, with my hands on the contacts. I want you to notice something."

Donovan's voice cut in, "I don't know if you can see this. There's a big Marine Corps helicopter coming in fast, to the right of this view. There—boy, it hit like a rock! Wait a minute. Here come parachutists! They're drifting down all over the place. Can you see that, Chief?"

Cardan could now see in the sky well beyond the fallen power lines the parachutes blossoming out in what appeared to be different shades of gray and drifting to the south. Big planes were gliding down fast overhead.

Maclane said urgently, "This is important, Chief. You see that mess of burning trash blown out of the cars over there?"

Cardan tore his gaze from the parachutes, and looked at the overturned cars. "You mean the front seat cushion, and some uphol-stery ripped half-off a door? What of it, Mac?"

"Watch it."

Cardan briefly glanced up at a plane that was banking steeply, toward the road. The plane blew up in a blast of black smoke, and Cardan looked back at the burning car, and growled. "What's the point of this, Mac?"

"Just watch."

A small piece of blazing upholstery flapped sharply, then tore away, and blew along the road in the wind, twisting and tumbling. It stopped, and momentarily seemed to lean against the wind, then rolled away, and stopped again, on an empty stretch of road.

Cardan frowned as the strip of cloth flapped in the air, rising slowly above the roadway, *but remained stationary and did not blow back with the wind.*

Cardan watched intently.

The cloth flapped in the air, as if held on an invisible pin.

Maclane said, "I've been trying to tell Don, I can influence this picture."

Donovan suddenly groaned, then cursed in a low voice. Cardan snapped his attention back to the scene in the distance, beyond the power line, but could see only a confused whirl of motion. He handed the headset he was using to Maclane, and put on the second headset of the circuit Donovan was using.

The confused whirl Cardan had seen beyond the power lines now sprang into clear view. Men in battle dress were running forward, then dropping to the ground to take aim at a line of cylinders rolling toward them. Cardan could see mortars, machine guns, 3.5-inch rocket launchers, and some weapon or device that he didn't recognize. At first glance, he felt a grim sense of pleasure. Then he looked again.

The men were struggling with their weapons. There was no sign of rifle, mortar, or machine-gun fire, and the rockets were falling short and failing to explode. The men glanced up at each other, then looked out over the lowland.

The cylinders were closer now, and faint blurs flickered at the snouts of their guns.

Close by, directly in Cardan's field of view, chunks of dirt and snow flew up. Then the smoke blew away, and he could see endless puffs of black erupt across his field of view in a continuous churning that stopped thought, and left him looking on blankly as men, guns, and equipment blew into fragments.

Then the cylinders were rolling by.

Behind them walked coveralled individuals seven or eight feet in apparent height, carrying like tommy-guns large-breeched, long-muzzled weapons, with which they methodically shot the wounded.

Then they had passed by, too, and there was nothing left but fragments, motionless figures, torn uniform cloth lifting in the wind that swept across the lowland, and dirt falling down the sides of shell-holes.

Cardan took off the headphones, snapped on the intercom, and said, "Miss Bowen, see if you can get General Whitely for me."

"Yes, Mr. Cardan."

Donovan got to his feet, and put his headphones on the table, "I can't watch that any more."

"Somebody has to keep an eye on it," said Cardan, "so we'll know if anything new develops."

"I'm going to watch it from a little closer range," said Donovan.

Cardan opened his mouth. Donovan went out, slamming the door.

Cardan got out a fresh cigar, stuck it in his mouth, and lit it. He blew out a cloud of smoke. "That's the trouble with having a bunch of individualists around. When the crisis comes, they all boil off in their own direction."

Maclane took off his headset. "The only one to boil off in his own direction so far is Donovan."

"Wait a while," said Cardan.

The intercom buzzed. Miss Bowen said, "Mr. Cardan, the men are back with the groceries."

"Have them put the stuff down in the subbasement. How about the men who went out to the sporting goods stores?"

"They aren't back yet, sir."

"O.K. Keep trying to get Whitely."

"Yes, sir."

Maclane, holding the headset in one hand, was squinting at the wall. "I wonder, Chief," he murmured, "what Donovan's planning to do?"

Cardan glanced at Maclane, and took a fresh grip on his cigar.

Maclane said thoughtfully, "No ordinary car will get him near the place by now, I suppose. But our steam car can do it. And they'll be *sure* nothing we have can move."

Cardan looked at Maclane sourly. "Mac, listen a—"

Maclane abruptly tossed the headset on the table and jumped up.

"Stay at that set!" Cardan ordered.

The door slammed as Maclane went out.

"Lousy individualists!" roared Cardan. He now had two circuits giving a close-range view of the action, and no one to do the watching but himself.

The intercom buzzed. Miss Bowen said, "The men with the sporting goods are back, Mr. Cardan."

"Good. Have them put them down in the subbasement, and leave a few men to keep an eye on things."

"They're on the way up here right now, sir."

"Oh," said Cardan coldly. "Well, when they get here, send them in."

"Yes, sir."

"And keep trying for Whitely."

"Yes, sir."

Cardan picked up the headset Maclane had dropped, and studied the remaining wisps of smoking upholstery from the wrecked car. He eyed them thoughtfully, and adjusted the cigar in his mouth. Watching one particular bit of upholstery intently, he willed it to move to the left. A puff of wind blew it to the right and backwards. Cardan's teeth tightened on the cigar. Drawing all his conscious awareness into a tight focus centered on the wisp of blackened cloth, he commanded it to move forward, toward him. A puff of wind carried it farther away. Cardan absently took out his cigar. Then he centered his entire consciousness on that little bit of cloth, till he was aware of nothing else. The view seemed to waver and enlarge as Cardan focused his mind on the cloth, seeing each separate fiber, taking hold of it as he became fully aware of its every visible characteristic, and lifted it up and forward, toward him, against the wind, and held it in the air. He turned it from side-to-side before him, over and over, winding it into a tight ball and spreading it out flat almost as if it were a finger on a hand that he controlled through the direct action of nerves on muscles.

Somewhere in the background, Cardan could hear voices. He drew a deep breath, and carefully took off the headset. He felt somewhat like a man awakening from anesthesia, or from a vivid dream. But his last glimpse with the headset on showed him the bit of cloth fluttering down from a position well upwind of the smoldering wreckage of the cars.

Miss Bowen was saying urgently, "Mr. Cardan, I have General Whitely on the line. And the men are back from the sporting goods stores, and they're quite insistent—"

Cardan picked up his cigar. "Put Whitely on, then let them in but tell them to be quiet."

Miss Bowen put the phone in Cardan's hand, then stepped outside to quiet angry voices.

"Hello?" said Cardan into the phone.

The door opened, and Cardan's men shoved in, rifles and shotguns thrust out in all directions.

"Bugs?" Whitely's voice jumped out of the phone.

"Right here," said Cardan, holding up his hand to quiet his men.

"Listen," said the general, "they've stepped up the power of that circle. We can't get anything through or over, and what we had inside is used up."

"What about missiles?"

"We attacked them hand-to-hand a little bit ago, Bugs. Not a gun would fire. As a last resort, we had a nuclear device in there, and if nothing else worked, we intended to set it off. We set it off. Nothing happened."

Cardan frowned. "How about missiles?"

"We've tried missiles. They seem to get through, but they don't explode—unless you want us to beat them to death with warheads."

Cardan set his cigar in the tray. "What are you going to do?"

"So far we've been fighting blind and off-balance. There are too many unknowns. We don't know who we're fighting, what they've got, or what they'll spring on us next. They've knocked us into a kind of punch-drunk stupor, and the only way out of it I can see is to get in there fast, smash their airhead while it's still little, and grab enough material and prisoners so we can start to figure out what's going on."

"What are you going to fight them with?"

"We're going to try to get at them close-range with gas and anything else that's not based on explosives. But, Bugs, how do we get close enough to do it in time? You drove through that barrier. How many of those steam cars do you have?"

"Just one, and I'm pretty sure someone just took off in it. The devil with that. Listen, Tarface."

"I'm listening."

"What you want is steam locomotives. Get after every roundhouse and railroad repair yard for one that isn't torn down yet. Get in touch with the Canadians. I think they're still using them, and theirs will be in good shape. There's a track that runs only a few miles to the east of that landing site, and—"

The general's voice cut in abruptly. "I've got the picture, Bugs. Thanks."

There was a click at Cardan's ear. He set the dead phone in its cradle and looked up at the men across the desk, bristling with guns. The powerfully-built, belligerent towhead stood directly in front of Cardan, and seemed to be the spokesman.

The door opened up, and Maclane came in, looking furious.

Cardan glanced at Maclane. "Don went off in the steam car, did he?"

"He whizzed right out of the parking lot as I was yelling to him to wait a minute."

"So you could run out with him, eh?"

"It's a free country," blazed Maclane. "You don't own me!"

There was a mutter of sympathy from the rest. Cardan was on his feet and had Maclane by the collar before he knew what had happened. "You fool, do you think I *want* to own you!" He gave him a shake, and let go. "Get out! Beat it, the lot of you!" He sat down, threw his dead cigar into the wastebasket, and pulled out a fresh one. When he looked up, they were all standing there, watching him pugnaciously.

He paused with the cigar in his hand and eyed them one-by-one. They looked back unflinchingly. "All right," he snarled. "Donovan has gone roaring off on his own, and you want to, too. Do you think *I* don't? But we've got something better here." He jerked a thumb at the circuits. "Mac was telling me he could influence the picture! When he left a minute ago, I discovered *I* could influence the picture. Do you know what that 'influencing the picture' means? What's the only way to move the image of an object on an ordinary TV screen without distorting the rest of the picture?"

Maclane, his eyes glinting, said, "Move the object itself in the studio."

"Right. And it seems to me exactly what happens here."

Smitty scowled. "So therefore, what?"

Cardan lit the cigar. "So therefore Mac can move a small light object down on that highway. So can I."

The big towhead said, "We'll never beat them by moving 'small light objects'! We've got to go down there and smash them!"

"What with?" said Cardan contemptuously.

"With what we've got. We can figure out what to do when we get there."

Cardan blew out a cloud of smoke. "If you think you're a one-man armored division, go ahead and try it. Maybe you can succeed where a paratroop battalion and nuclear missiles fail."

"All right, then, what *do* we do?"

"If you'll shut up for a minute, I'll tell you."

The towhead was watching him as if he had a bonfire lit behind each eye. Cardan blew a cloud of cigar smoke in his face, eyed the rest of the men, noted that all of them looked tense, and some appeared so keyed up as to be ready to spring at his throat any time. Cardan knocked the ash off his cigar and growled, "I don't know if you realize it or not, but one basic principle of either war or business competition is to hit your opponent's weak point. If you go charging out there with those guns, you're going to run against him where he's strong. Another basic principle is to do what your opponent doesn't expect, and isn't ready for, and get him off-balance. If you go after him head-on, you'll be doing exactly what he *does* expect, and he'll polish you off by simple routine. Now, if you want to go, go ahead."

The men glanced at each other uneasily. There was a brief silence. Smitty said, "What's your idea, Chief?"

Cardan glanced at their faces, saw they were all listening intently, and said, "It isn't just how much power a man has that counts. A lot depends on how he uses it, and where he brings it to bear. The armed forces have the power to flatten the opposition down at that highway, but they can't bring their power to bear. They're tied up. They've been hit by devices they can't strike back at. Now, what do you think that circuit there represents for our side?"

"Sure, but you said yourself, all you can do is move a little light object with it."

Cardan grinned. "That's all."

"But look, Chief—"

"Benjamin Franklin said, a couple of hundred years ago, 'There is no *little* enemy.'"

The men were squinting from Cardan to the circuit. Maclane scowled, and put his hands on the contacts.

Cardan said, "In the first world war, the British outnumbered the Turks in Palestine. But the Turks were dug into a system of trenches. The British couldn't bring their superiority to bear. Then Lawrence of Arabia went to work on the Turkish communications. Once he had these worn to a thread, the British threatened an attack in one direction, secretly switched their forces, and smashed through elsewhere. The British Army won the actual victory. But first Lawrence and the Arabs wore the opposition down and drove them to distraction."

The men all looked thoughtful. Smitty was massaging his chin with his hand. "We're like Lawrence, and the Armed Forces are like the British?"

"Exactly."

The towhead said curiously, "But if we can only move small light stuff, how does that help?"

Cardan said, "A pin is a very small light object. Do you know any man who can do efficient work with a little light pin stuck in him? And yet—he'd better do efficient work, with the Armed Forces closing in on him."

"H-m-m," said the towhead.

Maclane, his hands on the contacts of one of the sets, said, "Whatever we're going to do, Chief, we'd better hurry up and do it. They're setting up some kind of framework of long shiny rods on the highway. They're working as if they want to get it set up in a hurry."

Cardan snapped on the intercom.

"Miss Bowen, we're going to move down into subbasement. There's a switchboard down there, so we can keep in touch with the outside. The telephone lines are underground, so if worst come to worst, we should be able to keep in touch with the outside for quite a while. Are you willing?"

"Yes, sir."

Cardan looked up. "Let's go."

They went out the door in a rush, and headed downstairs.

The "subbasement," Cardan was thinking, was the reason for one of the worst squabbles he'd ever had with the major stockholders of the company. Every feature of it had infuriated them, from the massive, heavily-reinforced ceiling, to the small production facilities and self-contained water, sewage, and power supply. Why, the big stockholders demanded, should the profits of the company be sunk into this slab of masonry instead of turned back into useful production, or distributed in dividends?

In reply, Cardan mobilized the small stockholders, played the national anthem, waved the flag, puffed the Cold War into an imminent threat of missile and bombing attack, and scattered smoke, dust, and confusion in all directions. He squeezed through a violent stockholders meeting with a narrow margin of control and well-heeled opponents breathing fire and brimstone down his neck.

Cardan knew the subbasement was still spoken of acidly.

About the kindest name for it was "Cardan's Folly."

And Cardan knew that there was still a few diehards who automatically voted against everything they thought he wanted, just in commemoration of that subbasement fight. But he also know that the majority of the big stockholders were again behind him, with one reservation "So long as he doesn't want *another* bomb shelter."

As the massive doors slid back, Cardan eyed the subbasement approvingly, then walked in with the rest of the men.

Smitty, carrying one of the sets, said curiously, "Chief, why did you build this?"

"I thought we might need it."

"But why?"

"With people waving H-bombs and missiles around, what's wrong with having a hole to crawl into?"

"*I* think you had some kind of hunch."

Cardan shifted the cigar in his mouth, and blew out a noncommittal cloud of smoke. Overhead, the lights faded out, then snapped on more dimly. Someone called, "Power's been knocked out!"

Underfoot, there was a faint vibration as the subbasement generators began to turn over.

Cardan glanced around. Canned goods were regularly kept stored away down here, and now he noted a large pile of fresh groceries. "Good," he said approvingly, and gave directions for putting the food away.

Maclane, he saw, was at a table with a group of men huddled around a number of sets.

The towhead said, "What about these guns, Chief? We got the whole assortment—shotguns, rifles, air guns, CO_2 guns. You ask for it, and we've got it. We even picked up a few of these slingshots that shoot ball bearings."

Cardan nodded approvingly. "Sort 'em out, with the right ammunition by each weapon. I think the CO_2 guns and those slingshots are going to be the handiest."

"You figure we've got a siege coming up?"

"Not if I can help it," said Cardan. "But you never know."

The lights had now come on brightly once more, and Cardan again glanced at Maclane huddled with a little group at the sets.

Everything seemed under control, so Cardan spent several minutes seeing that everyone was inside, and that the subbasement was sealed off from the rest of the building, then he activated the TV pickups that enabled the men inside to see what was going on outside the building. He set some men to watch the screens, had others practicing with the weapons, and made arrangements for them to change off later on. Miss Bowen told him that most phone lines out of Milford had been knocked out, but a roundabout route was apparently still in operation for emergency use. Cardan nodded, and put her to work with the groceries and canned goods, in a corner fitted with a large, awkwardly-arranged collection of outdated cooking appliances that struck Cardan as the ideal kitchen.

"Hey, Barbara," shouted Smitty, with a grin, "Suppose we're marooned down here—the last woman on Earth, plus umpteen men."

Barbara Bowen grinned and picked up a can. "There won't be too many left after I serve my first meal. How do you open this, anyway?"

Smitty winced, and then Cardan saw Maclane gesturing to him frantically.

"Look at this," said Maclane, and Cardan put on one of the headsets. Around the table were other circuits and other men wearing the headsets, but they vanished as Cardan abruptly saw a view down the highway from the north, the traffic jam of cars in front of him in the background, a large lattice of bright metal bars growing up on the highway directly in front of him, between his point of view and the jammed traffic, and large gray-faced men pacing back and forth holding the ends of cables that looped skyward to where floating pieces of machinery edged long bright rods into the growing lattice.

Maclane said, "It's now or never, Chief. That Lawrence of Arabia stuff sounded good upstairs, but we're up against trouble now. I've got an awful hunch that if they once get that grid completed, we aren't going to stop them, ever."

Cardan looked over the grid. To him, it appeared to be just a big metal framework. That it was being fitted together with great precision seemed clear enough, but what could it *do*? Then he noted the cables running out to the framework, and paused to consider. The thing *looked* harmless. But so did a live wire, or a stick of dynamite with the fuse burning short. He studied the tense concentrated expressions of the workers operating the control cables that ran up to the overhead machines that handled the long rods. Some of these creatures had a look that appeared to Cardan like barely-suppressed jubilation.

Maclane's voice said tensely, "I can't even budge one of those rods. I've tried to swing it when it's being lowered into place. But I can't move it at all."

Cardan growled, "You can get a good grip on something light, can't you?"

"Sure, but how will that stop them?"

"You see that cat-faced clod just guiding a beam into place?"

"I see him."

"He's got a good thick head of hair. Take hold of a few strands, fasten your attention on them, and *pull*."

"Yes," said Maclane thoughtfully. "Yes, now I get it."

Cardan glanced around at the hill sloping up to one side of the highway, the ditch carrying run-off water at the base of the hillside, and on the other side of the road, the flat lowland with the wrecked planes and downed power lines. Not finding just what he wanted, he continued to look around, and his gaze passed across the traffic jam of deserted cars, some overturned and still smoking, and one with its transmission smashed, and gears and roller bearings strewn over the pavement beside it.

Cardan centered his attention on this smashed transmission, and his viewpoint seemed to slide forward as he studied the roller bearings, and then dwelt minutely and exclusively on each one in turn. After a while he had much the feeling of a man who has examined the operation of a complex machine, one element at a time, and now sees the thing as a whole, and has a good idea what he can do with it. Then as Cardan focused his attention on them, one-by-one, the bearings began to roll.

For an instant, he felt the same startled sensation he had had years ago, when he first pressed the accelerator of a car, and it abruptly moved forward with him. Then he was no longer thinking of the uneasy unfamiliar sensation, but was concentrating wholly on what he wanted to do.

The bearings rolled together in a small heap. Then, like wasps rising from an underground nest, they began to lift into the air. Cardan sent them, fast and low, down the highway toward the huge grid.

Beside the grid, one of the cat-faced machine-operators abruptly slapped at the back of his head. Beside Cardan, Maclane made a low noise in his throat. The operator jerked again, and twisted around angrily. Several of the other operators opened their mouths to shout as the rod overhead began to teeter dangerously.

Cardan's bearings were approaching rapidly.

The operator spread one hand over the top of his head, and with the other on the controls steadied the rod-shaped beam. A small fistful of hair visible between his spread fingers straightened out abruptly. This time the alien did not jump, but quickly moved his hand further over to ease the pain. Overhead, the beam paused, then started down again. Several more strands of hair straightened out painfully. The beam overhead stopped again. The operator, obviously fighting to keep himself under control, moved his hand again, then once more carefully began to lower the beam. Apparently to get a better view of it as it lowered, he took a step backward.

Cardan slid the bearings in under the raised foot as it came down.

The foot slipped, and shot back.

The alien took a lightning hop backwards with his other foot.

Cardan shot the roller bearings forward.

The other foot slipped.

The powerful figure of the alien landed on its knees, braced on one hand, with the other hand still gripping the controls at the end of the long cable that looped down from the machine.

Cardan looked up. Overhead, the machine had tilted and twisted sidewise, in such a way that the rod it held should have whipped forward and struck the grid. But another handling machine, controlled by one of the other operators, had taken hold of the end of the rod, and held it back. The rod was bent, but the grid itself wasn't damaged.

Maclane's voice said, "They've apparently got that thing finished except for one last beam."

Cardan was studying the controls that worked the handling machine. The operator had five fingers and a thumb, and each one of them disappeared into a hole in a thing like a partially flattened bowling ball on the end of the cable that dangled from the machine. Cardan brought up several of his bearings and rapped them sharply against the knuckle of the alien's index finger.

The handling machine jerked sharply upward.

The machine operator, in a display of vigor and resiliency, sprang back to his feet, glanced at his hand, and began to shout a warning to the others.

Cardan changed direction on the roller bearings, and shot about half of them into the open mouth.

A succession of spasms passed across the catlike face. The creature clapped a hand over its mouth, and suddenly dropped to the ground.

The control cable dangled free.

Cardan slammed a bearing in the index-finger hole of the control box.

The handling machine shot skyward.

Using his remaining roller-bearings like so many fingers, Cardan experimented with the control box. The various studs at the bottoms of the finger holes respectively raised the machine, moved it forward, moved it to the right, rotated the whole machine counterclockwise, or tilted it forward. The harder the pressure, the more rapid the motion. The thumbhole had two separate studs, one of which, Cardan found, reversed the action of the finger-controls. That was all he wanted to know.

Maclane gave a low exclamation. "They've finished it!"

Cardan, swinging the handling machine back and down, had the impression of a dull flash from below. When he had the machine well back and at about the height of the grid, he glanced forward.

Rolling out from under the raised grid, was a thing like a heavy tank blown up to several times its natural size, and fitted with an assortment of unconventional antennae atop its massive turret. Around the grid, them machine operators were grinning widely.

Cardan pressed one of the studs of the control box. The handling machine began to move forward. Cardan pressed harder.

Beneath the grid, a kind of fog sprang into existence as the monstrous tank rolled clear. A vague shape began to loom through the fog.

Cardan lifted the machine slightly as it gathered speed.

Below, someone was running, and waving his arms. Somewhere, someone raised a weapon. One of the antennae atop the tank began to swing around.

Cardan pressed harder on the control stud.

The machine slammed headlong into the grid. There was a sense of rending vibration, then a blinding flash.

For several seconds, Cardan couldn't see. Then he could make out the warped structure of the grid, tilted and bent. Around it, a number of figures were lying motionless. Several handling machines drifted nearby, their control cables untended. The foglike appearance that had been under the grid was gone now, and so was whatever had been looming through it. But the monster tank was swinging its turret around and slowly elevating what looked like an enormous gun. The turret stopped moving. At the mouth of the gun, there was a blur.

Miss Bowen's voice reached Cardan. "Sir, General Whitely is on the line and wants to talk to you right away."

"Take a message if he wants to leave one. I can't talk to him now."

Somewhere there was a thud, and a heavy, dull boom. Cardan felt the concrete floor beneath him move perceptibly.

The turret of the huge tank began to move again.

Cardan looked around, saw where the first machine operator had been violently ill, and recovered several of his roller bearings.

There was another blur at the gun mounted on the turret of the tank.

Maclane said, "Look. On the mall."

Behind the tank, creeping up the grassy strip between the double lanes of stalled traffic, came Cardan's steam-powered car, with Donovan crouched at the wheel. As Cardan stared, the steam car glided closer, steadily closing the distance between itself and the monster tank.

There was a heavy boom, and the earth jumped beneath Cardan.

The turret of the tank began to move again.

Cardan had the controls of one of the handling machines, and gently easing it to the side, and up.

One of the antennae atop the tank turret moved around. There was a faint shimmer in the air around it. The handling machine glowed near the spot where the control cable entered it, and suddenly blew apart.

Cardan immediately got control of another machine, and jerked it fast to the side.

The antennae turned slightly, and the machine blew up.

Cardan got another, and dropped it fast, to put it directly in line with a group of aliens running toward the grid. Keeping right in line with them, so the tank could not fire at him without having them in the line of fire, too, he sent it hurtling with increasing speed straight at the antennae.

The handling machine blew apart, as did a gun carried by one of the running figures. The remaining figures dove for cover.

Cardan was left with two handling machines, neither one of which, he was sure, could get anywhere near the tank. Nevertheless, he took control of one, and without moving it, looked around.

From somewhere around him, there was another dull boom, and the floor moved slightly underfoot.

The turret of the tank was swinging slowly around again.

At the rear of the tank, a figure dragged itself up.

Cardan blinked. Moving out on the slanting plate over the huge tread, Donovan hauled up on a rope a five-gallon can of gasoline.

Far down the grassy strip in the center of the highway, one of the big cylindrical vehicles came rolling around the bend.

"Mac," said Cardan, "see if you can do anything to that cylinder down at the bend."

Donovan, oblivious to the cylinder, pulled out a big wrench, and studied the tank. Nearby, a short pipe was thrust up, with a U-shaped piece at the top. Donovan methodically unscrewed the U-shaped piece, then started to empty the can of gasoline down the pipe.

The various antennae atop the tank swiveled around.

Cardan experimented briefly with the controls, then sent the handling machine straight back toward the grid, seized one of the rods, and wrenched and twisted at it like a dog tearing at a stick.

The motion of the tank's antennae wavered, and Cardan could guess the frame of mind of those inside. They had to protect the grid, but if they blew the machine up while it was at the grid, that would damage the grid. And while this new problem confronted them, Donovan was still pouring in gas.

Down the grassy strip, the cylindrical vehicle came to a sudden stop, then jockeyed around to bring its forward gun to bear on Donovan.

From a snowbank near the cylinder, a small chunk of dirty white flew out, and went in through the cylinder's view slit.

Atop the tank, Donovan threw a lighted match down the pipe after the gas, and jumped over the side.

A streamer of flame shot up out of the pipe, puffed out in a flash around the base of the turret, and was followed by black smoke.

Cardan jerked one of the rods loose from the grid, gripped the end like a flail, and went for a cluster of armed figures running up the highway. Spinning the machine, he whipped the long rod in a circle, and scattered powerfully-built, heavily-armed figures in all directions. After a few minutes of this, he had the highway completely to himself.

He glanced down at the far curve, where the front of the cylindrical vehicle suddenly dropped open, and a massive, feline-faced figure sprang out, and jumped down the bank at the end of the road.

"What happened to him?" said Cardan.

Maclane said, "He's tired of getting gritty snow ground in his eyes, ears, nose, and mouth."

"Good work. Where's Don?"

"He's disappeared amongst those cars, somewhere."

Cardan looked around. In front of him sat the large tank, with smoke rolling out of it. Nearby, the grid was bent badly out of shape, but still standing. Beside it hung one handling machine, its control-cable dangling. Cardan still had control of another one of the machines. Neither on the hill above the road, nor on the flat land below it, was there any sign of opposition. The sun was just setting, and long shadows were reaching across the road. Far to the south, a plume of black smoke was just coming into view on the horizon.

Maclane said wonderingly, "Just a little bit ago, they had us almost licked—and now they're finished?"

"Don't count on it," said Cardan. "This is like one of those fights where one side wins the first few rounds, and the other side wins the next few, and the whole thing is still in doubt." Cardan got out a fresh cigar, and stripped off the wrapper. He stuck the cigar in his mouth unlit, and growled, "There's something funny here. Where are the others?"

From down the table, one of the men spoke up. "Chief, these sets are focused on different places. Mac figured it was better to leave them that way than go nuts trying to focus them all over again. There's a lot of action going on here. You want us to fill you in?"

Cardan said, "Good idea. What places can you see?"

"Their ship, the road about two miles north of the traffic jam, the hill above the road, and a stretch of flat farmland below the road."

"What's going on at their ship?"

"A bunch of them have just come out wearing spacesuits, apparently to keep us from getting at them. They've got some crates and a long low machine—it looks like a metal-working machine of some kind—on a frame mounted between two of these cylinders they travel around in. The side bars of the frame attach to fittings on the sides of the cylinder, and at the front there's a movable plate that allows for a limited turn in either direction."

"Which way are they headed?"

"Toward the road."

"Are they armed?"

"Yes. And the spacesuits will make it harder to hit them with small stuff."

"How about on the hill, above the road?"

A different voice said, "They're busy here, Chief. It looks to me like they're getting set in case there's a counterattack. They've laid out two parallel cables, about six feet apart along the forward slope of the hill, for as far as I can get a view of it. Above the cables, and well spread out, they've got the cylinders partly dug in, covered with brush and moss, and so located that they can sweep the face of the hill with crossfire if anyone starts up. I don't know what the function of the cables is, but you can't get at the cylinders without crossing them. And if there's a pause at those cables—well, the cylinders have a nice clear field of fire."

"How about up the road?"

"Nothing doing right now, Chief. Some cars tried to get through here about half-an-hour ago, though. There are a couple of cylinders lying in wait here, and they blew the cars to bits."

"Is the road blocked?"

"The northbound side is. One lane of the southbound side, and about two-thirds of the grass strip, are unblocked."

"The cylinders haven't tried to completely block the road?"

"No, I think they may want to keep it partly open for their own purposes."

"How about the flat farmland below the road?"

The pugnacious towhead spoke up. "Chief, that crew from their ship are crossing it right now. What do you say I let the acid out of their batteries?"

Cardan blinked. "Do what?"

"I got a good look into one of these cylinders a little bit ago. The power to run them comes from some place. It looks to me as if the bottom third or fourth of the cylinder, at least in the center, is some kind of storage battery. If I let the fluid out, they'll be stranded."

"How are you going to do that?"

There was a silence, then the towhead said hesitantly, "I know how this sounds, but I can get through the metal."

Cardan removed his cigar.

The towhead said earnestly, "Sure, Chief, all you do is loosen a tiny bit at a time, then another and another, and when you get the rhythm of it, you can eat right through the metal. It's not a *big* hole, to start with, but you can enlarge it the same way."

Maclane muttered, as if the thought had just hit him, "Boy, we really let the genie out of the bottle this trip. Listen, Chief, how are we going to keep all this quiet afterward?"

Cardan shook his head, "One mess at a time." He took a fresh grip on his cigar.

The towhead said urgently, "What do you want me to do? They aren't going to wait while we argue over it."

"Let them through," said Cardan. "But if they try to go back, ruin them."

"Does that hold for just these, or for all of them?"

"If you see something really unusual, let me know. If you have to act fast, do what you think best. Otherwise, let them all go through without too much trouble *toward* the highway. But tie them in knots if they try to get back to their ship."

"Why?"

"So we can cut them off from the ship. The more of them out in the open, the better."

"I get it."

Maclane said, "Chief, that machine is just coming into view. I don't know if I like the looks of it."

From beside Cardan's shoulder, Miss Bowen said apologetically, "General Whitely left a message, Mr. Cardan. Would you like me to read it to you later?"

Cardan looked at the machine being hauled up on a frame carried between two of the cylindrical vehicles. It was still down on the flat land below the highway. Cardan couldn't recognize the machine, but supposed its purpose must be to straighten out the grid. As Cardan watched, the forward cylinder tried to start up the base of the embankment at the shoulder of the highway. After a short run, the cylinders ground to a stop. Both cylinders flung back dirt and rocks, then stopped, rolled backwards, and tried a longer run. This time they got about halfway up the bank, threw out an avalanche of stone and dirt, and then came to a stop, wheels spinning and apparently unable to go forward or back. Spacesuited figures milled around, then began to shove back at the forward cylinder.

Cardan studied the scene of confusion, and said, "Keep an eye on them, Mac. They must be getting desperate, and there's no telling what they'll do." He took off his headset, and turned to Miss Bowen. "What did Whitely have to say?"

Miss Bowen grinned at her notebook. "Do you want the exact words, or just the sense of it?"

"Just the sense."

"He said he'd run across a Civil War locomotive that had been repaired for some centennial, and he's rushing a trainload of troops north with it. He's found a few other steam locomotives here and there, and the tracks are being cleared while these locomotives come in to hook up with trains of specially-equipped troops. Several more locomotives are racing down from Canada, and he thinks the worst of the transportation problem is whipped. Now what he's afraid of is another landing before this one is crushed, and he's trying to get things set up in case it happens. Other countries have offered help, but the general thinks we can finish them off ourselves tomorrow, provided you can keep them tied up tonight."

"Provided *what*?" said Cardan, sitting up straight.

"He said that he knows you're doing something to them," said Miss Bowen, "and he can finish them off tomorrow provided you can keep them tied up tonight."

Cardan growled, "Did you—"

"Sir," Miss Bowen objected, "I didn't tell him a thing. He said something about ultra-high-altitude photographs, and then he said that no one could get into the mess these aliens are in without help."

Cardan lit up a cigar. "This poses quite a problem," he said. "If he knows that much, he's going to try to find out the rest of it. And we can't tell him the rest of it."

Miss Bowen said hesitantly, "Sir, if it's for national defense—"

Cardan puffed at the cigar and said nothing.

Down the table, someone said, "Chief, I hope you aren't going to sit on this."

Cardan said, "Maybe you'd rather have the government sit on it."

There was a rustle of faint movement, followed by silence, that told him that had a suddenly intent audience.

"I can see it now," said Cardan, eying the glowing tip of his cigar. "Bureaus, agencies, regulations, committees, boards, advisors, directives, appropriations, cutbacks, crash programs, reappraisals, closed hearings, progress reports, security clearance, secret files—"

Several of the men groaned, and Cardan said, "*I* couldn't squash this if I wanted to. The work would just go quietly on in cellars and attics, regardless what I said. With the government, it's a different matter. Consider the size and expense of the defense programs, for instance. This one device puts the whole business on the edge of being obsolete. What good, for instance, is a liquid-fueled ballistic missile when someone miles away and out of sight can get at the fuel lines before the missile takes off? What good is a naval vessel if the pressure to the turbines that drive the vessel can be leaked out by someone out of sight and reach in the distance? All calculations are thrown into doubt. The whole point and purpose of gigantic sections of industry employing millions of men, becomes questionable. Do you think the government won't be tempted to sit on this?"

There was a low angry murmur.

Cardan said, "And while that problem has everyone in a state of indecision, what are our cat-faced friends going to be doing? Let's just imagine for a little bit that we aren't us, here. Let's imagine for a minute we're the general staff of some interstellar feline race expanding into this region of space. Earth has been scouted, found suitable for colonization, and a force landed sufficient to throw the inhabitants in chaos. After a good start, the landing force gets smashed to bits. What is this feline general staff going to do when word of that comes in?" Cardan glanced around. "Just imagine we are that general staff.

What do you say? Shall we forget the planet? Or shall we go back with twenty times the force?"

There was a tense silence.

Then from down the table, someone said with conviction, "Go back and finish the job. Otherwise there'll be trouble later on."

Cardan nodded slowly. "That's what I think, too."

There was a slow stirring in the room. Miss Bowen said, "But—if every man in our armed forces had one of these circuits—"

Maclane shook his head. "It's easy to see with this, once it's focused. But to hold your mind concentrated long enough and hard enough to *move* something—I don't know."

Cardan handed Miss Bowen his own headset. "Here, try it." He watched Miss Bowen sit down, slip on the headset, shut her eyes, frown, and ask for pointers. Maclane, wearing a headset that showed the same scene, gave her advice. Miss Bowen's attractive features gradually grew pale, and her face tense. At length, she blurted, "But what do you *do*?"

"Just keep your mind on one small object."

"I'm dizzy with watching one small object."

"Then you—watch each part of it in turn, see it all, and take *hold* of it, mentally."

She bit her lip. The minutes dragged by. Abruptly she slumped, her features twisted, and she reached up to take off the headset. Then with a plainly violent effort of will, she brought her hand down again, and sat up straight. The color seemed to drain from her face. All visible trace of emotion vanished, like ripples on a lake when the air becomes intensely calm. Gradually, the calm lengthened out. Still she sat, with a look of intense quiet.

Then she relaxed, and after a moment smiled, and reached up to take off the headset. Her eyes opened and gradually focused, and her face was that of pretty woman waking from anesthesia.

"Well," she said smiling. "I did it. It was little, and it was light. But I moved it." She drew in a careful breath. "And I'd rather learn shorthand all over from the beginning then to do *that* again."

Cardan laughed. "It gets easier with practice."

Miss Bowen shook her head, and stood up. "I had no idea it was like that."

Maclane said, "I keep thinking, Chief, this isn't going to be everybody's dish. If we try to handle it the way we would handle . . . say . . . a new kind of rifle, there's going to be a lot of confusion, and all at the wrong time. Maybe we'd better keep it quiet, develop it ourselves, and not to be too anxious to hand it over till we know what we're doing. So far as defense is concerned, we've tied this crew of aliens in knots, just on the spur of the moment. If sixteen times as many come down on us in half a year . . . well, by then we ought to be sixteen times as tough—provided we keep working on it."

Cardan nodded, and looked down the table. "How does that sound?"

There was a unanimous murmur of agreement.

"O.K." said Cardan. "It remains to be seen how we come out of this present mess, and then there's the problem of getting Whitely off our track. But at least we know what we're trying to do." He glanced at Miss Bowen. "When Whitely called up the last time, did he have anything else to say?"

"He wanted to know how the enemy device operates that keeps gas or Diesel engines from working, or guns from firing properly."

Cardan frowned. "Tell him he won't find that out till he captures them. How should I know?"

"He wanted a rule of thumb explanation he could give so people will know what to expect."

"Oh. Say that the enemy has a device that sets up what you might call a damping field. Any release of energy creates a reaction in the field, and this reaction tends to choke off the release of energy. The more sudden and violent the release of energy, the greater the reaction of the field. A slow smooth release of energy isn't affected too much, but a violent explosion is sharply choked back by the reaction it sets up."

Maclane said, "Chief, excuse me. This crew is slowly getting that machine up onto the road."

Cardan could hear the rapid movement of Miss Bowen's pen on her note pad as he put the headset back on, and saw that the space-suited figures, using a winch, had the big machine almost up the bank. They had set up tall, apparently self-contained, lights on poles, and several of the aliens were studying the warped grid.

Cardan immediately tried the technique of cutting through the strands of the cable the winch was slowly turning around. At first, he had no luck at all, but then he got a tiny speck of metal loose, then another and another. A fine stream of powder began to sift down from the cable. He said, "Mac, we're going to want to keep these birds from getting back to their ship. If Whitely is going to capture whatever operates this field, we're going to have to keep the ship from escaping with a part of the puzzle."

"I'm willing," said Maclane. "What do you want me to do?"

"Make up some more of these sets, and focus them in a line from here back to that place where we were hunting last fall. You remember that hollow maple tree on the edge of the woods?"

"Chief, that must have been three or four miles from this place."

"What's to prevent us from taking that handling machine near the lattice, grabbing one of those lights on poles, jamming a couple of the finger-controls on the handling machine, and relaying it from one place to the next?"

"It will take time," Maclane said.

"This grid," said Cardan, "attracts them like garbage attracts rats. They don't like to give it up when they seem so close to winning. I think I can string them along here for a couple of hours."

"Then we switch what's in the maple tree into their ship?"

"That's the picture."

"We'd still have to get them out of those spacesuits."

"Don't worry about that," said Cardan. "We'll get them out."

"O.K., then," said Maclane, "if you think you can handle this end alone."

In the glare of the floodlights at the road, the cable suddenly parted. The end whipped back and snapped two of the spacesuited figures into the ditch. The machine rolled halfway back down the bank, to stick in the same holes it had just been dragged out of.

Maclane said, "I guess you can handle it all right." A moment later he got up. "I'll get these other sets focused as fast as I can."

The night passed slowly. Once again, the winch drew the machine up the bank, and this time chocks were driven under the wheels every foot or so as it went ahead.

Cardan located a vital pin in the winch, and cut it away so that it sheared off. The winch unwound and the wheels jammed back onto the blocks.

Cardan could see the intent feline faces behind the faceplates as they replaced the pin.

When the machine was again almost at the top of the bank, Cardan snapped the cable for the second time.

The spacesuited figures ran out a new cable, and again dragged the machine to the top of the bank.

Cardan cut through the fitting that supported the right rear corner of the framework stretching between the two big cylindrical vehicles. The frame tipped, and the machine slid halfway off onto the bank.

The spacesuited figures stared at it for a long moment, then slowly hooked cables to it, and began to winch it up the bank on its bottom.

Cardan looked the situation over intently. He wanted to keep the aliens from actually accomplishing anything, while letting them come close enough so they wouldn't turn to something new and harder to block. But he thought all the trouble at the embankment had about brought them to the end of their patience. One more delay there and they'd try something else.

Studying the stalled cars, it occurred to Cardan that there was a lot of gasoline in the tanks of all those cars.

He glanced around and saw that the machine was coming up the bank slowly and heavily. He had a certain amount of time to work.

Methodically, he cut through several of the car bodies into the gas tanks, and liberally doused the interiors with gasoline. He stripped the soaked upholstery into long strands, rectangular sheets, and wads of various sizes, which he built into a low mound in a shadowy place as close to the grid as he could find. Next, he stripped the insulation from a wire under the dash of another car, and touched the bare wire to the dash. A spark jumped.

Cardan looked around, and saw that the machine was now up the bank. Several of the spacesuited figures lifted off a panel to expose the controls, while others pulled out long thick cables, and began dragging them over to the grid.

Cardan brought a small square of gasoline-soaked cloth next to the bare wire as he again moved it against the dash. The cloth burst into flames. He whipped it forward to ignite the pile of soaked upholstery. From this he lifted blazing squares and strips of fire, which he wrapped around the alien's helmets and faceplates, and dropped onto the controls of the big machine, followed by sodden wads from which streamed fingers of fire as the blazing gas ran out.

In the midst of this chaos, there flashed out from some place on the far side of the traffic jam, a number of long hunting arrows.

Maclane's voice said, "I'm ready for that handling machine, Chief."

Cardan located the handling machine, knocked over all but one of the tall floodlights, seized that last one with the handling machine, and passed it to Maclane.

Off over the flat land to the east, as he did this, he saw a plume of fire and sparks racing steadily northward. That, he realized, must be the general's Civil War locomotive, bringing fresh troops to the scene.

Cardan glanced at the highway, and saw half-a-dozen motionless figures lying sprawled under the big grid, long feathered shafts jutting from their spacesuits. Others were behind the machine, firing into the jam of cars. Cardan stripped pieces of blazing upholstery from the pile, and wrapped them around the air hoses of the space-suits. As the hoses burned through, he stuffed wads of gas-soaked padding into the hoses. As the aliens flung these out, he jammed and unjammed the valves of their suits, giving them just enough air to struggle out of the helmets.

One of their last shots into the traffic jam had blown a car apart. Cardan spotted the car's battery amidst the wreckage, and trans-ferred the battery acid from the battery to the invaders, draining it down the backs of their necks.

Just then, one of the big cylindrical vehicles rolled down the hill, crossed the highway, and started down the bank and across the flat farmland. It was followed by another, and then another. Cardan glanced out into the dim distance to the south and southeast, saw gouts of flame leap out. Whitely, he realized, must have dropped troops off there as a diversion, and these troops were using flamethrowers on the enemy outguards.

Overhead, a bright light on a pole passed rapidly over the high-way, illuminating a seething brown pile on the handling machine that carried it. The aliens below were struggling out of their suits. One of them jumped over to try to get at the wires that ran out from the machine. An arrow streaked out, and this time Cardan saw where it came from—a slit under a raised cover on the side of the disabled monster tank.

A few moments later, Maclane said, "The bees are in the ship, Chief. And, boy—the aliens are out of it!"

"Any trouble?"

"Not much. I just had to move the queen, and the rest came along. They weren't in a good mood, though, believe me." Maclane was silent a moment, then said, "What a shambles. And these are the people who almost had us whipped a few hours back."

"When it started out," said Cardan, "they could hit us without our striking back. Now the situation is reversed."

"I hope they don't get it reversed again."

"Their time's running out. Whitely's closing in on them. If he does it the way I think he'll do it, he'll draw them off first by hitting them from the south and southeast, then he'll come down on them like a ton of bricks from the north."

"What do we do?"

"Keep them miserable. And somehow we've got to get Donovan out of that giant tank and away from here. He's in there firing out arrows at anyone who tries to get near the grid, and that's fine, except that the gas may get him when Whitely attacks."

"I think I can get a message to him, Chief. He knows Morse, and I can bang and scrape a piece of metal on the tank for dots and dashes."

"Good. Go to it."

A file of cylinders started down the hill, and began to cross the road. Cardan went to work to sabotage them as they passed.

In the east, it was starting to get light.

Maclane had persuaded Donovan to get out, and Donovan had just disappeared around the bend in the steam car, when from the opposite direction Cardan noticed a kind of fog begin to drift across the scene.

Maclane said, "Here it comes, Chief."

The fog began to thicken, rolling across the road and flat land below. Far off in the distance, there was a sudden blaze of light.

Cardan shifted his cigar, and watched intently. The glare, whatever it was, reminded him of thermite. Then he remembered the two cylinders that had been on guard up the road.

Somewhere up the road, twin beams of light reached out through the fog, and rapidly approached, followed by two more sets of lights.

A cylinder rolled across the road, its gun swinging uncertainly around.

A burst of flame sprang out at the cylinder, and it rolled aside and smashed down the embankment.

Through the gray mist moved an old high-wheeled steam car, a man in a gas mask crouched at the wheel, and another in the seat behind him.

Behind this car came two more, and as they pulled to the side, men jumped off two long flat-bed wagons drawn behind the cars. In the mist, the gas-masked figures dropped over the bank and disappeared.

It wasn't much over an hour later when Miss Bowen said, "General Whitely's on the line, Mr. Cardan."

Cardan glanced around the room. All but one of the circuits had been disassembled, the parts put back in storage bins, and the boards burned up.

Whitely's voice jumped out of the phone. "Hello, Bugs. Where are you?"

"Inside the Milford plant."

"I've got aerial photos here, and the industrial section of Milford's knocked flat."

"Then I guess we got into the subbasement just in time. How are things where you are?"

"We're rounding them up, what's left of them. Say, Bugs, they had quite a run of bad luck, you know that?"

"So I gathered from your last message." Cardan studied his cigar and waited.

"We'll be in to dig you out as soon as we get this cleaned up. We're anxious to know what you did it with."

"Did what with?"

"You know what I mean."

"Don't rush too fast getting here," said Cardan. "This place is well-shielded and we've got a good food supply."

"Don't try to dismantle it, Bugs. We can use it, whatever it is. And we'll be there as fast as we can get there."

Cardan said irritatedly, "The viewer we had was upstairs, and upstairs has been blasted to bits. Talk sense, Tarface."

The general said in a low hard voice, "It's going to be like that, is it?"

"Like what?"

"You know what I mean."

"Maybe you'd better spell it out."

"I'll spell it out in private."

Cardan drew on his cigar. "Before you go running off half-cocked after some figment of your imagination, Tarface, you'd better get a good grip on that equipment the aliens were using. There ought to be enough stuff there to make you happy, provided you don't accidentally shut off the field and get blown up with your own nuclear device."

"I've thought of that long since," said the general coldly. "The fact that a man is in uniform doesn't mean that he's a fool."

"I'm sorry, Tarface," said Cardan.

After a brief silence, Whitely said, "It's all right, Bugs. But I don't understand your attitude." There was a pause. "And I don't think I like it."

Cardan's eyes narrowed. "We've known each other a long time, Tarface. But don't ever get the idea you're going to tell me what to do, or I'll tie you in knots and beat your brains into your boots." Cardan sat up, warming to the subject.

A small voice came out of the phone. "I'm sorry Bugs. I got carried away."

Cardan cut off his next sentence. "That's O.K. I know how it is."

"Listen, we'll be in to dig you out as soon as we can."

"Don't take any unnecessary risks. We're all right here."

"O.K. And thanks, for whatever it was."

"You're welcome, for whatever it was."

The general laughed. "So long, Bugs. We'll be seeing you."

"So long. Tarface."

Cardan put the phone back in its cradle.

Maclane handed him the headset of the one remaining circuit. "I thought you might want to take a last look, Chief, before we disassemble it."

Cardan looked at the miserable collection of feline-faced giants, chained together, and being loaded into trucks.

Cardan studied the scene for a moment, then handed back the headset.

Maclane said, as he started to disassemble the circuit. "It's an imperfect world, where you can have a thing like this and not be able to use it freely and openly."

"Imperfect," said Cardan, "but it's still ours. And as long as that's so, some day things may be different."

"I'm not so sure," said Maclane. "I've been thinking about it, and I'm afraid it would cause terrific dislocation."

Cardan nodded. "Sure," he said. "It will cause dislocation. But there's a precedent for that. Remember, they used to clap certain people in prison, excommunicate them for heresy, jeer and make jokes about them. What they were doing caused dislocation, too. Therefore it had to be stopped, or so it seemed."

Maclane scowled. "You mean, witches practicing witchcraft?"

"No," said Cardan. "I mean, scientists practicing science. Think what happened to Galileo."

Maclane said somberly, "New things throw people off balance. They don't like it."

Cardan nodded. "Taking a step forward throws the human body off balance, too. But it's a good sign when the first steps are taken, however hesitantly.

"When someone starts to walk, even with screams of fear and rage, he's growing up."

Not In The Literature

Alarik Kade had not spent fifty-eight years of his life on The Project without acquiring an instinct for a day that is really going to go sour.

Signs and portents a tyro would scarcely connect up often gave him the first powerful indications. Things like the hungry redjacket drill that droned down the ventilation pipe around 0266 the night before, popped through a rusty spot in the screen, then whined around the room, banging into concrete floor, ceiling, and walls at random till it picked up the heat radiation from Alarik, huddled under a light comforter with the pillow over his head.

The drill hit the comforter, and Alarik sprang out of bed in a rush. The ring of night-glow dots around the lamp base guided him quickly to the lamp, but where was the striker? As Alarik groped around the tabletop, he could hear behind him the *zzt-zzt* and half-hysterical whine as the drill got into the warm covers and stabbed around in all directions for some place to draw blood.

Cursing under his breath, Alarik felt the cold curving surface of a pewter water pitcher, the smooth back of a closed razor, a slim volume containing logarithms to the base eight, a handkerchief, a thick book of well-tested pragmatic formulas and their constants, an ashtray with gold-plated model of an early turbine plane, a glossy brochure telling why he should buy Koggik Steel, a progress report he should have read last night and hadn't, a .50 Special Service Revolver with all four barrels full of rust, a Lawyer Skeel mystery with

423

three shapely girls on the cover, which he shouldn't have read last night but did—but no striker.

The whine of the drill was growing increasingly petulant. At any moment the thing might detect Alarik with its heat-sensitive nose and come for him. What would happen then, he thought, would be that in trying to hit the drill, he would knock the pitcher over and soak the book and papers on the table. With a sense of grim satisfaction in his foresight, Alarik set the pitcher on the floor, close to one of the table's massive cross-braced legs, and then felt of the tabletop again.

A little beyond where the pitcher had been, his three out-stretched fingers felt the flaring squeeze-grip of the striker.

Just then, the whine grew suddenly louder. Alarik ducked, banged his head, and the striker clattered to the floor. The drill smacked into the wall behind him. Alarik groped for the striker. The drill took off in a new line and hit him squarely in the back.

The room seemed to take a somersault.

Alarik came to with his face in the concrete and the last dregs of the drill's knock-out poison fogging his mind. His head ached, he could hear a noise in his ears like the roar of a waterfall, and there was a throbbing bump on his back about half the size of his fist.

Dizzily he pulled himself to his feet.

The way things had happened so far assured him he was in for a rough day. Whether it would be a real record-breaker, he told himself, remained to be seen.

He took a step forward, and put his right foot squarely into the water pitcher. His foot slid in smoothly and tightly and in clutching for support he knocked the razor off onto the floor. As he gripped the edge of the table, a muffled banging whine told him a fresh and hungry drill was blundering down the vent pipe.

Keeping a tight grip on his emotions, Alarik lowered himself to the floor and felt for the striker. His hand closed instead around the open blade of the razor. He gingerly shut the razor, slid it out of the way under the table, and heard it hit something with a metallic *clink*.

Alarik groped under the table, found the striker, stood up with his weight resting on his left foot, squeezed the striker once to see the cluttered tabletop by the light of the striker's sparks, managed to get the glass shade off the lamp without breaking anything, turned the knob of the rack-and-pinion mechanism to get the fragile mantle up out of the way, opened the gascock, and squeezed the handle of the striker. The flints scraped across the ridged steel, the gas lit with a *pop*, and Alarik triumphantly put on the chimney and lowered the mantle. The mantle lit up in a dazzling glare that showed a second redjacket drill, as big as Alarik's thumb, pushing in through the ventilator screen.

Alarik sprang forward to kill it, slipped, and landed on the floor. The drill streaked around overhead, Alarik's right arm and leg jerked up in a self-protective reflex, the water pitcher stuck to his right foot emptied itself in his face, and just then the drill detected the promising heat of the lamp. The drill whizzed around in tight circles, shot down the chimney, and whipped the mantle to bits. The room fell dark, and the gas jet settled down to incinerating the drill. A column of greasy smoke rose from the lamp chimney, and a powerful choking odor filled the room.

All this left Alarik Kade, Chairman-Director of the Special Project, half-choked and with one foot in a pitcher, picking the smoldering remains of one drill out of the lamp while still dizzy from the bite of another, and with the muffled hopeful buzz of yet a third standing the hair on end all over his body.

That was how the day started.

And experience told Alarik that with a start like that, it was bound to be a day he would never forget—if he lived through it.

The sunlight, when Alarik came up into it, after finishing out the miserable night, lit up a day that, on its surface, at least, looked good.

For one thing, there was not a cloud in the sky. That meant reasonably good ground observation. He glanced up, and saw, far overhead, the glint of the shiny aluminum gondola of *Sunbird*. The name made him uneasy, reminding him of the hydrogen that had been substituted for helium in the hope of getting a little more precious lift for high-altitude observation. A brief dazzling flash told him that *Sunbird's* signal mirrors were working properly, and that in turn meant that the aggravating difficulties with the seals of the remote arm were taken care of, at least for the present.

Off over the flat bright sand to his right, at the end of the long runway, the big turbine plane was being slowly wheeled around. Judging from the slowness with which it was turned, it already had its load of fuel and water, and being perfectly reliable, no one was worried about it. Slung under its midsection like a babe clinging to its mother was one of his two big headaches.

To his left, like an upright giant dagger with nearly conical blade and an almost cylindrical haft, stood The Beast. This was his other, and much larger, headache. Contradictory emotions of love and hate welled up in Alarik as he looked at it. No one could work on The Project for all this time without feeling a little of both these emotions.

As Alarik gazed at the shiny form, a hurrying figure coming toward him from the base of The Beast drew his attention.

Alarik nodded in foreboding. Now it would start. He had been allowed this moment of beautiful tranquility in order to give a contrasting background against which the day's misfortunes would stand out to better effect. As a check, he glanced around toward the turbine plane. Sure enough, here came a second hurrying figure. To further test the auguries, he glanced up. A tiny cloud was materializing just about on a line between Observation 10 and the projected path of The Beast as it arced out over the ocean. That would foul up the whole launch, unless the cloud moved on.

But the cloud showed no sign of moving on. It seemed to be shredding away on one end, and forming again on the other end, and at the same time gliding steadily forward, so that the net result, fantastic as it might seem, was just the same as if it didn't move at all. But it was getting bigger, he was sure of that. Alarik squinted at the cloud, then shook his head. Even in this modern day, the only truly intelligent life form in the universe had no more control over the weather—or real basic understanding of it—than on the distant day when a remote ancestor peered out the burrow mouth and some spark of intelligence suggested that that smoldering stubble from the grass could be put to use.

What had it been, thought Alarik, the fear of some digging enemy, or—

The chain of philosophical speculation was snapped as two hurrying pairs of feet arrived from opposite directions.

"Sir, the triggering clock is seventeen sixty-fourths off, halfway through the cycle, and the An. Comp. boys say she'll burn up on re-entry. We've tried re-setting, but that throws the clock off on both ends, and Comp. tells us then she won't go into orbit. We've got a new clock checked out, but all the control wires have to be reset, and that's going to take the rest of the morning. If we lift off this afternoon, she'll land in the pick-up area at night, unless we reset the clock. But if we reset that clock, we won't be able to lift off till tonight."

"What about Ganner's magnesium flare?"

"Sir, we tried it out three times last week and it worked fine. We installed it last night and ran a test check on a Pup rocket. Nothing happened."

Alarik gripped his chin. "It came down with no signal?"

"Oh, the siren was on. And this morning the ocean was red for a hundred spans in all directions from where she hit. The underwater sound ship picked up a good solid *ping* from the noisemaker. But all that stuff is too slow and uncertain. When the boys got there, she was sunk."

"Scrub the flight. We'll try again tomorrow."

"Sir, Weather says—"

Alarik glanced at the cloud. There was now a smaller cloud trailing it, and the first cloud looked bigger. He looked away angrily.

"When did Weather ever know what it was talking about? If we don't get clear weather for a month, that's just so much more time to perfect our equipment. And get me the name of the contractor who sold us that clock."

"Yes, sir." He turned and sprinted back toward the gleaming shaft of The Beast.

Alarik considered that he had got off easy. What if the clock had gone sour after she took off? The odds were that with his luck the An. Comp. boys would be wrong and instead of burning up on re-entry, she would make a freak re-entry, and come down through the roof of a metropolitan temple with the chief priest in charge and the benches crammed with notables.

Someone cleared his throat, and Alarik realized he wasn't safe in the burrow yet. He looked up and waited.

"Sir, the Babe's got a malfunction."

"What is it this time?"

"The hydraulic columns that control the impact-fuse-igniters. There's an overflow for excess temperature. Well, somehow air worked back into the lines, and now they're spongy. As sure as anything, we're going to get up there, let her loose, and dig ourselves a crater."

Alarik could hear more feet approaching, this time from behind.

"How long," he said, "to bleed the lines?"

"Considering how cramped it is in there, it's an all day job. What we need is some simpler way to ignite the tubes."

"I know. We've got research teams working on it. But for now, we'll just have to put up with more delay."

"Yes, sir. We should be able to get off tomorrow for sure."

Alarik nodded, and turned to find his assistant, Kubic, holding a small earnest-looking man by the arm.

"Sir," said Kubic, "this fellow claims to have some reliable method of setting off fuses with constant-length wires."

Alarik shrugged. "It's been tried. I doubt that if our teams of trained chemists couldn't find the ideal solution, a lone researcher could."

Kubic nodded. "Yes, sir, I know. But we've had so much trouble—"

"No doubt about that," said Alarik with feeling. He glanced at the newcomer.

Kubic glanced at him, too, then cleared his throat. "Any hole in a hurry," he said.

The fellow certainly looked unprepossessing. But then, you could never tell with a chemist. Some of the best dispensed with appearance and pretense entirely. You just couldn't tell.

"All right," said Alarik. "Go ahead. What's your solution. Remember, these wires curl back through both hot and cold regions alike. The fuses don't ignite easily. It takes a sharp crack to ignite them. They aren't supposed to ignite one at a time, but a bunch together. And we don't want any fishnet of wires in there. The thing has to be reasonably simple. To keep your tension constant is no easy problem."

"I know." The newcomer beamed and nodded.

"We don't want any maze of springs and pulleys. The present system is bad enough, what with the need for special heat-resistant plastics, double-lines, heat-stable liquids, and so on. A terrific amount of the highest type of chemistry has gone into it."

"I realize that," said the newcomer. "I don't claim to be a true chemist. I just like to follow my interest. I've been sort of an amateur chemist since childhood, and . . . well, I got to playing around with strips of zinc and copper one day, and put them into some dilute sulfuric acid, and for some reason, I laid another strip of copper across the tops of the strips standing in the acid."

Alarik smiled. "And you got bubbles on the copper strip. It's a standard experiment."

"Yes, but I wondered about it. *Why* did I get bubbles?"

"It's a well known chemical fact. Immerse copper and zinc in acid, let there be contact, and bubbles form on the copper. The bubbles are hydrogen gas." Alarik smiled tolerantly. "Go ahead. What next?"

"I wondered, why must there be *contact*?"

Alarik blinked. "What's that?"

"Bubbles formed *when I joined zinc and copper strips*. Why did these strips *have to be joined*?"

Kubic glanced at Alarik's frown, and said hastily. "The Director's time is limited. Now, if you'll come to the practical aspect of your idea—"

"Wait," said Alarik. "He's got a point. Why *does* there have to be contact? I performed that experiment, too, but that question never occurred to me." He looked at the man with new respect. "I would say that you must be a natural-born chemist. You are, I suppose, associated with the university nearby, at Kerik Haven?"

"No, no." A stricken look crossed the visitor's face. "Please, I am nobody. All that matters is this discovery, which I happened across purely by accident."

Kubic cleared his throat, and said uncomfortably, "The fellow is a janitor at the University."

"Well, in that position, he could, I suppose, observe, experiment, learn—"

"In the Dance Workshop," said Kubic.

Alarik frowned.

Their guest hung his head. "I was thrown out of the Chemistry Program as a student. I hung on, got a job as a janitor, and they threw me out of that job, too. But I've got a friend in the stockroom. He helps me get what I need."

Alarik considered the possibility that the man was a suppressed genius. It had happened often enough in the past, heaven knew. But in this enlightened age, such things were said to be impossible.

Chemical talent was searched for eagerly, coaxed along with scholarships, rewarded lavishly with high pay.

Their visitor seemed to sense Alarik's line of thought. "Please," he said, "don't think that I am trying to present myself as a chemist of any kind. I think . . . I think I have some skill, some insight, but it is of a different type. At school, my teachers told me that I asked the wrong questions. I disagreed. I was more combative then." For a moment, he lifted his head. His eyes flashed. Then he shrugged, and looked down at the dirt. "It's all gone now." There was bitterness in his voice. Then he smiled suddenly. "But I can solve your igniter problem for you."

"How does this wire of yours work?" said Alarik.

"Well, to explain it completely, I would have to describe to you a great deal of work I did with the two strips of metal." A wary look crossed his face. "But I've found that it's better not to go into that."

Kubic said, "Just tell us the practical details."

"Well, essentially, it is this. You run a wire from the pilot's compartment back to the fuse. When the pilot wishes that particular fuse to ignite, he presses a button."

Alarik frowned. "This is a very stiff wire."

"No, not especially."

"Then it is a reasonably stiff wire enclosed within a casing?"

"No. Oh, well, yes. There is a fibrous sheath over the wire."

"How will that stiffen it?"

"It doesn't need to be stiff," the newcomer answered.

"Then what moves it?"

"It doesn't move."

Alarik scowled at him. Kubic frowned.

"Then," said Alarik, "why does the pilot punch the button?"

"Because—He does it to—Well, that's what I'm coming to."

"Wait a minute," said Alarik. "A push is communicated along this wire, is that right?"

"No, sir."

Alarik stared at him. Suddenly he snapped his fingers. "It *twists*, is that it? You've found a way to convert a push into a twist, and then—"

"No. No, it *doesn't* twist. It doesn't move at all."

"*Doesn't move at all?*"

"That's the point. It *heats.*"

Kubic groaned.

Alarik shook his head. "No good. No, it won't work."

"But why not? Heat will trigger off the fuse."

Alarik felt faintly sick. He glanced at Kubic, and jerked his head toward the gate. That, he thought, was the trouble with these unsung geniuses. They wanted to sing for an audience and they didn't even know the scale.

Kubic put his hand firmly on the man's arm.

"Ah, I see," said the fellow suddenly. "Not the *whole* wire. Just the *end.*"

Alarik forced a smile. "It happens to be the *other* end we're interested in."

Kubic turned him around, and led him off forcibly.

Alarik could hear them in the distance. Kubic's voice was a series of low monosyllables. The other man's voice rose in loud complaint, and as the wind happened to be from that direction, he could hear him almost to the inner gate.

"But," the man cried, "it's the *fuse* end I'm talking about!"

Kubic muttered something or other.

"No, no, you don't understand! Friction has nothing to do with it! It's *not* heat conduction along the wire! That's not *it!*"

Kubic paused to take a better grip on his guest's sleeve.

Alarik frowned. If it wasn't friction, what *was* it? Here is a man who pushes a button attached to a wire. The wire is not stiff, but is enclosed in some kind of sleeve. The wire gets hot. Then it would burn the sleeve, wouldn't it? But wait a minute. Only the *end* gets hot. The rest of the wire doesn't move at all, doesn't twist—*How* does the end get hot?

"No! No! No! No!" came the voice, climbing higher. "It isn't that at all! I can show you!"

Alarik came to a sudden decision. He was hung around the neck with chemists of the most exalted rank. They all thought alike. They were the elite of the elite, but maybe he needed a fresh mind. What if the man's approach *wasn't* truly chemical? Just let it work, that's all. He cupped his hands to his mouth to shout to Kubic.

Abruptly the visitor ripped free of Kubic's grip. His voice carried in an almost hysterical shout:

"You're hidebound! You're blind as bats, the lot of you! I've begged for just a chance to *prove* there's such a thing as current, and there *is*! I can prove it! It's staring you in the face! But you won't listen! You fools! A *current* flows through that wire, and when it goes through the constricted end, *then* the end heats! No, it's not chemical. You can't argue against it because it's not chemical! It's potentially just as great as anything that *is* chemical! I try to tell you, *it's a whole new field of knowledge!*"

Alarik lowered his hands. He shook his head and shrugged. He glanced around at the towering evidence of chemistry in a chemical world. Chemistry was the study of matter, and matter was everywhere. Everything that was, was made of matter. There was nothing else, *could* be nothing else but matter. Oh, there was light, and sound, and lightning, but the best minds held that these were just disturbances in matter, or in finer forms of matter. There was the field of atmospheric chemistry, for instance, and the field of aetheric chemistry, but there was some doubt as to whether these fringe studies, particularly the latter, were really chemical at all.

How, all considered, could any other field of knowledge possibly *hope* ever to compare with the study of matter? Builders, mechanicians, physicians—all had important work to do, but they admitted they were only quasi-chemists, not truly chemical. Only the mathematicians held aloof, proclaiming a loftier discipline. But in actual practice, they were tied in knots. They couldn't accomplish a thing without a thousand trials, errors, and reservations. Matter just was not amenable to their theories, except in rare special cases.

He shrugged.

A last shout carried back on the wind:

"I'll show you! It's bound to come out some day. Current *does* flow!"

That decided it. What could flow through a solid metal wire? There was no space for anything to flow on the inside, and on the outside anything would fall off—or else ooze through the spaces in the fibrous sheath and drip out. Solid matter was largely incompressible. Therefore nothing could flow through it, because to flow, there must be space. And you couldn't have a current without something that flowed. And nothing could flow where there was no space.

Kubic came back, shaking his head.

"I'm sorry, sir. I didn't realize. The fellow's a fanatic."

"Well, it was worth a try. I thought for a minute there he had something."

"He acted plausible enough. But he blew up on the way out. Talked all kinds of gibberish."

"Yes, he didn't make much—Wait a minute!"

"Sir?"

"Listen. Suppose we use a stiff wire, inside a conduit of close spiral spring, and rotate that inner wire very fast, with pressure, against a narrow abrasive head applied to the fuse case?"

"Hm-m-m, you mean the friction will generate heat?"

"Sure it will. Now, of course, it isn't a very chemical procedure. It's just a piece of mechanism. But that's how we've progressed in The Project over the past hundred years or so. One little brick on top of another. In time, we'll get there."

"Yes, sir. But I don't know. Good mechanicians are as rare as shock-proof lamp mantles. You remember, twenty years ago, when we were using spring triggers on the fuses. That seemed pretty good till they complexified it up to the point where we couldn't recognize it any more. Then they got that hydraulic idea, and—Well, I don't know. One thing just seems to lead to another. It seems as if this is all taking too long. We go around in circles. Somehow, it's like trying to pull nails with a wrench. Where the devil do you take a hold? There's a tool missing from the kit somewhere."

"It's been a bad day," said Alarik, scowling. "Of course, over the long view, there *is* progress. And, occasionally, there's a real breakthrough. That new fuel, for instance. And, best of all, the superrefractive coating. Then, it was no small improvement when we hit on dissipation-cooling, and all the refinements of that. But I know, somehow these big advances don't make the dent they ought to."

Kubic glanced around at various massive structures that stretched off to north and west as far as the eye could see. "Well," he said, "it keeps unemployment down, I'll say that for it. But something tells me a lot of our effort here is at a tangent to the problem."

Alarik nodded. "I'll tell you what," he said. "We'll press this rotary-fire principle, and see what comes of it. We can send a routine payment check to this fellow you brought in. After all, he suggested the idea, whether he meant to or not. He, at least, *claims* to develop some new method. He may be a fanatic, but then, you look at some of the early chemists—"

Kubic nodded approval. "Good idea, sir. To tell the truth, *I* don't see why there has to be contact to evolve those bubbles, either."

"Take care of it now," said Alarik. "You never know when something will happen and we'll forget all about it."

Kubic's eyes widened. "Sir, look there—"

Alarik looked up.

"The devil with it. Get going, I'll take care of this."

Sprinting across the field from the bulk of The Beast came what looked like the whole maintenance crew. Alarik gave Kubic a shove, to start him in the right direction, and Kubic ran off to disappear behind a protecting buttress that led back to the Administration Building.

Alarik studied The Beast. Was that a wisp of smoke he saw, puffing out from under the drive ring?

Mechanicians, builders, brace men, clockers, supervisors, chemical technicians—the whole crew pounded across the field as if their lives were at stake.

That *was* smoke under the drive ring.

As he watched, a white plume billowed out, traveled slowly around the circumference, and wreathed the daggerlike base in smoke. Another plume joined the first, then another and another. The curving near-cylindrical top rode above the billowing clouds with no visible support.

Alarik held his arm out, stabbed his forefinger at the earth, and shouted, "*Ground!*"

All the workmen but the crew chief disappeared in a series of flying dives.

The crew chief, breathing hard, tears streaming out the corners of his eyes, ran to Alarik and saluted.

"Sir, I'll stay up and take my medicine. It was my fault. I—"

Thunder traveled across the field.

Alarik knocked the crew chief down the nearest hole and dove after him.

Pink brilliance reflected dimly on the sides of the tunnel.

"What happened?"

"The inside clocker—He's new. I shouldn't have let him down alone. We can't use any kind of lamps in there. He had to work with just a glow plate."

"*What happened?*"

The earth began to shake.

"Go on," shouted Alarik, "*what happened?*"

"He bumped the master pull wire, where it comes in out of the sheath from Control. The safety was pushed down, and by mistake, the tip must have been over the wire; the pin popped up out of the hole, the safety let go, the arming spring knocked the lever around, the safety came down and hit the taut wire, and that sprang the lever. We could hear it—Wham! Wham! Wham! Then she started."

Alarik swore.

The crew chief shouted above the roar. "He's still in there. *He's in there now!* The weight-savers dropped the ladders and weather covers loose. He couldn't get out. We just got down ourselves before the tower got jerked away."

The tunnel lit up in a pink glow, and they eased back around a corner.

"It's too complicated," the crew chief shouted. Then it was too loud to hear, and the uproar was too much to talk in anyway.

Alarik lay in the hole, his body one living ache. Gradually, awareness returned.

Well, he thought dully, there she goes. The faulty clock is still in her. The gliders and the *Sunbird* may get some data, but it's meaningless with that nonstandard clock in there. At intervals, The Beast will shoot out luminous vapor clouds, and that may help in the tracking—maybe. But where would she come down?

There must be some better way than this, he thought. It can't be this complicated. This was like trying to tie up a handful of marbles with a ball of string. When it got this complicated, it meant you were trying to do the job with tools or materials that weren't fitted to the work.

The roar was just about all gone now.

There was a thud, and Kubic came around the corner of the tunnel in a crouch.

"Sir, are you all right?"

"In a sense," growled Alarik. "How was it?"

"Beautiful. It looked beautiful. Actually, it was terrible, but it looked fine."

"Well, that's something."

"I got that pay voucher made out."

Alarik froze. Suddenly, ignoring the staring crew chief, he jumped up and grabbed Kubic by the arm.

"The devil with all that," he said. "I'm sick of this stuff!"

"Sir? You want me to cancel it?"

"No, no! Go on out there! Go get him! Grab him! Bring him back!"

"Yes, sir," said Kubic with alacrity.

He went up out of the hole in a rush.

Alarik climbed up into the open air. Far overhead was a small bright dot, gradually growing fainter.

As it disappeared, he could hear a determined voice carrying across the field, speaking of "currents" as something real, actual, and usable.

Alarik looked around. For a moment, he felt guilty. What he had in mind was unchemical. Therefore it was chicanery, fraud, quackery, unprofessional—

"The devil with it," growled Alarik. Years of accumulated frustration weighed on him like lead.

His hands opened and shut like those of a man badly in need of a hammer and he eyed the sky in supplication.

"Just give me," he said earnestly, "a tool to fit the job."

Acknowledgements

Eric Flint, Baen's editor of these stories, has suggested that the writer (Anvil) might like to put something personal—an introduction, preface, afterword—something—in this latest book of the series, this being possibly the writer's last chance to say whatever he might like to the reader.

I appreciate the suggestion—but think there are reasons to hesitate about author's prefaces, introductions, and afterwords. For a fiction writer, these extra nonfiction passages can be surplus baggage—an unintended hurdle between the reader and the story, and a free chance to put one's foot in one's mouth. Better, perhaps, to just get on with the story.

There is, however, one type of nonfiction section, inserted by the writer, that may be well justified, if not on the ground of special interest to the reader, at least on the basis of justice—that there are those who deserve some recognition, some expression of appreciation or gratitude, from the writer. That is the Acknowledgements section, in which the writer thanks some of those who have helped. The reader may just glance this over, but it does give the writer a chance to show appreciation—and it may benefit those who are thanked, for a reason anyone can sympathize with—If we help someone, we like it to be appreciated.

As with most books, a lot of people deserve credit for this series. Some have already been thanked by Eric Flint, who mentioned, in his Afterword to *Interstellar Patrol II*: Henry Cate III, along with Henry

Cate, Jr., and Jim Budler, Matthew Class, Dave Gerecke, Robert Klein, Dave Lampe, Mary Qualls, Mark Rubinstein, Peter Sims, Simon Slavin, Mark Stackpole, and Joe Webster. I'd like to add my thanks and appreciation to Eric's.

Also, as most of these stories were published in other books or magazines before being collected for Baen Books, I'd naturally like to thank all those who first selected and published them—although I am reasonably sure most of them would just smile and say, "Thanks, but it was our job." Still, those who do their job deserve appreciation.

There are, moreover, those who particularly deserve credit. Some may have passed on, but, as we are often told, the good that people do lives after them—and so, gratitude and appreciation also survive.

There is a book titled *The Rickover Effect*, which suggests the impact of Admiral Hyman Rickover on nuclear power and American industry—and so on the outcome of the Cold War. Admiral Rickover may no longer be with us, but the effects of his thought and actions are with us.

It is the same with anyone who lived through the Second World War, and saw how easily Nazi Germany absorbed the Rhineland, Austria, and Czechoslovakia, conquered Poland, seized Norway by surprise, then smashed the French and British armies, to conquer France and threaten the invasion of Britain. That was, to us now, long ago; but the effects of the resolve of Winston Churchill and Franklin Roosevelt, and of the millions who followed them, are with us still.

In science fiction, too, we have those who have a great and often not fully realized influence. John W. Campbell is often mentioned as a great editor, though this is only a part of the truth. An original and independent thinker, he was aware of and concerned with events outside of his personal responsibility, and he was unafraid to risk appearing to be wrong.

And while it may not be the job of writers to judge editors, still, we can be grateful to all those who know their job and do it. And, also often unsung, there are great agents.

At the time when I was sending out stories, and often having them sent directly back, I sometimes received in the mail, an invitation from one or another agent. Many came from an agent by the name of Scott Meredith, who seemed to have a very large agency. In time, I answered what I supposed was a form letter, and Scott Meredith replied—the beginning of what was, especially at the beginning, a slightly bumpy relationship, since I had one idea of what it should be, he had another, and I imagine the editors had theirs.

But the advantage of this soon became clear, as Scott introduced an element of order into what could be a chaos. He had an excellent foreign sales department, so that the same story that sold in the U.S. might resell in Britain, France, Italy, Germany—a marvelous arrangement for an American writer. If an editor was backward in his pay rate, or unconscionably slow to respond, Scott was not backward to point it out. He seemed a rare factor in the writing business—someone who, though seeing both sides, was often on the side of the writer.

When Eric Flint phoned to ask whether I would be interested in having these stories republished, I was surprised, but interested— which leads us to a nearly final statement of gratitude—not "final" in that I have run out of those to be grateful to, and hopefully not final in that there might be others in the future, but final in that, for these Acknowledgements, it is approaching the last recognition of gratitude when I thank Eric himself, an excellent writer and first-rate editor, who largely organized the books made from these stories.

I also want to thank David Weber, for his marvelous Introduction to *Interstellar Patrol*, and the late Jim Baen, the capable and inspiring publisher of Baen Books.

And there is still one more thank-you on this brief and incomplete list—to Joy Crosby, my wife, my first reader, whose mere look of boredom on reading a story guarantees it will be rewritten or forgotten, and who typed hosts of stories written (and often unintelligibly corrected) in longhand.

Each of these thank-yous deserves to be expanded to do justice to those thanked; and for each person thanked, there are many others who deserve to be thanked, including the first editor who explained his rejection of a story, and the writer of the most recent (well appreciated, though often not well answered) reader's letter.

Most deserving of thanks, of course, are the readers, the other half of a book or story, without whom there is no point writing. But how do you truly thank a reader? Perhaps only by writing another story.

Christopher Anvil